# TAN
# LINES

Read the first Summer:
BEACH BLONDES

More beach reads from Simon Pulse:
The Au Pairs series
Melissa de la Cruz

*Honey Blonde Chica*
Michele Serros

*Surf Ed.*
Karol Ann Hoeffner

*Shirt and Shoes Not Required*
Todd Strasser

*Partiers Preferred*
Randi Reisfeld

# TAN
# LINES
## a SUMMER novel

## KATHERINE APPLEGATE

Simon Pulse
New York  London  Toronto  Sydney

For Michael

SIMON PULSE     alloy**entertainment**

An imprint of Simon & Schuster Children's Publishing Division

1230 Avenue of the Americas, New York, NY 10020

*Sand, Surf, and Secrets* copyright © 1996 by Daniel Weiss Associates, Inc., and Katherine Applegate

*Rays, Romance, and Rivalry* copyright © 1996 by Daniel Weiss Associates, Inc., and Katherine Applegate

*Beaches, Boys, and Betrayal* copyright © 1996 by Daniel Weiss Associates, Inc., and Katherine Applegate

All rights reserved, including the right of reproduction in whole or in part in any form.

SIMON PULSE and colophon are registered trademarks of Simon & Schuster, Inc.

Designed by Ann Zeak

The text of this book was set in Bembo.

Manufactured in the United States of America

First Simon Pulse edition June 2008

20  19  18  17  16  15  14  13  12  11

Library of Congress Control Number 2008923442

ISBN 978-1-4169-6134-5

These titles originally published individually.

0310 OFF

june

# The Magic of Prom Night and Other True Myths

The doorbell rang at seven o'clock on the night of Summer Smith's senior prom. While Summer's mother ran to the door with her camera in tow, Summer stood calmly at the top of the stairs.

Wiser, worldly girls with diplomas and cars of their own had told Summer what to expect from her senior prom. In all her years of high school, they vowed, nothing would be as magical. Not homecoming, not the Christmas dance, not senior skip day, not the day she cleaned out the banana peels from the bottom of her locker for the very last time. Not even the great moment when the principal handed Summer her diploma. Nothing could compare to senior prom, these girls claimed. Things *happened* that night.

But Summer suspected that senior prom was just another high school ritual, even if it did feature giant paper pom-poms and boys in pastel cummerbunds. It was just a dance, just a corsage, just a chance to play dress-up. Not magic.

She'd even considered skipping the whole expensive event, since Seth, her boyfriend, lived far away. Besides, her good friend Jennifer was in a temporary state of guylessness, and it seemed only right not to go. Solidarity and all.

But in the end, Seth had convinced Summer that, as an official senior, it was her obligation to attend the prom. And Jennifer had promised that she was not going to slit her wrists just because she had to miss some stupid dance.

She glanced down at her long black velvet dress, sleek and sophisticated, slit to the thigh in a style that was both sexy and very practical for dancing. Her blond hair was swept up in a simple French twist. Her mother, with some trepidation, had lent Summer her diamond earrings and pendant. Jennifer had helped her do her nails and even her toenails. Summer was wearing her favorite perfume, a fresh, lemony scent that reminded her of Florida, where she'd first met Seth.

Her mother opened the door, and there stood Seth,

looking impossibly older and grave in a form-fitting black tux. He gazed at her and blinked.

"You look . . . so beautiful," he whispered in a voice full of sheer amazement.

"You look . . . so beautiful, too," Summer said, and then she laughed.

Her mother snapped a million or so pictures of Seth pinning on Summer's corsage while he tried very hard not to touch anything off-limits. Out the living room window, Summer could see a black stretch limo filled with their friends waiting at the end of the driveway.

Seth took her arm.

He said it again: "You look so beautiful."

It was an I-can't-believe-my-eyes kind of voice.

And for the first time Summer wondered if maybe those older, wiser girls had been right after all.

## Pen Pals at a Prom Are Not a Pretty Picture.

So what if the crepe paper in the Hyatt ballroom kept falling on the dancers? So what if the band played Kanye West—badly—whenever the chaperons sneaked outside for a cigarette break? So what if the punch tasted remarkably like Gatorade?

None of that mattered. It was still incredibly romantic.

Except for one tiny little nagging detail.

Summer laid her head on Seth's shoulder as they swayed slowly to the band's cover of "You're Beautiful." She tried to concentrate on the feel of his arms around her. She tried very hard not to think about the letter in her purse that was threatening to ruin her entire evening.

If only she hadn't seen it as she and Seth were walking out the door, she'd be dancing in blissful ignorance. But no, Summer *had* noticed the envelope addressed to her in the pile of mail on the hall table. She'd seen the return address. She'd seen the name Austin Reed. And after considering whether to faint or not, she'd grabbed the note and stuffed it in her purse while Seth was busy promising Summer's mom he would behave himself that night.

As she danced, Summer once again told herself not to overreact. It was probably just a "Hi, what's up, drop me a line sometime" note. The kind of letter a friend wrote to another friend.

Only Austin wasn't exactly a friend.

Summer put her arms around Seth a little tighter. He hated to dance, but he was pretty good at it. She rubbed her cheek on the stiff, cool fabric of his tux and closed her eyes.

She and Seth had been together almost a year. Like all couples, they'd had their ups and downs. There'd been jealousies and misunderstandings the past summer. During the school year, with Summer living in Minnesota and Seth in Wisconsin, there'd been too-quick weekend visits and too-long phone calls.

And over spring break, when Summer and Seth and their friends had spent the week on a yacht in Florida, there'd been . . . well, complications. Complications of the male variety, which Summer didn't like to dwell on.

The point was, she was there with Seth at that moment, and all was well. Better than well.

It was just a letter, nothing more.

"What?" Seth whispered in her ear, sending a shiver down her spine.

"Did I say something?" Summer asked, loudly enough to be heard over the wailing lead singer.

"You sighed."

"Oh." Summer gazed up at him. "I was just thinking about how much we've been through."

"It's been worth it, though." Seth stroked her hair gently. "And now it'll start to get easier. We'll have the end of the summer in Florida, and then college together in Wisconsin." He grinned. "And after that, who knows?"

The song ended, but couples still swayed lazily. Seth leaned down and kissed Summer for a wonderfully long time.

"Let's go outside," he whispered. "There's something I've been meaning to ask you."

"What?" Summer asked.

"Wait till we're outside," Seth said with a mysterious smile.

She took his hand as they drifted off the dance floor and past the long table filled with cookies and a big plastic punch bowl. Parents stationed behind the table watched them pass with discreetly approving smiles.

"I have to go pee," Summer said.

"I'll wait with the other abandoned males," Seth said, nodding toward the group of guys waiting patiently near the ladies' room.

"Don't let her go," a guy in a red cummerbund warned. "She'll never come back. It's like the Bermuda Triangle in there."

The rest room was packed with girls adjusting straps, bemoaning runs, retouching blush, respraying hair.

"Please, Summer, save me." Mindy Burke grabbed Summer by the shoulders. "Please tell me you have some deodorant in your purse."

Summer held up her tiny beaded black purse as evidence. "Does this look like it could hold anything?" she asked.

"Perfume?" Mindy pleaded. "I'll take anything. I can't believe I've been planning for this prom for, like, decades, and I forget my deodorant. I am such an idiot. Anyone have any perfume? Hair spray?"

"Please, Mindy, tell me you're not going to use hair spray on your pits," someone groaned.

When she reached a stall at last, Summer locked the door. The air was thick with mingled perfumes.

She opened her little beaded purse. It was hardly worth carrying—she'd barely managed to fit a comb, a quarter, and a box of Tic Tacs into it.

And, of course, Austin's letter.

*Austin T. Reed,* read the small print in the left corner of the envelope. It spoke to her like a voice, like *his* voice—soft and caressing and full of trouble.

She pulled out the letter. Notebook paper, torn on one edge. A coffee stain on the bottom.

Her hands were trembling, and she didn't know why.

*May 14*

*Summer, my beautiful, unforgettable Summer. Of course you are surprised to hear from me. Probably as surprised as I am to be writing you.*

*I know I left you abruptly in the middle of your spring break with nothing but a scribbled letter, a pair of mouse ears from Disney World, and, undoubtedly, a lot of questions.*

*I'm writing to tell you that I have discovered some of the answers.*

*I told myself I left you because I was afraid. Afraid of hurting you. Afraid of getting involved when I knew I might have inherited my father's nightmare, the awful disease that is stealing his life away.*

*But now I wonder if maybe I wasn't also afraid of what I was feeling for you, it was so intense and complete. And although I might have been able to handle it, I wasn't so sure you could. Not when you still had feelings, as you obviously did, for Seth.*

*On one score, at least, I can stop being afraid. It seems I have some good news and some bad news. The good news: I had the genetic testing done and I'm clean. I won't get Huntington's like my dad did. The great gene lottery smiled on me. I don't know why me and not my brother. I've stopped asking, because I never seem to be able to come up with an answer.*

Summer closed her eyes. She felt tears coming. Her mascara was supposed to be waterproof, but she couldn't afford to take the chance. She took a couple of deep breaths.

Someone pounded on the door. "Did you fall in or what?"

"Just a second," Summer said. Her voice was quavering. She found her place in the letter.

*Anyway (and this is the bad news, although I hope you see it differently), I'm going to reappear in your life and further complicate it.*

*I can't stop thinking about the feel of your mouth*

*on mine. I can't stop thinking about the way you
felt in my arms. I want to be a writer, so why can't
I find a way to put my feelings about you into
words?*

*I know you said you're heading down to Crab
Claw Key after graduation. I'll be there, waiting,
whether you want me to or not.*

*I remain hopelessly in love with you.*

*Austin*

Summer took a shuddery breath. She folded up the
letter neatly and put the little square into her purse.

"Summer, you okay in there?"

"I'm fine," Summer called.

She'd thought she had put Austin out of her mind.
Well, not out of her mind, exactly. He appeared in her
dreams with startling regularity. But out of her heart,
at least.

She'd chalked him up as a spring fling, a momentary
slip. He'd been a stranger in need of help, a guy about
to visit his very sick father and perhaps learn that he too
was destined to be very sick. She'd been a good friend.

A good friend who couldn't seem to stop kissing
him.

Seth had found out about them in the worst possible way. He'd seen them together, and he'd made
accusations she couldn't deny.

Eventually, though, he'd forgiven her. She didn't deserve his forgiveness, but he'd given it willingly. She'd been so grateful to Seth for a second chance to make things work.

Diana, Summer's cousin, had warned Summer that if she didn't get her priorities straight, she was going to lose Seth to someone who appreciated how wonderful he was. And Marquez, Summer's best friend from Florida, had told her the same thing.

They were right, of course. Seth was wonderful.

And if Austin was wonderful, too, in different ways, well, that really wasn't the point, was it?

With a sigh, Summer unlocked the door and made her way through the crowd.

"Turns out hair spray does not make a good deodorant," Mindy reported. "My pits are, like, permanently attached to my dress." She peered doubtfully at Summer. "What's wrong with you? Someone die?"

"Someone's *not* dying, actually," Summer said.

She captured a place at the crowded mirror.

Her mascara was definitely not waterproof.

# 3

# I Dos and I Don't Knows

Behind the hotel was an enclosed courtyard with a pool and a Jacuzzi. Seth led Summer to a pair of chairs near the pool. Austin's letter sat in her dainty little purse like a slowly ticking bomb.

Why did the existence of that note make her want to confess to sins she hadn't even committed? After all, during spring break Summer had told Seth the truth—that she'd had real feelings for Austin, and that if he hadn't left so suddenly, she wasn't sure what she would have done. She'd been honest. Belatedly, but still, that counted for something.

So why did she feel so guilty now, because of a single piece of coffee-stained notebook paper?

Seth glanced around, then cleared his throat. The wide patio was empty. A soft, cool breeze rustled the trees. The moon shimmered on the surface of the turquoise pool.

"It's not exactly the ocean," he apologized, "but it'll have to do."

"Seth," Summer asked, "is something wrong?"

"Nothing's wrong. As a matter of fact, everything's perfect. I just want it to stay that way."

"So do I."

"Have I told you in the last two minutes how beautiful you are tonight?" Seth whispered.

"You look pretty great yourself. This tux thing is good on you."

"Maybe I could get a job at a fancy restaurant, wear one all the time."

"It wouldn't be the same covered with mustard stains."

Seth grinned. "I can tell you're an ex-waitress. You think you'll work at the Crab 'n' Conch again when you go back to the Keys?"

"The Cramp 'n' Croak? I don't know. It wasn't exactly fulfilling, but the tips were good."

Summer sighed. Soon, very soon, she'd be back in Florida for the summer. She couldn't think about it without recalling Austin's promise—or was it a threat?

*I'll be there, waiting, whether you want me to or not. I remain hopelessly in love with you.*

"Well, if Marquez is working with you at the Cramp," Seth said, "you'll have a lot of fun, even if it isn't the most fulfilling job on earth."

"We can't all have big la-di-da internships like certain people."

Seth smiled. "They can call it an internship all they want. I'm still going to be just another boat grunt."

"A boat grunt building ultralight racing sailboats," Summer corrected. "It beats the heck out of asking 'Do you want fries or coleslaw with that?' a hundred million times." She squeezed his hand. "You should be really proud, Seth. They had dozens of applicants for that internship."

"I know. It's just that it means I'll be separated from you for part of the summer. California is so far away." He gazed off at the pool. Yellow lights glowed beneath the surface like the eyes of great fish. "Before long, you're going to be back on Crab Claw Key hanging out with Diana and Marquez just like last summer. I can't imagine not being there with you. And . . ."

"And?" Summer prompted.

"And I'm not sure I can stand being apart. I know we'll be going to college together next fall, but still . . . it seems like such a long time."

Summer nodded. Three months and then college

with Seth. It didn't seem like such a long time, really. They'd decided on the University of Wisconsin together. Seth wanted to go to college where his father and grandfather had gone. Summer hadn't felt strongly about a particular school as long as she and Seth could be together. She'd applied to some other colleges, even a difficult liberal arts school down in Florida, but in the end Wisconsin had seemed like a good compromise.

"Three months isn't so long," Summer assured him.

Seth's deep brown eyes were filled with longing and worry. "I just want to know we'll always be there for each other."

"Of course we will be, Seth," Summer whispered. "You know I love you." *And if not so long ago I thought maybe I loved Austin, too . . . well, that's over with,* she added silently. *Forgotten.*

Seth nodded. "I also know I almost lost you over spring break."

"Just because I had feelings for someone else doesn't mean I'm not totally in love with you."

"I know that," Seth said. "People can have feelings for more than one person at a time."

Something in his voice told her he really understood. It was strange, the way he was capable of putting himself in her place so easily. Sometimes she almost wished he'd been angrier about Austin, less understanding.

It would have made the guilt easier to bear.

"What happened over spring break made me realize how important you are to my life, Summer. And, well . . . I know this is, like, the corniest thing in the world to pull, but here goes."

Seth reached into his jacket pocket and removed a small black velvet box.

Instantly Summer knew what it was. She stopped breathing. Before she could sort through all her panicky reactions, Seth was down on one knee.

"God, I feel like such a dork," he said. "But you gotta do these things right."

When Summer opened her mouth to speak, he hushed her, placing a finger over her lips. "Before you go into logic overdrive, hear me out, okay?"

She nodded. Her heart was sprinting madly in her chest, but she kept her face expressionless.

Carefully Seth opened the little box. A small diamond on a simple gold band caught the moonlight.

He took her hand. "Look, I know that it would be absolutely and completely crazy for us to get married now. I *know* that, I really do. Maybe it's even crazy to get engaged now, but—" Seth gave a helpless, endearing shrug. "I guess I just don't care. Sometimes you do the stupid, crazy thing."

He caught Summer's surprised look and laughed. "Okay, so that's not the first thing you'd expect to hear

from a guy who color-codes his sock drawer. But I just
*know* in my gut this is the right thing for us, Summer.
It doesn't mean we'd have to get married right away. I
mean, I think we should finish college first, don't you?"

Summer moved her head slightly. It was not really
a nod, just an acknowledgment of the question.

"All I want this to be is a private symbol between you
and me that says we love each other and we always will."

Summer stared at the ring. Her mother's ring looked
just like this one. Small. Simple. Her mother hadn't
really wanted to bother with it, she'd told Summer.
She hadn't needed a symbol, hadn't wanted to waste
the money. Summer's dad had bought one anyway.

And now her parents were separated. Her dad lived
in an apartment near his office. He used plastic spoons
and forks from take-out places. The empty rooms
echoed when you walked through them.

Her mother slept in the guest bedroom now. At
dinnertime she kept forgetting not to set a place for
Summer's dad.

Carefully Seth removed the ring from its little box.
"Summer?" His voice was trembling. "Will you marry
me?" He looked up at her and smiled. "Someday?"

Before she could answer, he slipped the ring onto
her left ring finger. It was a little tight, and he had to
push to get it past her knuckle. But there it was, shiny
and important. It felt heavy on her hand.

The ring glimmered, a seductive promise. It was simple and easy.

It promised that even though her parents had messed up, and even though she'd messed up with Austin, things didn't always have to be that way. It promised that it would always be there, a tight gold reminder on her finger, making life easy just as she was heading out into the big, cold world.

It promised that sometimes it was okay just to do the stupid, crazy thing.

It promised to make Austin go away.

"Summer?" Seth whispered. "Will you?"

She looked at Seth with tears in her eyes. When she tried to say yes, no sound came out, so she had to nod instead.

# 4

## Crab Claw Key, Florida. There's No Place Like Home. Sort Of.

"Welcome home, engaged person."

Summer's cousin Diana swung the door to the stilt house wide open. It creaked loudly, just as it always had.

Summer stepped inside, set down her bags, and breathed deeply. The Florida air was thick and hot, like steam from a teapot. It carried a hauntingly familiar scent, part mildew, part salty ocean tang, part rotting wood, part sweet hibiscus. Not a great smell, some people would say. But to Summer, it was CK One and baby powder and Chanel No. 5 all rolled into one. It was her signature scent: Stilt House No. 1.

She'd spent the previous summer there, sharing the

space with Diver, her brother, and a territorial pelican named Frank, and although she didn't own the place (her aunt Mallory did), Summer thought of it as her own. The little bungalow was a squat and homely affair, but it was a historical landmark of sorts—rum smugglers had used it during Prohibition in the 1920s. The building sat above the water on wooden stilts. A rickety walkway wrapped around the house, then ran a hundred feet back to the grassy shore. Beyond that sat the huge home where Diana and her mother lived.

"A plant!" Summer exclaimed, noting the big philodendron on the middle of the wobbly kitchen table.

"From Mallory," Diana explained. She never called her mother Mom. "She had some other stuff done, too. New comforter on the bed, new silverware and glasses."

Summer opened the cupboard above the sink. "Matching glasses! No more Lion King and Slurpee cups. This is excellent."

"Well, you're practically a married woman now," Diana said, sitting on the bed in the far corner of the room. "Married women have utensils, Summer."

Diana kicked off her sandals and sat cross-legged on the bed. She looked as stunning as ever. Long dark hair, gray, unsettling eyes the color of the ocean on an overcast day. Although they were cousins, Diana had been adopted, a fact that always seemed embarrassingly obvious to Summer when they were together. Diana, who was a year older, exuded confidence like a character who'd walked off the set of *Gossip Girl*. Which was not to say she hadn't had her share of troubles. Diana's confidence masked a tendency toward deep and dangerous depression.

"For the record, Diana," Summer said, "I am not practically married. Jeez, I just graduated from high school a few days ago."

"But you're wearing a rock on your left hand." Diana grinned. "Or should I say pebble?"

"I already told you." Summer plopped her suitcase onto the bed. "Seth and I are not engaged, exactly. We're more like . . . engaged to be engaged. Semi-engaged."

"I don't think you can be semiengaged. It's like being semipregnant or a semivirgin." Diana eyed Summer up and down. "Hey, that isn't what's going on here, is—"

"Give me a break!" Summer groaned. "I am definitely *not* pregnant and definitely still virginal, not that it's any of your business."

"Maybe that was the idea, though." Diana wiggled her eyebrows suggestively. "Think maybe Sethie had ulterior motives? Figured if you're practically married, you'd say what the heck . . ."

"You've known Seth since he was a little kid."

Summer unzipped her suitcase. "What do you think?"

"No," Diana conceded, "that doesn't sound like Seth. He's the most wholesome, all-American guy I've ever met."

"You don't have to make him sound so boring."

"I don't think Seth is boring, Summer," Diana said. Her voice took on a strange, wistful tone. "I think he's pretty great, actually." She stood and went to the window. The drone of a motorboat filled the air. "That's why," Diana added, "I thought it was so odd, the call I got a couple of days ago."

Summer looked up, a bunch of T-shirts in her arms. "What phone call?"

Diana opened the little window over the kitchen sink, taking her time. She turned, shaking her head sorrowfully. "The phone call from Austin Reed. The one telling me to pass along the message that he'd see you soon."

Summer dropped her shirts on the bed and closed her eyes.

"Summer, Summer, Summer." Diana clucked her tongue. "If we're going to be roommates soon, you have to keep me updated on your romantic escapades. How am I ever going to cover for you?"

"You don't need to cover for me."

"I did during spring break," Diana pointed out. "After Seth found you and Austin in, shall we say, a compromising position, wasn't I the one who had to go around pretending Austin and I were hot for each other?" She sat on the bed and began carefully refolding one of Summer's T-shirts. "Not that it was such a terrible sacrifice, given that he bears a striking resemblance to Ethan Hawke. But it was kind of a waste of time, since Seth figured it all out anyway."

Summer looked at her cousin. "Diana, that is over," she said firmly. "Seth understands what happened. He forgave me." She shrugged. "And if Austin wants to try to get in touch with me, I can't exactly do anything about it, can I? What do you want me to do, get an unlisted phone number? Maybe I could go into the witness protection program, get a whole new identity."

"Okay, okay. Don't bite my head off."

"Sorry. I guess I'm just tired, after flying down and everything. I had graduation a few days ago, and then yesterday I saw Seth off to California. I feel like my entire life is changing, and I can't keep up with it."

"Have you talked to Seth since then?" Diana asked with interest.

"Last night. He said Newport Beach is great and he's really psyched about the boat building internship. But he wishes he were here."

"So do I," Diana said. She paused. "I mean, for your sake, it would have been great."

Summer sighed. "Come on." She pointed to the door. "I want to check out the view."

"Nothing's changed. Except I think that pelican of yours is actually fatter, if that's possible."

They stood on the weathered deck, leaning gently on the ancient railing. The small island was shaped much like a crab's claw, with the two "pincers" enclosing a sparkling expanse of turquoise water. Motorboats vied with sailboats and gulls for space on the little bay, and postcard-perfect palm trees hugged the shoreline.

Frank was perched on the railing. "Hey, Frank, remember me?" Summer asked.

He responded by pooping on the walkway, then eyeing both girls with obvious disdain.

"You two really have a rapport going," Diana commented.

"Frank was mostly Diver's friend."

"I guess you . . . haven't heard from Diver or anything?"

Summer shook her head.

"He and Marquez are pretty hot and heavy these days. You're bound to see him, you know."

"I know," Summer said softly.

Diana kicked at a loose railing. "You really could come stay up in the main house, Summer. Mallory's in and out on book tours, and we have, like, a hundred extra rooms."

Summer glanced back at her aunt's ornate pastel house—the perfect dwelling for a successful romance novelist. "I like it here," she said.

Diana shuddered. "Roughing it. I just don't get it."

"It's not just that. This place has lots of memories."

"Well, pretty soon we'll find something cool for ourselves. I can't wait to move out of Mallory's." She nudged Summer. "Maybe you and I should scope stuff out, then let Marquez in on it. She has no taste."

"She just has wild, out-there taste."

"Like I said."

For a few moments they didn't speak. The waves lapped at the slick wooden stilts with gentle insistence. Summer hadn't realized how much she'd missed that soothing sound.

"Summer," Diana said, breaking the spell, "are you sure about Seth? Really sure?"

Summer looked out at the familiar, endless vista of blue-green waves. "I'm sure."

"How do you know?" Diana asked. "I mean, I'm not sure I've ever really been sure." The uncertainty in her voice was unnerving. Diana usually radiated confidence like a force field. "Sure enough to wear a ring like that one, anyway."

Summer hesitated. She and Diana, despite being cousins, were not that close. But it would be nice to confide in someone, and why not Diana? They were going to be roommates for the next three months. It wasn't as though Summer was going to have any secrets for long.

"The truth is," Summer said, choosing her words with care, "I don't know what 'sure' means, exactly. I just know that when I saw this ring, it made sense. I was feeling overwhelmed, I guess. You know, with graduation and college and my parents splitting up, it felt like the whole world had been turned upside down. And then I saw Seth holding this ring in the moonlight, and bam, everything was right-side-up again." She touched the little diamond. "It made all the pieces fit together. I could see my life, college and being with Seth and everything else, and it felt good, you know?"

Diana frowned. "So you got engaged because you were feeling confused? I'm not sure that qualifies as the best reason on earth, Summer."

"That's not the only reason," Summer protested, so loudly that Frank took off in a huff. "I love Seth. Totally."

Diana watched Frank resettle in a palm tree farther down the shore. "Sorry. I guess I just don't understand. But if you're happy, then I'm happy for you."

"I'm definitely happy."

"Then I am also definitely happy, once removed." Diana gave her a quick hug. "I'm glad you're here, you know that?"

"Me, too."

"I'll let you get unpacked. We're going to the beach with Marquez this afternoon, okay?" Diana started down the walkway. "Oh, by the way, Austin mentioned a letter he sent to you. He wondered if you got it."

"Um, yeah. Prom day."

"Prom?" Diana paused. "Isn't that when you and Seth got engaged?"

"So?"

"So nothing. I was just noting the coincidence, that's all." Diana smiled. "Well, anyway, welcome back to paradise."

On the big-screen TV in the Olans' sunken living room, a yoga instructor was breathing deeply.

Diana's mother lay on the plush cream carpeting, trying to maneuver an ankle into position. When she saw Diana, she grabbed the remote and muted the TV.

"If I had Ted Turner's money, I'd have inner peace, too." Her mother sat up with a groan. The back of her puffy, lacquered hair was flat. "Summer settled in?"

"Yep."

"Hey, the Institute called. It's on the machine. They want you to sub for one of the other volunteers."

"Thanks. I'll call them." Diana hesitated. "You don't need to, um, bring that up with Summer or anything."

"What? Your volunteering with the kids? How come?"

Diana shrugged. "I don't know. It's just not anyone's business, okay?"

"If you and Marquez and Summer get a place together for the summer, you're not going to have any secrets. When I was in the dorm at college, the girls on my floor even started getting our periods at the same time. Isn't that wild?"

"Well, gross, anyway."

Her mother sighed. "I wish you girls would just stay here this summer instead of renting some seedy dive."

"Mallory, we have to get some seedy dive so we can feel like we're properly suffering. It's a rite of passage."

"If you suffered here, you'd have a Jet Ski and an espresso maker. Besides, I'm hardly ever here."

"When is your next book tour, anyway?"

"Pretty soon. West Coast, plus some of those other states. What's that one that's shaped like a square?"

"Wyoming? Colorado?"

"Yeah, one of those."

"You're not going anywhere near Newport Beach, are you?"

"There's a schedule Kara sent me on the table over there."

"Mind if I look?"

"Why? Are you and Summer planning a big party in my absence?"

Diana rifled through the mass of papers on the table. "Actually, I was thinking I might go with you." She located the itinerary. "Laguna Beach, Newport Beach, Long Beach, Los Angeles. Excellent. Mallory, how about a little quality mother–daughter time?"

"Why?"

"Why? Because we are mother and daughter. You wound me."

"Uh-huh. What gives?"

Diana patted her mother on the head. "You're going to the land of Rodeo Drive armed with credit cards, and you wonder why I want to come along?"

And if Diana just happened to stop by and say hello to Seth while she was in the neighborhood, so much the better. There was nothing wrong with a simple hello, was there? It would be an innocent get-together, nothing more.

Nothing at all like their not-so-innocent get-together last New Year's.

"Call Kara and she'll arrange the tickets."

"I'm not exactly sure yet," Diana said. "I have to wait and see how things go. It depends."

"On what?"

Diana shrugged. "Well, for one thing, I want to get

things settled here with Summer. The apartment hunting and all that. I just want to make sure everything's
definite."

*Like which guy Summer's decided on,* Diana added
silently. Summer could deny it all she wanted, but
Diana could tell she wasn't over Austin, not by a long
shot.

It wasn't fair—not to Austin, not to Seth, and not
to Diana.

A shudder ran through her as she remembered the
way Seth had held her that New Year's night. Long
months had passed since then, but she could still hear
his whispered, hypnotic voice and feel his lips on hers.

She'd tried to let it go. She'd written him long, passionate, embarrassing letters, but she kept every one in a
little cardboard box. She'd dialed his number on lonely
nights, but she'd always hung up at the sound of his voice.
Out of a sense of loyalty and guilt, she'd even done her
best to help get Seth and Summer back together.

But what exactly had her honorable intentions gotten her? Summer was halfheartedly engaged to Seth
while still infatuated with Austin. And Diana was left
out in the cold.

She headed off to the kitchen. "Want some
chocolate-chip cookies? It's a much more direct route
to inner peace."

# 5

# Ex-boyfriends and Ex-brothers

"Sunscreen, Dr Pepper, beach towel, romance novel, sunglasses, Blistex, brush."

Summer surveyed her beach bag with satisfaction. After nine long months of Minnesota weather, it was nice to get back to the basics. She consulted the mirror in her bathroom. The two-piece bathing suit she'd bought to wear over spring break still fit, more or less.

She checked the clock on the ancient stove. Diana would be waiting for her up at the main house. Well, she could wait another minute or two.

Summer grabbed the phone book from the kitchen cupboard. It was tiny compared to the fat white pages back in Bloomington. But as she'd hoped, Aunt

Mallory had supplied her with the newest edition, hot off the presses.

She sat at the kitchen table, turned to the *R*'s, and scanned. *Ranson, Redman, Ruiz*. Nope, back a little.

*Reed, Aaron M.*

*Reed, Augusta.*

*Reed, Carl.*

Summer breathed a sigh of relief. No *Reed, Austin*. Could be he hadn't moved down there after all. Could be he'd been calling from Missouri, where his family lived.

Could be he was living a couple of blocks down the street and he'd just gotten his phone the week before.

Summer closed the phone book with a groan. Maybe she'd call information later. Maybe not.

Maybe, when you felt the hand of fate swooping down at you, it was better not to know exactly when or where it was going to hit.

"Can you believe it? Here we are, just like last summer," Marquez exclaimed. "Only Summer's wearing an engagement ring, I'm about to be the first person in my family to graduate from high school, and Diana . . ." She sat up on her beach towel and lowered her shades. "Well, Diana's leaving her coffin much more frequently these days."

"One other change," Summer noted. "You have

lost so much weight, Marquez. You look fantastic."

"Fantastic as in 'Marquez was such a whale before, and now she looks more like, say, a manatee'?" Marquez asked. "Or fantastic as in 'Marquez was such a pig before, and now she looks like, say, Ms. Slender Teen Cuban-American of Crab Claw Key'?"

"How about second runner-up?" Diana suggested.

Marquez tossed a handful of sand at her. "It's not like I'm fishing for compliments, exactly. It's just that after J.T. broke up with me, I felt like such a complete loser, and now I'm starting to feel like the new, improved Maria Marquez."

"How did you do it?" Summer asked. "You've lost a *lot* of weight, Marquez."

"I know." Marquez laughed with pleasure. "I look down at my thighs sometimes and I think, whoa, somebody call the cops and file a missing-person report."

"But how?" Summer persisted.

Marquez shrugged. "Running on the beach, mostly. Plus my neighbor was throwing away her old exercise bike, so I grabbed it out of the trash. That's cool, because you can exercise while you watch Letterman."

"You exercise that late?" Summer asked.

"She exercises constantly," Diana said, with that hint of disapproval that always ticked off Marquez.

"Way to be sensitive," Marquez said, rolling her

eyes. "I'm cursed with fat-thigh genes. Some of us have a lonely battle to wage."

Diana flipped the page of her newspaper, fighting the ocean breeze. "I just think you're getting a little obsessed, that's all."

"I wouldn't expect you to understand, Diana. You're the only person I know who can eat an entire pound cake and actually *lose* a pound." Marquez shook her legs. There was still a trace of cellulite here and there. Another inch gone would be nice. Two would be better.

"Well, I'm very proud of you," Summer said.

Marquez grinned. Man, it was nice to have Summer back. Diana was the kind of friend who took work. She was critical and just a little too smart for her own good. Not that Summer wasn't smart, too— but she had the good sense to accept you the way you were, no questions asked. She was the perfect hanging-around, all-purpose best friend.

Diana held up her yellow highlighter in triumph. "I've found it! Listen to this." She folded her newspaper and marked an ad. "'Three-bedroom, two-bath charmer on Coconut Key, ocean view, beach access, Jacuzzi, pets okay.'"

"How much?" Summer asked eagerly.

Diana cleared her throat. "Twenty-two hundred."

"A *month?*" Summer cried. "That's, like, my entire income last summer waiting tables."

Diana shrugged. "I was just fantasizing. Okay, so we'll downsize a little."

"Try a lot," Marquez advised.

"How many bedrooms?" Diana asked. "Maybe we should get an extra for visitors." She cast a grin at Summer. "What if Seth and Austin show up at the same time? We'll need extra room, won't we, Summer? Or at least a very big bed."

"Austin?" Marquez repeated.

"He's ba–aack!" Diana said. "He wrote Summer. He called Summer. And he promised to see Summer very soon."

Marquez grabbed Summer's arm. "You *are* kidding! The same Austin Reed who almost caused you to break up with Seth?"

"Yes, that would be the one," Summer replied dryly. "Now can we drop it?"

"Right. You know me better than that."

Summer reached for her sunscreen and re-coated her arms. "I believe we were discussing our apartment," she said, sending Diana and Marquez a frosty look.

Marquez knew what that look meant: Let it go for a while. Fine, she could take a hint. But one way or another she'd get the truth out of Summer eventually.

"It should be quaint," Summer continued. "I want my first real apartment to be something I'll remember forever." She paused. "Of course, in a way the stilt house is my first official apartment."

"Doesn't count," Diana said, tapping her highlighter against the paper. "It's your aunt's." She frowned. "You know, Mallory did say we could live at our house this summer, but I told her we wanted to suffer."

"Let me get this straight." Marquez sat up. "You said no to a free gigantic house with big-screen TV and a billion bedrooms?"

"Don't forget the espresso maker," Diana said.

"I hate espresso. But I love money, and this could save us a bundle."

"Marquez," Diana said reasonably, "Mallory would be there. A maternal unit would be living in your midst."

"Yeah, I see your point. She is a little nutty."

"She's way past nutty. She's trail mix. She's—"

"Okay, we'll rent." Marquez didn't want to get into that again. Diana was very generous with her money, which she had way too much of. But she just didn't get *not* having money. It wasn't that she was insensitive, exactly. It just didn't occur to Diana that not everybody's mother was a bestselling novelist who drove a Mercedes.

And really, Mallory wasn't so bad. Or was it the fact that Marquez's parents were moving to Texas the day after next that made having a mom around seem tolerable? It was fine to complain about your mom, until you started thinking about what it would be like not to have her around to complain about.

"Marquez?" Summer asked. "You okay?"

Marquez adjusted her sunglasses. "Me? Yeah. Hey, I'm about to be an official graduate of John F. Kennedy High. Of course I'm okay. I'm way okay."

Diana rolled onto her side, observing Marquez with that annoying look that made Marquez feel as though her head were transparent. "Wasn't there something you wanted to discuss with Summer?" she said pointedly.

"You know, it's not like I've ever had trouble moving my mouth, Diana."

"You get no argument here," Diana said. She jerked her head at Summer.

"What?" Summer said. "Tell me, Marquez."

Marquez stared off at the ocean. A gang of seagulls was squawking uproariously over some shared bird joke. Laughing gulls, they were called. Summer's brother had taught her that. Diver knew all about birds and animals.

Summer nudged Marquez with her foot. "What, Marquez?"

"It's about Diver," Diana said softly.

Marquez took a deep breath. "See, the thing is, Summer, with you coming to my graduation tomorrow . . ." This was way too hard. Marquez hated getting stuck in the middle of other people's problems. But there she was, stuck big-time.

"You want to know about Diver." Summer bit her lip. "If I'll be okay if he comes, too."

Marquez nodded. "If you don't want him there, he's really cool with it. He understands. I mean, he's the one who ran out on your family. He's the one who's been holed up here in Florida for the last few months."

"It's fine, Marquez." Summer smiled, but Marquez could see the effort that went into it. "I wouldn't ruin your graduation for anything."

"And the party at my house after," Diana prodded. "He'll be there, too, Summer."

"It's okay," Summer said, more insistently this time.

"I was a little worried," Marquez admitted, "when you went to talk to him over spring break and didn't go through with it."

"It wasn't the right time," Summer said flatly.

"And now it is?" Marquez pressed.

"It'll have to be."

"He misses you, you know."

"I guess he should have thought of that before running out." Summer's voice was biting.

"Still, it'll be great having you both there tomorrow," Marquez said soothingly.

"I wish Diver could have been there for mine." Summer gave a tense smile. "It was hard. My mom and dad didn't even sit together."

Marquez played with the edge of her beach towel. She knew Summer blamed Diver for their parents' separation. Wrongly, Marquez felt, but she wasn't about to tell Summer that. The girl was bummed enough.

The laughing gulls were sniping at each other, nipping at feathers as they fought over a piece of seaweed. This wasn't going to be easy, dating Summer's brother while living with Summer. It was going to make Marquez the go-between and conciliator. The UN of the Smith family.

Marquez groaned. Could World War Three be far off?

# 6

# A Big Day for Marquez, a Bad Day for Summer

"There she is," Diana whispered. "Our little graduate."

Summer and Diana waved frantically from their seats in the bleachers. Marquez waved back.

John F. Kennedy High was a much smaller school than Summer's, and its size translated into a much more informal graduation ceremony. For one thing, it was being held outside, on the football field, while Summer's had been inside the cavernous gymnasium. For another, this was Florida, and it was nearly ninety-two degrees outside. That meant the assembled spectators were dressed in Crab Claw casual: shorts, T-shirts, even bathing suits.

By comparison, Summer, in her ribbed blue tank

dress with a straw belt, was dressed up. Diana was wearing a denim miniskirt with a halter top. But the rest of Marquez's family, her parents and five brothers, were wearing their stiff Sunday best. This was a big occasion for them. Marquez's parents had come to the U.S. from Cuba when Marquez was just a little girl. They'd had nothing but the clothes on their backs and their hopes.

"You must be very proud of Marquez," Summer said to Mrs. Marquez.

"Look at her sitting there, so serious," her mother said with a laugh. She had the same huge eyes, naturally olive complexion, and dark tangle of curls as her daughter. "You'd think she was going to the dentist."

"Maybe she's worried about Diver showing up," Diana pointed out.

Summer glanced down the bleacher rows. Still no sign of her brother. She felt a terrible mixture of relief and sorrow. She knew how much Marquez wanted to have Diver there that day. But Summer really didn't want to face her brother, not yet.

She'd tried over spring break. She'd gone to the wildlife sanctuary where Diver lived and worked. She'd come within a few feet of him. But the words just hadn't been there.

Diana nudged her. Marquez's mom and dad were kissing and whispering. Summer fingered her diamond ring. They looked so happy. Was it possible to stay in love when you were old enough to have a daughter graduating from high school? Summer's parents hadn't.

True, Summer's mom and dad had suffered in ways most parents only had nightmares about. Diver had been kidnapped from them as a child. And when he'd finally been reunited with them, the strain had been more than he could handle. He'd left after only a few months of halfhearted effort and returned to Florida.

And after he was gone, the fights between Summer's parents had begun. "It's your fault for pushing him too hard." "It's your fault for not pushing hard enough." "If only you'd tried harder." Each whispered accusation was another broken thread, until the whole fabric of Summer's life had unraveled before her eyes. The week before Summer left for the Keys, her mother had set up an appointment with a divorce lawyer.

A small woman bustled onto the dais and tapped the microphone. "Welcome, friends and family of our wonderful graduating seniors!" she exclaimed. She went on to extol the virtues of the graduating class. They were the adults of the future, the hope of tomorrow, the shining beacons in a troubled world.

Listening to the familiar words, Summer found it hard to believe she herself was a high school graduate. In three short months she would be a real, live college student at the University of Wisconsin. It seemed impossible.

She tried to imagine herself walking to class with Seth past the pretty brick campus buildings she'd visited earlier that year, but the image wouldn't stick. It didn't feel like *her* school, not the way Bloomington High had seemed like her personal campus by the time she was a senior.

Sometimes she imagined herself on another college campus—Carlson, the one in Florida that her English teacher had encouraged her to apply to. She'd been accepted, but Seth hadn't, and that had pretty much ended that discussion. Besides, it had been just a whim. It was a tough school, too rigorous for Summer. She would never survive the academic competition. And of course she wouldn't dream of going to college without Seth.

Diana nudged her. She pointed to the football field.

Striding across it toward the bleachers was Summer's brother. His hair was a shimmering sun-streaked blond, his tan dark. He scanned the bleachers with intense blue eyes.

His gaze locked on Summer, and her heart stuttered. He didn't smile or turn away. He just looked at her with his open, hopeful, accepting, beautiful face.

She wanted to do something, maybe wave or smile. But she just sat there, stunned, frozen by old pain.

Slowly Diver made his way up the crowded bleachers until he came to Marquez's family. He took a seat at the other end, as far as he could get from Summer and Diana.

Marquez saw him and gave a little wave. He waved back, grinning broadly. He did not look at Summer again.

Summer couldn't help looking at him, though. He was wearing the suit her parents had bought for his halfhearted job-hunting efforts back in Minnesota. He'd refused to wear it, saying it cramped his style and that if he couldn't get a job wearing jeans, he didn't want a job. There'd been a fight about it, a long one. Summer had taken her dinner to her room that evening to avoid the sharp words.

And now there he was, in ninety-plus degree heat and humidity that would wilt a piece of steel, and he was wearing the stupid suit.

Sure, he could wear it there, then, when it didn't matter anymore.

When it was too late for her parents to see it.

"They make a cute couple, don't they?" Diana said early that evening.

Summer nodded sullenly. Marquez and Diver did look great together as they danced on the Olans' wide, sloping lawn. The graduation party was in full swing, packed with Marquez's classmates and family members. A popular local band played on the patio. Mallory had called in her favorite caterer to provide the food. Colorful Japanese lanterns swayed from the trees in the twilight, and tiki torches burned at the edge of the water.

"We're starting to get party crashers," Diana said, noting the swelling crowd.

"This is probably the best graduation party on the key," Summer pointed out. "Marquez is really grateful that you went to all this trouble."

Diana shrugged. "You know Mallory. Any excuse for a party—and she adores Marquez." She sipped from a paper cup of lemonade. "Still, it would be nice if Marquez could at least say thanks."

"I think money stuff is kind of tough for her. Her parents lost the gas station, and now they're moving. She's not even sure she can swing college tuition."

Diana nodded distractedly. "Speaking of tough situations," she said, eyeing Summer, "you haven't said two words to Diver yet, have you?"

"I haven't said one word. It's like we're invisible to one another. Which is fine by me." Summer winced at the anger in her voice.

"Uh-oh. Mallory's waving me over. That can only mean a catering crisis." Diana brushed off her skirt. "Want to come?"

"Yeah, I'd be a lot of help in a catering emergency." Summer rolled her eyes. "We don't have caterers in Bloomington. We just nuke some Jeno's pizza rolls and call it a day. I'm going down to the stilt house to change into some shorts."

"You're not going to hole up and pout, are you?"

Summer pretended indignation. "I'm a high school graduate. High school graduates do not pout."

"Nobody ever told *me* that."

"It's at the bottom of your diploma, in really fine print," Summer said.

She crossed the wooden walkway to the stilt house. With each step the raucous music and swell of voices receded a little. The truth was, she *did* want to hole up in her house until the party ended—or at least until Diver left. But how long could she keep that up? What was she going to do when she and Diana and Marquez got a place together? Ban Diver? Lock herself in the bathroom every time he showed up?

"Hey, Frank." The pelican was sitting on the railing near her front door. He blinked and fluttered a wing.

Inside the stilt house, the music was just a throbbing bass line, like rhythmic thunder. The kitchen was cool and shadowy. Summer didn't turn on any lights.

On the kitchen table, the little yellow Post-it note sat like an accusation. Her aunt Mallory's scribbled, cryptic message was barely legible. When Summer had found it that afternoon after the graduation ceremony, it had taken her a minute to decipher her aunt's shorthand: *Austin cld. Cn't wat 2 C U. No #*. She was grateful, at least, that Aunt Mallory hadn't made an issue of it in front of Diana and Marquez.

It was too bad Austin hadn't left a number. It would have given Summer a chance to warn him off, to announce her engagement and send him on his way. Now she was stuck with this feeling of foreboding, waiting for the other shoe to drop.

She rifled through her ramshackle dresser, trying to locate her khaki shorts. In her new place, maybe she could have an actual closet of her own.

Suddenly she heard a gentle, tentative voice outside the open window.

"Hey, guy. Did you think I forgot you? Look, Frank. I scarfed you some anchovies."

Summer closed her eyes. Diver. Only he could be standing on her walkway, chatting with a pelican.

She crouched behind her dresser. Maybe he didn't know she was there. Maybe she could keep it that way.

"I'll bet you're glad Summer's back, huh, Frank?"

From her position on the floor, she could just make out Diver's silhouette against the velvety purple sky. He had his back to the railing. His jacket was gone, and his tie hung loosely around his neck. He might or might not have been looking into her window. She couldn't be sure.

"We had a lot of good times here," Diver mused. Summer wondered whether he was talking to himself, to Frank, or to her. "Remember sitting on the roof, you and me and Summer, watching the sun come up? The whole sky was on fire."

Summer did remember. She remembered the way they'd sat together in silence, awed and humbled, like two lone visitors in the world's largest cathedral. Diver had been a mystery to her then, just as he still was.

"I miss this place," Diver said, almost whispering. He was peering through the window. "I miss you, too. And Summer. I miss her a lot."

Summer stifled a sob.

"I guess she's kind of mad at me. Not that I blame her."

Another sob, this one audible.

"Maybe if we could talk," Diver said. "Maybe I could explain."

Summer sniffled.

The door creaked. She saw two tan bare feet sticking out of black pants. She looked up.

Diver stood there in the shadows. His hand was out. He was holding a handkerchief.

Summer took it and blew her nose. She sniffled again.

Diver turned on the kitchen light, then straddled a chair.

She started to give the handkerchief back.

"It's Jack's. He gave it to me when he bought the suit." Summer sat very still on the floor, her back against the dresser. She looked at the handkerchief. In the glare of the overhead light, the white linen almost glowed. Her throat felt as though she'd swallowed gravel.

"Mom got a divorce lawyer," she said, twisting the handkerchief in her hands. She didn't look at Diver.

She waited for him to say "It's not my fault" or "So what?" She had answers for those words. She'd practiced them in her mind, all the angry things she would say to Diver when she finally had the chance.

"Because of me," he whispered. It wasn't a question. It was a statement of fact.

Summer looked up. Diver's face was expressionless.

"Why didn't you—" She choked back a sob. "Why didn't you stay, Diver? Why didn't you try a little harder to belong? The rest of us wanted so badly to make it work."

"Because I didn't," Diver said. "Belong. Because . . ." He opened his hands, palms up, as if he expected the right words to fall into them. "I knew I wasn't going to stay. I figured it was better to leave sooner rather than later. I didn't want you all getting more . . . attached."

"Attached?" Summer cried. "Attached? You're not some stray dog we picked up off the street. You're my brother, you're their son. Doesn't that mean anything to you?"

Her voice echoed in the little room. Diver folded his hands together. He thought for a long time. "I didn't have your life, Summer. To me, Jack and Kim are just nice people. I grew up with other, not-so-great parents. I didn't have your perfect life."

"Do you have any idea what it did to Mom and Dad to lose you? And then to . . . to find you again, to have you back in their lives, and then to have you just vanish again? You leave a note on my bed that says 'I'm sorry,' like that somehow evens the score?"

Summer realized her hands were shaking. She climbed to her feet, pacing back and forth to use up the wild energy fueling her anger. "After you left, it was nothing but Mom blaming Dad and Dad blaming Mom for not handling you better. Then it was like they got tired and gave up. Well, I blame *you,* Diver. It wasn't because Dad pushed you to get a job and Mom bugged you to cut your hair. It was *you.*"

She dropped onto her bed and bent over, burying her head in her hands.

After a moment Diver joined her. He touched her hair, then pulled his hand away. "It wasn't just the job, Summer," he said softly. "It was other things.

They wanted me to tell them who my other parents were."

"You mean your kidnappers."

"I was only two, Summer. They were my parents to me." He sighed. "Jack and Kim wanted to press charges, to prosecute them."

Summer wiped her eyes. "And you have a problem with that?"

"I want to let it go."

"You want to let everything go, Diver. You just want to escape. You can't live your whole life that way."

Diver stood. "I guess it's the only way I know how."

He turned to leave. At the door he paused. "Keep the handkerchief. It's more yours than mine."

On the walkway, Summer heard him stop to talk to Frank, but she was sobbing too hard to hear what he said.

# 7

# Up on the Roof

Summer awoke the next morning before dawn. She put on shorts and her blue and gold Property of Bloomington H.S. Athletic Dept. T-shirt and made herself a cup of herbal tea.

The air outside was cool and wet. The sun was just a secret, glowing on the horizon. Waves lazily stroked the stilts beneath the house.

Summer climbed up the ladder that led to the roof, the way she had the year before with Diver. The shingles were rough on her skin, like cats' tongues. She sat very still. Now and then she sipped her tea. But mostly she just sat and waited.

With Diver the previous summer, watching the

dawn unfurl had been a wonderful moment. Spiritual, almost. They had shared something too big for words.

She wished it had gone better with him the night before. She didn't regret what she'd said. In fact, she'd been relieved to finally cut loose and drop her anger at his feet. Maybe Marquez was right. Sometimes it did help to just go ahead and be angry, instead of tying your feelings up in polite little packages with pretty ribbons, the way Summer had learned to do.

But now she was left with a gaping hole where the anger had been. She felt diminished. Smaller than before. Watching Diver walk away, his shoulders sagging, she'd felt awful.

But what could she do? Pretend he hadn't failed her family? Pretend he hadn't hurt her?

She heard footsteps on the dock, and her pulse quickened. She hoped it was Diver, then instantly regretted hoping. Slowly a figure materialized in the gray haze.

It definitely wasn't Diver.

"I come bearing the gift of muffins."

It was Austin, holding up a white paper bag. Summer's heart fluttered.

He looked pretty much the way he had when she'd first met him on her flight to Florida over spring break: tattered denim jacket, worn jeans, a couple of tiny silver hoops in one ear. He had submitted to a haircut, she could tell, but his dark brown hair was still operating by its own rules. He hadn't shaved in at least a week, though his faded T-shirt was wrinkle-free, a concession, she supposed, to her.

Austin was not the kind of guy you'd bring home to Mom. If Mom was feeling charitable, she might see a sensitive, tortured, down-at-the-heels poet. If she wasn't, she'd see her worst nightmare, the boy who was going to corrupt her innocent daughter and leave her brokenhearted.

"Austin." It was all Summer could think of to say.

He stood on the deck below her, gazing up in rapture as if he were having a religious moment.

"When I remembered your being this beautiful," he said, "I told myself I was crazy, no girl was that perfect. Now I see I was right all along." He grinned broadly. "Of course, when I imagined you, you were generally *in* a house, not on one. But what's a preposition in the grand scheme of things? May I come up?"

Summer gave a small nod. Austin tossed her the bag of muffins. They were still warm. She did not like what she was feeling—tingling skin and liquid bones and a stomach freed from gravity, the kinds of symptoms generally associated with the early stages of the flu. The symptoms she remembered from her early days with Seth.

They were not feelings she wanted to be having. She told herself to stop having them.

She was not listening.

Austin crawled across the roof and settled next to her. The spot where his shoulder was touching hers burned.

"So," he said. "We meet again."

Summer hugged her knees and nodded.

"You haven't gone mute in the meantime?"

She shook her head. Her voice was lodged in her throat like a piece of hard candy. She didn't dare try it.

Austin turned to look at her. She could smell his shampoo, or his aftershave, or his deodorant—something, anyway, that was lime-scented and exotic.

"You got my messages?" he asked.

Summer nodded.

"And my letter?"

Another nod, this one conveying regret and annoyance, she hoped.

"And would it be out of line to wonder if you'd give me a hello kiss?"

This time the nod was vehement.

"I see."

She'd forgotten how compelling his voice was, how full of wild promises.

"Well, can you at least hand me the muffins?"

Summer did. Austin took one out. The fragrance of blueberries wafted through the air.

A coppery halo glowed on the horizon. Summer fixed her gaze on it. She practiced the words in her mind like lines in a play.

"I'm glad you're okay," she said at last.

This time it was Austin who didn't speak.

"I thought you were afraid to take the test," Summer said.

Austin stared at his muffin, a bemused look on his face. "I was. Scared like I've never been scared."

"What made you change your mind?"

"Something you said, actually."

"Me?"

Austin touched the back of her hand with his fingertips. "You asked what if I went through life assuming I was going to get my dad's disease, and it turned out I was wrong? Afraid to get involved with anyone, afraid to take the chance. It would just be so ironic. So I had the genetic testing done after all." Austin gazed out at the drowsy ocean. "And lo and behold, the gods smiled on me."

"What did your family say?"

"My mom was thrilled, my dad . . . well, he's too out of it to really understand, I'm afraid. My brother—"

"The one who tested positive for the gene?"

Austin nodded. "Yeah. He was really glad for me,

but I could tell he was thinking, 'Why me and not him?' Which was pretty much what I was thinking. Life doesn't make a whole lot of sense sometimes." He turned to face her. "But that's something I'm starting to realize, Summer. Life doesn't always make a whole lot of sense. Sometimes we don't know exactly why we do what we do." He took her hand, but she slipped out of his grasp. "Which is why I've moved to the Keys."

Summer blinked. "You've moved to the Keys," she repeated very slowly, as if she were just learning English.

"I got a job waiting tables over on Coconut Key. You know, a little ways up the coast?"

Summer knew. It was one of the places Diana and Marquez wanted to go apartment hunting.

"Why are you doing this, Austin? Moving here, following me? You run off at spring break and tell me to have a nice life. You leave without any explanation—"

"Actually, I left a very articulate note," Austin interrupted. "Not to mention the photos from our Disney World trip."

"Without any explanation," Summer persisted, "and I get my life back together with Seth, and now you show up and go, 'Hey, by the way, my genes are okay, and I've decided to move in next door'?" She held out her left hand. The little diamond caught the faint pink morning rays. "Do you know what this is?"

"Cubic zirconia?"

"It's an engagement ring, Austin. Seth and I are engaged. Do you know what that means?"

"Um . . . I'm guessing I'm probably not invited to the bachelor party?"

Summer didn't smile.

Austin sighed. "I saw the ring right away, Summer, and yes, I know what it means. I just don't happen to care. Jewelry as an expression of commitment does not impress me. Besides, one thing a brush with mortality teaches you is to live for today."

*"Carpe diem,"* Summer said. "I remember."

He flashed her one of his most charming smiles. "Anyway, I happen to like it here. You've got sun and ocean and pelicans"—he gestured at Frank— "and I've got a job I can stand, and a not-too-bad apartment, except for the roaches you can saddle up and ride. Even without you, it's a nice place to be." He took her hand, covering the ring, and this time he wouldn't let go. "Of course, with you it would be perfect."

"There won't be any me."

"That's what you said on the Skyway to Tomorrowland at Disney World, and then you kissed me like I've never been kissed before."

"You must have had very limited kissing experience."

Austin leaned a little closer. "As it happens, I've had a lot of experience."

His lips were so close. The guilt and the recriminations evaporated. Even thoughts of Seth evaporated. All she felt was a terrific pull, as though she were a speck of steel and a million magnets were tugging her closer and closer.

"Just one kiss," Austin whispered, "for old times' sake."

Summer closed her eyes to the rosy horizon and Austin's dark gaze. She could feel her pulse throbbing through her temple like a marching band.

If she stopped thinking and just felt the pull, guiding her closer, it felt so sweet. It felt so good, so right, if she just didn't think. . . .

# 8

# I Think We Have a Really Bad Connection. . . .

"You still there, Seth?" Diana asked as she headed toward the stilt house, phone in hand.

"I'm here."

"Sorry, I slipped and almost dropped the phone. The grass on the lawn is really wet."

She made her way down the sloping lawn. The dawn light cast long shadows. The yard was filled with the remains of Marquez's party: crumpled napkins, overflowing trash barrels, a discarded T-shirt, a pair of sandals, a handful of wet crackers.

"We had a great party last night," Diana said. "Really crazy. Wish you could have been here."

"Me, too," Seth said. His voice was fuzzy. The connection was pretty bad.

"What time is it there, anyway?" Diana asked.

"Way too early," Seth said. "I couldn't sleep."

"How come you're calling? Is anything wrong?"

"No . . . I just, you know, wanted to tell Summer hi and stuff. You know."

And stuff. "Yeah, I know." Diana's grip tightened on the phone.

"She doing okay? Summer, I mean?"

Diana stopped suddenly as the sloping roof of the stilt house came into view.

Well, well. What an interesting sight this was. Her little cousin on the roof, in what appeared to be a very passionate embrace with Austin Reed.

"Diana?" Seth's voice was tinny and indistinct.

Diana put the receiver to her ear. "Yeah?"

"I said is Summer doing okay?"

"Oh, yeah. I'd say she's doing just fine, Seth. You don't have to worry about Summer. She can take care of herself."

She took a few steps onto the walkway that led to the stilt house, then held up the phone. "Summer!" she called.

Diana watched with grim satisfaction as Summer and Austin disentangled frantically.

"Diana?" Summer yelled back. "Did you want something?"

"It's Seth," Diana waved the phone.

Summer's mouth dropped open. Austin rolled his eyes. After a moment he climbed down off the roof, then helped Summer down. When he reached for her waist, she pushed his hands away irritably.

Diana sauntered down the walkway. She could see Summer working up an excuse, a logical explanation for why she happened to be playing tonsil hockey with someone other than her fiancé.

"Just a sec, Seth," Diana said. "Summer's a little busy."

There was a pause on the other end of the line. "Diana?" Seth said at last. "I never really got a chance to thank you for straightening me out over spring break. I was so angry about seeing Summer with Austin that I guess I couldn't see the forest for the trees, you know? You were right. I couldn't exactly get all irate when you and I had done the same . . . well, anyway, thanks."

"Sure," Diana said softly as she neared the stilt house. "Anytime. I'm a regular marriage counselor. Oh. I almost forgot." She paused in front of a stricken-looking Summer. "Congratulations on your engagement. I'm sure you two will be very happy."

With a knowing smile, Diana passed the phone

to Summer. Austin's face was impassive, but Summer looked so terrified and confused that Diana almost felt sorry for her.

Almost.

Diana turned on her heel and headed back to the main house. Summer's too-animated voice chirped away like the birds in the trees.

All too vividly Diana could picture Seth out in California in his dark little apartment. Near his bed would be a picture of dear old Summer. He would kiss it at night, he would dream about her, he would fill his fantasies with her.

In the meantime, Summer was busy filling her fantasies with Austin.

Kind, sweet, good-hearted Seth. He deserved better than that.

He deserved someone like Diana.

Maybe it was time to give Mallory's assistant a call about that ticket to California.

After Seth hung up, Summer clutched the portable phone tightly, as if she were holding his hand. His last *I love you* rang in her ear like a shrill alarm.

Austin was leaning with his back to the railing. "I take it that was my competition?"

"Seth is not your competition. You have no competition."

Austin smiled.

"You know what I mean."

"You didn't mention me," Austin said accusingly.

"You didn't come up." Summer glanced over her shoulder nervously. "I'm afraid Diana thinks we were . . . you know."

"But we weren't you-knowing. We had you-know interruptus." Austin raised his brows. "Although I got the feeling you would have you-knowed if you-know-who hadn't called."

Summer felt the guilt boiling up inside her. It was bad enough before, when she'd been attracted to Austin over spring break. But now she was an engaged woman, a woman with a great big symbol on her left hand (well, maybe not so big) that told the world she'd found Mr. Right.

Summer joined Austin at the railing. Vivid dawn colors spilled across the surface of the bay. A silver fish popped into the air like a wingless bird, then gently splash-landed.

"I'm going to tell you something, Austin," Summer said evenly. "Just so you understand." She cleared her throat.

"I'm all ears."

"After you left me, I told Seth the whole truth. About how I felt about you, I mean." She stole a glance at Austin. His hopeful gaze made her stiffen, but she pressed on. "I told him that if you had stayed, I wasn't sure what I would have done. I told him that . . . that I'd had real feelings for you."

"I knew you did," he said. The sound of triumph in his voice told her he hadn't really been so sure.

"But then time went on, and you were gone, and I realized just how much I'd always loved Seth. I realized that I want to spend the rest of my life with him."

"You can't possibly know that," Austin scoffed.

"Why not?"

"Because for starters, it's crazy to talk about your whole life that way." Austin looked down into the placid water. "Who knows what your whole life even means? I don't presume I'll live till the ripe old age of ninety with my high-school sweetheart. In my family, it just hasn't worked out that way for some of us. Our genes have other ideas."

For a moment Summer wondered if he was going to cry, but his mouth hardened into a tight line of resolve.

"And besides," Austin continued, "just because you have a high school diploma, Summer, doesn't mean you understand the workings of the universe. You haven't had enough experience to make a life-changing decision like getting engaged."

"Oh, and you have? How many girlfriends are enough to know, Austin? Three? A dozen? A hundred?

What if girl number one hundred and three is the right one, and you settle for number one hundred and two?"

Austin looked at her and sighed. "All I know is that I am madly in love with you, right now, this instant. I don't know where either of us will be or how we'll feel next October, or five years from now . . ." His voice trailed off. "Or for however long we're around. I can't make promises, Summer. Promises are like that glitter on your finger. They can get lost way too easily. Look at all the divorces in the world. You think those people didn't mean it when they said 'till death do us part'?"

Summer moved her left hand, watching her diamond flash softly. In her parents' wedding album there was a picture of her mother gazing fondly at her own diamond ring. It had caught the dazzling light of the photographer's flash, making it look far bigger than it really was.

"How can you settle for Seth when you haven't even given me a chance?" Austin asked.

"There's a difference between settling and making a choice, Austin. I've made my choice."

He shrugged. "Well, it's not like I'm going away. I don't give up easily, Summer. I almost lost you once already."

"I think you should probably go now."

"You can keep the muffins."

"Thanks."

"You still getting a place with Marquez and Diana?"

She nodded.

"Whereabouts?"

"We haven't decided."

"You wouldn't move without leaving a forwarding address, would you?"

She smiled a little. "You bet I would."

"I'll find you." Slowly Austin turned to leave, then hesitated. "I guess you're not up for a good-bye you-know?"

"How about a handshake?"

Austin took both her hands in his and held tight. He looked down at her ring. "Before long, that ring will be off your finger," he said confidently.

"It's never coming off," Summer replied.

She didn't sound nearly as confident.

# 9

# Anchors Aweigh

"Five more minutes," Marquez vowed, waving to Diver as she ran by him on the beach. She was still feeling exhausted from her graduation party the night before, but exhaustion was no excuse not to exercise.

Diver was sitting on the white sand in his swim trunks, watching her with a look that said he just didn't get it. Well, Diver didn't have to get it. He was naturally lean and could eat whatever he wanted. Whereas Marquez could eat a potato chip and watch it instantly take up residence on her hips.

Marquez picked up her pace a little, although she was so winded she was sucking air like a vacuum hose.

She nodded to a jogger passing her on the wet sand. She'd never had a clue how many people were up at the crack of dawn like this, dashing across the beach as though they had a bus to catch.

She'd flirted with exercise over the years, of course. Read the magazines that told her "Twenty Minutes a Day Is All It Will Take to a Shapelier You." Mostly she'd just rolled her eyes at all the people trying so hard to turn themselves into Cindy Crawford clones.

But now things were different. Marquez wasn't sure why. They just were.

Exercise was only the beginning. Marquez had bought one of those little food scales so that she could tell how many ounces of Grape-Nuts she really was consuming. She'd learned to cut up her food into tiny bits and savor it, morsel by morsel.

And it had paid off. She'd heard it in the compliments of friends and casual acquaintances. She'd felt it in the way what she called her "fat jeans" hung slackly from her newly thinner hips.

Of course, Diana said she was losing too fast. And Diver said it, too. But what did they know? They were congenitally, pathologically, unfairly thin people.

Diver, strangely, hadn't once said anything about her new and improved look, which just told Marquez the obvious: She was still way too fat. She couldn't exactly expect him to compliment her. A guy as gorgeous as Diver was practically accosted by beautiful girls everywhere he went.

Marquez gulped at the air, arms and legs pumping, sweat trickling down her chest. When she reached the little dock that signaled her turnaround point, she allowed herself to slow up just a little. Her thighs and calves were searing with pain, but that was the price she had to pay for all those surreptitious Milky Ways over the years.

She turned, veering past a giddy Labrador retriever out for a run with its female owner, and headed back to the spot where Diver sat anchored to the sand.

That's what he was, her anchor.

The word had come to her that morning, after loading the last chair into the cramped U-Haul and kissing her mother and father and brothers goodbye. *Thank God for Diver. Thank God he's there for me right now. My parents are leaving, and my house is being taken over by strangers. I'm done with high school, and I'm not sure I can swing college. And my ex-boyfriend is out running around with a girl who looks like Kate Moss on Slim-Fast.*

*Diver is my anchor.* That's what Marquez had told herself while tears had streamed down her face and she'd promised her mom and dad and brothers all kinds of things. I'll write every day, I'll take my vitamins, I'll get a nice job, I'll eat more, yes, I promise I'll eat more.

She'd watched the U-Haul grumble away down the tiny palm-lined street where she'd grown up. Then she'd climbed in her ancient Honda and hightailed it up the coast to Diver's place.

She was getting Jell-O legs, all wobbly and uncertain. The sand made running so hard, but that was good. Hard was good because hard meant more calories were being burned away. She hadn't eaten that morning, which was even better. That way the exercise wasn't wasted on her disgusting, never-ending appetite, the little weak beast inside of her.

Diver smiled as she neared. He was so intensely handsome. She knew that when people saw them together, they never dreamed she and Diver were boyfriend and girlfriend. They were so mismatched. It wasn't just because he was a golden boy from Swedish and English stock and she was Cuban-American. It was because he was a perfect, chiseled specimen of humanity and she was a shapeless blob of tan-colored Play-Doh. But that was going to change.

She loved Diver with all her heart. She was going to keep him, somehow. Somehow she would find a way to be sure he never left her, the way J.T. had left her.

Marquez dropped onto the sand beside Diver. Her head was swimming as though she'd just spent an hour in the spin cycle of her parents' old Maytag. She put her head between her legs and tried to breathe.

"Hey," Diver said, rubbing her back, "you okay?"

"Fine. Just . . . winded."

"You sure?"

"I'm fine. It's the price we jocks pay." Marquez wiped the sweat off her brow and checked her watch. "Man, I should get going soon. Diana and Summer and I are going apartment hunting today." She dropped her head onto his hard, sun-warmed shoulder. "I wish you weren't so far away. This drive is murder. I don't suppose you'd like to be a fourth roommate?"

Diver laughed. "My sister wouldn't like that."

"She'd get over it." Marquez grinned. "And you could share a room with me. Think of the possibilities."

"I've thought of the possibilities," Diver said, kissing her softly. He had a way of brushing his lips over hers that sent ripples of longing down to her toes. It was as intense and fleeting as a flash of heat lightning.

Marquez wished Diver would say, "Yes, sure, I'll move in with you," but of course he wouldn't. Not with Summer there. And probably not even if Marquez had a whole place to herself. Diver was a loner. He liked his privacy. He wasn't ready for a relationship like that yet. And maybe Marquez wasn't either. She sometimes spent the night at Diver's, but they never did anything, never crossed the line. Sure, they made out for long, passionate, wonderful hours. But that was as far as it ever went. It seemed to be the way Diver wanted it.

Marquez wasn't sure what she'd do if Diver were more like J.T. With J.T., it had always been like a game of keep-away, with Marquez dodging and scolding and finding a billion different ways to say, "No, I'm not ready for that, J.T."

But with Diver . . . she wasn't so sure. Maybe it would make them closer. Maybe then she would be sure she could hold on to him.

"There's something I've been wanting to tell you," Diver said, trailing a finger through the sand.

"How much you adore me?"

"You know I do." Diver smiled tolerantly. He always just assumed Marquez understood how he felt, as if she were a mind reader. He hoarded words like gold, doling them out with care. "There's a new wild-life rehabilitation center opening down on Coconut Key. They're looking for help, and I thought I might apply. . . ."

Marquez's heart jumped. "Diver, if Diana and Summer and I can find a place there, then you and I would be in the same town. That would be fantastic!"

He nodded. "It would be." He glanced over his shoulder at the makeshift tree house he'd been living in for the last few months. "I'd miss it here, but it would be good to be near you. And I can't stay here forever. This new job would mean more training." He made a face. "Summer said I can't hide out and escape forever. It made me . . . think. Don't tell her that, though."

Marquez squeezed his hand. "Apply, okay? I'd feel so much better if you were closer."

"Okay," Diver said. He kissed her again, and she shivered a little.

After a while she stood on reluctant legs. "Where are you going?" Diver asked.

"I got my wind back. I thought I'd do another lap."

He pulled on her arm. "Stay here," he said softly. "No more running for a while, okay? Let's just sit and watch the waves."

Marquez hesitated. "I'll be back before you know it," she promised. "The waves can wait." She took off down the sand before he could answer.

Two more laps, Marquez thought as she ran. She could pull off two.

Maybe even three, if she really tried. The waves could wait. And so could Diver.

# 10

# In Search of the Perfect Apartment

11:35 A.M.: *Quaint 2 BR, 1 bath apartment.*
*Tub with feet, fireplace, charm to spare.*
*Must see to believe!*

"Well," Summer said, clearing her throat, "I see it, but I don't believe it."

"At least they weren't lying about the tub," Marquez said. "It has feet, all right."

Diana sighed. "So do the rats."

"We'll think about it," Summer told the manager.

12:15 P.M.: *Immaculate 1 BR, den.*
*No smokers. Won't last.*

"So, yes or no?" the caretaker asked. She took a long drag on her Marlboro.

"I was sort of wondering where the den was," Summer said. "We were going to use it as a second bedroom."

The woman pointed.

"But that's a closet," Marquez protested.

Another satisfied puff. "It's got a door on it, right?" the woman asked hoarsely.

Marquez nodded.

"It's got an outlet in it, right?"

"You mean, to plug stuff in?" Summer asked.

The woman rolled her eyes. "First apartment, huh?" She jangled her keys. "It's got an outlet, it's got a door, it's a den. Yes or no?"

"We'll think about it," Summer said.

1:20 P.M.: *Sunny bungalow, pets okay,*
*eat-in kitchen, AC, steps to beach.*

"It's hot in here," Diana said.

"Sweltering," Marquez agreed. "I thought this place had air-conditioning."

Summer pointed to the ceiling fan.

"Oh," Marquez said wearily.

"Beach access, too." The manager jerked his thumb. "A mile and a quarter up the highway."

Summer checked the ad. "Just a few steps," she quoted.

"Yeah," Marquez muttered, "if you're the Jolly Green Giant."

"We'll think about it," Summer told the manager.

2:10 P.M.: *Beautiful, quiet, secure 2 BR, 2 bath. Walk to shops. Caring management.*

"It really *is* beautiful," Summer murmured as Diana parked her car.

"And quiet and secure. And you really could walk to downtown," Marquez added excitedly.

A balding middle-aged man appeared from behind the building. Gold chains sparkled around his neck. His huge stomach strained at the buttons of his sweat-stained shirt.

He gave an enthusiastic wave. "Well, well, it's my lucky day," he called. "You the gals who called about the apartment?"

"I'm guessing that would be the caring management," Diana said with a sigh.

"We'll think about it," Summer called.

Diana floored the gas pedal.

"The thing is, I'm about to be homeless." Marquez sipped at her diet Coke that afternoon. The girls sat at a wobbly table, the rental ads spread between them.

The air in the little café was sultry. The restaurant was on the bottom floor of a yellow house located on a tiny cobblestoned street filled with shops and restaurants that backed onto the water.

"You're not homeless. You can always stay with Diana or me till we find a place," Summer assured her.

"The new people are moving in next Monday," Marquez said sullenly. "I have to have all my stuff out by then."

Diana folded the paper and pushed a damp lock of hair off her forehead. "Man, it's hot. We could have at least picked a restaurant with air-conditioning."

"I think it's charming," Summer said, "in a tacky sort of way. There's a bookstore attached to the café and everything."

"I do like Coconut Key a lot," Marquez said. "There's more to do than there was on Crab Claw. There are restaurants and a movie theater and a mall. And it's a college town. FCU's here, so Diana and I would be all set this fall—assuming, that is, I can get together enough cash to cover books and stuff. And there'd be a lot more people our age than on Crab Claw." She grinned. "More male meat on parade."

"Summer doesn't need more male meat," Diana said dryly. "She's getting plenty. If anything, Summer needs to go on a vegetarian kick for a while."

Marquez looked at Diana curiously, then at Summer. "What's she talking about?"

Summer shrugged uncomfortably. She really didn't want to get into it.

"Summer had a little visitor this morning," Diana said, smirking. "Or I guess I should say a big visitor. How tall is Austin, Summer? About six-two?"

"Austin came to see you?" Marquez cried.

"He lives around here now," Summer said flatly.

"You *are* kidding." Marquez peered at Summer. "Whoa, wait a minute. You are *not* kidding?"

"What are the odds?" Diana said, leaning back in her chair with a cool smile.

"He just said hello," Summer said. "He brought me some muffins."

"Hmm . . . is that what they call it in Minnesota?" Diana inquired. She leaned toward Marquez. "He brought her muffins in a major way, if you get my drift."

"Diana!" Summer nearly shouted. "We were not kissing, if that's what you're thinking. We were . . . thinking about kissing, I admit, but that's all. At the last minute we didn't. And even if we had kissed— which we didn't—it would have been just for old times' sake."

She finished her speech just as the waitress approached. She was a pretty black girl about their age, wearing the worn expression of someone near the end of her shift. She placed plates of hamburgers and fries in front of Diana and Summer.

"You sure you don't want anything?" she asked Marquez.

"I'm fine," Marquez said.

"I've got plenty of cash, Marquez," Diana offered, "if—"

"I'm not destitute, I'm just not hungry, Mom."

"Okay, then. You need anything else here?" the girl asked.

"Yeah," Marquez muttered. "An apartment would be nice."

The girl shook her head. "It's tough finding anything on Coconut. You've got students and retirees and snowbirds all fighting for the same real estate." She snapped her fingers. "You know, though, there might be a place . . . but no, it's kind of weird. You're looking for a three-bedroom?"

"We're looking for anything with a roof and a toilet," Summer said.

"I'd settle for a Porta Potti," Marquez said.

"You mind if I sit?" The girl straddled a chair. "Sorry, I'm breaking in new Docs. I'm Blythe, by the way."

"That's Diana," Summer said, "that's Marquez, and I'm Summer."

"Cool name." Blythe smiled. "The thing is—" She lowered her voice. "There's a place here. On the top floor. I probably shouldn't say anything, 'cause it might be taken, but it's sort of cool, in a weird way. It's this converted attic, so all the walls are slanted, and I think maybe there are only two bedrooms. There's a little pool out back, and you can see the ocean, which is great. The landlady—my boss—is completely wacky, but it's a great location and dirt cheap. I live on the second floor."

"You think we could take a look at it?" Summer asked hopefully.

"See, there's this new guy working here—he is so gorgeous, incidentally, and the girls are falling all over themselves. But anyway, he might be taking it. I don't know. I haven't worked with him in a few shifts. Could be he found another place."

"This would be so perfect," Marquez cried. "We'd be right in the center of town, and the ocean's right there, and I'd be close to Di—" She snapped her jaw closed.

"Close to what?" Summer asked.

"Or should we say *whom*?" Diana asked.

*"Who,"* Marquez corrected.

"No, *whom,*" Diana said.

"I'm pretty sure it's *who*—"

"Who, what, which, whatever, just tell us what the deal is!" Diana snapped.

Marquez rolled her eyes. "I didn't say anything because I knew it would freak Summer out." She paused. "The thing is, Diver might be moving down here. There's a wildlife place, like the one he works at, opening up, and he's going to apply. So it's not definite or anything. Besides, he's going to be around, Summer, one way or another."

"I know," Summer said, tearing at her napkin. "It's okay, Marquez. I have no right to interfere in your love life."

"Well," Blythe interrupted, looking a little uncomfortable, "I've got ketchup bottles to fill."

"Sorry," Marquez apologized. "We got sidetracked there on personal stuff."

"I know how that goes." Blythe stood and pushed in her chair. "Tell you what. I'll ask my boss about the place. If Austin doesn't want it, maybe you can go on up and take a peek. It's probably a mess—"

"Austin." Summer said it in a very low voice.

"Yeah, he's the new guy."

"Tall, dark, looks like trouble?" Diana asked.

Blythe grinned. "That's the one."

Summer pushed back her plate. "We are outta here."

"Wait a minute, Summer," Marquez pleaded, grabbing her arm. "Can't we at least take a look at it?"

"I am not living where Austin works," Summer declared. "No way."

"I take it you know Austin?" Blythe asked.

"Oh, she knows him, all right," Diana said.

"Oh. Like, *knows* him."

"Only I'm trying very hard not to know him anymore," Summer said sternly. "I'm sorry, Marquez, but we'll just have to keep looking."

"We've *been* looking." Marquez crossed her arms over her chest. "I don't see why your personal life is the only deciding factor here. I am practically broke and soon to be homeless. I need a job and I need a place, and I need them fast. And between avoiding Austin and Diver, you're going to end up making us live in Maine or something."

Summer looked at Marquez with concern. Her hand was shaking just a little, and she looked near tears. It wasn't like Marquez to get so worked up. Usually she'd just laugh it off and tell Summer to lighten up.

"You know," Blythe said, "if you need a job, there's always something here. The tips are nothing special, but you can scarf all the food you want."

"I could have a job *and* an apartment, maybe," Marquez said, glaring at Summer and managing to make her feel completely crummy.

"Marquez has a point," Diana said. "I mean, if you and Austin are just friends, Summer, what's there to worry about?"

Summer caught the gleam in her cousin's eye. She knew what Diana was implying. If Summer was really committed to Seth, what was the problem?

Marquez was looking at her with hope, Diana with challenge. Fine, then. She could handle it. She could handle Austin Reed just fine.

"Ask your manager if the apartment's available, would you, Blythe?" Summer said at last.

"And if it is?" Marquez challenged.

Summer took a deep breath. "And if it is," she replied, "we'll think about it."

# Constellations and Other Very Important Stuff

"Seth? Hi, it's me." Summer lay on her bed in the stilt house. Through the open kitchen window she could see the night sky, heavy with stars. The wind was up, and the waves grumbled loudly as they hit the shore. "I'm in the stilt house."

"Is anything wrong?"

Summer could hear the concern in Seth's voice. She tried to imagine him in his new apartment in California, the one he shared with other guys from the boat building company. But she couldn't even seem to conjure up a decent image of his face.

"Nothing's wrong, no." She reached for the photo on her nightstand of Seth and her at the prom. They'd posed for the photo shortly after Seth had proposed. They looked breathless and dizzy, as though they'd just climbed off the world's fastest roller coaster.

"How's the apartment hunting going?"

Summer set the picture aside. "Um, we found one, maybe. It's on Coconut Key, and Marquez and Diana really love it. But I'm not so sure."

Seth laughed. "Like you three will ever agree on anything. Why don't you like it?"

"Well, it's on the top floor of this house, an attic, really. So the walls are all slanted."

"And?"

"And that's it. Who wants to live in a place where you have to walk tilted all the time?"

"Well, I guess I can see your point. This place I'm sharing isn't exactly a palace. It's right near my job, which is cool, but sharing an apartment with three other slobby guys isn't paradise. I wish it were you instead."

"I miss you."

"I miss you more. How's your ring holding up?"

Summer held out her hand. The diamond winked at her in reproach. "So far, so good. I almost took it off to do the dishes today, but I was afraid I'd lose it."

"Don't lose it, whatever you do. It wiped out my savings."

"I love you, Seth."

"I love you, too."

"I should hang up. It's late."

"Okay. I'll call you next."

"You hang up first," Summer said.

"No, you."

"I love you," Summer said. She started to disconnect, then hesitated. "You still there?"

"Yeah."

"Okay, this time I'm really hanging up." She heard Seth saying "I love you" again as she clicked off the phone.

Summer closed her eyes, listening to the relentless waves. *What's wrong with the apartment? Well, I'll tell you, Seth. It's just a few steps away from Austin, and something tells me that's not exactly the ideal location.*

After a few moments Summer reached for the phone and punched in her phone number in Bloomington. Was it really her number anymore? Where was home now? The stilt house? The University of Wisconsin, where she and Seth would be going to school that fall? Some slant-walled attic apartment on Coconut Key?

When she heard her mother's voice, Summer's eyes pooled with tears. "Mom? Did I wake you?"

"No, I was just putzing around, waiting for Leno to come on. You okay, honey?"

"I'm okay. I just . . . I miss you, is all."

"Oh, I miss you, too, hon. This house is just so empty now, with Diver and you . . . and your dad . . . gone. I feel sort of abandoned."

"Are you holding up all right?"

"Oh, you know. Good days, bad days. Hey, guess what I did today? I got an application to U of M. I'm thinking of going back to school, maybe getting my master's in social work. What do you think?"

"I think that's fantastic, Mom."

"Me, too. Although it scares the hell out of me. Wouldn't that be so crazy—mother and daughter in college at the same time?" She laughed a little too hard.

"I wish I were home. I'd take you out to celebrate."

"Well, I'll see you plenty this fall. UW's just a quick drive. I'll force you to come visit me in my dorm room."

"You're not really getting a dorm room?"

"No, no." A pause. "But the thing is, honey . . . Dad and I are going to go ahead with the divorce for sure. And when everything's finalized, well, we both agree there's no point in keeping this big old house."

Summer took a shuddery breath. "You're going to sell the house?"

"We have to, Summer. It just wouldn't make sense to keep it. Maybe I'll get one of those condos in

Edina—you know, the fake gingerbready ones out by the mall?"

"Those are cute," Summer said without feeling.

"Don't be sad, honey."

"I'm not. I mean, I am. But I'm sadder for you."

"Don't be. I'm a tough old broad."

"You're not so old," Summer said. She gazed out the window. The stars were cluttered in the sky like tossed silver coins. She wondered how astronomers made sense out of them all. Seth knew lots of constellations—Orion and Aquarius and Pegasus, all those.

"Mom?"

"Hmm?"

"Did you ever think, when you married Dad, that it would turn out this way? Did you have any doubts that maybe he wasn't the right one, maybe there was someone else even more . . . right?"

Her mother laughed. "Oh, I suppose so. I think everybody does. Everybody who's honest with herself." She hesitated. "Your dad and I were so young when we got married. How can you make a decision at the age of nineteen that's supposed to last the rest of your life?" She paused again. "It's something you should think about, too, sweetheart."

Summer took a deep breath. "I know," she said. "I will."

After she hung up, Summer closed her eyes and hugged her pillow and tried to picture Seth. But to her frustration, Austin kept making unannounced appearances. Finally she turned her attention to the stars hugging the horizon. She thought maybe she saw Orion, but it was hard to tell.

She'd have to ask Seth. He would know for sure.

"Just one more thing," Marquez promised.

Diver looked at her incredulously. He'd been packing her Honda all morning, despite heat in the low nineties. His shoulders and chest shone with sweat. His face was flushed. He looked as frustrated as Diver ever really looked—mellow, by most people's standards, but Marquez knew better.

"I can't leave Geraldo behind."

"Geraldo," Diver repeated. "The mangy, smelly, stained stuffed elephant you keep on your bed?"

"That mangy elephant knows all my deepest, darkest secrets."

Diver smiled grudgingly. "Well, then, bring the dude along. So what if I have to ride on the roof?"

"He'll fit. He's mushy."

"Where will he fit, exactly?"

He pointed to the car in the driveway of Marquez's soon-to-be-former house. The entire backseat and trunk overflowed with art supplies, half-dead plants, clothes in Hefty bags, framed paintings from Marquez's art classes, photo albums, a handful of mismatched pots and pans Marquez's mother had left for her, sheets and pillows, and a huge cardboard box marked Very Important Stuff.

"There's room on the passenger side," Marquez said. "Geraldo can ride on your lap."

Diver wiped his brow with the back of his arm. "It's a good thing that I love you."

When they were finally done lugging things out to the car, Marquez stood in her vast, empty bedroom, which had been a ground-floor ice cream parlor once upon a time. The hardwood floor was spattered with color, a Crayola-box palette of drizzles and splashes. But it was on the walls that Marquez had truly left her mark. Giant murals extended from floor to ceiling, the once bare brick covered with dazzling scenes. Palm trees and birds, sunsets and sunrises, anything and everything that she'd felt like painting over the years. There were names, too, a graffitilike maze of friends and teachers, movie star crushes and boys of the month.

"Jared Leto, huh?" Diver murmured, his arm draped around Marquez's shoulder as they studied a wall.

"Just a passing phase."

Marquez caught a glimpse of herself in the full-length mirror on the back of her closet door. She was wearing a pair of old shorts she'd almost given up on. Now they hung loosely on her. Still, her butt looked disgustingly huge. She tugged down her baggy T-shirt, hoping to disguise the awful truth.

"What was there?" Diver pointed to the thick layer of black paint in the corner, where bits and pieces of red letters still poked through.

Marquez shrugged. "J.T. He got spray-painted out of existence."

"I wish it were that easy," Diver said softly.

Marquez looked at him. "What do you mean?"

"Nothing. Just that it takes time, that's all." He moved close to the wall, running his fingers over the glossy layers of paint. "Where am I?"

"There, next to Summer's name."

"Linked by blood and paint."

"Let's go," Marquez muttered. Suddenly she couldn't stand it anymore. She could imagine the new people coming in, bitching about the way she'd ruined the room, painting over the walls in some sunny pastel. Well, it would take about a hundred layers of off-white latex to cover *those* walls. She could take some satisfaction in that, at least.

They left the house quietly. Marquez locked the door behind her. "You'll have new walls soon," Diver assured her.

"Not like those." Marquez climbed into the front

seat of her Honda. The sun-heated vinyl seat burned her thighs.

"Well, at least you managed to talk Summer into taking the apartment," Diver said as he climbed in beside her, Geraldo clutched in his arms.

"After two more wasted days of searching," Marquez said with a grin. "That girl can be stubborn. But she caved in the end."

Diver nodded thoughtfully. "She can be tough to get through to."

"Family trait," Marquez said affectionately, patting Diver's knee. "It's in your blood."

"Maybe. I don't know, though. My dad . . . my other dad . . . he was stubborn, too."

"You mean the one who took you?"

Diver nodded.

"How about his wife?"

There was no answer. Diver was busy trying to reattach Geraldo's right eye.

"Diver?" Marquez said gently. "If you ever wanted to talk about them, you could. You know that, right?"

"I know. But that's over. I want it to go away."

Marquez started the car. She wasn't going to push it. She and Diver were alike that way. They didn't like to dissect things and dwell on them, the way Summer and Diana did. When Marquez felt bad, she liked to drive or dance or paint. A couple of times, when she'd felt really low, she'd even tried drinking. But that had left her with worse feelings and horrible hangovers. So now she stuck to her art, mostly.

Diver, when he felt bad, just stared at the ocean and climbed inside himself. It made Marquez feel a little lonely when that happened, but she understood why he did it, and she didn't push.

"Well, good-bye, house," she said softly, backing out of the drive. She wiped away a tear, feeling annoyed. It was just a house, not a shrine.

She drove down the narrow streets of the key, passing familiar landmarks along the way. The spot where her brother Miguel had broken his wrist skateboarding. The corner of Palm and Lido, where she'd kissed her sixth-grade crush on a dare. The Crab 'n' Conch, where the food was lousy and the service wasn't a whole lot better.

"I think I may have a job," Marquez said as she braked at the four-way stop in the center of town. Two guys shouldering a red surfboard sauntered past. "Waiting tables at this café place on the ground floor of our apartment building. The landlady owns it. She says I can pick up shifts, see how I do."

"Great," Diver said. "If I get that job at the wildlife rehab center, we'll both be gainfully employed."

They'd just started across the intersection when she

heard someone yell. Marquez knew it was J.T. even before she turned to see him. His new girlfriend, the one Marquez had discovered him in bed with, hung off his arm. She was giggling loudly.

J.T. waved. "Hey, Marquez, where you goin' with Geraldo?"

Marquez hit the gas, ignoring him.

After a few blocks, Diver asked, "You all right?"

"I'm fine," she said. Her body felt tight with compressed energy. Maybe she'd go for a run later, a long one.

"It'll get easier."

"Look, it's over with me and J.T., okay? I don't really want to talk about it."

Diver played with Geraldo's eye. "Okay. I know how that goes."

Marquez cranked up the radio. Green Day, nice and loud. She drove as fast as she figured she could get away with. The backseat was piled so high with stuff that she couldn't see out the rearview mirror, but that was okay by her.

She wasn't planning on looking back, anyway.

# 12

## Diamonds Are Not Always a Girl's Best Friend.

"You know, I'm starting to sense what this apartment needs," Diana said as she dug a camera out of a cardboard box. "I think it's called furniture."

"We have a mildewy couch left by the previous tenants," Summer pointed out. "Plus a mildewy chair and a mildewy table. And the landlady said she's got plenty of mildewy mattresses in the storage shed."

Diana aimed the camera at Summer. "You're right. It's not like we don't have a decorating motif. Mildew goes with everything. By the way, smile. I'm breaking in my new camera and recording our move-in for posterity."

Summer stuck out her tongue, and Diana clicked the camera.

Marquez and Diana had been right about one thing, Summer thought: It *was* a quaint apartment. Despite the sloping roof, the place was surprisingly big. It featured one large bedroom flanked by a bathroom, with a smaller bedroom on the other side. The kitchen, which was really just an extension of the living room, was even more dated than the one in the stilt house. But the polished pine floors gleamed, and the arched windows let in plenty of light, even affording a view of the ocean.

If it weren't for the little Austin problem, it would have been just about perfect.

"Knock, knock, male coming, everyone decent?" Marquez called from the stairway.

Summer busied herself dragging a suitcase into one of the bedrooms. She wished Marquez could have at least let them get settled in before bringing Diver over. But sooner or later, Summer knew, she was going to have to get used to seeing him.

She took a deep breath and headed back into the living room. Diver was holding a box of silverware and a big stuffed elephant. He met Summer's eyes reluctantly.

"Smile," Diana commanded, turning her camera on Diver, but he didn't react.

"Look, you two," Marquez said, marching across the room with two plastic bags of clothes in tow, "I love you both, and you're just going to have to get used to being in the same room together. I'm tired of tiptoeing around your feelings. Summer, say hi to your brother."

Summer toyed with her diamond ring, avoiding Diver's gaze. "Hi."

"Diver, say hi to your sister."

"Hi," he said softly.

"There." Marquez dropped the bags. "Now, was that so difficult?" She wrinkled her nose. "What is that smell?"

"It's our decorating theme," Diana said. "Early American mildew."

"Man, let's open some windows, already."

"They *are* open."

"Doors, then." Marquez swung open the louvered French doors that opened onto a wide balcony. "Look at this view," she said. "This is so fantastic."

Summer, Diana, and Diver joined her on the balcony. An ornate wrought-iron fence wrapped around the veranda. Trumpet vines, thick with bright orange flowers, wove in and out of the railing. An ancient oak tree shaded the porch, its limbs heavy with Spanish moss. The entire street below was lined with little shops and restaurants in turn-of-the-century buildings.

"How could you not have wanted to live here?"

Marquez asked Summer. "What a great location. And my new job is right downstairs." She sighed. "Of course, it's not exactly like my old house."

Summer patted her back. "I bet it was hard to leave your murals, huh?"

Marquez shrugged. "I'll do a new one here. Maybe something on the ceiling. Sort of our own little Sistine Chapel."

"Whoa," Diana said, making a time-out sign. "Before you start redecorating, let's try to do something tasteful. Like, say, putting that elephant out of his misery."

"Like your coffin's going to blend in, Diana."

Diana rolled her eyes. "I'm going to measure the living room," she said. "Maybe we can steal one of Mallory's leather couches."

"I think we should do this on our own," Summer said to Marquez. "Start from scratch."

Marquez elbowed her. "Did you smell that couch?"

"But if we let Diana borrow from home, it'll be like it's her place, not ours."

"You're right," Marquez conceded. "And I'm already feeling kind of placeless at the moment."

"Me, too. I talked to my mom last night, and she said—" Suddenly Summer realized Diver was listening intently.

"Said what?"

"Nothing. Just . . . well, she and my dad are selling the house." She shot a look at Diver, but he'd turned away. He was staring impassively at a bee drowsing near one of the trumpet flowers.

Just then there was a knock at the door. "Anybody home?" a voice called from the stairwell.

"We have company, girls," Diana announced.

Blythe was standing in the doorway, a plate of muffins in her hand. Someone was standing behind her. A guy.

With a sudden flash of horror, Summer realized it was Austin. Like Blythe, he was wearing a black T-shirt with Jitters, the café's name, on the pocket. He was carrying something small and square wrapped in tissue paper.

"Well, well, the plot thickens," Diana said, grinning slyly at Summer. "Come on in."

"We brought you welcome-to-the-neighborhood muffins," Blythe said. "Left over from this morning, but hey, they're still good."

"Great! I'm starving," Diana said, grabbing one.

"None for me, thanks," Marquez said.

"Me either," Summer said, glaring at Austin.

"Told you she wasn't the muffin type," Austin whispered loudly to Blythe.

"Sit, everybody," Diana said. "You have your choice

of mildewed couch or cardboard box. By the way, Blythe, this is Summer's brother and Marquez's boyfriend, Diver."

Blythe grinned at Diver. "Nice to meet you. Sorry I can't stay. I'm technically on duty, even though the café is totally dead."

"I can stay," Austin volunteered, dropping onto the couch. "I'm technically off duty."

"Thanks for stopping by, Blythe," Marquez said.

"Come by later," Summer added. "We might even have chairs and stuff." She turned to Austin. "We're a little busy here, Austin."

"Aren't you even going to open my housewarming gift?"

"No."

"Yes, we are," Diana said. She grabbed the present from Austin. "It's our first, if you don't count the muffins."

"It's really for Summer," Austin said, but Diana was already unwrapping the tissue paper. She held up a small frame. There were typed words inside.

"It's poetry," Austin volunteered, "e.e. cummings."

Marquez checked it out. "Nice," she commented. "I don't get it exactly, but I like the frame." She passed it over to Summer.

"Go ahead," Austin said. "Read it."

Reluctantly Summer scanned the words:

yes is a world
& in this world of
yes live
(skillfully curled)
all worlds
—e.e. cummings
"love is a place"
*No Thanks* (1935)


"It's very nice," she said politely.

Austin stretched out on the smelly couch. "Isn't it amazing how he could compress so much into those five lines?"

"But I don't get it," Marquez said. "What is she supposed to say yes to?"

"Take a guess," Diana said with a smirk.

Diver examined the poem. "No, it's not like that," he said after a moment. "It's more like saying yes to life, to . . . possibilities."

Austin nodded. "You ought to come to one of our poetry slams at the café sometime."

"Now *there's* a hot evening," Diana said. "Sign me up for sure."

Summer grabbed a cardboard box and began unpacking dishes wrapped in newspaper. "We really need to get to work, Austin."

"You're absolutely right." Austin sat up and clapped his hands. "Let's get down to business. Nice place, by the way. I almost took it, but it was too rich for my budget, and I don't need this much room. I live just a couple of blocks over."

"Oh, happy happy, joy joy," Diana said.

"So where do you want me?"

"Toledo would be nice," Summer muttered.

Austin laughed. "Alice, the landlady, told me you were thinking about painting the walls. She's got paint and brushes and stuff stashed in the storage room down-stairs. Want me to see what's available?"

"Yes," Marquez said.

"No," Summer said.

"What color?" Diana asked.

"I'll take that as a maybe," Austin said cheerfully. With a wink at Summer, he headed for the stairs. "Back in a minute."

Summer pointed an accusing finger at Marquez when he was gone. "Why did you tell him yes to the paint?"

Marquez shrugged helplessly. "I don't know. Maybe it was that poem. It just popped out."

"I *told* you guys this would happen," Summer grumbled.

Diana began arranging silverware in a drawer. "Relax, Summer. Nothing is going to happen unless you want it to." She sent her a knowing look. "That is, as long as you remember how to say no."

"Remind me never to move again," Diana groaned a few hours later. She stretched out on the bedroom floor, her legs propped up against the low, slanting ceiling. Marquez lay beside her, her head in Diver's lap. In the next room, Austin and Summer were laughing loudly at some private joke.

"Have some more pizza, Marquez." Diana pushed the box across the floor. "All you ate was, like, a black olive."

"I'm too bushed to eat," Marquez said. She checked her watch. "That's got to be a world record. We painted the living room walls and unpacked three people's stuff, and it's only five-thirty." She poked at Diana's head with her toes. "You sure you're okay with the room division? It's not really fair, me getting one all to myself."

"Sure it is. First of all, you're the one who'll be generating all the paint fumes. And besides, you'll have Diver visiting, probably. At least until he gets that job."

"*If* I get that job," Diver amended.

Summer's musical giggle floated through the open doorway. "For someone who didn't want Austin around, she sure is enjoying having him here," Diana muttered. "How long does it take them to paint four walls, anyway?"

"I really think Summer just wants Austin to be a friend," Marquez said.

"You didn't see what I saw on the roof of the stilt house," Diana said.

"I don't get why you care, anyway." Marquez yawned. "I mean, it's Summer's love life, not yours."

Diana sat up. She was grouchy and antsy, and she felt like causing some trouble. "I just worry about Seth, is all. I really like him. He's a nice guy, and he deserves better than—" Austin laughed loudly, interrupting her. "He just plain deserves better."

Marquez sat up, too. Her dark eyes were narrowed suspiciously. "Since when do you care so much about Summer and Seth's relationship?"

"I'm their friend."

"So am I, but I didn't arrange for them to have a romantic spring break getaway on a private yacht. You did." She crossed her arms over her chest.

"Mallory knew the owner. Big deal. I invited you, too." Diana grinned. "And you know I don't care about you, Marquez."

"Still, it seems a little weird—"

Summer's frantic scream interrupted Marquez. "No! Oh, my God, where *is* it?"

Seconds later Summer rushed into the room. Her

face and hands were smeared with white paint. "My ring! I can't find my ring!" She put her hands to her head, leaving a smudge of paint on her hair. "Help me, you guys!"

They followed her to the other room. Austin was scanning the floor. If he was smiling, it was hard to tell.

"Oh, no, oh, no, this is some kind of omen, isn't it?" Summer wailed. "Seth is going to kill me. He is going to totally kill me." She paced frantically back and forth, nearly knocking Austin over. "No, he's not going to kill me. I'll kill myself. It'll be less painful that way."

"Faster, too," Austin added.

"Would you please stop ranting long enough to tell us what happened?" Diana said.

"I . . . oh, God, I can't believe I was so *stupid*! . . . I took off my ring because I couldn't find any gloves and I didn't want to get paint on it." Summer peered under a sheet of newspaper. "So I took it off and put it on the windowsill in this Dixie cup."

"You put it on the windowsill?" Diana asked. "Wasn't that kind of asking for trouble?"

"Oh, fine, Diana, like I don't feel bad enough," Summer wailed.

"Sorry," Diana apologized. "But think how Seth is going to feel."

"I *am* thinking about how Seth is going to feel. First he'll feel terrible. Then he'll feel homicidal."

"Could be the other way around," Austin pointed out. "They say depression is anger turned inward—"

"Shut up, Austin!" Summer snapped. "You're the one who said it would be safe there. This is partly your fault."

"I don't see how I—"

"B-Because," Summer sobbed, "because the other day you said I wouldn't be wearing my ring before long, and you were right. You . . . you were . . . psychotic. No—"

"Prescient?" Austin offered.

"Psychic?" Marquez tried.

"I don't know. One of those *p* words." Summer sniffled. "Oh, it's not your fault," she admitted, "it's mine."

"So losing it was kind of a Freudian slip, you mean?" Austin asked.

"Please shut up," Summer sobbed.

"Really, Austin, you're not helping matters," Marquez said. She put her hands on Summer's shoulders. "Get a grip, okay? This doesn't *mean* anything. It just happened. Now, let's get organized. When's the last time you saw the ring?"

"A few minutes ago. We were talking about whether to paint the ceiling, and Austin and I were fighting over who got the ladder. Then I noticed the Dixie cup on its side."

Marquez put her head out the window. "The roof is almost level, just a little bit slanted. Maybe the ring fell onto the ground."

"I'll go look," Diver offered.

"Me, too," Marquez said. "Summer, you and Austin and Diana scour the bedroom. Check the rest of the apartment, too. Maybe it just rolled somewhere."

"You know, you could probably pick up a couple of extra shifts at the café and buy a new one," Austin said, grinning.

Summer groaned. "Maybe it wasn't the biggest ring, but it meant the world to me."

"That's obvious," Diana said sarcastically.

"What's that supposed to mean?" Summer demanded.

"Nothing," Diana said. "Let's everybody calm down and start looking. I'll check outside with Marquez and Diver. You two do the bedroom."

"We've already looked," Summer moaned. "It's totally hopeless."

Diana headed out the door. "Depends on how you look at things, I suppose," she said softly.

# 13

# Marquez Can't Wait, but Austin Can.

"Smile," Diana instructed, pointing her camera toward Marquez.

"I will not smile," Marquez said, panting. "I am sitting on an exercise bike, sweating like a giant porker. I am not in the mood to smile."

The sun had set, and the search for Summer's ring had long since been abandoned. Austin had talked Summer into going for a walk around town. Diana, Marquez, and Diver had stayed behind in the apartment. Diver was stacking cardboard boxes while Diana played with her camera and Marquez exercised.

"I'm warning you, Diana," Marquez barked. "Don't do it."

To Marquez's great annoyance, Diana snapped a picture anyway.

"How long are you going to ride?" Diana asked. "It's been, like, an hour."

"Come on, Marquez," Diver agreed as he broke down an empty box. "Hang out with us. It's been a long day."

"Another half-mile," Marquez muttered, feeling annoyed. It was going to take some time to get used to sharing her space this way. At home she'd had the entire downstairs to herself. She'd been able to paint or daydream or exercise to her heart's content. Without interference. Without commentary from some unfairly skinny audience.

Diana went to the kitchen window overlooking the backyard. "Summer and Austin are back," she reported. "They're heading for the pool patio. That was quite a long walk they took. Of course, she probably had to get over the terrible trauma of losing her ring."

"What is it with you and Summer and Austin?" Marquez asked breathlessly.

"Nothing. I just think after she made such an issue about not wanting to move here because of Austin, it's kind of strange that she's spent most of the day with him."

"I think you should leave that up to Summer," Diver said.

Diana held up her hands. "I'm just engaging in some idle speculation. Summer says she wants nothing to do with Austin, then she spends the day with him, loses her engagement ring, and spends more time with him. I think it's a little weird, is all."

Marquez stopped peddling. Sweat trickled down her forehead. Her feet felt glued to the pedals. She climbed off stiffly, like an old woman. The room spun for a moment. She grabbed the handlebars for support.

"You okay over there?" Diver asked.

Marquez nodded. "I'm feeling the burn."

"You're not supposed to exercise to the point of collapse, Marquez," Diana chided.

"Like you would know?"

"I read *Glamour*. I know these things."

"Yeah, well, I read the numbers on my bathroom scale."

Diana shook her head. "Hey, they're your muscles. I just happen to prefer less-strenuous exercise."

"Like aerobic check-writing."

Diver pointed to the couch. "Why don't you sit down and recover?"

"Can't. I'm all sweaty. I need to take a shower."

"The first shower in our new apartment," Diana exclaimed.

"You are *not* photographing it for posterity, either," Marquez said.

"I wouldn't mind a copy of that picture," Diver said.

Diana trained her camera out the window. "You think Summer's going to tell Seth the truth about the ring?" She paused. "Or about Austin?"

Marquez hobbled toward the bathroom. She felt disoriented, the conversation buzzing past her like a tennis match she couldn't follow. "What?" she asked.

"Summer. You think she'll tell Seth?"

Marquez blinked. "Anybody seen my backpack?"

"Over by the door," Diver said. "Marquez? You sure you're okay? You look kind of pale."

"I just need a shower." Marquez grabbed her backpack. "See you in a minute. And no unauthorized photos, Diana."

"Yeah." Diana laughed. "The tabloids would pay big money to see you in the buff, Marquez."

Marquez closed the bathroom door behind her. Diana's comment stung. It was just a joke, just Diana mouthing off as usual, the kind of teasing Marquez had done herself a million times. So why were tears burning her eyes?

She wasn't tracking, wasn't making sense. She was so, so tired.

She needed to clear her head. A hot shower would be good. Maybe the pills, and then a hot shower.

She locked the door and dug through her backpack for the little bottle.

She poured some into her palm. Little white pills. Her hands were shaking.

How many should she take? She should have asked.

She wanted to make them last. But when she ran out, she could always go back to the Cramp 'n' Croak. Willi, the day cook there, could always get her more, or if not Willi, plenty of other people she knew.

She put one on her tongue. Leaning her head into the old-fashioned porcelain sink, she turned on the tap and swallowed the pill.

That would be good for starters.

Marquez took off her clothes and stepped into the claw-footed tub. She pulled the curtain around her and turned the water on as hot as she could stand. The fine spray was like needles on her skin. The heat made her dizzy.

After a while she dried off and put on her terry robe. Already she felt a little buzzy. She wasn't sure what to expect. But she knew what she wanted.

She wanted the hunger to go away. She wanted to stop being so very, very tired.

She wanted to be thinner. Just a little thinner. And she didn't know why, but she just couldn't wait any longer. She had to make the need go away.

Her hair still dripping, she went into the living room and cuddled up next to Diver. Diana was out on the back balcony, camera in hand.

"You look better already," Diver said. He kissed her tenderly.

"Amazing what a shower can do for your outlook," Marquez said.

"Feeling any better?" Austin asked Summer.

"A little." Summer managed a halfhearted smile.

They were sitting in white chaises by the side of the little kidney-shaped pool behind the apartment. Thick palms filtered the rosy twilight rays. A tiny stone fountain featuring a decrepit-looking cherub trickled softly. The scent of jasmine was heavy in the air.

"I'm glad I wasn't working tonight and could be with you in your hour of need," Austin said.

Summer punched him in the arm. "I've had about enough of your sarcastic ring remarks."

"Hey, I'm the one who risked life and limb climbing out onto the roof to check the gutter. You know how old that roof is?"

"How old?"

"Real damn old, that's how old."

"Well, thanks. I'm glad you could stick around, too. For some reason, Diana seemed kind of mad at me about the whole thing. And Marquez has been really distracted lately. So I guess it was nice to have some moral support." She dipped her toe into the warm pool water. "Even if it was you."

"So you're sorry you told me to get lost when I showed up today?"

"I didn't exactly tell you to get lost."

"I recall some mention of Toledo."

Summer turned to face Austin. She thought for a moment. "Look, I won't deny I don't . . . mind having you around, Austin. And since it looks like there's no way to avoid it, with you working downstairs, all I ask is that we keep it just friends. Platonic. No complications. I have enough complications in my life at the moment."

"Platonic." He made a sour face. "Does that mean no touching whatsoever?"

"Under no circumstances."

He got up and stood behind her chair, grasping her shoulders in his hands. "What if I were to, say, give you a shoulder massage? Strictly therapeutic?"

Summer squirmed out of reach. "That would not qualify as platonic."

"Sure it would. Waiters give each other shoulder massages all the time after a long shift."

"No wonder you're so popular at the café."

"No, that would be because of my simmering sexuality and irresistible charm."

Austin reached for her shoulders again and began to knead them with slow, deliberate strokes. It felt heavenly.

"Feels good, doesn't it?"

"No," she lied. She glanced over her shoulder nervously. From there the third-floor balcony was barely visible.

"What?" Austin asked. "Afraid someone will see you?"

"No," she lied.

"Relax. Nobody upstairs can see us through all these palms. Besides, there's nothing wrong with getting a shoulder rub, Summer. We are consenting adults." Austin bent a little closer, still kneading. "Besides, if I wanted this to go any further, I'd do something like lean close. . . ."

Summer felt his hand gently gathering her hair to one side, baring her neck. She shivered. He leaned even closer. She could feel his warm breath. She wanted to move, but she couldn't.

"Then," Austin continued in his low, soothing whisper, like wind through leaves, "then I'd brush my lips against the side of your neck, like so. . . ."

She felt the soft warmth of his mouth touching her neck. For one horrible, tantalizing moment, she almost turned to face him. A few more inches and his mouth would be on hers—

What was she *doing*? She cleared her throat. "You know," Summer said suddenly, her voice shaky, "Seth proposed to me by a pool."

Austin laughed. "Whoa, you sure know how to dampen the mood."

"There was no mood, Austin. There's not going to be any mood."

"I believe this is called 'denial.' It's not just a river in Egypt."

"Very funny." Summer tried not to smile.

Austin ran his fingers across her shoulder blades. "If there is no mood, how come I'm still giving you a shoulder massage?"

Summer yanked free of his grasp. "You're not," she said crisply.

Austin shrugged. "Your loss. It's a great stress reducer, you know. And you're stressed out."

Summer rubbed her eyes. "You're right about that, at least. What am I going to tell Seth?"

"You realize I'm not exactly an impartial observer." Austin stroked his chin. "But if I were you, I'd probably hold off telling him. Maybe the thing'll turn up."

"I probably shouldn't take your advice, but in this case I happen to agree with you. I mean, there's no point in worrying Seth unnecessarily. In the meantime, I've got to get a job, and quick. Maybe I could earn enough to buy another one before I see him again. You think I could match it?"

"Oh, you can probably find one at any Kmart," Austin said with a laugh. "So, we still on for tomorrow? I really don't mind driving you to some interviews. Although there's always Jitters."

"I think I'll pass on Jitters." Summer hesitated. "In fact, I think I'll pass on the ride, too. I'll take the bus. Or I can wait till later and borrow Marquez's car or Diana's."

"Marquez is driving Diver back tomorrow. And you said Diana had errands to run. Let me drive you. I promise it will be entirely platonic chauffeuring. You need to start your savings account so that you can replace that ring. Although I do know a bubble gum machine where you could find a good match."

Summer stifled a smile.

"Go ahead," Austin challenged. "Laugh. I know you want to."

"I do not. I do not find you amusing."

Austin shook his head. "Yes, you do."

"You have such an ego for someone who keeps getting rejected."

For a moment Austin fell serious. His dark eyes surveyed her with longing so intense she could feel the pull of it. "I know how you really feel, Summer," he said softly. "I felt the way you kissed me over spring break. And I can wait a long time for something that good to happen again."

Summer touched his shoulder gently. "Then you're going to wait a very long time, Austin."

"You know what they say," he replied, the intensity replaced by a casual tone. "Good things come to those who wait."

# 14

## To Be or Not to Be a File Clerk; That Is the Question.

Summer awoke the next morning to a mattress that smelled like an old tennis shoe. Diana was up, her bed already made. The shower was running.

Summer padded out to the living room. Diver was on the front balcony, reading the morning paper.

"Hi," Summer said uncomfortably. "Mind if I borrow the want ads?"

She took a seat on one of the old wicker rockers the previous tenant had left behind. The morning sun was brilliant, the air filled with a rich, loamy smell from the carefully tended garden below.

Diver handed Summer the classified section. "Diana's taking a shower, I think. And Marquez is still asleep. She was kind of wired last night." He cleared his throat. On the street below, a group of tourists in gaudy T-shirts and wide-brimmed straw hats trooped by. "How did you sleep?"

"Okay. It's weird having just a mattress on the floor. It's also weird having one that smells like Grandma Smith's attic."

Diver smiled shyly. Summer studied the want ads. She felt stupid, bringing up a relative. In a strange way, it didn't feel as if she and Diver were related anymore.

"Remember that time—" Diver ran his fingers through his shimmering blond hair. "Remember that time you and I watched the sunrise on the stilt house roof?"

Summer nodded. "I remember."

"It was the best sunrise I ever saw."

"Me, too."

They fell silent. Summer scanned the ads. There wasn't much to choose from—pretty much the same stuff she'd seen advertised all week.

Just then Diana appeared on the porch. She was wearing a red velour robe and had one of her mother's towels wrapped around her head. Already she had on makeup.

"If I'd known you talked in your sleep, Summer, I would have roomed with Marquez." Diana leaned over the edge of the railing and inhaled the sweet-smelling air. "All night long. 'Oh, please, Austin' and 'Yes, yes, Austin.'"

"I did not!" Summer cried, horrified.

Diana nodded. "Jeez, Summer. You think you know someone. . . ."

Summer felt her cheeks heating. She *had* had a dream about Austin, and a pretty juicy one at that. Could she really have—

"Oh, relax, don't look so frantic. You slept like a log. Although you do snort sometimes."

"I do not snore."

"Not *snore, snort*." Diana made a little hoglike noise. "Don't worry. It's kind of endearing."

"You're certainly in a good mood," Diver said.

"I'm going shopping. Need I say more? But I'll be back this afternoon if you need the car for job hunting, Summer."

"That's okay. I'm covered." Summer chose not to mention her chauffeur for the day. There was no point in getting Diana started. "Here's what I've narrowed it down to. A restaurant called Kaboodles needs a lunch waitron. A pancake house on the edge of town needs one for breakfast, but I think they make you wear a frilly pink apron."

"Skip that one," Diana advised. "Pink is not your color."

"Those of us who work for a living don't pick our

jobs that way," came a hoarse voice from the living room.

"Marquez!" Diana exclaimed. "You look . . . not quite human."

Marquez joined them on the porch, slouching against the ivy-covered wall. There were dark, shiny circles under her eyes. "I had a rough night."

Diana grinned at Diver.

"No, not like that," Marquez said irritably. "I just couldn't get to sleep. I was tossing and turning like crazy. Diver slept on the couch." She nudged Summer. "So, what were your other choices?"

"Oh." Summer glanced at the paper. "The newspaper needs a part-time proofreader, which could be dangerous, since it involves spelling. Oh, yeah—there's a place down the highway that needs a file clerk. Something to do with dolphins, which might be cool."

"Filing for Flipper. Take that one," Marquez advised.

"No, don't," Diana said forcefully.

Everyone looked at her in surprise.

"I mean, I know that place. The Dolphin Interactive Therapy Institute, right?"

Summer nodded. "So?"

"So it's like a really long drive from here. How would you get there? The buses aren't exactly reliable.

And I think it's in this rickety building, really scuzzy-looking and . . ." Diana trailed off.

Summer and Marquez were gazing at her in bafflement.

"What gives, Diana?" Marquez asked.

Diana sighed. She wasn't going to find a way out of this. "I . . . um . . . I volunteer there."

For a moment no one spoke. "You?" Marquez demanded. "*You* volunteer?"

"It's no big deal, okay? It's just something I do."

"What do you do there, Diana?" Summer asked, as surprised as Marquez was by this revelation.

Diana shrugged off the question. "Just . . . stuff. Work with the kids. Mostly they're abused and kind of messed up. They spend time with the dolphins, and sometimes they start to open up."

Marquez's mouth was hanging open. "I don't understand. This is . . . like . . . *nice,* Diana."

Diana sighed again. "I knew I shouldn't have told you."

"I think it's fantastic, Diana," Summer said, touched by the faint blush on Diana's cheeks. Diana *never* blushed. "So I guess you wouldn't want me hanging around, huh?"

Diana adjusted the tie on her robe. "It's not like that. It's just . . . you know, it was kind of my private place. I did it all last year, too, and you guys never caught on. But I knew with us living together . . ." She sighed. "Go ahead and apply, Summer. It's not like I own the place. Anyway, I gotta get ready. I've got a full day at the mall planned."

"What's the occasion?" Marquez asked.

"You don't need an occasion to shop, Marquez. But I'm on the lookout for some traveling clothes." She started to leave, pausing in the doorway. "I'm going out to the West Coast with Mallory for a few days. She's got a big book tour, and I thought she might want some company. We're leaving tomorrow."

"Whoa, hold on." Marquez grabbed her by the sleeve. "You're spending time with your mother *deliberately*? This is too much to deal with. Somebody get me a chair."

"I've got a lap here," Diver offered.

"I'd crush you," Marquez said. She stared at Diana in disbelief. "I'm having information overload here. You volunteer with needy kids *and* you're going to hang out with your mom for no reason? Where is evil Diana? Who are you and what have you done with her?"

Diana favored her with a smile. "I can see why this would be difficult to grasp. I'm a complex woman, Marquez. Whereas you are, well, your basic one-celled organism."

"Where will you be on the West Coast, Diana?" Diver asked.

"Oh, I don't know. La-la land. Beverly Hills. Places with Armani and Donna Karan boutiques."

"Newport Beach?" Summer asked. "That's a little south of L.A."

"Is that where Seth is working?" Diana asked.

Summer nodded. "Maybe you could say hi to him. He'd probably love to see a friendly face."

"I don't know," Diana said. "There probably won't be much time. But for you, I'll give it a try."

Marquez eyed Diana doubtfully. "Suddenly she's Mother Teresa. Man, I need a cup of coffee. You are definitely full of surprises, Diana."

On the street below, someone honked. Austin pulled up in an old red Karmann Ghia convertible. "Your chariot awaits," he called.

Diana smiled coolly at Summer. "It seems," she said, "I'm not the only one who's full of surprises."

Summer slumped into the passenger seat of Austin's car. It was noon, and the sun was merciless. "Well, so far I'm oh-for-four. At this rate I really will have to pick up shifts at Jitters. Although they'd probably tell me I'm underqualified. Or overqualified. Or they'll keep my application on file. Or tell me to come back next week when the manager's in . . ."

She lay back against the headrest. The sun beat down on her face. Her skirt was damp and wrinkled.

Her blouse stuck to her back. Her shoes hurt. There was no way around the fact that job hunting was a full-time job. And the pay was lousy.

She cast a furtive glance at Austin. He was wearing cutoffs and no shoes, and a pair of near-black Oakleys was hiding his eyes. He'd taken off his shirt to soak up the sizzling rays. He was even more firm and well muscled than she remembered from spring break.

Austin started up the car. "What did the dolphin people say?"

"When I told them I was Diana's cousin, they couldn't stop raving about her. About how great she is with the kids, and all the progress she's made with some of their really tough cases." Summer kicked off her shoes and propped her feet on the dash. "It's weird. It's like this whole other side of Diana she's never shown to anyone."

Austin pulled onto the two-lane highway and headed back toward Coconut Key. The hot wind whipped their hair into a frenzy. "She's a strange girl, Diana. Very complex. There's something not quite trustworthy about her that makes her quite appealing."

"What do you mean? I trust her."

"Well, you know her better than I do, obviously. I just get the feeling that with Diana, there's always a little bit more to the story."

Summer watched the sea grass zipping past. The ocean was alive with sunlight. Even with sunglasses, she had to squint.

She thought about Diana's impromptu visit to California. It occurred to her that if Diana saw Seth, she might unintentionally slip and mention the lost ring . . . or even Austin. The very thought made Summer queasy. Maybe she should say something to Diana, just to be sure. Of course, chances were that Diana wouldn't even see Seth. Summer was probably worrying for nothing.

"So, anyway," Austin said, "think there's any chance the dolphin guys will hire you?"

"Oh, they were really nice, but I doubt it. Besides, I don't want to invade Diana's turf, you know? And we already live together. Working together . . . that might just be too much togetherness." Summer closed her eyes to the bone-melting sun. "And anyway, they have about a zillion applicants, and they were hoping for someone who could work part-time this fall. And I won't exactly be in commuting distance come September."

"Where *will* you be this fall, exactly?"

Summer opened her eyes. Austin was looking at her, but with his dark shades, she couldn't read his expression.

"I'll be a freshman at the University of Wisconsin."

"And why is that?"

Summer sat up a little straighter. "Because it's where I want to go to school."

"And why is that?"

"What are you all of a sudden, Joe Shrink?" Summer asked.

Austin shrugged. "Just curious."

"I'm going to UW because Seth and I were both accepted there, and it's a good school, and it's close to my home." She hesitated. "My home" sounded funny now that she was living in Florida again. But Minnesota was her real home. It was the place where her family was, the place where she'd been born. The place where she'd grown up.

"Why UW?" Austin pressed. "Why not, I don't know, the University of Minnesota? Or Michigan? Or Arkansas?"

Summer occupied herself putting her sandals back on. "Well, I did apply to some other schools. But Seth's dad and grandfather went to UW. It was kind of important to him to continue the tradition. And I didn't care where I went as long as—"

Austin looked over, lowering his shades to make sure she saw his skeptical expression. "As long as you were with Seth. That's so fifties of you. You're deciding the future of your education based on the desires of your boyfriend?" He shook his head. "You seem like such a feminist. And now you reveal this dark side."

"I *am* a feminist," Summer said, scowling. "And it's not just my boyfriend. My family's there, and the friends I grew up with. My best friend in Bloomington, Jennifer, is going to UW. Lots of people I know. Not just Seth."

"And what will you be studying way up there in Wisconsin? Going for a PhD in moo-cows?"

"I'm undecided." Summer crossed her arms over her chest. "How should I know what I want to be? I'm only eighteen."

"That, at least," Austin said with a grin, "is an enlightened answer."

"I'm so glad you approve."

"So the plan is, you go to UW, marry Seth, get a nice, bland job, maybe in the insurance industry— yeah, that'd be about right—then have nice, bland little Seths and Summers?"

"Something like that. Except for the insurance part. And the bland part."

They slowed as they neared the edge of Coconut Key. The town sprouted out of nowhere, a sudden, crazy hodgepodge of old houses with tin roofs and latticework porches. Many were on stilts or concrete pilings as a protection against hurricanes. Graceful herons walked the edge of the road in stately slow motion.

"So where else did you apply?"

"Some other schools in the Midwest," Summer said. "And one down here, just for the hell of it."

"Florida Coastal? The one Diana and Marquez are going to?"

Summer shook her head.

"Carlson?" Austin looked at her with renewed respect. "Isn't that a private experimental college?"

"It was just an idea. My English teacher suggested it. She said it would stimulate me or something like that. English teachers love to talk about stimulation. The intellectual kind of stimulation, anyway."

"And you were accepted?"

"It doesn't matter, Austin. I'm not going there. I'm going to UW."

They drove on in silence for a while. Summer closed her eyes. The sun was making her drowsy.

"Hang on." Austin took a sudden, sharp turn to the right onto a small dirt road lined by squat palms.

"Where are we going?" Summer asked, grabbing the door handle to keep her balance.

"Detour."

"What kind of detour?"

"A good detour." He gave her a cryptic smile. "Most detours are."

## Love at First Sight

"I think I'm in love," Summer murmured as she got out of the car.

"I knew you'd come to your senses eventually," Austin said.

"Not with you. With this place. Have you ever seen such a beautiful school? I mean, it looked good in the brochures. But this is amazing.

She started down a manicured stone path lined by magnificent palms.

"Wait up," Austin called, "I need to put on a shirt," but Summer couldn't wait.

Carlson's tiny campus was set at the very tip of

Coconut Key. Its white stucco buildings with red tile roofs were arrayed along the beach. The grounds were thick with exotic tropical plants in full bloom. In the center of the campus was the striking student union building, a huge mansion that had once been the winter residence of R. T. Carlson, an illiterate immigrant who'd grown up to be an eccentric but generous railroad baron. Upon his death, he'd requested that the land and residence be turned into a college.

Austin fell into step beside her. "What a beautiful, strange place," he said. "Check out the huge trees over there."

"Banyan trees," Summer said. "The roots grow down to form new trunks. They're from India. My English teacher said she used to attend poetry classes under the trunks. It's like a big tree house."

"So she went to school here?"

"Ms. Desai. She said it was the best choice she ever made." Summer paused to watch two students sitting by a fountain. "It's a real free-form curriculum. You don't declare a major. Instead you just take lots of different courses based on important works of literature."

"I've heard about it. It's tough to get into." He winked at her. "No sweat for you, though, huh?"

"My grades weren't that great. They must have liked the essay I wrote."

They sat on the shady steps of the main building. "So what was your essay about?" Austin asked, leaning back on his elbows.

"What I wanted from my education."

"And that would be . . . ?"

"Well, basically I said I wasn't sure, but that I thought if I had a good education, I would be able to make informed decisions. You know, make good choices in my life." Summer shrugged, feeling suddenly self-conscious. "Blah, blah, blah."

Austin touched her on the shoulder. "Don't make fun of yourself that way. I think that's exactly what you should want from an education."

Summer eyed him doubtfully. "If you're so pro-college, then why did you drop out of the University of Texas after only a semester?"

"Hey, do as I say, not as I do." It was Austin's turn to look uncomfortable. "I guess it was all the stuff with my dad. All of a sudden he's got this incurable disease, and there's a fifty-fifty shot I'm going to get it. Acing Rocks for Jocks just didn't seem to matter much."

"What were you going to major in?"

"Poetry." He grinned at her, a self-conscious, cockeyed grin that was sweet and self-deprecating. "Yes, I know. Business or medicine might make me more cash. No, they would *definitely* make me more cash. But my dad was a music major at Juilliard, and he turned out okay. His cello career was really taking off, until . . . well, anyway, I'm going to go back to school. I just need some time to regroup, is all."

The heavy stained-glass doors to the union opened, and a petite young woman with a long braid down her back appeared on the top step. She was carrying a massive load of books. As she started down the steps she dropped several. Summer and Austin leapt to the rescue.

"Thanks," she said. "I think I bit off more than I can chew."

"Need a hand?" Summer asked.

"That'd be great. I'm just heading over to Wilson Hall. Thataway."

They split up the books and started down a winding path toward one of the stucco buildings near the beach.

"I'm Cary Woo," the woman said. "I'm a TA in English lit."

"What's a TA?" Summer asked.

"Teaching assistant. I'll bet you're going to be a freshman, right? I'd remember you otherwise."

"You know everybody on this campus?" Austin asked incredulously.

"It's a tiny place. Everyone knows everyone."

Austin laughed. "The University of Texas was like a small city."

"That's how UW is," Summer said. "Really big."

"Well, that has its advantages," Cary said. "Lots

of variety. Me, I like the family feel of Carlson. It's a special place."

She opened the door to one of the little buildings. Big windows afforded a view of the white beach and the endless water beyond. "Plus," Cary added, "the view's spectacular. And if you want more excitement, there's always FCU, down the road. We share some facilities and library resources with them, so it's like having a sister campus."

"Two of my friends are going there." Summer dropped her load of books onto the wooden desk at the front of the classroom. The room smelled of chalk dust and sea air.

"Well, thanks for the help," Cary said.

"Anytime." Austin started for the door. "Summer? You coming?"

Summer hesitated. "Cary?" she said shyly.

"Hmm?"

"Are the classes here as hard as everybody says?

"Oh, yeah, they're tough." She laughed. "I mean, you work your tush off here. It's intense and it's focused. It's not the right college for everybody. You have to be very self-motivated, very into learning." She paused. "But it's worth it. It's something you'll take with you the rest of your life. It helps you define where you want to go, to make the right choices, you know?"

Summer glanced over her shoulder at Austin. He

was leaning against the doorjamb, thumbs hooked in his pockets, studying her carefully.

"Yeah," Summer said. "I guess."

A few steps out the door, Summer stopped in mid-stride.

"What?" Austin asked.

"Just a second. Wait here, okay?" She ran back to the doorway. "Cary?"

Cary looked up in surprise. "Back already?"

"I was wondering . . . if someone had applied here and been accepted but then said no and then decided she wanted to maybe go after all, what would that someone do?"

Cary smiled. "I imagine that someone would check in with admissions," she said.

"That's what I figured."

"Good luck," Cary said.

Summer nodded. "It's really hard here, huh?"

"It's really great, too."

Austin was waiting for her under a palm tree. "Forget something?"

"Not exactly," Summer said softly. "I may have overlooked something, though."

"Mind if I swing by my place?" Austin asked when they returned to his car. "I've got to work tonight, and I need to pick up my waitron clothes."

Summer looked at him doubtfully.

"Believe me, it's not a place for seduction, Summer. It's pretty much of a hellhole."

"Okay, then."

Austin's apartment wasn't a hellhole, but it did make Summer's place look palatial. It was a garage apartment, a tiny one-bedroom on a side street in the seedier part of Coconut Key.

"I've never seen so many books outside the library," Summer said, stepping over a cardboard box full of musty-smelling volumes.

"I had my mom ship them out. Cost me a fortune. But they're like friends, you know? I felt lost without them around." He yanked off his T-shirt. "Make yourself at home. I've gotta change. There might be something edible in the fridge, but I wouldn't put money on it. If it's moving, don't eat it."

Summer sat on the aging couch. She felt guilty being in Austin's apartment, although there was really no reason for her to feel that way. She picked up a volume of poetry off the floor. Rilke. One of Cary's books had been a volume of poetry.

Summer tried to picture herself sitting in one of Carlson's white stucco buildings. She would be carrying a heavy book bag. All her fellow students would be smarter. She would ask stupid questions, and they would be too polite to laugh, but they would snicker behind their hands.

Austin reappeared. He'd changed into his work clothes and run a comb through his windblown hair. He looked way too good to be going to a job waiting tables. He looked way too good for Summer to be in his apartment without a chaperon.

"Sorry I can't feed you. How about tomorrow night, though? It's my birthday. I could cook you up some lasagna or something."

"I don't think so, Austin."

He shook his head. "You're going to make me spend my birthday alone in this hovel? Have you no heart?"

She hesitated. "A platonic birthday dinner? No strings?"

"No strings. Just the best lasagna you've ever tasted."

"I guess." She fell silent, staring at the Rilke book she was holding.

"You're awfully quiet."

"I was thinking about that school."

Austin sat beside her. "You're thinking about reapplying, aren't you?"

Summer stared at him, aghast. "I didn't say that."

"You implied it. Implied applying." He touched her hand. "You are, aren't you?"

She closed her eyes. "Everyone is counting on my going to UW. Seth. My mom. Jennifer. All my high school friends. I have a dorm room picked out. I put a deposit down. It's too late to change my mind."

"It's never too late, Summer. Never."

Summer groaned. "How can I be so unsure about everything? How could I not know? I made a decision, and I have to stick with it."

"You made a decision based on inadequate information. You chose UW without seeing Carlson. Today you went there, and it felt right, didn't it?"

Summer nodded. "But I can't change my mind just because the campus is pretty."

"That's not why it felt right. It felt right because you saw yourself there and you realized you'd let your fear get in the way of making the right choice. You talked to Cary and you started to think, 'Hey, I could make it here.'"

"I'm not smart enough for Carlson."

Austin looked annoyed. "I guess the admissions people were just hitting the beer pretty heavy on the day your application showed up."

Summer rubbed the spot where her ring should have been. "I can't. What about my mom? She needs me right now. What about Seth? He's counting on our being together. I can't."

"I know you think I'm biased here, and I am." Austin took her fidgeting hands and held them still. "But you have to believe me when I tell you that you can't make decisions about your life because it will make your mom happy or some guy happy. Not even," he added with a sigh, "if that guy is me."

"I know that."

"But do you really?"

Summer thought of the classroom again. She pictured Cary asking her a question. Maybe a question about Keats, a difficult question, an unfathomably hard question, not at all like questions Ms. Desai had asked all year in senior English.

She pictured herself answering the question. No one in the class would smile. She would answer correctly. They would all be impressed. They would see that she had valuable things to offer. They would know that she belonged.

"If I could be wrong about college," Summer whispered, "I could be wrong about . . . anything."

Austin nodded. "Welcome to life," he said.

He was leaning toward her so imperceptibly that his lips were almost on hers before she realized that this time they really were going to kiss.

It was as if they'd kissed a million times, and as if they'd never kissed before. It was as if Austin knew just what she was feeling. It was as if he'd climbed right inside her mind and her heart to a place she'd never let anyone go before.

It was as if he'd seen the part of her that knew all the right answers.

# 16

# Dangerous Pictures, Dangerous Pills

When Diana got home from shopping, the apartment was empty. It was also hot, stuffy, and an incredible mess. Cardboard boxes were stacked everywhere. Crumpled newspaper littered the floor. One of Marquez's bras was stuck between the couch cushions. A stack of dirty dishes leaned precariously in the sink.

Was it any wonder Summer had lost her engagement ring in this chaos? Of course, Diana knew, there was a psychological element to it, too. It was way too symbolic, given Summer's flirtation with Austin, for it not to have been.

Diana tossed her shopping bags onto the couch. A skirt, two tops, a dress, a pair of shorts, some silver earrings, and the pack of photos from the one-hour lab at the mall. The only thing she hadn't gotten around to was picking up some shoes.

She checked her watch. Well, she could at least try calling him. There was a chance he'd be home from work by that time. Diana would have to get Seth's number from Summer's address book.

She rummaged through the pile of stuff next to Summer's bed and finally located the little blue address book. Summer had drawn red hearts around Seth's name. How very cute, Diana thought. How very cute and insincere. She copied Seth's number and address down on a piece of scrap paper and put the address book back where she'd found it.

Her eyes fell on a pair of Summer's shoes, brand-new leather ones with chunky lug soles that would look great with the black micromini Diana had just bought at Burdine's that afternoon. Would it be tacky to borrow your cousin's never-worn shoes while you were borrowing her slightly used boyfriend?

Diana slipped her foot into the right shoe. It was a little snug, but she could get by for a night if she had to. She tried on the other one. Her toe hit something hard, like a piece of metal.

Frowning, Diana took off the shoe and felt inside.

The minute she touched it, she knew she'd hit gold. Literally.

She pulled out the ring and held it up to the light.

It was too bad Diana didn't believe in signs. Because this one was a neon-lit, bigger-than-life, in-your-face sign if she'd ever heard of one.

She grabbed her cell phone, stretched out on her bed, and dialed the number she'd copied out of Summer's address book.

She slipped the ring onto her finger. She could not seem to stop smiling.

For a giddy second she thought about putting everything on the line, just telling Seth there and then how she felt. She never really had, except in those letters she hadn't had the guts to mail.

Wait, she told herself. Savor it. She had to wait till the time was right. In romance, timing was everything.

"Seth?" she said when he answered on the second ring. "You'll never guess who this is."

It was only two flights of stairs from Jitters to the apartment, but Marquez felt as though she were climbing Everest. She must have gained weight, must have. How else could she explain this heaviness in her limbs? Her legs and arms felt like big sacks of flour.

She'd worked her butt off at lunch and even stayed late, but still she'd only made a lousy sixteen bucks in tips. She was never going to make it through the school year this way. Maybe she could find a classier place to work or take on some more shifts. Maybe even pick up a second job for the summer.

At the door to the apartment, she fumbled for her key. Her hands had been shaking all day. Her breath came in sharp gasps. She definitely had gained weight. She was going to have to buy a new scale—if she could ever come up with the spare cash.

It was hot inside, and dark. The louvered doors were closed. She heard a muffled voice coming from the room Summer and Diana shared. The bedroom door was closed.

She wondered if the phone had been installed yet. But no, that was supposed to happen next week. It must be someone on Diana's cell phone.

Curious, Marquez put her ear to the door.

"Oh, come on, Seth. For old times' sake."

Diana? Talking to Seth?

"We had fun over New Year's, didn't we?"

Marquez leaned a little too hard on the door, making it rattle. Instantly Diana yanked it open. The phone was in her hand.

"Oh," she said, looking immensely relieved, "it's you. I thought maybe it was Summer. What were you doing? Eavesdropping?"

"I was just wondering who you were talking to, is all."

"When did you get home?"

"Just now." Marquez pointed to the phone. "Is that Seth?"

"Um, yeah. I was just . . . um, letting him know I'll be out west with Mallory. You know. In case we could all get together."

"You and Mallory and Seth."

"Yeah. You know, for dinner or something." Diana shoved the phone at her. "You wanna say hi?"

"I'm kind of beat. You tell him hi for me."

"Sure. I will." Quickly Diana shut the door behind her.

Marquez went to her room. Very strange, she thought as she shed her waitron clothes for her exercise gear. Diana's acting as though she'd been caught with her hand in the cookie jar. Marquez sometimes wondered if maybe there wasn't something a little odd going on between Seth and Diana.

Marquez tied on her sneakers. It wasn't anything she could put her finger on. Certainly not the kind of thing she'd ever mention to Summer, who had a vivid imagination when it came to problems of any stripe.

In the kitchen, Marquez surveyed the cupboard. She'd skipped breakfast and lunch, which was good, because she was clearly putting on the pounds again. She got out a piece of bread, a knife, and a plate. Carefully she sliced the bread into four squares. She sliced each of those squares into four more pieces.

She could hear Diana's laughter in the other room. It was probably nothing. And if it wasn't, Marquez didn't want to know about it. She had enough on her mind without getting into some mess between Diana and Summer.

She picked up one of the squares, placed it on her tongue, and hesitated. Just two. She would eat only two of the tiny squares. The rest she would save for dinner.

Marquez ate the bread very slowly. She put the other squares in a plastic bag and took it to her bedroom. In her top dresser drawer there were two other bags, each with their own squares of bread. She'd been good those times. She hadn't eaten any of the extra squares.

She'd just climbed onto her exercise bike when Diana emerged from her bedroom, looking flushed and hyper.

"So," Diana said energetically, "want to see what I bought today?"

"Not unless you got a bathroom scale," Marquez said. Slowly she began pedaling. Her legs did not want to cooperate.

Diana sat on the couch, studying Marquez as if she were an exotic zoo animal. "Didn't you just get off work?"

"Yeah, and I'm picking up a dinner shift tonight."

"Did you have lunch? There's some pizza in the fridge we could nuke."

"I already ate."

Diana frowned. "Marquez, I know you don't want advice from me—"

"You got that right."

"—but don't you think maybe you're overdoing it? The dieting and the exercising and working extra shifts."

"Not all of us can spend our days running up the credit cards, Diana," Marquez muttered. "Some of us have to work for a living." She was annoyed at the sound of jealousy in her own voice.

"If you need money—"

"I don't need money. As it happens, I still owe you from that credit card I used over spring break."

"Don't worry about that, Marquez."

"Look, Diana, I'm going to pay you back every penny, one way or another." Marquez pedaled harder. Sweat poured off her brow, and she'd barely started.

Diana opened the front porch doors to let in more breeze. "You look kind of worn out, to tell you the truth, Marquez. Your parents just moved, and you're working really hard. That can be awfully stressful."

"Did you learn that at your dolphin job? What, did they make you an honorary psychologist?"

Diana looked annoyed, to Marquez's satisfaction. She was silent for a few blissful minutes. Then she started in again.

"We've had a couple of girls there . . ." Diana pursed her lips, as if she wasn't sure whether to continue. "Girls with, you know, dieting problems. There's a woman who works with them, a counselor who's really cool. I could give you her name."

Marquez stopped pedaling. She could feel the anger moving inside her like a caged animal. "Are you suggesting I need a shrink because I'm trying to lose a few pounds?"

"It's not just a few pounds, Marquez. And maybe you can fool your family and Summer, but I'm around you more. I'm just saying that I could give you her name if you wanted to talk. I'd pay for it, too."

Marquez sent Diana her steeliest gaze. "I do not need your help running my life, Diana. If we're going to be sharing this apartment, let's get that straight right now. I'm not going to pry into your complicated little mind. I'm not going to ask why you're calling your cousin's fiancé. I'm not going to, because I've got my own life to keep track of, and that's hard enough. All right?"

Diana held up her hands. "Okay, okay. You're right. I'm sorry." She gave a shrug. "What do I know, anyway? I do a little volunteer work now and then, and suddenly I think I'm Sigmund Freud."

She headed for her room. "Just for the record, there's nothing going on between Seth and me." She smiled frostily. "But you're right. It's none of your business, anyway."

# 17

# Summer Goes to Dreamland, and Diana Goes to La-La Land

Summer checked her alarm clock. Three-twenty in the morning. Diana was snoring very loudly. And she claimed Summer made noise!

She rolled off her mattress and made her way across the floor, nearly tripping on an open suitcase. Diana was leaving early that morning for California. Aunt Mallory was picking her up, and Diana had been nice enough to say Summer could use Diana's car while she was gone.

Summer gently closed the door behind her. Marquez's door was shut. The main room was striped by yellow moonlight coursing through the louvered doors. The air was hot and sticky, even for a June night.

She located Diana's cell phone under a pile of

clothes. Carefully she punched in the numbers. Please, please, please, let it be Seth who answers, she thought. It wasn't as late in California, but he and his roommates got up early for work.

To her relief, the sleepy voice at the other end was Seth's.

"Hi, it's me, Summer," she whispered. "Did I wake you?"

"No." Seth yawned. "Well, okay, yes. But I'm glad you did. Is anything wrong?"

She sat on the couch, hugging her knees. "Not really. I just wanted to talk, is all."

For a sudden, vivid moment, she flashed back to that afternoon and the way she'd felt in Austin's arms. Guilt washed over her like an icy wave.

"This isn't about, uh, Diana, is it?"

"Diana? No, why?"

"Nothing. I was just wondering."

"She's coming out to California this weekend with my aunt. There probably won't be time, but I thought I'd give her your address, you know, in case they can stop by. Would that be okay?"

"Um, sure." There was a long pause. "Yeah, that'd be okay."

"I don't have to if you don't want. I could just tell her you're really tied up with work. I know Diana can be kind of . . . well, Diana."

"It's okay," Seth said, sounding a little edgy. "Whatever."

"You're tired. I should let you go back to sleep."

"No, don't go," Seth said quickly. "Don't go yet. I like just hearing your voice. What did you do today?"

"I went job hunting." With Austin. "Then I stopped by that college we applied to, Carlson." With Austin. Then I kissed Austin till I thought I'd pass out.

"What's it like?"

"Carlson? I thought it was pretty cool. I met a teacher there. A teaching assistant, really. She said it's true what they say about it being a tough curriculum."

"I'm glad I didn't get in, then," Seth said. "We want to have some fun during college, after all."

"What if . . ." Summer took a deep breath. "What do you think would have happened to us if we'd decided to go to different colleges? You know, like Mindy Burke and Joe McGrath? You think we would have been able to pull it off?"

"I don't know. It was hard enough with me living just a couple of hours away from you in Wisconsin. I can't imagine doing that for four years straight, can you?"

"No." Summer bit her lip. "I guess not."

Seth yawned again.

"We should hang up," Summer said. "I just wanted

to hear your voice for a minute. Sometimes it feels like you're so far away, and I feel so lost, you know?"

"I know. Me, too. But it won't be forever."

Summer felt a hot tear make its way down her cheek. "I love you, Seth," she whispered, and then she hung up before she started crying.

She lay on the couch, sobbing softly into the smelly old cushions, hoping she wouldn't wake Diana or Marquez. She didn't want to have to explain herself. She didn't want to try to explain how she was torn between two guys—one the safe and sweet choice, the other challenging and passionate.

Or how she was torn between two colleges—one the comfortable and simple choice, the other difficult and even scary.

She was even torn, she suddenly realized, between two places. The place where she'd grown up, where her family and long-term friends were, where the winters were bitter and the summers brief, and her adopted home there in the Keys, where the summers were sweltering but the sun never, ever stopped shining.

She closed her eyes and fell into a fitful, uneasy sleep.

She dreamed that she was in a classroom at Carlson. There was only one other student present—Austin. He was standing at the board, wearing his Jitters T-shirt, writing down an equation that explained the com-

plex physics principles involved in the act of kissing.
Summer tried to keep up, but she kept getting confused:

x/y
$2(x - y) \times (Summer - Seth)$
Austin = the right answer

Every time she raised her hand to get help, the telephone in her book bag would ring. And every time she
answered it, it was Seth, wanting to know what she'd
done with her engagement ring.

She got a lousy night's sleep.


Diana tiptoed out of the bedroom around six o'clock.
Summer, for some reason, was sprawled out on the
couch, softly snorting, as usual.

Well, no point in waking her. Quick, clean get-
aways were always the best.

Diana sneaked past the couch, her suitcase in tow.
She stole another guilty glance at her cousin. She was a
beautiful girl, in the wholesome, sunny way that guys
like Seth always fell for. She looked so sweet and guile-
less that Diana felt an annoying twinge of remorse.

It wasn't as though she hadn't tried to keep Summer
and Seth together, she reminded herself. Summer was the
one who'd allowed Austin back into her life. Summer
was the one who'd blown her chance with Seth.

Diana eased open the door. She could wait for Mallory, who would undoubtedly be late, down at Jitters, maybe have herself a latte and a cinnamon roll.

The door creaked like something out of a bad horror movie. Summer stirred instantly.

"Diana? Are you leaving already?"

"Yep. See you in a couple of days. The car keys are on my dresser."

Diana scooted out the door, but it was too late.

"Hey, wait."

She set down her bag with a sigh. "I'm kind of in a hurry, Summer."

"Sorry. I was just thinking you might want Seth's number and address, in case you have time."

Damn. Diana hesitated. She could let it go, pretend she hadn't called Seth, but Marquez might spill it.

"Not necessary. I called him yesterday to see if he'd be around."

"You did?" Summer sat up, rubbing her eyes. "But I just talked to him last night, and he didn't mention it."

Diana studied her manicured nails. "Well, we just touched base for a sec. He probably forgot, is all."

"Maybe."

"Hey, I borrowed your black shoes. Is that okay?"

"Sure. We're roommates. What's mine is yours."

Diana cleared her throat. "Well, I gotta run. Good luck with the job hunt—"

"Listen, one other thing." Now Summer looked fully awake, even wary. "If you do see Seth—"

"I probably won't. There won't be a lot of time, and you know Mallory—"

"But if you *do,* do me a favor and don't mention Austin. It would just worry Seth. You know how he is."

"I don't see why you'd care. It's not like there's anything going on between you and Austin, right?"

"Just don't mention him, all right?" Summer said pointedly.

"You know me better than that, Summer." Diana grabbed her bag. "Gotta run."

"And Diana? The same thing goes for the ring, right? I mean, who knows, it may still turn up."

Diana gave a fleeting smile. "It wouldn't surprise me at all."

# 18

## Summer Makes a Call while Diana Pays a Call

"You've been staring at that cell phone for hours, Summer," Marquez chided that afternoon. "Lift your feet, by the way. I'm in full sweep mode."

"Would you please stop cleaning already?" Summer pulled her feet up onto the couch so Marquez could rush past with a broom. "You're making me feel guilty."

"This place is a sty."

"Yeah, but since when is that an issue for you? Your old room was never exactly neat, Marquez. I remember one time it took you three days to locate your bed."

Marquez whisked dirt into a dustpan with frantic little strokes. "This is different. There are three of us slobs now. Although, to be fair, Diana is truly the queen of crap." She pointed toward a pile of cardboard boxes stacked against one wall. "Look at all that stuff. She's just waiting for the maid to show up."

Summer smiled wryly. "You're the next best thing."

"I work cheap, that's for sure."

"Are you okay, Marquez? You look kind of run-down."

"Did you and Diana get together and decide to gang up on me?" Marquez demanded, hands on hips. "Because I really do not need two extra mothers, thank you very much."

"Why? Did Diana say something?"

"Something along the lines of 'Stop working so hard, stop exercising and dieting so much,' which is way easy advice, coming from a rich, lazy, skinny person."

Summer could tell she'd hit a nerve. Maybe she'd back off, talk to Diana about it when she got back. She could even talk to Diver, although that would be kind of awkward. One thing was sure: There was no reasoning with Marquez when she got like this. It would be better to let her cool off, then try her again on a calmer day.

Summer made a space on the couch. "Come sit with me, Marquez. You could use a break. And I need advice."

"No offense, but I'd rather clean the sink."

"Okay, compromise. You clean the sink *and* give me advice."

Marquez grabbed a sponge and a can of Comet. "Does this have something to do with that phone you've been flirting with all day?"

Summer nodded. "I've been thinking about switching colleges. Going to Carlson instead of UW."

Marquez dropped her sponge, blinking in disbelief. "But that would be fantastic, Summer! Diana and I would be just down the street at FCU, and maybe we could even keep this place! And we'd all be together this fall—" She stopped in midsentence. "Uh-oh," she said, her voice hushed. "Seth."

"Seth," Summer repeated. She closed her eyes and groaned. "I feel like such a ditz, Marquez. I mean, I made a commitment to UW. And Seth and my mom and Jennifer and everybody back home, they're all counting on me. But when I visited Carlson yesterday, I realized how special it was. And the only reason I didn't pursue going there was because Seth didn't get in." She sighed. "No, that's not the only reason. I was afraid I couldn't cut it there. It's really tough, and I was sure I'd fail."

"And now you're not so sure?" Marquez asked.

"Now I'm starting to wonder how I'd feel if I never even gave it a chance. But I don't know how to choose,

Marquez. If I was wrong about UW, I could be wrong about everything."

Marquez picked up her sponge and occupied herself with the sink, scrubbing diligently. After a while she turned to face Summer. "This isn't about Austin, is it? About being close to him? I mean, you *are* doing birthday lasagna tonight."

"Platonic birthday lasagna," Summer corrected. She hadn't told Marquez about the unfortunate kiss incident. She was trying to convince herself it hadn't happened.

"Whatever kind of lasagna," Marquez said. "The point is, does this change of heart have anything to do with him?"

"No. I asked myself that, but no. It isn't even about you and Diana, or about staying here in Florida. I'm starting to realize I have to make decisions based on what I feel in my heart, not what will make everybody else happy." She clutched one of the stained old couch pillows. "Besides, no matter what I do, it'll be a mess. It's too late to make everybody happy. So that kind of just leaves me. But I'm not sure I have the guts to go through with it. Assuming, that is, Carlson will even consider my application this late."

"Well, how will you feel if you don't do it?" Marquez asked gently.

"I'll feel like I was afraid to do the hard thing. Like

I was afraid of failing. And that feels awful. But disappointing people because I'm confused and stupid and indecisive and idiotic, that feels awful, too."

Marquez set her sponge aside. "You are none of those things. Well, except maybe indecisive. And confused." She retrieved a small framed picture off the counter. "Here's my advice," she said, handing it to Summer. "Me and e.e., whoever he is."

Summer stared for a long time at the poem Austin had given her. "If I say yes to this, I'm saying no to so many other things."

"Like Seth. What will you do about him?" Marquez asked gravely.

Summer swallowed. Her throat was tight and dry. "Hope he understands? Visit him on holidays?"

"And what will you do about Austin?"

"I don't need to do anything about Austin. There's nothing that needs doing where Austin's concerned."

Marquez shook her head. "Sometimes I'm really glad I'm me and not you, Summer. Not usually. But sometimes." She hesitated for a moment. "Listen—" She hesitated.

"What?"

"Oh, nothing."

"What, Marquez?"

Marquez shrugged. "I was just wondering if

you knew that Diana called Seth yesterday."

"Yeah, she mentioned it this morning, when she was leaving."

"Oh." Marquez looked relieved. "Good."

"Why?"

"No reason. Just wondering, is all." She motioned to the phone. "Go ahead. Call the college before you lose your nerve."

Summer took a deep breath, then called information. "Could I have the number for Carlson College?" she asked.

She punched in the number. "Why does it have to be so complicated, Marquez?" she asked as the phone rang.

Marquez gave a dark laugh. "Girl," she said, shaking her head, "you are most definitely asking the wrong person."

Diana parked the rental car in front of a nondescript apartment building on the outskirts of Newport Beach. She checked the directions Seth had given her when she'd called him from her hotel room. Yep, she was in the right place. So why did she feel so wrong?

She checked herself out in the rearview mirror. A little more lip gloss, a touch-up with her brush. She was stalling, and she knew it. She wondered if Seth was watching her from one of the windows. He'd sounded neutral on the phone. Not encouraging, exactly, but not as though he was sending her definite "back off" signals either. He'd sounded like she felt: unsure.

Diana dropped her brush back into her purse. The packet of pictures was tucked inside. So was Summer's ring, in a little zippered pouch. Diana opened it and felt a shot of courage. Her secret weapon.

Summer's disloyalty was the reason this was okay. Summer didn't deserve Seth. Summer didn't want Seth.

She'd had her chance. Now it was Diana's turn.

Slowly Diana got out of the car. She looked good in her black mini and the shoes she'd borrowed from Summer. That was something, anyway. It should have given her confidence. Usually she approached guys with the secret knowledge that they were silently swooning over her. But with Seth, she couldn't be sure.

Before she could even knock, he appeared behind the screen door. She couldn't quite read his face through the screen.

"Diana," Seth said softly.

He opened the door, and she wrapped her arms around his neck and gave him a kiss—on the lips, yes, but nothing to scare him off. Just a taste of the possibilities, a reminder of what he'd been missing. His arms were harder than she remembered. He seemed taller, too.

Seth pulled away awkwardly, leaving her dizzy and

disoriented. He took a couple of steps back. "I, uh, I thought we'd maybe go get something to eat. You hungry?"

"Starved. That sounds great."

"I just need to grab my wallet and some shoes." He combed his fingers through his thick chestnut hair. "Did you have any trouble getting here?"

Diana clutched her purse a little tighter. "If you only knew, Seth," she said lightly. "If you only knew."

# 19

# You Learn the Most Interesting Things When You Clean House.

"You're late," Austin admonished as he held open the door. He had a kitchen towel draped over one shoulder and a wooden spoon in his right hand. "I was starting to worry."

"Sorry." Summer slipped inside. "I was debating whether to come."

Austin frowned. "Scared of my cooking? Or of me?"

"Both." Summer handed him the envelope she was carrying. "Happy birthday."

"It's either a check or a gift certificate. Just the right thing to send the message 'I care, but not a whole lot.'"

Summer headed for the kitchen, which smelled of tangy tomato sauce and garlic. "It's from the bookstore. I thought you could pick out a book you really wanted. You've got so many, and I didn't want to get you something you already had."

"Thanks," Austin said, sounding genuinely pleased. "It's the perfect present." He grinned. "Even if it is cold and impersonal."

Summer peeked in the oven. "Looks good."

"And only slightly burned."

As she stood, Austin slipped his arms around her. "Austin," Summer said firmly, "this is a platonic birthday meal, remember?"

He looked at her incredulously. "And was that a platonic kiss yesterday?"

"Look, I think we need to talk. How about a beach walk?"

Austin hooked his thumbs in his pockets. "Sure, why not? We'll work up a big appetite, which might not be a bad idea, given my culinary skills. Just let me go throw on a shirt without tomato sauce on it."

While Austin was changing, the phone in the living room rang. "Want me to get it?" Summer asked.

"Naw," Austin called from the bedroom. "Let the machine do the dirty work."

A moment later his answering machine clicked on. A soft voice, an older, more muted version of Austin's, filled the room. Summer felt uncomfortable listening, but there was nowhere to go to avoid it.

"Hey, it's me, your much older, much wiser sibling. I hope you're not picking up 'cause you've got better things to do, hopefully better things involving someone of the female persuasion. Let's see, what's up . . . I talked to Mom last week. Dad's worse, no surprise, but enough of that. Seriously, give me a call sometime, okay? I'm worried about you. The news hits hard for a while, I know. Let me know how you're holding up, Austin. It gets easier after a while, really it does. Anyway, have a good one. Happy nineteenth. There'll be many more. Believe me, there will."

The room went quiet. Austin appeared in the doorway, his face expressionless.

"Was that your brother?" Summer asked.

"Yeah." Austin brushed past her toward the door. "You ready?"

"What did he mean, 'Let me know how you're holding up'?"

"Who knows?" Austin held open the door. "He downs a couple of beers, he gets sentimental."

"And when he said it gets easier—"

"You know, my dad. He was talking about my dad, Summer. Now can we go already?" Austin snapped.

"Sorry."

"No, I'm sorry." Austin rubbed his eyes. "It's just

birthdays. They give me the creeps. I always feel like I have to live up to the high standards of happiness set by society."

"A walk on the beach followed by lasagna," Summer said, heading out into the soft night air. "That's not so bad for your nineteenth birthday, is it?"

Austin closed the door behind him and gazed up at the sky. "Platonic lasagna," he corrected. "Technically, it could be better."

Marquez grabbed the last two cardboard boxes and carried them into Diana's bedroom. The slob. It was a good thing Marquez had energy to burn. It was her day off, and she'd spent it in high gear, scrubbing and dusting and rearranging. The amazing thing was, she still had energy left. Maybe it was the pills. Or maybe it was because she'd eaten virtually nothing all day. No fat calories or carbohydrates to drag her down. She was practically floating around the apartment. If it weren't for her megabutt, she'd quite possibly be flying.

Near Diana's bed, she felt a little dizzy. The ceiling swirled and the floor buckled. She let the boxes tumble to the floor and dropped onto the edge of the bed.

Letters and papers covered the floor like snow. Damn. Now she'd have to clean up even more of Diana's mess.

She put her head in her hands and waited for the

dizziness to pass. It wasn't the first time. It had been happening more and more. At first it had scared her. But soon Marquez had realized it was a sign she was being good. It meant she was really accomplishing her goal. She could *feel* herself getting lighter. If her head felt light, could her body be far behind? She almost liked the dizzy feeling, the way it passed through her like a shimmering white wave of pure energy.

Out in the backyard, she could hear people splashing in the pool. Blythe and some friends. They'd asked Marquez to join them, but she'd lied and claimed Diver was coming over. The truth was, he was working late that night, but Marquez was okay with that. Lately she didn't much care about being around other people. They just got in the way, asked questions, gave her disapproving looks.

Marquez paused for a minute to count up her calories for the last twenty-four hours. She'd never been good at math, but somehow she'd developed the ability to compute calories down to the last piece of gum or carrot stick. It was a weird skill. It was a shame there weren't more career opportunities in calorie counting.

She tallied up the day and considered. Not bad, not great. If she didn't eat anything that night, she'd be doing okay.

Slowly Marquez got on her knees to scoop up the letters and papers she'd dropped. What a pack rat Diana was! Like anyone cared about her junior-year essay on *Silas Marner*. There were endless postcards as well, all from Diana's mother on her book tours, scribbled illegibly in red pen, not that Marquez cared what they said.

Marquez's mother had written her just once since moving. It had been on a piece of plain white paper in pencil, a busy note full of anecdotes about the family. At the bottom she'd written,

*Are you eating enough and taking your vitamins? Remember how much your mama loves you, Maria.* Marquez had tucked the letter inside her pillowcase. When she tossed and turned at night, she liked knowing it was there.

As she piled the last of the letters into their cardboard container, an odd return address on an envelope caught Marquez's eye. Why would Diana have kept a letter she'd written to somebody else?

Then Marquez saw the intended recipient: Seth Warner.

Marquez withdrew the letter from its envelope, feeling a weird mix of curiosity, indifference, and guilt. Her hands were trembling, the way they always seemed to lately. It was really annoying when she was trying to pour coffee. She'd come close to scalding several customers at Jitters.

The date at the top of the letter made her blink.

January fourteenth of that year. Just a few days after
Marquez and Diana had visited Summer and Diver and
Seth over winter vacation.

She started to read. The handwriting was precise
and feminine, but the letters kept blurring together,
and Marquez had to stop and close her eyes several
times.

> 1/14
> Seth:
> *This is my fifth letter to you. You haven't
> received any of them because I haven't sent any of
> them, and I probably won't send this one either.
> I'm not used to embarrassing myself, and I'm
> not used to being the one doing the chasing. Face
> it, I'm used to guys coming after me. This is a
> new experience. I'm sure you're smiling to your-
> self right now in that smug way you sometimes
> have.*
>
> *But anyway, here goes. I know you think
> what happened between us New Year's Eve was
> a terrible mistake. I did too, at first, because like
> you, I care about Summer. But now that I'm
> back in Florida and my head has cleared, I've
> started to realize something. It wasn't a mistake,
> Seth. Those feelings have been there between us
> for a long time, just waiting in the shadows. And*

*if it took breaking down on some icy highway in*
*Minnesota for us to figure that out, then maybe it*
*was fate.*

*The point is, I've always been in love with you,*
*Seth, and I just never had the nerve*


The letter ended there, abruptly. Marquez stared at
the words pitching and rolling on the page and tried to
make sense of them. Diana and Seth? New Year's?

Diana, in *love* with Seth?

Diana, who was in California with Seth at that very
moment.

She'd betrayed Summer during the winter. And she
was about to betray her again.

Marquez rubbed her eyes. She threw the letter into
the box with a groan. It was too much information.
She couldn't cope. She didn't like other people's problems, and these were other people's problems with a
vengeance.

What was the etiquette when Friend A stole Friend
B's boyfriend and you knew about it? Would it be better to tell Friend B and hurt her? Or to keep your
mouth shut, like a sensible human being?

She remembered how grateful Summer had been
over spring break when Seth had forgiven her for her
indiscretions with Austin. No wonder Seth had been
such a saint! And Diana . . . Diana had actually tried

to get Seth and Summer back together. What had that been about? Guilt? No, Diana wasn't the type to feel guilty. She wasn't even really the type to feel, but maybe there was another side to her that Marquez didn't see. After all, Diana had been feeling *something* when she'd written that love letter to Seth.

Marquez clenched her fists. She felt angry for Summer, who'd been lied to and betrayed by Seth and Diana. It wasn't fair. Whatever her faults, at least Summer had tried to make things right with Seth and to keep Austin at bay. Meanwhile, Diana was busy doing her very best to seduce Seth away.

Marquez stood slowly. The world spun for a moment. She needed to clear her head before she decided what to do about this.

Exercise. She would exercise for a while. That was easy, this wasn't. She would ride her bike. She would not go anywhere near the fridge. She would ride longer and faster than she had the day before.

Later she would decide what to do about Diana and Seth and their betrayal. But first things first.

If she rode long enough, she might even burn off the apple she'd had for breakfast.

# 20

# A Picture's Worth a Thousand Lies.

"You're not eating anything." Seth pointed to Diana's untouched plate.

"Oh, I'm just not very hungry," Diana said quickly. "Jet lag, I guess."

Seth consulted his watch. "It's dinnertime in Florida." He cocked his head to one side, eyeing her up and down. "I guess this is kind of slumming for you, huh? The guys and I have lunch here every day. The fish is fresh, but I know the place isn't much to look at."

Diana took in the little restaurant, with its tacky marine decor. She hadn't really noticed it until that moment. She'd been too busy looking at Seth. He was even more attractive than she'd remembered, which was saying something. His deep brown eyes always hinted at a smile, and his smile always hinted at some tantalizing and very sexy possibilities.

Or maybe she was just imagining things. Was Seth bored? Uncomfortable? Did he even remember the night that was burned into her own memory?

She stretched out casually, letting her foot just graze his leg under the table. He didn't move. Good. That was a good sign. He would have pulled away if he'd felt really uncomfortable.

Or maybe he just hadn't noticed her foot. Or her.

"You probably would have eaten better if you'd stuck with your mom in Laguna Beach," Seth said.

"But I prefer the company here," Diana replied, sounding more seductive than she'd intended.

Seth took a swig of his Coke. "It would have been cool if Summer could have come along, too."

Oh, yeah. Way cool.

"She was pretty busy," Diana said, "what with job hunting and getting settled in. Seeing old friends, that sort of thing." She ticked off the seconds as she waited for Seth to ask which old friends, but he wasn't biting.

Instead she shifted position a little, her right foot still making contact with Seth's shin. "You know, when I was leaving this morning, Summer and I were talking," Diana said casually. She toyed with a french fry. "And she said you hadn't mentioned that I'd called you to tell you I was coming." She dipped the fry in ketchup, taking her time, then popped it into her mouth delicately, the picture of innocence. "And I was wondering how come."

"How come?" Seth echoed. It was his turn to shift in his seat. "Uh, no reason. You know. I guess it just didn't come up."

"I was starting to worry," Diana said, playing with another french fry, trailing it across her plate, "that you'd told her about what happened between us."

Seth's eyes went wide. "Wh—Why would I do that?" he sputtered. "That was ages ago. It was just a fluke, just a—" He ran out of steam. "No, of course I never told her."

"A fluke." Diana considered the word. "A fun fluke, though, wasn't it?"

A new thought seemed to occur to Seth. "Diana, you didn't *tell* her, did you?"

"Of course not."

"Or tell Marquez, because Marquez would keep her mouth shut for about three seconds flat—"

"No, Seth." Diana reached across the table and took his hand. The feel of his rough fingers made her shiver. "I care about Summer, even if she doesn't . . ."

"Doesn't what?"

Diana pulled her hand away. She had him. Now to

reel him in, nice and slow. "Nothing. I was just babbling. Hey, I almost forgot. I brought some pictures of
our new apartment. Want to see?"

Seth pursed his lips, still mulling over her words.
"Sure."

Diana opened her purse. "Now, keep in mind this
is a new camera I was experimenting with, so don't
expect miracles. But it'll give you the idea." She withdrew the packet of photos, which she'd carefully organized on the plane trip for maximum impact.

She handed him the first photo. "That's our place
from the outside. There's a café and bookstore on the
bottom floor and apartments on the upper levels. Cute,
huh?"

Seth nodded. "Not bad. Although it's kind of a
comedown from your mom's house, isn't it?"

"Well, it doesn't have a Jacuzzi, no. But then,
it doesn't have Mallory either." She passed him the
next photo. "That's the inside, the day we moved in.
I believe I captured Summer and Marquez in all their
sweaty glory. Sorry you missed out. Two flights of
stairs, no elevator, ninety-six degrees."

Seth gazed fondly at the picture. "Is that Diver in
the corner?"

"Yeah. He helped out."

"How's Summer doing with him?"

Diana shrugged. "They're tolerating each other,

at least." She handed him another photo. "That's the backyard view. The pool's a little scuzzy, but you get the idea."

"Who's that? It sort of looks like Summer, but it's hard to tell with all the palms."

Diana checked the photo. "Yeah, that's Summer."

"Who's with her?"

Not too fast. Nice and easy. "I can't tell," Diana said. "Some guy, it looks like."

Seth set the picture aside, unperturbed.

Diana passed him the next picture with calculated nonchalance. "And that's the inside of Jitters, the coffee place downstairs." She added a careful pause. "You know, where Marquez and Austin work."

She waited, flipping through the photos, counting the seconds until Seth absorbed it all.

One one thousand, two one thousand—

"Austin," he repeated. It was barely a whisper.

She had to be careful not to overplay her hand. Diana looked at him, eyes wide, making certain she was conveying her horror. She dropped the photos onto the table with a little gasp—a nice touch, she thought.

"Oh, Seth. Oh, God, I just assumed you knew. . . ."

"He's there, on Coconut Key?"

Diana nodded. She reached out for his hand, but he yanked it away.

"Is that all?" He was seething. She could see the anger in the tight muscles of his jaw. His words came out like the urgent release of air from a pierced tire. "I mean, he's just there, is that all? Are they . . . is she, you know . . . spending time with him? Being with him?"

Diana didn't answer. She closed her eyes and sighed to make it clear she was far too decent to tell him what he didn't want to hear.

Seth pounded the table. "Tell me, Diana,"

Diana rifled through her pictures, as if she didn't know quite what she was looking for. It was right where she'd placed it, at the bottom of the pile.

"Here," she said, pleased and a little shocked when actual tears sprouted in her eyes. She almost hated to hurt Seth this way, but it was, after all, for a greater good.

For a long time he stared at the picture without moving. She was surprised when he suddenly leapt up.

"I have to use the phone," he said, tossing the photo down. Before she could say anything, he was rushing off.

She picked up the picture. The composition was a little off, the focus a little hazy, the palm leaves distracting. Still, she'd managed to nicely capture Summer's rapturous smile as Austin massaged her by the pool.

When the phone rang, Marquez decided to ignore it. Diana's cell phone was on the couch, miles away, and

Marquez was on the exercise bike with miles to go. She wasn't sure how long she'd been riding. She knew her legs weren't going very fast, but it didn't seem to matter. She couldn't really feel them anymore. She couldn't feel her body much at all. She was weightless, floating, unattached.

The ringing continued. "Go away," Marquez muttered, but the damn phone kept chirping away incessantly.

At last she climbed slowly off the bike. Her legs nearly gave way, but then she righted herself. Sucking in air, she dragged herself over to the couch and picked up the phone.

"What?" she demanded.

"Marquez? Is that you?"

The voice was fuzzy and faraway, the way Marquez felt inside her head. "Who is this?" she asked, panting.

"It's Seth. Seth Warner. Are you okay? You weren't—I mean, I didn't catch you and Diver in the middle of something—"

"Seth. Imagine that. Is Diana there, too?"

"Um, yeah. We're at a restaurant. Listen, is Summer there? I really need to talk to her."

Fragments of Diana's letter came back to Marquez. She should say something, shouldn't she? Defend Summer? Yell at Seth?

Marquez opened her mouth to speak, but the words

had evaporated. Her stomach twisted and lurched. She wondered vaguely if she was going to be sick.

"Marquez?"

Marquez closed her eyes and willed the queasiness away. It had happened before. It was nothing to worry about.

"Marquez, are you there?"

"Seth, Summer isn't here right now. And I have to go."

"But I really need to talk to her."

"Bye, Seth—"

"Just tell me this, Marquez." The edge in Seth's voice finally caught her attention. Was he crying? Or angry? Or both? "Just tell me this. Is she with Austin?"

The dizziness came again, grabbing her hard, shaking the breath from her. The room was dancing past, and she could not keep up.

"Yeah, Seth," Marquez said. She had to lie down, hang up the phone, make Seth go away, make the awful ache in her gut go away. "She's with Austin."

She hung up on him, tossed the phone aside, and tried to stand. Water. A glass of water would be good. No calories.

She was halfway to the sink when her legs gave way and she fell to the floor. Her eyes closed and then, finally, the world stopped its wild dance and stood perfectly still.

# 21

# Decisions, Decisions . . .

Summer dug her toes into the cool, wet sand and sighed. The waves surged and receded in a soothing rhythm, but she didn't feel soothed at all.

Austin sat beside her, close enough for their shoulders to touch.

"Look, I know the lasagna was bad, but was it bad enough to send you into a coma?" he chided.

"Sorry. I guess I haven't been very talkative."

"I know rocks that are more expressive." Austin laced his fingers through hers. "Especially given that this is our second walk of the evening. During the first one you sounded like you had something to say."

"I did. Do."

"But you didn't seem to get around to saying it."

"I'm just . . . trying to sort everything out, Austin." Summer closed her eyes to the silver blanket of stars. "It was hard enough coming to a decision about Carlson today. I came here tonight sure I was going to tell you I never wanted to see you again, but somehow it hasn't been as easy as I'd thought it would be."

"You do know what's standing in your way, don't you?"

"My incredible indecisiveness?"

"No. Our incredible kiss." Austin leaned close. His eyes were bright with moonlight. "Here's the deal, Summer. Seth is the University of Wisconsin. Safe, logical, a good, all-around choice, if a little dull. I, on the other hand, am Carlson. Demanding, difficult, challenging, and a really great kisser."

"I think you may be stretching the analogy."

"You've made one good decision today. Why not go for two?"

Austin cupped her chin in his hands. She felt the same exquisite, tantalizing free fall she always felt when she was close to him. She felt the same irresistible draw, the pull like gravity claiming her.

She stared up at the sky and tried to think of Seth, but her thoughts got lost in the crush of stars. How did he make sense of them, finding pictures in the glittering maze? Why did some people always seem to know just where to look and just what they wanted, when it was so hard for her?

"Where's Venus?" Summer asked.

Austin blinked. "Could we stay on the subject here? Let's stargaze later."

Summer lay back on the sand, one arm under her head. How had she known that it was a good idea to try for Carlson? It wasn't as though there'd been beacons and marching bands and red flags guiding her to the answer. It had been more like a soft glow, a delicate bubble of feeling that said, "This will feel more right than any other choice you can make." And it wasn't as though she still didn't have doubts. Carlson might not take her. Her mom might be furious. Seth most definitely would be furious.

But the little bubble of feeling was still there. Somehow she knew that doing the thing that scared her, the hard thing, was the right thing.

She looked at Austin. He was gazing down at her with obvious longing. He was gorgeous and complicated and wonderful, and she was probably in love with him.

The stars overhead were impossible to know. But Seth had taught her that if you started with a guidepost or two—the Big Dipper, for example—you could learn to navigate them.

Love was a guidepost like that. But when you loved

two people, there had to be something more. Summer closed her eyes and searched for a little bubble of feeling, something to hang on to.

Seth had forgiven her once before. Seth had stood by her. Seth had loved her longer. Seth had placed a diamond ring on her finger because he loved her that much.

Loyalty, honor. They were big, important words, but they were there inside her, softly glowing like candles in a far-off window.

She wanted Austin. She loved Austin.

But she loved Seth, too, and she owed him her loyalty in a way she didn't owe Austin. She'd made a vow to Seth. And if she hadn't honored it as well as she should have so far, well, maybe it wasn't too late to try.

"Summer. God, you're beautiful," Austin whispered, but as he brought his lips to hers she at last knew the right thing to say.

"It's time for me to go home," she said. "I'm going to call Seth." She kissed Austin on the cheek, a kiss filled with regret and longing. "I'm sorry, Austin. But that's my choice."

Diana stared out of Seth's bedroom window, watching the ocean come and go. It would be dark soon. She couldn't see any stars yet, but the sky was turning a bruised purple.

"I'm sorry, Seth," she said for what had to be the hundredth time.

After he'd called Marquez, they'd gone back to Seth's apartment at Diana's suggestion. He'd cried a little, ranted some. Then he'd fallen silent. He'd been lying on his bed staring up at his ceiling, lost in contemplation for way too long. This wasn't working out the way she'd hoped. She hadn't counted on all this messy emotion.

"I don't believe it." Seth sat up, eyes bright, as if he'd come to an obvious conclusion.

"I thought Marquez told you—"

"I don't care." Seth crossed his arms over his chest. "I don't believe it. Summer wouldn't betray me this way. If she's hanging out with Austin, it's because they're friends."

"Maybe," Diana conceded. "But then why didn't she tell you about him?"

"Because . . . because she knew how upset I'd be. She didn't want me worrying when we were so far apart."

His voice had taken on a plaintive, hopeful quality. It made Diana feel pity and frustration. He just wasn't getting it. She was going to have to use her secret weapon, and she didn't want to. Not anymore. It seemed . . . cruel, somehow.

"Summer wouldn't do something like that. She wouldn't," Seth insisted, as much to himself as to Diana.

"Seth," Diana said reasonably, "she already did it once. Have you forgotten spring break?"

"But she told me about that. She's not the kind of person who would keep a secret—"

"Not like you, you mean?"

Seth looked at her like a wounded animal.

"You never exactly mentioned New Year's to Summer, did you?" Diana added.

Seth closed his eyes and sighed deeply. "I know. I know. I'm a hypocrite."

"Well, then, so am I." Diana went over to the bed and sat beside him. Not too close, but close enough. She touched his hand.

"I don't regret what happened between us, Seth. Do you?"

Seth stared through her as if she were a pane of glass. He didn't answer.

"She wouldn't do it," he said at last. "We were engaged, Diana. She was wearing my ring."

Diana took a long, slow breath. "I want you to know something, Seth. I didn't want to do this. I didn't want to come here and tell you these things. But in my heart, I knew you deserved the truth. You deserve a whole lot better than this. A whole lot better."

She reached for her purse. Slowly she unzipped the little pouch.

When she took out the ring and held it in the air,

Seth didn't react. He just stared at it, mesmerized, as if she'd performed a fantastic, impossible magic trick.

"She hasn't worn it for a long time, Seth," Diana whispered.

Slowly he pulled his gaze from the ring to Diana. His eyes were hard and dark.

"You certainly came prepared," he said. "You brought everything but fingerprints, Diana. 'Gee whiz, Seth, didn't Summer mention Austin?' Why'd you even bother with the innocent act? Why not just trot out the evidence like the FBI?"

Diana looked away. "I thought you liked innocent," she said. "It always worked for Summer."

Seth yanked the ring from her grasp and threw it across the room. In one swift move he pulled Diana down on top of him.

She could still hear the ring rolling slowly across the floor as they began to kiss.

july

# 1

# Meanwhile, Back at the Ranch . . .

Summer could still hear the waves crashing slowly onto the sand as Austin bent down to kiss her.

It had been an hour since they'd left the beach and walked back to her front porch. An hour since she'd told him, finally and absolutely, that it was over between them.

His warm lips brushed hers. She backed away a step. "Austin—"

"It's my birthday, you realize," he said, with just the hint of a smile.

"Under the circumstances, I don't think kissing would be a good idea."

"A harmless good-night kiss, nothing more." He

ran a finger down her bare arm. The bright yellow porch light turned his dark eyes amber.

"I really don't think—"

"Okay, then." Austin hooked his thumbs into the pockets of his worn jeans. "I'm going to go for the last-ditch, cross-your-fingers, Hail Mary pass. The mark of a truly desperate man."

In spite of her resolve not to be further charmed by Austin, Summer laughed. "And that would be . . . ?"

"An appeal to your merciful nature—the pity kiss. It's the least you can do, Summer. You've just tried to end our relationship. On my birthday, no less."

"I haven't just *tried* to end it, Austin. I really have."

"I've heard that before, though, haven't I?"

"But I mean it this time." Summer crossed her arms over her chest. "I—" She paused when she heard footsteps approaching from the pool area in the backyard.

It was Blythe, a tall, stunningly pretty black girl who lived on the second floor of the building. Someone was with her, a girl Summer had never seen before. They were both wearing bathing suits, with damp towels wrapped around their waists.

"Hey, guys, how's it going?" Blythe started up the steps, leaving wet footprints in her wake. "Hope we're interrupting something."

"You're not," Austin replied glumly. "Unfortunately for me."

"What a waste," said the second girl, eyeing Austin appreciatively.

"Down, girl, he's taken," Blythe warned. "Caroline Delany, this is Summer Smith and Austin Reed. Caroline's from Virginia. She and I used to be counselors at a summer camp there. I haven't seen her in ages."

"How long are you staying?" Summer asked, grateful for any reprieve from her conversation with Austin.

"Oh, a couple of weeks, a couple of months," Caroline replied. "As long as Blythe can stand me."

She had a sweet smile, Summer thought. With her short blond hair caught back with a little barrette and her slight build, she looked younger than the rest of them, almost vulnerable.

"I told Caroline if she gets on my nerves too totally, I'll force her to pick up my shifts at Jitters. That'll get rid of her," Blythe teased. "Hey, that reminds me. Marquez isn't working tonight, is she?"

"I'm pretty sure she has the night off," Summer said. "Why?"

"We asked her to join us down at the pool, but she said Diver was coming over. She seemed kind of down, so I went back to check on her about an hour ago. But when I knocked on your apartment door, no one answered. Guess she and Diver decided to go out."

"I thought Diver had to work late tonight,"

Summer said, frowning. "I hope Marquez is okay."

"She *has* seemed a little stressed out," Blythe said. "I mean, I hardly know the girl, but at work she's been either totally hyper or totally zoned, you know?"

"I know. I've been worried about her too. She's been on this major exercise binge. I swear I never see her eat anything anymore."

"Wish I had that problem." Caroline patted her rear. "But I never met a fry I didn't like."

The two girls headed inside. "There goes every man's fantasy woman," Austin said with a smirk. "Never met a guy she didn't like."

"*Fry,* you sleazebag. See how easy it will be to get over me? You're already scoping out the possibilities."

Austin's grin vanished. "Not likely, Summer. You're irreplaceable." He shook his head sadly. "You're making a terrible mistake, you know. How many guys are you going to find who'll say nauseatingly corny things like that? Out loud? In public? Even without being threatened with bodily injury if they don't?"

Summer took a deep breath. "This is the right thing for me, Austin. I feel good about this decision. I really do."

She wondered if she sounded convincing. She wondered if she herself was convinced.

The truth was, she didn't feel good about this decision at all.

The truth was, she wanted Austin. She loved Austin.

But she loved Seth too, and she owed him her loyalty in a way she didn't owe Austin. She'd made a vow to Seth. And if she hadn't honored it as well as she should have so far, well, maybe it wasn't too late to try.

Seth had loved her enough to place a ring on her finger. And if she'd accidentally lost the ring, well, maybe it wasn't too late to replace it.

With a remarkably similar one, she hoped.

"I'm not going to just walk away," Austin said. "I'm not going gently into that good night . . ." He groaned. "Damn. That's a bad sign. When I'm desperate, I start quoting poetry."

"At least it wasn't a dirty limerick."

Silence fell. Suddenly the air seemed suffocating, with its thick, sweet scent of jasmine and heavy wetness. Night noises filled the emptiness—crickets and frogs thrumming, the ebb and flow of the nearby surf, the rustle of palm trees catching the occasional tendril of breeze.

Austin took her hands in his and held on too tightly. "Summer, look . . . I . . . what if I told you I need you right now?"

The lost, childlike sound of his words made her ache. His eyes shimmered with tears.

"Austin . . . don't."

"What I mean is—" Austin paused. "I can't lose you right now. I already feel like I'm losing everything."

His father. That's what he meant, Summer knew. Austin's dad had a hereditary illness called Huntington's disease. He was confined to a hospital bed, unable to communicate, slowly dying. Austin's brother had inherited the gene that caused the disease. Austin had recently been tested for it too. Fortunately, he'd been luckier than his brother.

"I will always be here for you, Austin," Summer whispered. "Anytime you need to talk—you know, about your dad or anything else—I'm here. It's not like we can't be friends."

"We *are* friends. Friends who happen to be in love with each other." Austin leaned against the porch rail. He stared past her into the velvety darkness.

He was so different from Seth, Summer thought. Intense, surprising, independent. Something about Austin told you he didn't give a damn what the world happened to be thinking about him. His looks just added to that impression: longish brown hair that refused to behave, a perpetual hint of beard, a couple of tiny silver hoops dangling from one earlobe, an ever-present and charming smirk.

And yet there was a wistfulness about Austin as well. Summer always had the feeling he'd lost something and was desperately trying to recapture it. What it was, she didn't know. He was still a mystery to her. An almost irresistible one.

Seth, on the other hand, was pretty much an open book. Steady, protective, reliable, completely faithful. He was the boy next door. She was the girl next door. And it seemed inevitable that someday they'd get married and have little kids next door of their own.

Austin squared his shoulders. He looked calmer, as if he'd come to some conclusion.

"Maybe this is a good thing." He said the words slowly, measuring each one. "I've often wondered if coming here to the Keys to be near you was a good idea. I talked myself into believing that if it was good for me, it would be good for you. . . ."

The cool, distant look in his eyes told Summer that he was already pulling away from her. Good, she told herself. That was what she wanted.

"But you deserve better than I can give you, Summer. I come with a lot of . . . well, limitations. I'm like one of those crappy plane tickets, full of restrictions, where you can only travel to certain places at certain times of the week . . . and for only so long."

"What limitations, Austin? I don't understand. What are you talking about?"

He shrugged. "Limitations. We'll let it go at that, all right?"

"You are not a crappy ticket," Summer said softly. "You are most definitely first-class round-trip to Paris."

"No. I'm more like one-way to Kalamazoo. On Greyhound. Sitting next to a guy who smells like bad cheese while he drools on your shoulder. But let's quit while we're ahead. This analogy is in danger of collapsing under its own weight. The point is, maybe this is all for the best." His tone was resigned and flat. He sounded deeply tired. "Maybe Seth is the guy for you. I doubt it, but then, I'm biased."

For some reason Summer was reminded of the message Austin's brother had left on his machine earlier that evening.

"It gets easier after a while," he'd said, "really it does." He'd had the same resigned, weary sound that Austin had right at that moment.

She touched his arm. He gazed at her fingers on the taut muscle of his forearm and smiled a little. "So. One last pity pucker for the road?"

Summer kissed him softly. She tried not to think about the longing and sadness and regret churning inside her. She tried not to sob when one of Austin's tears dampened her own cheek.

She was being faithful to Seth. She was doing the

right thing. She was being honorable and loyal and steadfast and true.

Sometimes doing the right thing hurt like hell.

"So long," Austin whispered as she pulled away.

She closed the door behind her so he wouldn't hear her cry.

# 2

## Hard Questions, No Answers

Summer slowly climbed the three flights to the apartment she shared with Marquez and Diana.

It was a great place—a charming attic apartment in a Victorian house, complete with two porches, one overlooking the bustling main street, the other directly over a small pool in the backyard with the ocean a little ways beyond. The house was located right in the heart of Coconut Key, which boasted two great colleges and endless miles of pristine white beaches.

It was the perfect tropical paradise, except for one tiny problem: Austin. It was bad enough he'd moved to the Florida Keys to be close to Summer, but he even worked at a café on the bottom floor of her apartment building. How was she ever going to avoid seeing him?

It was way too easy to imagine the awkward encounters, especially when Seth came back from California. But it wasn't as though she could move. They'd just signed a lease for the summer. And Marquez and Diana loved the apartment.

It was impossibly complicated and impossibly sad. Summer sniffled as she fumbled for her key.

"Marquez?" Summer called as she unlocked the door. "It's me, and do I ever need a Chunky Monkey fix."

No answer, but the lights and the stereo were on.

"Diver? Are you guys in the bedroom?"

Summer took another step. The apartment was eerily quiet. "Marquez?" she whispered.

The first thing she saw was the hand.

Marquez's hand, jutting out from behind the couch.

Summer gasped, and her heart shot into her throat. She ran to Marquez's side.

Blood trickled from a cut on Marquez's forehead. Her usually dark complexion was chalky. She was wearing her exercise sweats. A towel lay by her side.

Summer took her friend's hand. It was cool and limp.

Oh, God, please don't let her be . . .

Summer felt for a pulse.

Nothing.

She tried again, watching to see if Marquez was breathing.

Finally Summer found a pulse, saw a shallow breath.

The phone—where was Diana's cell phone? Their apartment phone hadn't been turned on yet. Frantically Summer dug under the couch cushions.

Damn it, where was the phone?

She sprinted to the hallway. "Blythe!" she screamed down the stairwell. "Call 911! Blythe!"

Blythe's door flew open. "What's wrong?" she demanded. She was still in her bathing suit.

"It's Marquez! She's fainted! I think she was exercising. She must have passed out and hit her head. Call 911 for me, right away!"

"It'll be okay," Blythe said calmly. "Go back to Marquez. I'll be right up as soon as I call."

Summer ran back down the hall to the apartment. She grabbed a blanket off the couch and gently covered her friend.

She looked so small. Tough, unstoppable, crazy Marquez. Summer squeezed her limp hand. Marquez's arm was light, just a slender stick of bone. Summer hadn't realized how thin she'd gotten.

So thin, so quickly. Why hadn't she noticed? They'd all been so busy encouraging Marquez about her weight loss. Maybe they'd been too encouraging.

Blythe and Caroline appeared in the doorway. "They're on their way," Blythe reported. "I'll bet she just got light-headed working out, that's all."

"She'll be okay, Summer," Caroline said.

Summer brushed Marquez's thick hair away from her face. "I hope you're right," she whispered, but she wasn't nearly so certain.

*Marquez? Can you hear me, hon?*

*She's been slipping in and out. Her BP's up. One-ten over sixty. Pulse is still a little thready.*

*Marquez? I'm Dr. Mary Lewis. Almost the same first name as you, although your friend tells me you don't use it. Open your eyes, Marquez. Do you know where you are?*

*Come on, Marquez. Stay with us here.*

*You hit your head, Marquez. You're in Fairview General, the hospital on Coconut Key. Sounds to me like you got a little carried away on the exercise bike and fell off and hit your head. Just took a couple of stitches. You won't even notice them. Marquez?*

*I haven't gotten anywhere with her, either. She hears okay, she just won't . . . Hey, you sure she fell off a bike?*

*That's what her roommate told the admitting nurse. Why do you ask?*

*Just something she said. The only thing, actually. Something about diving.*

*Hmm. I doubt it . . . I mean, her clothes were dry, her hair was dry.*

*Maybe I got it wrong.*

*Marquez? Listen, I need to ask you some questions so we can be sure we give you the right medications, okay? You need to help me out on this, Marquez.*

*Have you been taking anything? Drugs of any kind?*

*It's okay to tell us. We just want to help you, hon. And we can't help you unless you tell us the truth.*

*How about it? Cocaine, crack? Maybe some amphetamines? Speed?*

*Come on, Marquez. Work with us here. We're not the bad guys, okay?*

*We're getting nowhere. Where's that roommate of hers? Maybe I'll try her.*

*Waiting room, I think. Want me to get her?*

*I'll go talk to her. Give me a full blood workup, and let's keep Marquez here overnight for observation.*

*I'll be back later, Marquez. Maybe you'll feel like talking more then.*

*What's that? Did you say something, hon?*

*Something about diving again, I'm pretty sure.*

*Diving! Right. No diving for you anytime soon, kiddo. About the last thing in the world you need right now is more exercise.*

# 3

## Best Friends, Brothers, and Other Troubling Mysteries

"Diver!"

Summer ran to meet her brother as he entered the waiting room. She hugged him, then pulled away, suddenly self-conscious.

"Marquez—"

"She's okay," Summer assured him. "I talked to the nurse a little while ago. They're going to keep her overnight, just to be on the safe side."

"Thank God. I was so scared." Diver sank into a yellow vinyl chair.

"The nurse said Marquez's doctor wants to talk to us, but then we can probably go see her."

Diver combed back his long sun-streaked hair. His

dark blue eyes were clouded with worry. "I wish I could have gotten here sooner. I must have broken twenty traffic laws on the way."

"My neighbor Blythe and a friend of hers drove me over. They're down in the cafeteria."

"Summer—" Diver hesitated. "Why does the doctor want to talk to us? Marquez just fainted, right? You're not keeping something from me, are you?"

"No, of course not. I don't know why she wants to talk to us." Summer sighed. "I've been kind of worried about Marquez lately. She's seemed so stressed out."

"Yeah. I've been worried too."

"But you know Marquez—you say one word to her and she bites your head off."

Diver leapt from his chair and began pacing the small room. "She's been exercising constantly, and she hardly ever eats. She never ate well. Marquez thinks a bag of Doritos and a Diet Pepsi is a well-balanced meal. But lately . . . I never see her eat anything."

He reached the end of the room for the second time and spun around. Summer almost smiled. She'd never actually seen someone pacing before. Her usually mellow brother looked like one of those anxious expectant fathers in a TV sitcom. Only there was nothing funny about this.

Diver took another turn. "Marquez means everything to me. If anything ever happened to her . . ." He glanced at Summer, then looked away.

Summer thought she saw guilt in his eyes. And why not? Why was it so easy for Diver to care about Marquez? Why, when it had been so hard for him to care about his parents—Summer's parents—and Summer herself?

A tall young African-American woman in a white coat, a stethoscope draped around her neck, strode into the waiting room.

"Summer Smith?" she asked.

Summer nodded. "I'm Summer. And this is my brother, Diver."

"Diver? Ah, so that explains it. Marquez was asking for you. I'm Dr. Lewis." She sat on the couch with a sigh. "Take a load off. I need to ask you a couple of questions."

"Marquez will be okay?" Diver asked.

"In the short term, yes." The doctor leaned forward, hands clasped on her knees. "Look, I won't beat around the bush. Does Marquez use anything?"

"Use?" Summer repeated.

"Drugs. Coke, maybe, or amphetamines? We're running her blood work right now, but she came in with the pulse rate of a hummingbird, and drug usage would fit with some of her other symptoms."

"Marquez would never use drugs," Summer said automatically.

Diver looked away.

The doctor pursed her lips. "Has she been exercising excessively lately, losing a lot of weight? Maybe bingeing and purging . . . you know, throwing up after meals?"

"She's been on a real exercise jag, yeah," Summer said. "And she's lost a lot of weight really fast. We've all told her a zillion times how great she looks—"

"I found some pills," Diver interrupted. His face was pale. "She told me they were just over-the-counter stuff, diet pills someone at work gave her. I made her throw them away. I figured . . . I thought she was okay."

"Well, she's not okay," Dr. Lewis said grimly. "Marquez could be on the road to a serious eating disorder. I'm going to give her the name of a support group that meets once a week here at the hospital. Your job is to encourage her to get some help, got it?"

Diver rubbed his eyes. "I told her how beautiful she was. I told her she didn't need to lose any more weight—"

"It's not about losing weight, Diver," the doctor said gently. "For people with eating disorders, it's all about getting control over their lives. This is the only way they know to do it. Has Marquez been under a lot of stress lately?"

"Her family lost their house and business and moved

to Texas. They were really close," Summer said. "And
she didn't get into the college she wanted, and she
caught her boyfriend in bed with another girl—"

The doctor cast a dark glance at Diver.

"No, not Diver," Summer added quickly. "Her *former* boyfriend. And she's been having money problems
and working what seems like quadruple shifts."

"So the answer is a definite yes," the doctor said as
she stood. "Look, it's important for her friends to be
supportive, but in the end what Marquez really needs is
professional help. Do what you can, okay?"

"We will," Summer promised.

"Can we see her?" Diver asked.

"Of course. Maybe she'll be a little more talkative
with you than she was with us. They're taking her up
to the third floor, east wing."

Diver and Summer headed to the elevator. "I
should have done something," Diver said. "I should
have known."

"I was thinking the same thing."

"I can't let anything happen to her, Summer."

"I was thinking that too."

Marquez's room was lit only by a small light over
her bed. Beneath the peach blanket, she looked impossibly frail. Her hair fanned over the crisp pillow in dark
ribbons.

When they stepped through the door, she closed

her eyes. Her lower lip trembled. "I'm sorry," she whispered, and then Diver and Summer ran over and hugged her and yelled at her and cried with her, and then they did it all over again.

"You don't have to walk me down," Summer told Diver as they waited at the elevator half an hour later. "I'm sure I can find the cafeteria. I'll just follow the smell of overcooked cabbage."

"I don't mind. I wanted to talk to you alone. We need to really keep an eye on Marquez, okay? You and me together, I think we can pretty much cover her all the time."

The doors slid open. Diver stepped into the empty elevator, but Summer just stood there, contemplating him.

"What?" Diver demanded, hands upraised.

"Nothing." Summer entered the elevator and jabbed the button for the first floor.

"No, what?"

"It's just . . . I look at you here with Marquez. You practically arm wrestle the night nurse into submission till she agrees you can sleep in Marquez's room. You're ready to turn into the Pill Police to help her. And the way you were just so . . . so *there* for her tonight."

"Is there a problem with that?"

"No. I'm really glad for Marquez. I love her too.

She's my best friend, don't forget. It's just that—" She shrugged. She was tired. She shouldn't have started this. She was upset about Marquez and upset about Austin. She most definitely shouldn't have started this. She and Diver had already had this discussion.

The doors opened. Diver stepped into the empty corridor. "It's just that I couldn't be there for Jack and Kim and you back in Minnesota, right?"

Jack and Kim. He could never, ever bring himself to call them Mom and Dad.

"I'm sorry I brought it up. I'm tired, is all. We've done this, Diver. Let's not go through it again."

Summer followed a sign that pointed toward the cafeteria. But Diver persisted, trailing her down the hallway. Other than the occasional nurse or orderly, the hospital seemed deserted. Summer checked her watch. It was so late. She wondered if she should call Seth in California when she got home. It was three hours earlier, but he'd probably be in bed already. Still, it would be nice to hear his voice after this awful night.

"Summer." Diver grabbed her arm, forcing her to a halt. "Jack and Kim are my biological parents. But they were my parents for only two years. I had other parents—" His voice caught. "Bad parents, but still, parents."

"They kidnapped you, Diver. I'd say that rates right up there on the bad-parent scale."

Diver grimaced. "When you found me last summer, it was too much too fast. You pushed so hard. You wanted me to be the brother you'd lost, Jack and Kim wanted me to be the son they'd lost . . . I don't know. I couldn't live up to your expectations." He paused, searching for words. "With Marquez there aren't any expectations. That's why I can be there for her. It's easier."

"That's always the deal with you, Diver. You always do what's easy. You walked out on Mom and Dad without even giving them a chance because it was easy, and now they're divorcing. I'm glad it was easy for you." She choked back tears. "It wasn't so easy for them."

"Please, Summer, whatever there is between us," Diver said, "whatever bad blood, we need to work together to help Marquez."

"Marquez is my best friend. I'm not the one who needs lessons in loyalty—" She stopped when she saw Blythe and Caroline come through the doors of the cafeteria.

Blythe waved when she saw them. "So? How's she doing?" she asked, walking over.

"She'll be fine," Summer said, trying to collect herself. "She just, uh, overdid it."

"Thank God. Someone needs to slow that girl down a little. Oh, Diver, this is Caroline—"

Caroline gasped. "Oh, my Lord!" she shrieked. "I swear, it really *is* you, isn't it?" She grabbed Diver by the shoulders. "Paul? Paul Lamont? Don't you recognize me?"

Diver shook off her grip and took a step backward. "You've got the wrong guy—"

"Car, this is Diver Smith, Summer's brother," Blythe interjected.

Caroline frowned. "Wow, this is really eerie. I mean, you look *exactly* like this next-door neighbor of mine who—well, never mind, it's a very long story. Are you *sure* you never lived in Virginia? Positively sure?"

Diver offered up one of his patented charming smiles. "I'm sure I'd remember if you'd been my neighbor," he said. "Sorry to disappoint you."

Caroline frowned. "But I—"

"Gotta go," Diver interrupted. With a quick glance at Summer, he headed off down the corridor, practically jogging.

"Boy, I could have sworn that was him," Caroline said. She nudged Summer. "You're absolutely sure he's your brother?"

Summer sighed. "You know, Caroline, sometimes I really wonder."

# 4

## What Diana Wants, Diana Gets.

The apartment seemed terribly lonely when Summer got home. The truth was, it wasn't really even "home" yet—she and Diana and Marquez had just moved in a couple of days earlier. And now, with Marquez in the hospital and Diana in California, it felt alien, as if Summer were staying in an empty hotel. A hotel with a really cheesy interior decorator.

After a long search, Summer located Diana's cell phone and dialed Seth. By now she knew the number by heart.

Seth was doing an internship for a company in California that built racing sailboats. He shared an apartment in Newport Beach with some guys from the sailboat company.

Summer wondered if he and Diana had managed to get together that weekend. Diana was in California with her mom, a romance author who was on a book-signing tour. Summer had encouraged Diana to stop in and say hi to Seth if she could find the time. It wasn't nearly as good as visiting Seth herself, of course. But at least she could get the lowdown on Seth's apartment, his roommates, that sort of thing. And more important, she could get a feel for how he was faring without her. It was so hard to read people over the telephone.

The phone rang three times before someone finally picked it up.

"Hello?" The voice was low, throaty, a little annoyed. A girl's voice.

Summer winced. Seth had two guy roommates. This was probably someone's girlfriend. She hoped she wasn't interrupting anything.

"Um, I'm sorry to call so late. Is Seth Warner there?"

A long pause. "Summer?"

"Yes?"

"It's me, Diana."

"Oh, I . . . I didn't recognize your voice. You sounded sleepy."

"Well, it *is* late."

"So you caught up with Seth okay, huh?"

Another pause. "Oh, yes. We had a very interesting evening, actually."

"You want interesting? We've just had the evening from hell here. I came home tonight to find Marquez passed out on the floor—"

"Oh, my God! What happened?"

"She's okay. Just a cut on her head. She's staying overnight at the hospital for observation. But the doctor says she needs some counseling."

"The dieting, right?" Diana sighed. "I already tried to get her to see someone."

"You did?"

"Right before I left for California. She wasn't interested. Damn. I knew she was in trouble."

"Diver thinks we're going to have to keep an eye on her, all of us."

"Yeah." Diana sighed. "Assuming she'll let us." She fell silent.

"Well, um, I guess if you could pass me on to Seth—"

"Seth?" Suddenly Diana's voice was animated. "Yeah, hold on a minute. He's right here."

Summer heard whispered voices, some shuffling, then the sound of someone grabbing the receiver.

"Seth?"

"Yeah, I'm here." The edge in his voice startled Summer. "Where were you tonight, anyway? I called before."

"I—at the hospital. Marquez—"

"Diana just told me. I'm glad Marquez is okay. I meant before that. Where were you before?"

With Austin, Summer answered silently. With Austin, saying good-bye.

Suddenly a terrible thought came to her. What if Diana had told Seth that Austin was living on Coconut Key? Summer had asked her not to mention it. But if it had slipped out accidentally, Seth, being Seth, would no doubt be assuming the worst. . . .

"Seth, what's wrong? You sound kind of weird. Are you upset about something? Is everything okay?"

A short exhalation of breath, then silence.

"Seth?"

"Look, Summer, I'm flying back to Florida with Diana. I've got a little cash saved, and Diana's going to front me the rest till I can pay her back. I've got to see you."

"Oh, Seth, that's so fantastic! I need to see you, too, so badly."

"I'm flying back with Diana day after tomorrow, if I can get a flight."

"How long can you stay?"

"I don't know. As long as it takes."

Summer frowned. "What do you mean? Are they giving you time off work this soon? What about the internship?"

"Screw the internship. I just have to see you, okay?"

"Me too. It's like you read my mind. I hate being separated this way. It's so hard."

He didn't answer.

"Seth?"

"Yeah?"

"I love you, Seth."

"Do you?" Seth whispered. "Do you really, Summer?"

"Of course I do," she said. The line hissed with static. "Seth? This is the part where you say 'I love you' back."

"You already know that," Seth said softly, and then the line went dead.

Diana watched Seth as he hung up the phone. His smooth bare chest glistened in the moonlight. He was so beautiful. And so close to being hers completely.

"Are you sure about flying back?" she asked softly. "Maybe you should wait, let things sink in. You're awfully upset right now."

"I'm not ending this over the phone. I want to see her. I want to hear her tell me to my face that it's over."

Diana began kneading his tight shoulders. "I don't know . . . maybe you're right. Maybe it's better to get this over with quickly. Better for you and for Summer."

"And for you?" he asked caustically.

She let it go. He was angry at her for telling him the truth. It would pass. She could wait. All that mattered was that she was the one in his room at that moment, touching him in the darkness. Not Summer.

"She said she loved me." He said it pleadingly, a question that needed answering.

Diana brushed the nape of his neck with her fingertips. She had to choose her words with care. If she handled this right, Seth would turn to her when he realized it was really over with Summer. But if she pushed too hard, he'd come to see Diana as part of the messy breakup and leave her behind when he left Summer.

"I think Summer probably does love you, Seth, in her way," Diana said carefully.

Seth turned to her. "I have to be sure," he said. "I've got to see her one more time before I . . . you know. Before I end it."

"I know," Diana said. "I understand."

That wasn't what she'd had in mind. She'd pictured a long-distance breakup, courtesy of AT&T. The usual, with lots of accusations and sobbing and Kleenex. Then Summer would fall into Austin's arms—where she'd spent plenty of time already—and Diana would stick around a while longer to provide Seth with the necessary aid and comfort. By the time his internship was over and he returned to Coconut Key to finish out the summer, they'd all be the best of friends.

Or at least on speaking terms.

Or at least no one would be facing homicide charges.

But if Seth went back to Florida right away, there could be problems. Summer could string him along the way she had the last time, when he'd caught her with Austin. Seth was vulnerable that way. He'd fallen for Summer's promises before.

And then there was the little matter of the engagement ring. That had been a gamble, sure. Diana knew it was only a matter of time before Summer heard about Diana's little ruse.

She'd be furious, of course. First, that Diana had found the missing ring and held on to it. And second, that she'd used it as evidence of Summer's infidelity.

Diana knew what would happen. Summer would explain to Seth how she'd really lost the ring accidentally, and Marquez would back her up. She'd beg Seth to reconsider and give her another chance.

No, the ring maneuver had probably not been one of Diana's smarter moves.

On the other hand, it had gotten her this far. Into Seth's arms.

"Lie down," she whispered. "I'll give you a massage. You're so tense, Seth. You need to relax."

She straddled his waist and ran her hands over his back in slow, deliberate strokes. Her own muscles were as tight as his. She felt anxious and a little guilty.

She could have any guy she wanted. She didn't need these underhanded tricks, this seduction routine. She could look at a guy, crook her finger, and have him running to do her bidding.

Any guy, that is, except Seth.

"Feel better?" she murmured.

"You don't have to do this, Diana."

"I want to."

Maybe it would work out okay after all. They'd fly back, and Seth would see Summer and Austin together, the way Diana had seen them so many times. After all, Austin worked in their building. He would be impossible to avoid. Even if Summer tried to cover up her relationship with him, it would just be a matter of time before Seth caught a shared glimpse, a subtle touch . . . something that would give Summer's true feelings away.

It would be the final nail in the coffin. The end of Summer and Seth.

The beginning of Seth and Diana.

Diana trailed her long nails down Seth's spine.

"Seth, I don't think it would be a good idea for you to tell Summer I was the one who told you about Austin."

"Don't you think she'll figure that out on her own, Diana?" Seth said sarcastically.

"All Summer knows right now is that you have a sudden desire to fly home and see her. You'll see for yourself what's going on with her and Austin when you get there. You'll see your ring is no longer on her finger, and that's all you'll need. She doesn't have to know I was the one who started it all."

"What do you care what Summer thinks? I mean, after what we just did . . ."

"You're not sorry, are you?"

"At the moment I don't feel anything, Diana. Except maybe like shoving my fist through the wall."

"She's not worth that kind of anger, Seth. And as for my caring what Summer thinks . . . look, I don't approve of the way she's treated you or I wouldn't have come to you this way, but I've got to keep living with the girl. I just signed a lease for the summer. Besides, she's my cousin."

Seth rolled over so that she was sitting on his chest. He looked up at her with a smile that threatened to turn into a sneer. "So then you get it all, huh, Diana? No blame, plus me. What a deal."

"I don't get you, Seth, not the way I want. I know

you're still in love with Summer. You'll probably always be in love with her."

"Not after this," he said bitterly.

"I know it hurts." Diana combed her fingers through his hair. "I'm so sorry."

Seth stared at her, shaking his head. "I have to tell you, Diana, I just don't see what you get out of this arrangement."

She bent down, brushing her lips against his. "I'm so glad you asked. Allow me to explain."

# 5

# To Sleep, Perchance Not to Dream

Diver shifted in the uncomfortable chair beside Marquez's bed. She was sleeping soundly, her mouth open slightly, exhaling in long, slow breaths.

He wished he could be so lucky. All night long he'd been slipping in and out of the same awful dream. Each time he awoke he was bathed in sweat, his heart hammering wildly, his teeth clenched.

He'd had the dream a million times. He knew it by heart, every plot twist, every bizarre turn. Sometimes he even knew it was a dream while he was dreaming.

It should have been reassuring. Like an old TV rerun.

But every single time it was utterly, completely terrifying.

He walked softly to the window and peered through the blinds. No hint of dawn. No reprieve.

He wondered what time it was. Sometimes he actually wished he wore a watch, like normal people. But then, nothing about the life of Diver Smith was normal.

Diver. Jonathan. Paul. Sometimes he wondered what his name really was.

He'd picked up the nickname Diver when he was living on the streets, sleeping on the beach at night and diving under piers to hide from the beach patrol. Before that he'd been Paul, the name his parents—or the people who'd kidnapped him and pretended to be his parents—had called him.

And before then, until the age of two, he'd been Jonathan. That was the name he'd been born with. The name on his birth certificate.

By the time Summer had been born, Jonathan was already just a name in the newspaper, a black-and-white photo on the side of a milk carton. It was the name she'd grown up afraid to say out loud for fear of what it might do to her fragile, desperate parents.

Diver went back to his chair. He was tired, so tired, but if he closed his eyes, he'd go back to that place he couldn't bear to see, not even in his dreams.

It always started the same way. The playground. The tiny yellow sneakers on his feet. The red ball.

He let his lids fall. He listened to Marquez's steady breathing. In, out, in, out . . . if he concentrated on that soothing sound, maybe he could sleep peacefully, dreamlessly, for once. . . .

But there it was. Cracked, chewed-up red rubber, as if it had been a dog's ball at some point.

Diver knew he would throw the ball. And the part of him watching the dream knew that by throwing the ball he would change his life forever.

It flew. Pretty far, it seemed. It bounced dully on the faded grass. It rolled over to the fence and lay there against the chain link.

A man was standing by the fence. His face was hidden. A woman was in a car nearby, the door open. She was crying, but her face too was hidden.

He ran to get the red ball. He picked it up.

The man reached over the fence to grab him.

He floated, helpless.

In his chair, Diver moaned softly. This was the part of the dream he dreaded. There would be detours down black highways, lonely houses with echoing corridors, years that blended into years in the space of a dream second.

There would be the funeral, his seven-year-old self in a stiff, too-big suit, the sickly sweet smell of lilies in the air. He would see his mother, his mother who really wasn't his mother, in her peach dress, her face thick with powder. His father would lift him up to the casket, and he would scream.

More detours, more highways, more houses. And then, always and forever, came the fire.

It never hurt in the dream. He walked calmly, feet cool and bare, over sizzling embers. He breathed in the poisonous fumes as though they were crisp mountain air. He could see through the sooty veil of smoke, parting it like a curtain.

And what he saw, every time, was his father, his father who was not his father, lying under a burning support beam. His clothes were ablaze. His hair, even his skin.

He could see his father. He could walk effortlessly through the burning house and touch him. But whenever his father's mouth opened to scream, he could not hear him.

He could not hear him because by that time Diver was always the one who was screaming.

"Diver, hon, wake up! Diver!"

His eyes flew open.

No smoke. No fire. Marquez was sitting up in bed, rubbing her eyes.

"The dream again?"

Diver nodded. His throat burned. His eyes stung.

Sometimes he woke from the dream absolutely certain he was in the middle of a raging inferno.

But of course that fire was over. It had been extinguished long ago.

And so had all record of the boy named Paul.

"Come here," Marquez whispered. She patted the mattress. "Come sleep with me."

Diver stood shakily. He climbed onto the bed and crawled under the sheets. Marquez's body was warm. She felt small against him, breakable.

He should have known she was getting too thin. This was his fault. He didn't know how to take care of people. He couldn't be trusted.

He was crying. He hadn't cried like this in a long time, perhaps years. Maybe not even since the fire.

Marquez took his hand. "It's okay. You're with me now. It was just a dream, Diver. It wasn't real."

But it was real. He couldn't tell Marquez that. He couldn't tell anyone, ever.

Because if they found him, it would be the end.

He ran his fingers over the scar on his hip, the flesh hard and rubbery where the burn had healed badly.

When Marquez had asked about it, he'd told her he'd tipped over a pot of boiling water on the stove as a little kid. She'd laughed and said, "I bet you were a handful. I bet you were a beautiful kid. Don't you have any pictures?"

"No pictures," he'd told her. "My parents weren't exactly the sentimental type."

After a long while he stopped crying. Marquez was asleep again, breathing in, out, in, out, slowly and steadily. He lay beside her and watched her breathe until the first pale hints of dawn appeared.

# 6

# Summer Is Definitely Not a Morning Person.

The midmorning sun poured through Summer's bedroom window, painting the walls a brilliant gold. She squinted, then burrowed beneath her blanket.

She'd had a lousy night's sleep, filled with unsettling dreams. She didn't remember them, not exactly. But she knew Seth and Austin had been featured stars. It was probably just as well that she couldn't recall the details.

Summer forced her eyes open. Even with the flowered sheet over the window, the light was blinding. Maybe she should think about getting real curtains.

Florida light. Nothing like the milky Minnesota sunlight she'd grown up with. This was go-to-the-beach-and-bake sun. It made you want to grab your sexiest bathing suit, your darkest shades, and the trashiest novel you wouldn't mind being seen with in public and head for the ocean. . . .

Reality check.

None of that was on the agenda that day. Her first priority was getting Marquez home from the hospital and giving her a nice lecture on the Five Basic Food Groups and Why We Must Eat Them.

Following that, if there was time, Summer needed to hit the streets and do some more job-hunting. She was getting increasingly desperate. Most of the good waitress jobs were taken, and waiting tables was her only marketable skill—unless you counted the fact that she typed about eleven words per minute, only slightly faster than an untrained chimp.

She climbed out of bed, shielding her eyes from the glare. A glance in her mirror made her shudder. She had major morning hair.

Should she call the hospital, she wondered, or would Marquez call her? The doctor might even have released her already.

Summer turned on the radio. Coldplay. Excellent bed-making music. The least she could do was have the apartment nice and neat for Marquez's return. Marquez had been on a real cleaning jag lately. Very un-Marquez-like, and a little disturbing, actually, since she'd always been so messy that she made Summer feel organized.

Diana's side of the room was already clean. Her bed was crisply made, her side of the closet neat. Her still-unpacked boxes were piled in tall stacks against the wall. One box was out of place—old letters, it looked like. Summer shoved it into the closet. She glanced at a postcard of Paris from Diana's mother. It surprised Summer a little that her cousin saved things like that. On the surface, at least, she wasn't exactly the most sentimental person. But even Diana probably had a softer side.

Diana would return the next day, and with her, Seth. He'd sounded so strange on the phone the night before, so distant. Summer knew she should have been thrilled he was coming back for a visit, even a short one. But she couldn't help feeling uneasy.

One way or another, Seth was going to find out that Austin was living on Coconut Key. With Austin working downstairs at Jitters, it was just a matter of time. That would lead to a lot of pointed questions, along the lines of "Why the hell didn't you tell me this?"

Add to that the fact that she'd reapplied to Carlson College, right there on Coconut Key. If she was accepted again, it would call into question all the plans Seth and she had made: going to the University of Wisconsin together, spending all four years there together, then getting married. . . .

Her hand flew to her mouth. She'd almost forgotten.

She touched the bare spot where her engagement ring should have been. She could *feel* its absence, a phantom sensation, the way they said you could still feel a missing limb long after it was gone.

What would she tell Seth about the ring? "It could have happened to anyone, Seth. I was just painting the apartment, and I took it off and put it on the window-sill so I wouldn't get paint on it, and then it just sort of vanished. . . ."

Seth would never understand. He would never understand because if he'd been wearing the ring, he would never in a million years have taken it off.

Of course, she thought with sudden bitterness, guys didn't even wear engagement rings. Only girls. What was that all about? How come girls were the ones stuck with the awesome responsibility?

It was too much . . . Austin, college, the ring. Seth would never forgive her for her many and assorted sins.

Well, that was one more chore to add to the day's list. By the end of the day, she had to find a perfect replica of her engagement ring. Preferably one under ten bucks.

After a cup of hot tea, Summer called the hospital. Marquez had already been discharged. Summer hoped she was coming straight home to rest up. But knowing Marquez, she would probably head directly to Jitters to work a double shift, then throw in a triathlon for good measure.

Diver had been right about that, at least. They were going to have to keep a close eye on Marquez. Very close.

Someone knocked softly on the door. Summer ran to get it, thinking it was Diver and Marquez. She'd swung the door wide open before she realized it wasn't Marquez at all.

"Austin."

He was carrying a bouquet of yellow daisies. His eyes were bloodshot. His hair was tangled. He needed a shave.

Obviously he hadn't slept well either.

"Thought you were rid of me, I know. May I?" He stepped inside before she could answer.

"They're very pretty," Summer said with a nod at the flowers, "but I can't take them, Austin."

"Good thing. They're not for you." Austin tossed the bouquet on the kitchen counter. "They're for Marquez. Blythe told me what happened when I got in for the morning shift today. I went out and bought them on my break."

"That was very thoughtful. I'll be sure to see she gets them." Summer started to fill a glass of water for the flowers, then rolled her eyes. "God, I just realized I look like crap."

"Day-old crap," Austin amended. "But so do I." He shrugged. "Breaking up is hard to do."

Summer ran to her bedroom to put on a robe. When she returned to the living room, Austin was on the back balcony, gazing down at the sparkling pool. Or at Caroline, who was stretched out on a lounge chair, glistening with suntan oil.

"Heartbroken, you say?" Summer asked wryly.

He turned to her. Gently he combed her tangled hair with his fingers. "Completely," he whispered.

Deep inside her something stirred. She closed her eyes and took a step back.

"Austin, I think you should go. It's too hard . . . I can't keep seeing you this way. We need to make a clean break." She tightened the belt of her robe. "The thing is, Seth is flying back here tomorrow for a visit, and, well . . ."

Instead of getting angry, Austin just shook his head. He almost looked amused. "You'd like me to keep a low profile, is that it? Maybe just disappear from the scene entirely? I hear Canada's nice this time of year."

"I only meant—"

"I know what you meant, Summer. You want me to make it easy on you—"

He was interrupted by a knock at the door. "That's probably Marquez," Summer said, running for the door. "She doesn't have her keys."

Marquez practically flew into the room, followed by Diver. "Home, sweet home!" she cried. "Man, I have *got* to take another shower. I still reek of hospital."

Summer gave her a long hug. "You look good. How do you feel?"

"Scarred for life." Marquez pushed back her hair to reveal a small Band-Aid on her forehead. "My brilliant modeling career is over before it started. Whoa, flowers?" She grabbed the bouquet and inhaled deeply. "You shouldn't have."

"I didn't. I mean, I was going to, but I sort of overslept. They're from Austin. He's out on the porch."

"What a sweetheart."

"Not really." Austin came in and gave Marquez a kiss on the cheek. "I have ulterior motives. I'm hoping to pick up some of your shifts."

"No way." Marquez laughed. "I am back on active duty as of tonight."

"Marquez," Diver said sternly, "the doctor said to take it easy."

She rolled her eyes. "Okay, okay. You can have

my dinner shift tonight, Austin. But that's it. I'm broke. When I get that hospital bill, I will be beyond broke."

Diver wrapped his arm around her protectively. "I told you I'll help with that. I'm a wealthy man now."

"You're a less destitute man," Marquez corrected.

"I got that job at the new wildlife rehab center," Diver explained. "Called them this morning, and they were ready to put me to work yesterday."

Summer frowned. With Diver working close by, she was going to be forced to see even more of him. "Congratulations," she said neutrally.

"I need to find a place in town as soon as I can."

Marquez nudged him. "I told him we wouldn't mind a male roommate for a while, right, Summer?"

Summer shrugged. "Sure. I guess. You should check with Diana first, though. She'll be home tomorrow. With Seth."

"I believe that's my exit cue," Austin said. He winked at Marquez. "Glad you're okay, kid." He opened the door, then hesitated. "Hey, Diver, a brilliant thought just occurred to me. If you're stuck, you could always double up with me at my place. It's the size of a postage stamp, but the roaches are the size of poodles. So it sort of evens out."

"That'd be great, Austin," Diver said. He cast a sidelong glance at Summer. "Easier than staying here."

"Yeah, at my place you can belch to your heart's content and scratch yourself with impunity." Austin grinned. "Chicks don't approve of that kind of thing."

"Chicks don't approve of saying 'chicks,' either," Marquez said, giving him a playful sock in the arm.

"Stop by anytime, Diver," Austin said.

"How about tomorrow afternoon?" Diver asked. "That'll give me time to get my stuff together."

"Great. It's over on Palm Avenue." Austin gave Summer a wistful smile. "Ask Summer. She knows just where it is."

# 7

# Look Who's Not Talking

"I told you we should have come to Woolworth's first!" Marquez held her discovery high. "*Voilà!* I give you the Hope Diamond!"

Summer examined the ring in its little black velvet box. "More like hopeless."

"The price is right. Seven ninety-five."

"This is never going to work, is it?"

"Summer, we have been to every jewelry store and drugstore and antique store on the key. Where else can we go?"

"Crappy Fake Diamonds R Us?" Summer examined the ring carefully. "You know, it *does* look an awful lot like the one Seth gave me."

"You don't suppose . . . ?" Marquez grinned. "He always was kind of cheap with a buck. Buy it, Summer. Seth's coming tomorrow. This is as good as it's gonna get."

"I'm sorry. Am I wearing you out? Diver was right. You should have stayed home and rested this afternoon."

"I am not an invalid, Summer," Marquez nearly shouted. If Summer said one more sweet, solicitous thing to her, she was going to scream. "Although you'll be one soon if you don't shut up."

"The doctor said—"

"I fainted. I overdid it a little. Okay? Since when is it a federal crime to try to lose a little weight?"

Summer snapped her mouth shut, but Marquez could practically see the words fighting to escape from her tightly pressed lips.

"Diver has already given me the lecture, Summer. You're off the hook."

Summer examined another ring, pouting.

"I know the drill, okay? Eat my veggies. Exercise in moderation. Stop counting calories. I'm beautiful, I'm perfect, I'm already too skinny, I'm the Cuban-American Kate Moss."

Summer just looked at her, worry written all over her face. Marquez's own mother had never looked at her with that much concern.

"Oh, all right, go ahead, get it over with," Marquez groaned. "I can see you're going to explode otherwise."

"It's just that you really had us scared, Marquez. I mean, it's easy for *you* to crack jokes." Summer's lower lip trembled. "*I'm* the one who found you lying there. I'm the one who thought you were . . . you know . . ." Summer sniffled. "And all I could think of was that if anything happened to you—"

"You'd get to have my bedroom?"

Summer sniffled louder.

"What, then? My stereo? My car?"

"It's not funny, Marquez."

"You're as bad as Diver. He was all weepy too. Jeez, one little teeny fainting spell. Is your whole family this emotional?"

Summer wasn't smiling. "Okay," Marquez relented, "I promise I'll be good, okay? Really, I promise."

"And you'll go to that counseling group?"

"You are going to make someone a really obnoxious mother someday. You will be the mother of all mothers."

"Marquez."

"I don't see what good it'll do. They'll all be sitting in a circle having . . . you know, *feelings*."

"It won't kill you to try it, Marquez."

"There may be hugging involved."

Summer wasn't budging.

"God, all right. One time. And in return you promise to shut up about this?"

"I promise." Summer was beaming. "One more thing. I told Diver I'd be sure you had lunch."

"Sure, fine. Whatever."

"And one more thing."

"Do you understand the phrase 'pushing your luck'?"

Summer hesitated. "The doctor asked if maybe you'd been taking something."

"Something?" Marquez echoed sarcastically.

"Um, pills. You know." Summer looked embarrassed in that sweet midwestern way she had.

"Diver already asked me that, Summer. The answer's no. I mean, please."

"Okay." Summer didn't look entirely convinced.

Marquez took a deep breath. She couldn't take all this nosing into her life. She felt as though she were suffocating. They didn't understand that she had it under control. But the more they poked at her, the less control she'd have.

Still, if she fought too hard, they'd be all over her even worse than they were already. Between Diver and Summer, she'd feel as though she had a twenty-four-hour guard.

Better to humor them. Get them off her case.

"Buy the ring, then we'll eat something," she said wearily. "I'll be outside. I need some air."

"You're okay?" Summer's hand was on her shoulder.

Marquez shook it off. "I just need some air. That's all. Just some air."

"This isn't exactly what I had in mind when I said lunch," Summer said half an hour later as they sat down on the beach.

"Chili dogs?" Marquez plucked off a piece of bun. "It's classic beach food. Besides, I had a craving."

"Well, that's a good sign, I guess."

They stretched out on the fine white sand, letting the waves tease their bare feet. It was late afternoon, and the crowds had thinned to a few die-hard sun-bathers and some surfers trying to ride the halfhearted waves. The air still shimmered with heat. The sky was a pale, washed-out blue.

"I wish we had our suits on," Summer said.

"Speak for yourself," Marquez replied. She was wearing a pair of long, baggy shorts and one of Diver's big T-shirts, but even in her camouflage clothes she knew she looked like a beached whale. She cast a glance at Summer, who had on a crop top and khaki shorts. She was one of those naturally, unfairly thin girls who could eat anything without gaining an ounce. Summer was irrefutable evidence that life was not fair.

"So," Summer said, changing the subject, "you think Seth will believe the ring?" She held out her hand, displaying the little pretend diamond. "I wish it fit better. It's kind of big."

"Tell Seth you lost weight." Marquez shook her head. "I don't get why you don't just admit to him that you lost it."

"I will. If I don't find it, I will. But it's only been a few days, and it could still turn up in the apartment somewhere." Summer took a bite of her chili dog, then wiped her mouth with the back of her hand. "And you know Seth. He's so sensitive. He'll think it means something, my losing the ring. Besides, he and I will have enough to discuss."

"Austin, you mean."

Summer lay back on the sand with a sigh. "Austin."

Marquez watched a seagull bobbing on the waves. Once again she tried to remember the phone call the previous night. Seth had called, she was pretty sure of that. She'd been exercising. She'd been a little out of it, winded, fuzzy. He'd asked her . . . at least she *thought* he'd asked her . . . if Summer was with Austin.

What had she told him? Had she told him the truth?

Why couldn't she remember? Was it the pills? Maybe it was because she'd hit her head so hard.

Why would she have told him the truth? It wasn't Marquez's style to butt in where she didn't belong. She would have said something vague, some half-truth, wouldn't she?

"Yeah, Seth. She's with Austin." She could almost hear herself saying it.

Marquez glanced at Summer. Her eyes were closed.

Quickly Marquez tore off a hunk of her chili dog and buried it in the sand. Some seagull was going to dine well that night.

"Summer, why do you think Seth is coming back?" Marquez asked. "His internship's for another month, right? And it must cost a fortune to get a ticket on short notice."

"He said Diana was fronting him some money." Summer rolled onto her side. "I'll tell you the truth. He sounded funny on the phone. Sort of . . . cold."

"You don't suppose Diana told him about Austin?"

"I asked her not to. But you know, it's not like there's anything to tell, really. I told Austin I want him out of my life. And I can't help it if he chooses to live in the same town I live in."

"Still, it's not like you mentioned it to Seth. He'll

be freaked when he finds out. After all, you fell for Austin over spring break."

"I know. I blew it. I was just trying to keep things simple, and the more I tried, the more complicated things got. I should have told Seth the truth right from the start."

"Hey, everything will be fine. That ring could easily pass for one costing twice as much." Marquez laughed. "Which is to say fifteen bucks and some change."

"Too bad I don't have a job. Maybe I could have afforded a better fake stone. Oh, well. I've got another interview coming up."

"As what?"

"As . . ." Summer hesitated. "As, um, a companion."

"Dogs are companions, Summer. Being a companion is not a job for a person."

Summer tossed some sand on Marquez's leg. "It involves running errands for some nice young guy who's recovering from a car accident. At least I hope he's nice. I'm just about out of job options."

"There's always Jitters."

"Not with Austin there."

"What about that clerk job at Flipper for Freaks?"

"The Dolphin Interactive Therapy Institute," Summer corrected. "They never called me back. Could be they noticed I can't type, take dictation, or operate a copy machine. Or make coffee without a recipe book."

"How about your sunny disposition? Besides, I'll bet that with intensive training you could master the coffee."

"It's probably just as well. That's sort of Diana's thing. She's been volunteering there a long time, and you know how she is. She has her own private world she doesn't want anyone intruding on."

Marquez sneaked another wad of chili dog under the sand. "Diana and volunteering. It's hard to say those words in the same breath. It's like *Satan* and *bake sale*. It just doesn't quite work."

"I think Diana has a sweeter side we just don't get to see."

"Visible only with the aid of an electron microscope."

Summer laughed. "Like there's this box of letters she's got in our room. Did you see it? Full of old stuff, postcards from my aunt Mallory, that sort of thing. Would you ever in a million years have dreamed Diana would save letters from her mother?"

Marquez blinked. Letters. The box of letters. She'd dropped it when she was cleaning up Diana's room. The letters had scattered all over. When she was picking them up, she'd seen it—a letter from Diana to Seth, never sent. A love letter.

"Marquez? You okay?"

"Yeah. I've just got sun-stun."

"Me too."

She could tell Summer. Maybe it was her duty. If Diana and Seth had been together over New Year's . . .

If Diana was still in love with Seth . . .

If Marquez had told Seth that Summer and Austin were together the night before . . .

If, if, if. Her head was spinning. What if she was wrong? She hated getting involved in other people's messes. She hated the way people poked into hers.

It was perfectly possible that Seth would show up the next day and everything would be fine. Besides, if Marquez needed to confront anyone about all this, it was probably Diana.

Now *there* was a happy thought.

She shoved the last of her chili dog under the sand.

"I'm stuffed," Summer said.

"Me too."

"I'm glad you ate. I feel like I did my duty."

"Mission accomplished," Marquez said softly. She smoothed the sand with her hand.

She'd wait and see what happened with Summer and Seth. Sometimes the best thing to do was just bury your problems.

# 8

## Diamonds Aren't Forever

Through the plane window Diana watched the familiar line of islands unfurl, a string of green pearls in a blindingly bright blue ocean. It was a sight that always comforted her, but that day she was too jumpy to care.

She laced her fingers through Seth's. He didn't react, didn't tighten his grip. But he didn't pull away either. He was in neutral, noncommittal. He'd been that way since talking to Summer.

She knew the signs. She'd pulled the same act with far too many guys—being cool, unreachable. Seth was holding back, and it made her angry. But she couldn't push. She would just have to watch this movie unfold and hope it had a happy ending. For her, anyway.

"Seth?"

He looked at her, not quite smiling.

"What are you going to say when you see Summer?"

He pulled his hand away. "I'm really not sure, Diana. I guess I'll just give her a chance to tell me her side of the story."

Her side. That was not a good sign. It meant he was weakening. It meant he wanted to find a way to forgive Summer.

"What could she possibly say in her defense?"

"I don't know," Seth snapped. "I just want—" He looked away. "I want to know that she really doesn't love me anymore. I want to hear it."

Again Diana took his hand. She could say it now. The way she'd tried to say it in her letters. It wouldn't be so hard just to whisper the words, would it? "I love you, Seth." Would that be so hard?

"I—" The rest got caught in her throat.

"What?"

"I just wanted to say I'm glad I can be here for you. And I'm glad we had the last couple of days together. It was good, wasn't it?"

He gave a terse nod.

"Don't let yourself get hurt any more, Seth. Just remember that you've been through this before with

Summer. She already told you once it was over with Austin. You can't trust her."

This time Seth squeezed her hand. He held on so tightly that it hurt, but at least it was something.

In her mind she tried out the words again.

I love you, Seth.

She wondered if she'd ever have the nerve to say it out loud.

Seth saw her lying there by the side of the pool, asleep. She had on the two-piece bathing suit she'd bought for spring break, the one he'd helped her pick out. He'd sneaked into the dressing room and stolen a glance over the door, then a kiss.

Seth walked along the cement pathway toward the sparkling blue-tiled pool. No one else was around, although he had a sneaking suspicion that Diana and Marquez were spying on him from the third-floor balcony.

Summer's body glistened with oil. Her hair, spilling over the side of the lounge chair, caught the late afternoon sun like spun gold.

He paused and wiped his brow. It was humid in southern Florida, much hotter than in California. Already he'd forgotten what summer heat in the Keys was like.

He tried to summon up the rage he'd felt for the past two days. The feeling of betrayal—gut-wrenching, absolute betrayal—he'd felt when Diana had shown him the photo of Summer and Austin. Worse still, the emotion he'd felt at the moment when she'd shown him Summer's ring.

He'd shopped every jewelry store in Eau Claire before deciding on that ring. It wasn't the fanciest or anywhere near the biggest. But it had seemed to him, when he'd found it in the little jewelry store downtown, to be perfectly Summer. Simple, sparkling, clear, honest.

He had known instantly that it was the diamond that belonged on her finger.

It had cost a hell of a lot more than he'd planned on. He'd worked double shifts at Subway, shoveled mountains of snow, even picked up a paper route from a friend.

But it had been worth it just to see the expression on her beautiful face that night at the prom.

If he closed his eyes, he could see Diana's hand holding the ring, the symbol of his vanity and stupidity. How could he ever have believed Summer would be his forever? How could he have been fool enough to trust her after the way she'd betrayed him with Austin over spring break?

Another picture came unbidden to him: a picture

of Diana, hair tangled, face flushed, lips swollen from his kisses.

But that was not what this was about.

This was about Summer and her betrayal.

This was about the ring she no longer wore.

He was only inches from her now. To his annoyance, his eyes filled with tears. He looked weak, coming back to Florida. He was signaling that he wasn't ready to give her up, and already that was revealing way too much.

He knelt beside her. How many times had he kissed those lips? Even in his anger he wanted to kiss her again. Just one more time.

She stirred. Her eyes opened.

"Seth?" she whispered.

She sat up and put her arms around his neck. She smelled of coconut oil. Her skin was hot and damp.

She was going to kiss him, but he couldn't let that happen. If she did, he might forget why he was there and who was right and who was wrong.

He grabbed her hands to push her away.

And then he felt it. On her finger, where it belonged.

His ring.

# 9

# Black Widows and Avenging Angels

"Sit," Marquez commanded.

With a deep sigh Diana dropped into a chair at a window table. Jitters was quiet, with just a few customers sipping lattes while they read the afternoon paper. The front door was wide open, allowing in the humid air along with a host of flies. The tall palms lining the cobblestone street cast long shadows, shrouding the window in shade.

Marquez took a chair across from her. Her arms were folded over her chest. Her dark eyes were narrow slits. She looked like a simmering pot in serious danger of boiling over.

No matter. Diana was about to go nuclear herself.

Just a few minutes earlier Seth had kissed Summer. Diana had seen it with her own prying eyes.

After all he knew, how could he *kiss* Summer?

Diana stared out the window. Two lifeguards in red beach patrol swim trunks passed by, probably heading home for the day. A few steps behind them was a young couple. The guy was toting a beach umbrella and a cooler. The girl had her hand on his bare back. She stood on tiptoe to whisper something in his ear.

Diana thought of Seth, of the way his tight, muscular back had felt beneath her hands. The way his mouth had felt, skimming kisses along her neck.

She shook off the thought and turned back to Marquez. "So what is it you want to talk about?" she demanded. "Is there some reason we couldn't have done this upstairs in the privacy of our own apartment? I mean, I just got home, Marquez."

"We can't do this in the privacy of our own apartment because when we were up there you insisted on hanging over the balcony so you could eavesdrop on Summer and Seth."

"She was kissing him."

"In case you've forgotten, they're engaged."

"In case you've forgotten," Diana shot back, "Summer's been getting hot and heavy with Austin ever since Seth went to California—" She stopped herself.

She was nearly shouting, and Blythe was on her way over to take their order.

"Hey, guys. Back already, Diana? How was California?"

"Like Florida, only three hours earlier."

"Seth came back to see Summer," Marquez added.

"Cool. I'm anxious to meet the love of her life."

Diana rolled her eyes. "I'll have an iced coffee, Blythe. And one of those low-fat muffins."

"Marquez?" Blythe asked.

Marquez shook her head. "I already ate."

"It's on me," Diana said, softening her tone a little.

"No, thank you," Marquez said pointedly.

"How's your head, by the way?" Blythe asked. "You really had us scared the other night."

"Just a couple of stitches, no biggie."

"Sure you don't want a muffin? If I had your figure, I'd be scarfing 'em by the ton."

"Really, Blythe, I'm fine."

Diana waited till Blythe was gone, then said, "I'm sorry about what happened to you, Marquez."

"And oh, by the way, you told me so, right?"

"No, actually, I wasn't thinking that at all."

Marquez rolled her eyes. "One one thousand, two one thousand—"

"What exactly are you doing, Marquez?"

"Counting the moments until you give me The

Lecture. You know, the one I've already had from Diver and Summer about taking care of myself. How water isn't one of the five basic food groups, et cetera, et cetera, blah, blah, blah. That lecture."

Diana smiled gently. "No. No lecture." She saw the challenge in Marquez's eyes: I dare you to try to fix me. I dare you to take away my pain.

Diana had been there herself the previous summer, and for a long time before that. Maybe it hadn't been exactly the same pain, but she'd been stuck in a depression so dark it had threatened to take her down with it.

"I don't want to nag you and I'm not going to lecture you. But I do want to tell you that I've been . . . mixed up . . . before. And sometimes it helps to talk to someone who can be objective."

"No way."

"I didn't want to either. But there were some people at the Dolphin Institute who worked with the kids there. Counselors. And they helped me get through the stuff with Adam and Ross."

"Diana, *you* were nearly raped by your boyfriend's brother. *I*, on the other hand, got a little dizzy. I fail to see the comparison."

Diana tapped her fingers on the table. She was tempted to give up, but she knew that was just what Marquez wanted.

"I know you're strapped for cash right now," Diana said. "I'd really like to help you out with the counseling costs. It'd sort of be . . . you know, like things coming full circle."

"I am not interested in becoming your pet project. And no way am I taking any more of your damn money!" Marquez exploded, so loudly that customers looked up in alarm.

Diana held up her hands as if she were placating an onrushing bull. She couldn't handle Marquez's legendary temper just then. It wasn't the time or place. Later on she'd try again.

"All right, all right, whatever. If you don't want my help, though, keep in mind there are places that will do the counseling for free, or—"

Marquez pounded her fist on the table. "We are not here to discuss my battle with cellulite. We are here to discuss you. *You,* Diana. Predatory witch of the planet."

Blythe returned with Diana's coffee and muffin. "Listen, I wanted to ask you guys something, but I'm getting the feeling this isn't a good time. Am I right?"

"Yes," Marquez growled.

"No," Diana said. "What is it, Blythe?"

"I just wanted to tell you that I'm having a little party this evening. I get off in fifteen minutes, then I'm heading over to Turtle Beach to do a barbecue.

It's sort of for Caroline, this friend of mine who's visiting. And, well, I know you just got back, Diana, and Summer will probably be busy with Seth, but it'd be great if you could stop by."

"Thanks, Blythe," Diana said politely. She kept her gaze trained on Marquez as if she were an attack dog who might pounce if Diana let down her guard. "I'll pass the word."

"Great." Blythe grinned. "Now I'll let you get back to your argument."

"It's not an argument," Diana said.

Marquez nodded. "It's more like a nuclear skirmish."

"You don't have to tell me about it. Why do you think I don't have any roommates?"

Diana leaned across the table when Blythe was out of earshot. "Excuse me? Did I hear you right? Predatory witch of the planet?"

"Good point. I should have said universe."

"I'm impressed, Marquez." Diana took a sip from her coffee. "*Predatory* is a certified four-syllable word. Too bad you have no idea what it means."

"Oh, I looked it up, Diana." Marquez checked the door and lowered her voice. "It said 'See New Year's Eve.'"

Diana did not allow herself to react. She kept her expression carefully neutral. She took another sip of her coffee. She tore off a bit of her muffin.

On the outside she looked unfazed. Inside was another story. Her stomach was busily trying out for the Olympic gymnastics team.

How did Marquez know? How could she possibly *know*?

"I don't know what you're talking about, Marquez," she said, her voice as smooth as silk.

"I found the letter, Diana. The love letter you never sent to Seth. I know you're still in love with him. And it doesn't take a rocket scientist to figure out why you went out to California."

"And why is that?"

Marquez favored Diana with an arctic smile. "I'll give you a clue. It wasn't to spend quality time with mommy dearest."

For a fraction of a second Diana wanted to bolt. Run away, lick her wounds, regroup.

She was furious with Marquez for going through her private letters. She was horrified at the potential consequences if all this came out.

But mostly she was desperately humiliated to have been found out this way. Especially by Marquez, of all people.

Tears stung her eyes, which just added to the embarrassment. She looked away, biting down on her lower lip to keep it from quivering.

"Okay," Diana said at last. "So you know. Now what?"

"Now you tell me," Marquez said darkly, "how you could pull a thing like this with your own cousin. Summer is a stand-up girl, Diana. How could you do this to her? To me, sure. I could handle it—"

"Unfortunately, your taste runs toward guys with parole officers, Marquez."

"Not Diver," Marquez said proudly.

"Okay, he's the exception that proves the rule." Diana sneaked a quick dab at her eyes with her napkin. "Look, I know how this seems. But before you accuse me of any more mortal sins, you should remember this, Marquez. I tried like crazy to get Summer and Seth back together over spring break. I was the one who went to Seth and said, 'Look, you've made your share of mistakes, too, Seth. Give her a second chance.'" She took a shaky breath. "So he did, and what did he get for his trouble? Austin Reed, right back in the picture. You can say what you want, Marquez. But Summer's still in love with Austin. I'm sorry. I think Seth deserves better than that."

"So instead of Summer he gets Vampira, Queen of the Undead?"

"Instead of Summer," Diana whispered, "he gets someone who really loves him."

For the first time Marquez seemed to relent. She leaned back in her chair, toying with a package of

Sweet'n Low, lost in thought. "I'll give you this much. It's true that Summer's real confused right now. I think she has strong feelings for Seth and for Austin. But she told Austin it was over, Diana. I think she's worried sick about losing Seth." She gave a laugh. "I mean, we spent an entire day searching for a fake ring to replace her engagement ring."

Diana swallowed. "You did?" she asked, attempting nonchalance. "And did you find something?"

"Oh, yeah. It's a pretty convincing fake too. Turns out Seth could have spent seven ninety-five and saved himself a fortune."

She should never have taken that ring to California. She should have known that ruse would come back to haunt her.

She was such an idiot.

But she'd been desperate. And desperate times called for desperate measures.

"This just proves my point," Diana said, embarrassed by the plaintive sound of her own voice. "This is just the kind of unfair tactic Summer pulls. Why not just tell Seth she lost the ring? If there's nothing there, why not just tell him about Austin?"

"Because it would hurt Seth, Diana. Because she wants to protect him. I know that's a difficult concept for you to grasp, since you're a great believer in the black widow approach to mating. But that's how

Summer is. I'm not saying she's not making a mess in the process, but her heart's in the right place."

Diana looked out the window, watching the shadows shift with the breeze. "So now what? Now you're going to tell her everything?"

Marquez dropped her head into her hands. "I don't know," she said wearily. "I don't know what the hell to do. I hate soap operas. I watch *The Daily Show*, not *Days of Our Lives*. I don't know—you tell me."

"You're going to follow *my* advice?"

"No, I'm going to do the opposite of whatever you tell me to do."

"Marquez, I won't deny I'd hoped Seth would choose me over Summer. But if that's not the way it's going to work out, what good will it do for you to tell her the truth? If Summer finds out about Seth and me, it'll be over between them for sure."

Marquez lifted her head. "Yeah, but if I don't tell her, evil will go unpunished. I can't let you just walk away from this, Diana."

"So all of a sudden you're the FBI?"

"I like to think of myself as God's avenging angel."

Diana crumpled up her napkin and tossed it aside. "I'll be punished, all right." Tears came again, and this time she let them fall. "I won't get Seth."

Marquez nodded. "For once, Diana, it appears you

are actually telling the truth. Which worries me, since I believe that's one of the first signs of the apocalypse."

"Well, then, I'm glad we cleared the air." Diana shoved back her chair. "Just one more thing. If you ever go prying into my personal life again, you will be very, very sorry."

"I was just cleaning up your mess, Diana. The box of letters slipped."

"And you accidentally pulled that particular letter out of its envelope and accidentally read it. What are the odds of that, I wonder?"

"It was a real fluke," Marquez agreed.

Diana didn't smile. "You betrayed our friendship, Marquez."

"What friendship? We can't have one, not after the way you betrayed Summer."

"Fine. You won't see me grieving." Diana dropped a five-dollar bill on the table and walked away without another word.

Halfway upstairs Diana changed her mind. She headed outside and around the house, toward the backyard.

She should never have written that letter. Wasn't that the unwritten lesson of politicians? Shred all the evidence. Deniability was everything.

She paused behind a stand of palm trees. Summer and Seth were still by the pool, deep in conversation.

His hand was on her thigh, and he was gazing at her like a worshipful puppy. It was a miracle his tongue wasn't hanging out.

Diana had given him so much. She thought of their weekend together. His warm sheets. The dark night falling over them like a secret.

She'd shown him her heart.

She'd done that only once before, with Adam. He had betrayed her. It had taken her a long time to find a way to get even with him, but she had.

If Seth was just using her, if he was going to crawl back into Summer's arms, then Diana had nothing more to lose. Her self-respect would already be in tatters.

This time she already knew how she'd fight back.

That letter might come in handy after all.

# 10

## She's Not Gonna Wash That Man Right Out of Her Hair

When Diana returned to the apartment, she found Marquez in the kitchen doing dishes.

"Oh. It's just you," Marquez snarled.

"I'm taking a shower."

"By all means, keep me posted."

Diana made a beeline for the bathroom. She cranked up Marquez's portable radio, which sat on the orange crate that served as a makeshift table. Joan Osborne was wailing bitterly about lost love. Perfect shower music for the newly betrayed.

She gazed at her reflection. What was it about Summer that Seth found so irresistible? Or maybe the question was, what was it about Diana that he found so resistible?

Or maybe the question was, how could she have made such a mess of things?

Diana stripped off her clothes, turned the shower on as hot as she could stand it, and stepped under the spray. She wanted to wash off the hours of travel dirt she'd accumulated. And, if possible, she wanted to wash away the residue of ickiness she felt about Seth and her. It was equal parts guilt, distaste, and anger. She doubted a little Dial lather and hot water could remove it.

Diana surveyed the assortment of shampoos perched on the edge of the tub. It was amazing how much stuff in plastic bottles accumulated when you gave three girls one shower to share. Marquez was all Suave products, no frills. Summer bought anything that smelled good. Diana bought her shampoo and conditioner from salons, and the bottles always had pretend words such as *volumizing* on the label.

She selected something from the Body Shop that smelled like tangerines. It belonged to Summer. Swiping it was not as gratifying as Diana had hoped. It did not exactly make up for the awful poolside kiss she'd witnessed.

Someone knocked at the door.

"I'm in the shower, Marquez," she called.

The door opened a crack. "It's not Marquez. It's me, Seth. Can I come in?"

Diana peered around the shower curtain. "Is Summer coming too?" she inquired coldly.

"She's down in the laundry room. And Marquez is checking the mail." Seth glanced over his shoulder. "We have to talk, Diana. Now."

Diana motioned him in. "If Summer finds you in here, Seth, you're the one who gets to explain why we're suddenly into group showers."

Seth slipped in and leaned against the door. He crossed his arms over his chest. "She's wearing my ring," he reported in a low, ominous voice.

Diana rinsed off her hair. She turned off the shower and held out her hand. "Gimme a towel, at least."

"Sure. As soon as you give me an explanation."

"Seth, I'm wet and naked and not in the mood for an inquisition. The ring's a fake, obviously."

Seth passed her a towel, careful to lower his eyes.

"What, all of a sudden you're not interested?" Diana demanded. "As I recall it, you were plenty interested the other night."

She wrapped the towel around her and stepped out of the shower. She felt slightly ridiculous and extremely self-conscious.

Seth was staring at his hazy reflection. "A fake," he

repeated, watching himself say the word, as if he could locate the truth in the mirror.

"She bought a cheap ring to fake you out when she found out you were coming home. Marquez told me."

Seth stared at her. He had the tortured look of a math student tackling an unsolvable problem. "But why would she do that?" he asked in a whisper.

"How do I know? I've long since given up reading Summer's complicated little mind. She may seem like sweetness and light, Seth, but she's manipulating you all over the map. Now would you please go? I'm freezing my butt off here."

Seth's tone became hard. "How do I know the ring you showed me in California wasn't a fake?"

"Trust me. I can tell. My mother has more diamond rings than Elizabeth Taylor. It was your ring, all right."

Seth looked unconvinced.

"Play Columbo. Check the one she's wearing, Seth. See for yourself."

"I'm not sure I could tell. I mean, I'm no jeweler."

Diana felt herself losing patience. She adjusted her towel, took a deep breath, and prayed she wouldn't say something she'd regret. "Seth," she said softly, reasonably, "have you forgotten about Austin? Set aside the whole question of the ring. Assume I'm lying about it, although Lord knows why I would. What about *Austin*?"

Seth gazed at the yellowed linoleum. "You know, I could replace this for you guys," he said vaguely.

"*Seth.* Track with me here. What about Austin?"

He nodded slowly. "I know. I know I have to confront her about him. I just . . . wanted to hold her for a minute, be with her like nothing had changed."

"Nothing?" Diana exploded. "Everything's changed, Seth! Have you forgotten how furious you were this weekend? What happened to all your righteous indignation?" She lowered her voice. "Have you forgotten what went on between us? What was I? Just a cheap stand-in?" She went to him and grabbed his arms. "She loves Austin, Seth. Don't be fooled. I've seen them together, laughing and whispering. I've seen him with his hands all over her."

She could feel him tense. "I don't know what to believe anymore," he said.

"Believe your ears, Seth. Confront her. You'll hear her lies and then you'll know."

Seth gave a slight, almost imperceptible nod. "There's some kind of beach party tonight, Marquez said. I'll get Summer alone and I'll confront her. I will."

"I hope so, Seth," Diana said. "I can't go on this

way. And neither can you. Now beat it. I still have to volumize."

His gaze locked on her, seeming for the first time to see her. "You smell like tangerines," he said.

"You like it?"

"Yeah, I do. Summer's hair always smells like tangerines too."

## Diver Moves In and Austin Moves On

Austin lay sprawled on his dilapidated couch, watching as Diver unpacked his meager possessions.

"Man, you do live light, don't you?" he said. He took another swig of his beer, one of several he planned on consuming before the evening was over.

Diver shrugged. "A sleeping bag, a cup, a fork, a toothbrush, a bar of soap. What else does a man need?"

"A loaf of bread, a jug of wine, and someone other than thou," Austin replied. "Speaking of, want a beer?"

"I don't drink. It disturbs my *wa*."

"Your *wa*, you say?"

Diver shrugged. "My inner harmony. I used to think girls disturbed my *wa* too. But then I met Marquez."

"By the way, she called right before you got here. Something about a party over on Turtle Beach at sunset."

"Hmm. Want to come?"

"Nope. Gotta work." Austin consulted his watch. "As a matter of fact, I'm already late. And anyway, your sister might be at the party. As it happens, she's been disturbing my *wa* all to hell."

"I know. I'm sorry about that."

Austin watched Diver meticulously reroll his sleeping bag. It left a sprinkling of white sand on the floor.

"You're a man of few words, Diver," Austin said. "A fine quality in a roommate. Although I wouldn't have complained if you'd brought a state-of-the-art stereo along with your fork and your toothbrush."

"I didn't have electricity at my last place. It was in a tree."

"Somehow that doesn't particularly surprise me."

Diver scanned a pile of CDs on a bookcase. "I notice a lot of classical cello CDs."

"You into classical?"

"I'll listen to pretty much anything." Diver grinned. "Especially the ocean." He pulled a CD off the shelf. "You've got a lot of these. Caleb Reed. Is he good?"

"Was. He's my dad."

"He's . . . gone?"

"In a manner of speaking. He has Huntington's disease. He's what you might call going."

Diver nodded solemnly. He returned the CD to the shelf gently, almost reverently.

The simple gesture touched Austin. When the subject of his dad came up, most people mouthed platitudes or asked prying questions. But Diver knew better than to do either. Yeah, he was going to be an okay roommate.

Too bad he would also serve as a constant reminder of Summer.

Austin crumpled his beer can and stood a little unsteadily. "Well, I'm off to ply my trade. You got a key, right?"

Diver nodded. "You sure you don't want to come by the party tonight?"

"Real sure." Austin grabbed a pen and notepad for work. "Make yourself at home. I'll see you later."

Outside, the air carried the fresh tang of the ocean. Austin made his way down the winding streets of Coconut Key at a leisurely pace. He wasn't in any hurry. He didn't really care if they fired him at Jitters. One way or another, he was going to have to find a different job anyway. He couldn't keep working there, not with Summer so close by.

Maybe he should move to Boca Beach, up the coast. His dad was in the hospital there, and Austin could visit him more often. It would probably do more good for Austin than for his dad, who was pretty far gone.

Still, it seemed like the right thing to do. Stick around for the death vigil.

And while he was at it, get a glimpse of the future.

Suddenly the street began to sway. The beer and the sun were making him a little dizzy, he told himself— that was all. He leaned against a palm tree, the spiny trunk like knives against his back.

The reality of his situation hit him like that every so often, sneak attacks that left him winded and disoriented. He *knew* the truth, of course. Every waking moment he knew it. But he only *felt* it now and then, often when he least expected it.

He resumed walking, more slowly now. A beautiful blond girl in a string bikini skated past, but he barely noticed her.

He wondered, not for the first time, if he should have told Summer the truth. It wasn't as if she couldn't have handled it. She would have been great. A real trouper.

And it would have been nice, so nice, to have someone to share the burden with. His brother knew, and his mom, but it was different with them. They saw the world through the dark lens of their own experience. When his brother learned he'd inherited the same defective gene that had caused Austin's father's slow demise, he'd seriously considered killing himself.

No, they could see the world only in terms of their own genetic bad luck.

But Summer would have been different. She would have come up with hopeful things to say. "It will be years and years before you have any symptoms yourself, Austin. They're doing all kinds of exciting genetic research. You can't give up hope, not this soon."

It would have been great to hear someone say those things. Even if they weren't necessarily true.

But he'd lied to her. Said he'd gone to the genetics clinic and passed the test with flying colors. He'd wanted to spare her the knowledge. It would have been cruel to tell her.

Of course, if he'd really been noble, he would have walked out of her life for good a long time ago and never come back. It was probably wrong for him to have tried to get her back, knowing what he knew.

He paused in front of the Victorian house where Jitters was located. The café looked busy, full of loud tourists. He stared up at the third-floor balcony, Summer's balcony. There was no sign of her.

She was gone, lost to him.

He wondered if he could have fought harder to

keep her. Probably, he decided. But in his heart he knew it was fairer to her to let her go.

Maybe this was just how things were meant to turn out. He didn't bother asking why. He didn't try to find an explanation—fate, the stars, bad karma, bad luck. That was one thing his father's slow dying had taught him: Asking why was a waste of breath.

# 12

# The Case of the Incredible Shrinking Knuckle

Diver skirted the foaming surf, enjoying the feel of the wet, packed sand as it first resisted and then gave way to his feet. The quiet water was surprisingly warm. The first stars of the evening glittered low on the horizon, delicate pinpricks of golden light.

He loved the beach. It was home. Sometimes he wondered if he really had been born in Minnesota. Here at the edge of the world, where the land gave out and slipped into the sea, was the only place he truly felt at peace.

Two girls jogged by on the sand. As soon as they were past him, one of the girls let loose an earsplitting wolf whistle. Diver looked back, and they picked up their speed, giggling musically.

He shook his head. Will, one of the guys at his old job, had claimed Diver was a "babe magnet." And sometimes Diver wondered if there was some strange truth to it. Girls did seem to be awfully interested in him. It should have been flattering, he supposed. But it always made him a little uncomfortable when some girl, an utter stranger, made a move on him. How he looked on the outside, after all, had nothing to do with who he was on the inside. It always surprised him that girls didn't understand that better.

He stooped to pick up a nice unbroken shell. He heard the soft shuffle of footsteps in the sand and looked up to see a figure, a girl, approaching him with a determined gait.

He kept low, hoping to avoid another embarrassing flirtation. In the scant starlight, it took him a minute to register the short, stylish blond hair and pretty features.

Caroline.

Diver tossed the shell aside and stood. There was no need to panic. He'd brushed her off easily at the hospital. If she pressed any more, he'd just shrug and deny whatever she had to say.

"Paul. I was hoping you'd show up tonight."

She stood before him, hands on hips, much smaller than he was but intimidating nevertheless. She was wearing a black one-piece suit and a black nylon windbreaker. She very nearly blended into the night.

Diver gave a laugh. "Boy, I wish I could help you out. I mean, any guy in his right mind would have loved to have you for a next-door neighbor. But like I said, you've got the wrong guy. I've never even been to Virginia."

She smiled coolly. "That's too bad," she said in her smooth southern accent. "And here I went to all the trouble of having this faxed to me. On my vacation, no less. What a shame." Caroline reached into the pocket of her windbreaker and retrieved a neatly folded piece of paper. "Still, you might want to read it anyway. Just to be sure."

Diver took the paper from her. Even in the darkness, he could see it was a copy of a newspaper article.

"I know it's kind of dark to read, but you can probably make out the pictures just fine."

Diver didn't have to look. He'd saved the same clipping. It was yellow around the edges now and crisp to the touch.

The fire. What remained of his house.

And beside that photo, another, smaller one. From his seventh-grade yearbook, a blond, blue-eyed boy with an attitude, refusing to smile for the school photographer.

The caption read "Missing Youth, Suspect in Arson Death."

Caroline touched his arm. Her fingers were cool.

Her smile was pretty, believable the same way an arti-
ficial Christmas tree seems real from far away.

"I'd really like to talk to you, Paul."

It wasn't a request.

"I have nothing to say to you." Diver pushed
past her.

She ran to catch up and grabbed his arm. He
stopped.

"You know, I'm thinking that a murder suspect
doesn't really have a lot of negotiating room," Caroline
said, Sunday-school teacher sweet. "Tomorrow afternoon, your place."

Diver closed his eyes. "All right. Just . . . don't say
anything to anyone till then. Deal?"

"Oh, your secret's safe with me, Paul." She let go
of his arm. "It'll be fun. Just a couple of neighbors chatting about old times."

"I'm staying—"

"I know where you're staying." Caroline started
back toward the party. "I've done my homework.
Now come on. We've got a beach party to attend.
And I even promise to call you Diver."

Summer took Seth's hand and pulled him toward the
water. "Come on, you big baby," she teased. "The
water's incredibly warm. I know you're used to mellow Pacific Ocean water now, but this'll have to do."

She pulled Seth in while the others, sitting on the sand, laughed and applauded.

When the water was waist deep, Seth wrapped his arms around Summer and held her close as the gentle waves nudged them.

"This is nice," he said.

"Are you sure?" Summer asked. "You've been so quiet. Maybe it wasn't such a good idea, coming here to the party with all these people."

She glanced back at the beach. Blythe, Caroline, and some other people, friends of Blythe and people from the apartment building, were gathered around a small bonfire. Rihanna was playing on the CD player someone had brought along. Marquez and Diver were off by themselves, slow-dancing. Two other couples were dancing at the edge of the water, including Diana and some guy who was a high-school friend of Blythe's. The guy was cute in a gawky way, but he wasn't Diana's type. She was probably just being polite.

It had been a nice party, with good food and lots of laughs. And in a way it had been a relief to have a lot of people around to keep things from getting too difficult with Seth. It didn't hurt to have the whole defensive lineup there, but Summer knew it couldn't last much longer.

They needed to talk. All evening Seth had been watching her doubtfully and speaking too politely, as if she were his just-arrived mail-order bride.

Maybe it didn't mean anything. Diana and Diver had been quiet, too. Maybe it was just the rich food and the hot night air and the endless whisper of the waves lulling people into silence.

"I guess I haven't been very talkative," Seth admitted. "I've had a lot on my mind." He took a deep breath. "So. Tell me the truth. Have you missed me?"

She tried to ignore the edge in his voice. "Of course I have. Have you missed me?"

"More than you know. What have you been up to?"

Again the harsh tone. "You know, just . . . job-hunting, mostly. Unsuccessfully. I have another interview tomorrow, though." She crossed her fingers. "Maybe this time they'll take pity on me."

Seth stared at her hand, the crossed fingers, the little fake ring.

"Summer," he said softly. "I love you."

He pulled her close and kissed her for a long time. It wasn't like his familiar kisses. It was shy, the tentative, hopeful kiss of a first date.

He let her go and took her left hand. He cupped it in both of his and lifted it to his lips. His hands, to her surprise, were trembling.

He kissed her fingers, then pulled back, admiring her ring.

"It looks nice in the moonlight, doesn't it?" he said.

She nodded but said nothing.

"I was worried when I got it," Seth continued. "You know, would it fit, would it be the right one. But then I saw it and I knew. The jeweler told me it was one of a kind—did I tell you that?"

He reached for the ring, clasped the band with his fingers, and tugged a little. "It's loose. That's weird. I could barely get it past your knuckle, remember?"

Summer swallowed. "Guess I've lost weight."

"In your knuckle?" Seth laughed, but it wasn't exactly a happy laugh. He pulled a little harder on the ring.

Summer yanked her hand away. "Seth, you can't take it off."

"Why not?" he demanded. "Haven't you ever?"

"No. It would be bad luck. I'm sure there's some kind of old wives' tale about that. Like seeing the bride in her gown before the wedding."

Seth was staring at her. His dark eyes glowed in the moonlight. She shivered even though the air was hot. She had a queasy feeling in her gut, the one she got when she knew she was making a mess of things.

"Let me see the ring, Summer."

"Why?"

Seth held out his hand. Summer hesitated. After a moment she slipped the ring off her finger.

He held it up to the moonlight, the shining emblem of her stupidity and weakness.

Why hadn't she just told him the truth, told him everything? There was a lesson there somewhere. Don't avoid pain—just get it over with like an adult.

Or at least don't go buying replacement rings at Woolworth's.

Like a savvy buyer, Seth studied the ring, squinting at it in the darkness. He was looking for something. He *knew*.

How did he know? Could he have read it in her eyes? She wasn't exactly a poker face. Had he noticed the cheap setting? The loose fit?

Could Diana have let the truth slip?

He ran the tip of his index finger inside the band. "There's engraving," he pronounced. He seemed satisfied, but she saw disappointment in his eyes. "I didn't have your ring engraved," he pointed out flatly. "Did you have the ring engraved?"

"No."

"Then what does this say?"

Summer sighed. It was over. She'd been caught. She deserved her fate.

"I believe," she said quietly, "it says 'Made in Taiwan.'"

Seth drew back his arm. With a great heave, he hurled the ring far out into the black water.

It landed without a sound. Strange, Summer thought, for such a big moment. There should have been a huge splash, maybe even a tidal wave.

"Tell me it all," Seth said.

# 13

# They Say Confession Is Good for the Soul

They headed back to the beach and walked in silence for a while, until the noise of the party had evaporated in the night air.

"I was painting the door," Summer began.

She sat on the beach. Seth sat too, leaving a wide space between them. They both stared out at the black, sluggish ocean, avoiding each other's gaze.

"Painting," Seth repeated doubtfully.

"I'd already gotten some paint on the ring once," Summer said, "and I didn't want to get any more on it. I was afraid it might not come off."

"Not come off," Seth repeated again.

"Well, how should I know? I've never had a

diamond before. I'm not adult enough to have real jewelry, Seth. Before we got engaged, the most expensive thing I'd ever owned was that pin in the shape of Minnesota my aunt Ethel gave me. And I never wore that, except to family reunions. And Aunt Ethel's funeral. I mean, how the heck was I supposed to know?"

She took note of the hysterical pitch in her voice and resolved to stay calm. She was a criminal spilling it all to a cop. A penitent confessing to a priest. There was no point in getting all emotional about it.

"So you took off the ring—"

"And I put it on the windowsill in a Dixie cup, and the next thing I knew the cup was empty and the ring was gone. We searched the apartment for hours, and outside too. Under the window, in the bushes, you name it."

"The gutters?"

"Diver checked those."

"Under the bed, that sort of thing? It could have rolled anywhere, right?"

"Trust me, I looked. I was frantic, Seth. But I kept thinking that there had to be a logical explanation, that it'd turn up, that it *had* to turn up. People don't just suddenly lose their engagement rings, except maybe in movies." She sighed. "Of course, usually those are comedies."

"Go on."

"Well, the thing is, I didn't want to tell you because I thought you'd take it as some kind of omen. Like it meant something. Sort of a Freudian slip."

She stole a glance at Seth. He was nodding slowly, reserving judgment.

"So when you called and said you were coming," Summer continued, "Marquez and I went out and tried to find a duplicate ring. We must have gone to every store on the Key. And then finally, when I was just about to give up, I found the perfect imitation."

"The one I just threw into the ocean."

"We found it in the jewelry section at Woolworth's."

Seth winced.

"I mean, it's not like it was anywhere near as beautiful," Summer hastened to add. "But I thought it might be enough to get by until . . . until I found the real one. Which probably sounds incredibly stupid and naive, not to mention really, really chicken."

"Yeah. Especially the chicken part."

"I didn't want to upset you, Seth. I know how hard you worked for that ring. And I felt like such a jerk. The truth is," she sighed, "some squirrel probably ate it. Or some rat sneaked it away to its nest."

"That does seem possible," Seth said. "Some large, conniving rat."

"What?"

"Nothing."

"I'm sorry, Seth. I'm so sorry." She took a deep, shuddery breath. "But there's more."

The hard part. The really, really hard part.

Seth turned to her, waiting, his jaw clenched. He almost seemed to be anticipating her words. But of course he didn't know how awful they would be.

Summer looked away. "There's something you should know, Seth. It's like the ring . . . I should have just come out with it. But when someone you love is far away, it's harder. It's hard to say certain things over the phone." She groaned. "I have no excuse. I just didn't want you to get the wrong, you know, impression—"

"Say it already, Summer."

"Austin Reed moved here."

She waited for the furious, shocked accusations of betrayal, but none came. Seth just gazed out at the ocean, rocking slightly in the sand.

"He was here on Coconut Key even before Diana and Marquez and I found our apartment. He works at Jitters—you know, the café downstairs?"

"And?"

"And that's all."

"You've been seeing him?" His voice was choked.

"No, I mean yes, I mean I've seen him, yeah. He's sort of hard to avoid. But I made it very clear to him that whatever we had is completely over."

"Do you still have feelings for him? The way you did last spring?"

Summer considered. She'd told so many half-truths, done so much evading, that it was starting to come naturally to her. But she wanted to clear the air once and for all. Even if it meant causing more pain.

"I did have feelings for him, Seth. I don't think you can care about someone and then, bam, suddenly stop caring. But I realized something important when I was sorting through all this." She slipped her hand through his. "We are engaged, Seth."

"And this was news to you?"

She stared up at the vast expanse of stars. "Do you ever think about what that means? It means you and me, together until we die. It means loyalty to each other above all else." She smiled wistfully. "And it means forgiveness—at least I hope it means that."

For a while they didn't speak. The waves rolled back and forth over the sand, waiting, it seemed, as impatiently as Summer was waiting.

Finally Seth stood. He looked down at her. She could not read his expression.

"You should have told me all this."

"I know."

"How can we trust each other if we're not completely honest?"

"I know. I didn't want to hurt you. Again."

"It's going to take me some time, Summer. I have to sort through all this."

She nodded.

"Maybe—" Behind her she heard movement. She turned to see someone, a tall guy, walking down the beach at the water's edge. Stumbling was more like it.

"He looks drunk," Summer said.

"Plastered."

The figure grew larger, clearer. He was humming to himself.

Suddenly he stopped.

"Shummer," he said.

"Oh, God," Summer whispered.

Austin sauntered over, nearly tripping on his own feet.

"Seth, let me talk to him alone, okay? He's drunk. There's no telling how he might act."

"Maybe this is a good thing," Seth said darkly. "We can clear the air at last."

Austin paused before them, staring at Summer Wearily. "Shummer," he whispered.

"Hi, Austin," she whispered.

He stared unsteadily at Seth.

"You remember me, Austin," Seth said. "We met during spring break. It's me. Seth."

# 14

## The Whole Truth and Anything But

"I have to say, your timing's perfect," Seth said. "We were just discussing you."

"I'm flattered."

"Don't be."

"Austin," Summer said gently, "this isn't really a good time—"

Austin frowned, then swayed. "I came for the party. Diver said there was a party."

"The party's down the beach," Summer said, but Austin just stood there, eyeing Seth as though Austin were a scientist who'd just discovered a new and intriguing species.

Seth turned to Summer. "Isn't this the part where

we duel for the fair maiden? Is that what you want, Summer?"

"I'm really sort of a pacifist," Austin said. He swayed a little more, then plopped onto the sand with a grunt. "Could play poker for her, if ya want."

"No, that's too lowbrow," Seth said sarcastically. "How about earnings potential? What do you want to do, Austin?"

Austin lay back on the sand, considering. "You mean when I grow up?"

"A big if, I grant you. What's your game plan?"

"I'm going to be a starving poet. Suffer for my art. Then die a tragic early death. Or else I'll write for Hollywood."

"Well, I plan to become an architect and have my own firm someday. I'd like to see six figures by the time I'm thirty."

Summer crossed her arms over her chest. "Since when?"

"Since always."

"Seth, you're being ridiculous."

"Okay, then. We'll look at the whole picture. You want to have kids, Austin?"

Austin narrowed his eyes. "With you?"

Seth grimaced.

"Well," Austin said, "kids, I don't know. They're

kind of like a long-term commitment. But I wouldn't mind a dog. Maybe one of those big, sloppy pound dogs. . . ."

Seth rolled his eyes. "I'm getting at least two kids. A boy and a girl."

"So," Austin said, rolling onto his side, "you can just, like . . . order them from a catalog?"

Seth sighed loudly. "How about your education?" he pressed.

"I watch *Jeopardy!* every afternoon."

"I'm going for my advanced degree at UW."

"University of Weeniedom?" Austin let loose an impressively loud burp. "A nice enough little preschool, I guess." He glanced at Summer slyly. "Although I hear Carlson's even better."

"Say what?"

"Austin," Summer warned.

Austin sat up and waved Seth off extravagantly. "Never mind. Look, I came for the party, not for Shummer. You already won."

Seth glanced at Summer. "What do you mean?"

"She chose you and blew me off. Loyalty, honor, all that good stuff." He shrugged. His body was loose, jointless. "It's just as well. I'm what they call in insurance circles a 'bad risk.' "

Seth stared from Austin to Summer and back again. "You're telling me the truth, man?"

Austin offered up a goofy smile. "Yeah, I know, I had a hard time believing it too."

"I told you, Seth," Summer whispered.

For the first time Seth seemed to have come to a conclusion. He nodded firmly. "I believe you. I do." He reached out his hand to Summer. "Come on. Let's go back to your place."

Summer jerked her head toward Austin, who was lying on his back, arms spread, making sand angels.

"We can't leave him."

"Leave him," Austin advised. "He'sh fine."

"I can't, Austin. Remember that other time? The time you went swimming at night over spring break?"

It seemed like ages ago, but it had been only a few months. Austin had been upset over his father and gone swimming, half intending to drown himself. Summer had saved him, but not without nearly drowning herself in the process.

Seth let out a long exhalation, slowly shaking his head. He held out his hand to Austin. "Come on, buddy. We're taking you home."

"A threeshome?" Austin inquired.

Seth gave a rueful laugh. "Yeah, Austin. Something like that."

At two in the morning Diana eased open the door to the apartment. The lights were out, which meant Summer and Marquez were already asleep. Good thing. She was exhausted and angry and not in the mood for another episode of *The Seth and Summer Show*.

She locked the door behind her and tossed her keys on the counter. Moonlight streamed through the balcony doors.

She'd spent the whole evening watching Summer and Seth together. Hoping that Seth would take note, she'd even pretended to flirt with some guy named P.J., an old friend of Blythe's. When she'd danced with the guy, he'd smelled of licorice and sweat and held her too close. Diana had watched over her shoulder while Summer and Seth went swimming in the ocean. Swimming and kissing.

She wondered where Seth was staying that night. She wondered if she really wanted to know the answer to that question. She was starting to realize that ignorance was sometimes bliss.

"Where've you been?" a low voice inquired.

Diana jumped, her hand to her heart. Seth was sitting on the couch in the dark.

"You scared me, Seth," Diana hissed. "What are you doing lurking around there? Why aren't you with Summer?" She said the name with just the right touch of sarcasm.

"How about a little poolside chat, Diana?"

"I'm tired."

"We could do it here," Seth said in a hushed voice, "but I'm not sure you want Summer to hear what I have to say to you about you and her ring."

Diana sighed. She might as well get it over with. "Fine. Whatever. Let's go to the pool and you can tell me how you believe all Summer's nice little lies."

Seth didn't speak all the way down to the backyard. The pool was unlit, save for the silver moonlight frosting the water. A dragonfly struggled across the surface, unable to free itself from the water's hold. Diana knelt down and scooped it out. It buzzed away in wild loops.

"You lied to me, Diana." Seth said it wearily, like a disappointed teacher. His hands were on his hips.

When he wanted to, he could be downright parental, Diana reflected.

"Summer lost that ring. She didn't take it off because she wanted to break up with me."

"So that's the story," Diana said. She sat on the edge of the pool, dangling her legs in the warm water. "And you're buying it. Seth, you are nothing if not eternally gullible. You are the ultimate used-car salesman's fantasy. You'll buy anything as long as it comes wrapped up in a pretty package."

"One thing about Summer, Diana. Unlike you, she's a lousy liar. She told me how the ring disappeared while she was painting. The story was too Summer-like not to be true." He sat down on the edge of a pool chair, hands clasped between his knees. "The thing is, she didn't know the ending to the story. The part where you somehow found the ring and flew it all the way to California."

Diana's mind was in overdrive, searching for ways out of the corner she'd boxed herself into. But nothing could help her. She'd trapped herself. "Fine, whatever," she snapped, her tense voice betraying her outward calm. "Believe what you want to believe, Seth." She hesitated. "So . . . did you tell her about me and the ring?"

"No. I didn't see the point in hurting her."

"Very noble. Of course, there's still the little matter of Austin Reed."

"Funny you should bring him up. Guess who crashed the party this evening—Austin himself."

"Any bloodshed?"

"Sorry to disappoint you. He was righteously drunk. He told me just what Summer told me," Seth said, sounding way too much like a prosecutor going in for the kill. "She chose *me*. She wanted *me*, Diana."

"Interesting. Did he also tell you how he pawed her by this very pool a few days ago?"

Seth gave her a long-suffering look.

"You saw the picture, Seth. Austin and Summer, right here. Extremely close together. Some might say intimately close. And that's just the time I was able to capture it on film. Who knows what went on with them behind closed doors?"

"This is why you're so good, Diana." Seth wagged a finger at her. "There's just enough truth mixed in with your fiction to make it compelling. Summer's not wearing her ring, true enough. Austin's here in Coconut Key, true enough. And yes, I bought your version of events hook, line, and sinker. But it wasn't the whole truth. I'm starting to realize you're not very good at the whole truth, Diana."

"I told you the truth about my feelings for you." Her voice was soft and indistinct. "That was the whole truth."

"Maybe," Seth said. "I suppose I'll never really know."

She could hear, in his indifferent tone, his condescension. Seth was slipping from her grasp. Panic hammered at her. And when Diana felt panicked, she fought back tooth and nail, like any cornered animal.

She stood, eyeing him with cold disdain, waiting until she saw a hint of worry.

"You know, Seth," she said, "it seems to me that I'm not the only person here who has trouble with the concept of the whole truth. You've been known to leave out part of the story yourself."

"What's that supposed to mean?"

"It means you're a hypocrite. It means you used me. It means"—she turned to go—"this isn't over yet. You want the whole truth? Fine. You know what they say. Watch out what you wish for, Seth. You might just get it."

## Just One Big Happy Family

Marquez checked the mileage counter on her exercise bike. "Wimp," she muttered. A couple of days off and she'd completely lost her stride. Not only that, her morning weigh-in had been positively devastating.

She'd been eating, that's why. And to get Diver and Summer off her case, she'd completely blown her exercise strategy. If she let them have their way, she'd blimp up like a balloon at the Macy's Thanksgiving Day parade.

She pedaled even faster. Sweat trickled down her chest. Diana was still asleep, Summer was in the shower, and Seth was crashed out on the couch, oblivious. For once she could work off some calories without the diet narcs on her case.

At the beach party the night before, Diver had been all over her about going to counseling. When he talked to her at all, that was. For most of the evening he'd been busy gawking at that Caroline girl. Beautiful, skinny Caroline. All night they'd eyed each other.

Marquez was not an idiot. She could see what was going on. And if there'd been any doubt, the way Diver had clammed up was all the evidence she needed. He'd been quiet, even by his standards.

She was losing him, she was sure of it. Someday soon she was going to walk in on him and Caroline, just the way she'd walked in on J.T. and that slut.

Sure, Diver swore everything was fine, swore he loved her. But he was like Summer that way. Too nice to say the truth of things.

She'd just clocked another mile when Diana emerged from her bedroom. She had on her red silk robe. Her hair was mussed, and there were dark, shiny circles under her eyes. That was pretty rough around the edges for Diana. She usually arose looking as though she'd just had a *Seventeen* makeover.

"Is this fresh coffee?" Diana muttered, holding up the pot.

"I have nothing to say to you, Diana," Marquez replied.

"And that would be, like, a punishment?"

Summer came out of the bathroom dressed in a

slinky blue sundress. She took one look at Marquez on the bike and groaned. "You're not overdoing it, are you?"

"Not if the scale is any indication."

"Marquez—"

"All right, all right." Marquez slowed her pedaling. "I just need to cool down. What are you all dressed up for, anyway?"

"My companion interview."

"Seems to me you have plenty of companions," Diana said under her breath.

"What?" Summer asked.

"Nothing."

Summer leaned over the back of the couch and kissed Seth lightly on the lips. He opened his eyes. "Excellent wake-up call," he said, yawning. "Hey, you look great."

"Does anyone know if this is new coffee?" Diana demanded.

"I made it a while ago," Summer said. "It's probably kind of bitter."

"Perfect," Diana said. She popped a cup in the microwave, cast a dark glance at Seth, and headed for the bathroom.

"What's the matter with her?" Summer asked.

Marquez shrugged. "Let's just say some of her best-laid plans fell through."

"Well, I'm off," Summer said, grabbing her purse. "Wish me luck. Do I look like companion material?"

"You do to me," Seth said with a leer. "Hey, you sure this guy just wants you to, like, run errands and stuff?"

"No, Seth. He wants me to clean the house wearing a French maid costume." Summer rolled her eyes. "He was in a really bad accident. He's in a wheelchair."

"But his hands work, right?"

"Seth, please shut up. I am desperate. It's this or I get a job at Jitters."

"Whoa. Knock 'em dead."

Summer snapped her fingers. "Marquez. Before I forget, the nurse at the hospital said you should call to confirm that you're going to the counseling session tomorrow, remember?"

Marquez just kept pedaling. She suddenly realized that she'd already come to a decision.

"You're not backing out?" Summer asked.

"Look, maybe I'll go next week. I'm just not in the mood, okay?"

"But you promised."

"Well, I lied. God knows I'm not the only person around this place who's done it." Marquez was pleased when both Summer and Seth looked equally uncomfortable.

Still, Summer wouldn't go down without a fight. "Marquez, please go, for me. For Diver."

"Summer, I am a big girl and I don't want to be nagged. Nagging would *not* be a good idea." She gave Summer her best back-off look. "*Not,* I repeat, a good idea. Got it?"

Summer sighed. "We'll talk about this later."

"It's going to be a very brief, very one-sided conversation."

"We'll talk," was all Summer would say. She kissed Seth one more time. "I'm glad we're okay," she said.

"Me too. Real glad."

Before leaving, Summer cast one last disapproving, hopeful, plaintive, annoyed look at Marquez. It was amazing. The girl could convey more guilt trips with her blue eyes than all the nuns at Marquez's junior high combined.

When the door closed behind Summer, Seth sat up, rubbing his eyes. "What did you mean," he asked, jerking his head toward the bathroom door, "about Diana's plans falling through?"

Marquez climbed off the bike, testing her rubbery legs. "'Should auld acquaintance be forgot—'"

Seth gulped. "New Year's?"

"New Year's."

"You didn't tell Summer?"

"I haven't yet. But let me just say this. You and Diana had better behave yourselves, or I may be feeling a lot more talkative."

"There's nothing between Diana and me, Marquez."

"I guess she just flew out to California for the scenery?"

Seth actually flushed.

"Yeah, that's what I figured." Marquez wiped her brow with a towel. "Look, this apartment has more secrets in it than my eighth-grade diary. I can't even keep track anymore. Let's just keep things simple. You behave, I'll keep my mouth shut. Deal?"

"I love Summer, you know that."

"And Diana loves you. And Austin loves Summer, I'm guessing. You're like rabbits, all of you. In heat. In the spring. Just get a grip on the hormones, and I'll mind my own business."

Seth laughed. "You have my solemn oath that my hormones are under complete control."

"You're a guy, right?"

"Last time I checked."

"Then your hormones will be under control around the time you're six feet under."

Seth got up to pour himself a cup of coffee. He turned to Marquez, hesitating. "You know, that counseling stuff . . . Summer really thinks it might be a good thing to give it a shot."

"That," Marquez said, shaking a finger at Seth, "would be an example of business that doesn't need any minding from you."

"Sorry."

"Apology accepted. Now do me a favor."

"What?"

"Go in there and ask Countess Dracula to hurry up with her shower. I'm not speaking to her."

Seth grinned. "You're afraid of her?"

"Not as long as I'm wearing a clove of garlic around my neck. You?"

"No." Seth gazed at the door almost wistfully. "Diana's just complicated, that's all."

"Calculus is complicated, Seth. Diana's easy to understand. She's evil. Pure and simple."

"Well, I'm glad somebody understands her," Seth said wearily. "I know I never will."

Marquez nodded. "Were you . . . you know . . . ever really in love with her?"

"You think calculus is complicated?" Seth laughed sadly. "I'm still working on that one."

# 16

# References Available on Request

Summer checked the address she'd written on the paper. It was in an exclusive residential area, a private enclave on a sort of mini-island off the key.

When she'd called about the companion ad, a nurse had answered. The patient (as she'd referred to him) was eighteen. He'd been in a near-fatal car accident while visiting Germany. His family lived in New England, but they were renting this house in the Keys for his rehabilitation. He wanted to recover in private, away from prying eyes. He'd suffered injuries to his spine, his right leg, his face, even his vocal cords. He was partially paralyzed. He was a nice boy, quiet, not demanding like some of the nurse's former clients. He needed someone to read to him, run errands, keep him company.

Did Summer have a résumé? Any nursing experience? Any experience, period?

Summer turned the corner onto the small road that skirted the beach. The sun was searing, the sky cloudless. She wondered if this was a waste of time. She took out the résumé in her purse, the one she'd put together the previous night. It was handwritten, since she didn't have access to a computer, and on lined paper.


    Summer Ann Smith
    142 Lido Lane, Apartment 301
    Coconut Key, Florida 33031


    *Telephone:* I don't have one yet, but the phone company says this week for sure or next week for absolute sure. My cousin's phone is 555-8761 if you need to get in touch with me, but she'll probably answer. Her name's Diana.


    *Job Objective:* Companion.


    *Education:* Graduate of Bloomington High School, Bloomington, Minnesota.

*Activities:* High school honor society, three years; choir; yearbook; copy editor of *The Bloomington Bugle* (school newspaper).

*Job History:*

—Five years babysitting experience, including regular care for triplets. Played, changed diapers, made meals, supervised homework. Developed excellent supervisory skills and ability to make killer macaroni and cheese.

—One summer waiting tables, Crab 'n' Conch, Crab Claw Key, Florida. Served patrons, worked as hostess, did side work, took inventory, did extensive cleaning. Developed public relations skills and superior upper arm strength.

*Available for work:* Immediately.

*References:* Available on request.

Summer sighed. It looked, she had to admit, pretty unimpressive. Even she wouldn't have hired herself. And she was her own best reference.

It was her own fault for waiting till the last minute. She'd written the résumé the night before, after the beach party. She'd been worried and distracted after her big discussion with Seth and after escorting Austin back to his apartment.

Summer paused to slip off her sandals. She crossed the street and headed to the beach. She made it a policy to avoid wearing shoes whenever possible, and besides, the hot sand felt heavenly.

She passed the spot where she and Seth had talked during the party. She should have felt relieved after getting things out in the open with him. She'd thought making a clear choice would have simplified things, but after seeing Austin depressed and drunk, she'd felt awful. Maybe making a choice wasn't the hard part. Maybe living with the aftermath was.

Did she feel this way because she'd made such a mess of things? Or because she'd come to the wrong conclusion about Seth and Austin?

She watched a group of children racing to finish a sand castle. No, Seth was her fiancé. She loved him. She owed her loyalty to him.

She wondered if it was a good sign that she had to keep repeating the same mantra over and over again, reminding herself of the reasons she and Seth belonged together.

She crossed back to the street, put her sandals on, and turned down a private dirt road. A narrow wooden bridge spanned the water that separated the key from Eden Shores, where her job interview would take place.

Seth was leaving the next day. He'd told her he'd done what he needed to do, coming back to touch base with her. He was going back to finish up his internship. Then the rest of the summer would be theirs together.

She was definitely going to discuss the college situation with him before he left. Technically she could wait; after all, she didn't yet know if Carlson was going to accept her. But she'd learned her lesson about avoiding hard confrontations. Better to do it right away, even if her application was rejected later. He would be upset and would see it as a betrayal. But Seth would just have to understand that when it came to her education, she had to listen to her own heart.

At least she felt comfortable with this choice. She knew it was the right thing. Austin had helped her realize she'd decided against going to Carlson because she was afraid of failing there.

She would tell Seth that he could reapply to Carlson the next semester. Maybe if his grades at UW were good, Carlson would take him and they could still spend most of their college years together. But she was not going to go to UW just to make him happy or just because he hadn't been accepted to Carlson. Not even after all that had happened between them. She couldn't live her life trying to please Seth.

A uniformed guard in a gatehouse had to make a

call before she was allowed to cross the bridge. It was her first taste of Eden Shores, a place people in Coconut Key talked about in hushed tones. Lushly lined with palms, it was home to maybe two dozen estates, huge pastel fortresses with giant windows, giant pools, giant privacy walls, and giant Dobermans standing guard. A small but exclusive yacht club claimed the south end of the islet.

It made her a little uncomfortable. She'd never really known any rich people, unless you counted Adam Merrick, the senator's son she'd dated briefly the previous summer. He'd seemed like a perfectly normal guy—that is, if you could have two hundred bathrooms in your house and still be perfectly normal. Of course, in the end he'd turned out to be a complete dirtbag. It seemed that having money didn't necessarily mean you also had character.

The perfectly manicured main avenue was empty save for a few gardeners sweating profusely in the wet heat. Summer checked the address again. The house was at the end of a cul-de-sac, an imposing building made of peach stucco. She shook the sand out of her sandals, smoothed down her hair, and rang the bell.

The door swung open to reveal a portly butler. His few remaining strands of silver hair were combed over his shiny bald head. His bulging gray eyes reminded Summer of a cartoon fish. He nodded gravely. "May I help you?"

"I'm here about the companion job. My name is Summer Smith. I'm sorry I'm a little early, but I walked and I wasn't sure how long it would take, because I've never been here before."

The butler indulged a smile, the corners of his lips twitching just a bit. "Come in, Ms. Smith," he said, revealing a clipped New England accent. "You'll be speaking with Ms. Rodriguez on the lanai."

Summer followed him to an airy screened porch overlooking the ocean. It was furnished with white wicker rockers surrounding a rectangular lap pool. Green plants grew in abundance. Three ceiling fans moved lazily overhead.

"I assume you brought a résumé?" the butler inquired.

"Well, kind of." Summer handed her envelope to him. "It's pretty dorky. I mean, I don't exactly have a lot of companion experience, unless you count, you know, just hanging out with people."

He smiled. "Hanging out," he repeated, as if he'd never actually tried the phrase. "I shall pass this along." Chuckling under his breath, he left her alone.

"Excellent interview technique, Summer," she muttered. "Impress them with your total dorkiness right up front."

She gazed around the room, then peeked into the adjacent living room. There was something sterile about the house. It didn't have the debris of daily life about it—magazines, letters, photos of family members, dust, confusion, and clutter. Or maybe really rich people didn't make messes. Maybe they just had them removed by specially trained anticlutter SWAT teams.

"Ms. Smith?"

Summer spun around. A young woman, maybe just a few years older than Summer, stood in the doorway. She had short curly hair and thickly lashed eyes. She was wearing a crisp white uniform. "Oh, hi. I wasn't snooping. Just . . . you know. Okay, I was snooping."

"I'm Juanita Rodriguez. We spoke on the phone."

Summer shook her hand. "Somehow I thought you'd be older. I mean, you're a nurse, right?"

"LPN. Licensed Peon and Nobody. Have a seat."

"Thanks."

"I looked over your résumé," Juanita said, settling into a rocker next to Summer.

"Pretty pathetic, huh?"

"Not entirely. Me, I can't imagine tackling triplets." She smiled coolly, eyeing Summer up and down with obvious curiosity. "Actually, Jared—he's my patient— seemed quite impressed when I showed it to him. He asked to interview you himself."

"Impressed?" Summer laughed.

"Go figure." Juanita leaned forward, lowering

her voice. "I just wanted to prepare you. Jared's been going through a tough time from a rehab point of view. He's paralyzed from the waist down, and he suffered severe lacerations to his head, neck, and right hand. He's just now regaining the use of his vocal cords. He has to speak quietly, and you have to work to listen. It's like talking to someone with a very hoarse voice."

Summer nodded. "Is he still . . . you know . . . bandaged and stuff?"

"Most of his face is," Juanita said as she counted off the details on her fingers, "plus his right hand and his neck. And his right leg's in a cast. They need to put a new pin in his ankle soon."

Summer winced. "He must be in a lot of pain."

"As much emotional as physical. He's pretty much alone here. His family pays the bills, but that's all they do. It's a real shame." She blinked back tears. "The staff tries to be there for him, but I suggested a companion might be a good idea. Jared's been reluctant to go ahead, but I finally placed the ad anyway."

She stood, cocking her head at Summer, still sizing her up. "So. I just wanted you to know what you may be getting yourself into. By the way, it's live-in if you want it. There's a whole wing for the staff."

"I have an apartment," Summer said. "I just want a normal nine-to-five kind of job."

Juanita shook her head. "Let me tell you something, Summer. There is nothing at all normal about this job."

Summer watched her leave. She moved purposefully, like someone on a tight deadline. Summer had the feeling Juanita didn't think she was up to the job.

A few moments later, as a big wheelchair slowly rolled into view, Summer wondered if maybe Juanita was right.

# 17

## The Invisible Man

Sitting in the chair, erect, almost stiff, was a slender figure in a denim shirt. A white blanket was draped over his legs, one of which was in a cast. His right hand was wrapped in bandages nearly as thick as a boxing glove.

But it was his face—or what she could see of it—that made Summer's stomach lurch. It was swathed in so much white gauze that only his eyes, his ears, and part of the back of his head were visible.

Like a mummy, she thought. Trapped.

Summer tried not to react. She looked him directly in the eyes, went over, and took his left hand.

"It's nice to meet you, Jared," she said. "I'm Summer Smith."

His tight grip surprised her because he appeared so frail. He looked up at her. Staring out from the white bandages, his dark eyes were startling, like a snowman's coal eyes.

"Summer. What a wonderful name." His voice was like a whispering stream over gravel. He studied her hand and made a noise that might have been a laugh but sounded more like a cough. "Good upper arm strength," he quoted from her résumé. "I like that."

Summer smiled. "I lifted a lot of trays."

A pause followed. He stared at her blatantly. From anyone else it would have been rude, but Summer didn't mind—maybe because she was staring too.

"Well, I'll leave you two," the nurse said. "Buzz me if you need anything, Jared."

"Thanks, Juanita."

Juanita gave a nod to Summer. "It was nice meeting you, Summer."

"You too."

Jared waited until Juanita had closed the door behind her. "Juanita's great. But very protective," he said. "So. You live here on the key?" His voice came slow and hushed, like air hissing from a tire.

Summer nodded. "Right in Old Town. An apartment in a Victorian house."

"Roommates?"

"My friend Marquez and my cousin Diana."

He paused, nodding, as if this information required some time to digest.

"Family?"

She noticed he spoke briefly, as if long sentences tired him. Maybe they did. With all those tight bandages, his lips could probably barely move.

"In Minnesota. That's where I'm from. Bloomington. The Mall of America's there." She rolled her eyes. She was babbling again. She always babbled when she was uncomfortable.

Jared appeared to smile, though it was hard to tell. It seemed to be less a full-fledged smile than a slight shift of the bandages surrounding his mouth.

"Boyfriend?"

Summer hesitated. "Um, yes."

"I'm not surprised."

She stared at her hands.

"Sorry. None of my business."

"No, that's okay. I'm engaged," Summer said. "His name is Seth. I had a ring, but it's temporarily vanished. At least I hope it's temporary."

Jared moved a little in his chair, wincing with the effort. He took such a long time to speak that Summer found herself trying to guess his next words.

"He's very lucky," he said finally.

"Well, that's debatable," she said with a shrug, "but thanks."

"So. Juanita told you the duties?"

"A little bit. Running errands, reading, that sort of thing."

"Chess?"

"Um, I don't play, I'm afraid. But I'd love to learn. And I'm great at poker."

"Movies?"

"I love movies. TV too."

He was staring again. She felt a little like a painting that had just been unveiled.

"Questions?"

"Well, hours, pay, all that."

"What hours do you want?"

"I guess like any regular job. Nine to five. Although," she added with a smile, "if you could make it ten to six, that'd be cool. I have this tendency to oversleep."

"Make your own hours."

"Really? Wow. Well, okay, but I'm flexible. Like if you wanted to go down to the beach and watch the sunrise or something, I could set my alarm." She flushed. Maybe he couldn't leave the house. "Is that something you could do? Go outside?"

He moved his head—a nod, she thought. "We have a specially equipped van."

"I was thinking we could just, you know, go out in the garden or maybe walk down the street. I could push your wheelchair—"

"It's electric."

"Oh. Well, then, maybe I could ride with you." She laughed, then wondered again if she'd put her foot in her mouth. "I'm sorry. I guess I'm not sure what to say."

"You're doing fine," he said. "How's twenty an hour to start?"

"Twenty dollars? An *hour*?"

"Okay, twenty-five."

"That's like . . . wow. That's more than minimum wage by a long shot."

"It's not an easy job." For the first time Jared looked away, past Summer to the blue-green waves. "Does this . . . disgust . . . ?"

Summer hesitated. At first she thought he'd said "discuss." Then she realized with a start what he meant: Did this job disgust her? Did *he* disgust her?

"Oh, no," she exclaimed. "Why would you even think that? You were hurt in an accident. Why would I feel anything but . . ." She clutched at the air, searching for the right word. Not *pity*, that wasn't right. "Why would I feel anything but compassion? It could just as easily be me in that wheelchair as you."

"I don't think so," he said in a barely audible voice. He looked at her. His eyes seemed even darker. She wondered if they had tears in them. "Are you sure?"

"Wait a minute. Are you offering me the job?"

"I'd be grateful if you'd take it."

Summer grinned. "So when do I start?"

"Soon. Please."

She went to him and shook his hand, and then she saw for certain that he was crying.

# 18

## Truth or Dare

Diver opened the door even before Caroline could knock. She was wearing a pink dress, something frilly that Marquez would never have been caught dead in. When she sashayed past him into Austin's living room, she left a flowery scent in her wake.

"You might want to close the door," she advised, settling on the couch, feet demurely crossed at the ankles. "I assume we're alone?"

"Austin's at work."

"Sit, sit. We have so much to discuss, Paul."

Diver leaned back against the door, arms crossed over his bare chest. "Just say it, Caroline."

"Jeez, you've turned into such a sourpuss. 'Course,

you always were a little . . . odd." She batted her eyelids. "Still, who knew you'd fill out so nicely? I might have paid more attention to you if I'd known."

"What do you want from me?"

Caroline tapped her finger on her chin. "Not a man to mince words, are you? Like my daddy. He's a lawyer, did you know that? I had one of the clerks at his office do a little fishin' for me—bein' the boss's baby girl does have its advantages—and I came up with the juiciest little tidbits about you, Paul."

"Such as?"

Caroline pulled several pages of faxes from her purse. "Well, for starters, there's an outstanding warrant for your arrest, but then you knew that." She glanced up at him. "Arson, murder, you name it. And here I always thought of you as an underachiever."

"I didn't do it, Caroline." His voice sounded distant and hollow, as if someone else were saying the words in a far-off room.

"Hmm. That's going to take a little convincing, isn't it, Paul? What with the flammable liquid all over the place—"

"What liquid?" Diver demanded.

"The police found traces of a solvent that could have been used to start the fire." She consulted her papers, biting her lower lip in concentration. "Nothing conclusive, apparently, but still . . ." She shook her head, smiling sympathetically. "It doesn't look good."

"He was refinishing some furniture on the porch," Diver murmured. "Maybe that was it."

"Could be. But then there's the other matter of your history."

"What history?"

"You know. All those pesky domestic calls to the house." Caroline put her hand to her chest. "I can still remember police cars showin' up at all hours. My mama would look out the window and say, 'Paul's daddy's havin' a bad day again.'" She lowered her voice. "And that time your mama went with the police, her eye as black as night—I tell you, I will never forget it till the day I die. We were just little kids then. Maybe you don't even remember."

Diver clenched his hands. He remembered, all right.

"But then, even after she died, the way your daddy would take his hand to you! My Lord, he had a temper." She set the papers aside. "It's only natural he would come to a sorry end. Frankly, I don't blame you one bit."

"I didn't kill him," Diver said, but even as he said it he had a flash of the fire behind him, receding from view as he ran like he'd never run before, his feet bare on the dewy lawn, his head bleeding. Running away. His father's screams had been drowned out by the sounds of the fire devouring everything in its path.

What he should have said was, "I don't remember killing him."

"Paul? You look a little pale."

Diver went to the kitchen and splashed water on his face. He wondered if he was going to be sick.

As he dried his face with a paper towel, Austin's phone rang. "I'll get it," Caroline volunteered sweetly.

"Don't!" Diver cried, lunging for the receiver. But it was too late.

"Hello?" Caroline said. She looked over at Diver. "Yes, he's here. Just a moment."

Diver grabbed the phone away.

"Diver? It's Summer."

"This isn't a good time, Summer."

"Who was that? The accent sounded familiar. Is that Caroline?"

"Yeah. She was just leaving."

Summer paused. "Look, I need to talk to you about Marquez. She says she's not going to counseling tomorrow. I thought if we got together—"

"Maybe later."

"Diver," Summer said sternly, "I know you aren't thrilled about having me in your life. I'm not thrilled about it either. But you're the one who said we had to work together to keep an eye on Marquez."

"I know." Diver glanced at Caroline. "Why don't you come over in half an hour?"

"I can't. I might run into Austin."

"Fine. I'll meet you at Surfin' Sam's, that little restaurant on the water. Half an hour."

"Good. Hey, you okay?"

"Yeah. Never better."

He hung up the phone. "Your sister?" Caroline inquired. "I've been meaning to get together with her. I'm sure she'd love to hear me reminisce about you as a kid. All the time she missed . . . it's a real tragedy, your being kidnapped and all. What a life you've had."

"How do you know about that?"

"Blythe told me. She heard it from someone at work who knows Marquez and Summer. It fit together nicely, once I had all the pieces." Caroline clucked her tongue. "Very movie-of-the-week, really. At least you had the good sense to be kidnapped by someone with big bucks."

"What are you talking about? They didn't have any money."

"Oh, but that's where you're wrong, Paul." Caroline waved her faxes in the air. "Mind if I get a drink? The heat here is just wilting me."

She poured herself a glass of water and drank it slowly, letting him wait. "See, it turns out your mean ol' daddy had a big stash of money. Guess there was a lot of insurance on your mama—what did she die of, anyway?"

"Cancer."

"Well, he made a killing, pardon the pun, and you, Paul—Diver, I mean—are the only heir." She shook her head. "Darn the luck, though. You go to claim the money, and sure as night follows day, they'll arrest your pretty little butt for murder. Isn't life funny sometimes?"

Diver sat down. He no longer trusted his legs. He felt he should say something, but there was nothing left to say. He'd been running from the truth for years. The truth always had a way of catching up with you, though.

"So what's your point, Caroline?" he asked wearily.

"Well, you can see how awkward my position is. I mean, I *have* to turn you in, Paul. It's my duty as a citizen." She tapped her finger on her chin. "Of course, if we went in together and I told them a nice little story about how I woke up that night and looked out my bedroom window, how I saw you try to save your daddy by runnin' bravely back into the flames . . . well, you get the idea. I could turn you into a hero, Paul. They'd drop the charges, probably give you the key to the city."

"And your motivation for this would be . . . ?"

"Eighty percent of the insurance money." Her voice had lost its southern sweetness. "I was going to take it all, but I'm a good Christian. And I believe in giving even the worst sinner a second chance."

"This is blackmail."

"Go ahead and complain to the police. I dare you."

"They'll ask you why you didn't tell them all this earlier," Diver pointed out.

She shrugged. "Post-traumatic stress, isn't that what you call it? I'll tell them I blotted the whole awful episode right out of my mind."

She sat back against the couch and checked her watch. "So, what'll it be? The gas chamber or a ticker-tape parade? Seems like a pretty easy choice to me."

Diver closed his eyes. Sometimes, when he concentrated hard enough, he could still feel the heat of the fire sweeping toward him, enraged, like a living thing.

He opened his eyes. "You're right, Caroline," he said. "It's a pretty easy choice, all right."

# 19

## True Confessions at Surfin' Sam's

"Have a burger. It's on me," Summer said to Diver as he slipped into the chair across from her. "I'm officially employed. Not only that, I'm overpaid."

Diver said something, but she couldn't hear him. Surfin' Sam's, a beachfront burger joint that was little more than a large shack, was filled to the brim with tourists and locals. Most were in bathing suits, half were toting surfboards, and all were rowdy.

"What did you say?" Summer asked loudly.

"Congratulations."

"Thanks." She took a sip of her Coke. "Diver, what's wrong? You look sick."

"Flu, I think. I'm okay."

Summer reached across the table and felt his head. "You sure?"

"Positive, Mom."

"Fry?"

"I'm not hungry."

"This is totally none of my business," Summer said, "so you can tell me to back off, but what was Caroline doing at your place?"

Diver tapped his fingers on the table, glaring at her. "Back off."

"Oh, come on, Diver. You know darn well Marquez will tell me anyway."

"It's really not that interesting."

"Humor me."

Diver sighed. "Caroline was right, it turns out. We *were* neighbors way back when. Only it was when we were really little, and she had the place wrong. It was in North Carolina. My folks—my other folks—lived there for a while. So did her family."

"So who's Paul?"

"She got the name wrong too. Between you and me, Caroline's not all that tightly wrapped." He shrugged. "Paul was this guy who lived down the block from us. A real bully. Used to terrorize us both." He gave a lame laugh. "She stopped by, we reminisced. I think . . . you know, maybe she was coming on to me."

"Wouldn't surprise me. Every girl at Blooming-ton High wanted to be my friend while you were going to school there. You made me very popular. Temporarily." She pushed her plate aside. "You want my advice?"

He smiled grimly. "No."

"Whatever you do, don't tell Marquez about Caroline. The last thing she needs to worry about right now is the possibility of losing you."

"Why would she lose me?" Diver asked sharply.

"To another girl," Summer said. "There are lots of Carolines out there, lying in wait to prey on naive, unsuspecting guys like you. Why else?"

The waitress buzzed past and handed Diver a menu. "Thanks, he said, "but I'm just passing through."

"Too bad for me," she replied with a wink.

Summer rolled her eyes. "I rest my case."

"Look," Diver said, leaning close, "I need you to make Marquez understand that she has to take better care of herself. It's her responsibility."

"I've tried," Summer said. "I was hoping you could get through to her."

Diver combed his fingers through his hair. "I'm not the best one to give lectures on responsi-bility. I have a tendency to walk out when things get tough."

"At least you leave polite notes behind," Summer

said. "Allow me to quote in full: 'I'm sorry.' No greet-
ing, no signature. Succinct, to the point, no unnecessary emotion."

She saw the pain in his eyes and almost regretted
her sarcastic tone. They were there to talk about
Marquez, not to reopen old wounds.

"I need you to promise me something, Summer,"
Diver said. "No matter how you feel about me, you'll
always be there for Marquez, right?"

"Of course I will. She's my best friend."

He leaned back, studying her. "It's easy for you,"
he said.

"What?"

"Sticking around for people. Loyalty."

Summer gave a rueful laugh. "Not always. Ask
Seth."

"Still, when you say you'll stick by Marquez and
get her through this, I know you mean it. If I said it, it
would be just . . . words."

Summer gazed at her brother. Diver was talking
in riddles. He was good at that. Of course, he was also
good at talking to pelicans. He was like an onion: peel
away one layer of mystery and there was always another
one waiting.

"Diver," she said softly, "are you sure you're
okay?"

"I'm always okay. You know that."

Against her better judgment, she reached across the table and squeezed his hand.

"Have you forgotten you hate me?"

"I don't hate you, Diver. You just . . . disappointed me is all."

"It's a habit of mine."

"That's water under the bridge. The real problem is Marquez. I'll talk to her, make her see how worried you are. Maybe I can get through to her with a guilt trip—I'll say you're a wreck and that she owes you."

"She doesn't owe me. I owe her. She's the first person I've ever really let myself love since . . . you know. Since I was little."

"Since Mom and Dad," Summer said softly, waiting for the inevitable clarification, the "Jack and Kim."

But Diver simply nodded. "And since you."

The moment hung suspended in time, floating between them like a fragile soap bubble. Neither moved or spoke for fear it would burst.

At last Diver pushed back his chair. "Well, I need to go."

"I know you're worried about Marquez," Summer said. "But she'll be fine. You love her, and I love her. And she can count on us, right?"

"Right," Diver whispered, speaking not to her, it seemed, but to some secret part of himself.

# 20

# It's Always So Nice to Get Mail

When Summer got back to the apartment, it was empty. There was a note from Seth on the counter:

> *Hi, Summer—*
> *Marquez is at work, Diana's at her volunteer thing, I'm out ring shopping. Back from Woolworth soon. I love you.*

Summer smiled. She went to her room and changed into a pair of cutoffs and a T-shirt. The room was a mess. Apparently Diana had been on another reorganizing frenzy. There were boxes everywhere, papers on the floor, clothes on her bed and on Summer's.

Summer sighed. Maybe the problem was that Diana had grown up with a maid to clean up after her. Summer had to clear off a place on her bed just to sit down.

She felt like napping. She wasn't tired, really, but she wanted to sleep away the images that kept coming back to her, haunting her mind: Austin the night before, drunk, depressed, in pain because of her. Jared that day, trapped in a mangled body, willing to pay a stranger to be his friend. And Diver just now, unreachable as always, trying nonetheless to say he loved her.

At least that was what she thought he'd been trying to say. With Diver, it was difficult to ever really know.

She thought of Seth, out buying a ring at Woolworth's, and smiled. Sweet, reliable, solid Seth. Sometimes she didn't realize how lucky she was. At least with Seth she always knew where she stood.

She pushed back her sheets, tossing aside more of Diana's stuff. She should have known better than to share a room with her cousin. This bedroom was the size of Diana's old closet in her former house. *One* of her closets.

Summer grabbed a box of postcards and odds and ends off her pillow. Underneath it was a letter. She tossed it in the box and shoved the box onto Diana's side of the room.

With a sigh, she crawled under her sheets and closed her eyes.

Her eyes flew open.

*Seth,* the letter had said. The name had been written in Diana's careful, perfect handwriting.

Why would Diana have been writing Seth?

Summer climbed out of bed and went over to the box. She fished out the note and began to read.

> *1/14*
>
> *Seth:*
>
> *This is my fifth letter to you. You haven't received any of them because I haven't sent any of them, and I probably won't send this one either. I'm not used to embarrassing myself, and I'm not used to being the one doing the chasing. Face it, I'm used to guys coming after me. This is a new experience. I'm sure you're smiling to yourself right now in that smug way you sometimes do.*
>
> *But anyway, here goes. I know you think what happened between us New Year's Eve was a terrible mistake.*

Summer paused. She went over to her bed and sat down on the edge, clutching the letter to her chest. New Year's Eve.

*What happened between us New Year's Eve.*

She plunged to the letter's finish, like a reader who just had to know how the story ended.

> *The point is, I've always been in love with you,*
> *Seth, and I just never had the nerve*

That was it. No signature, no finish.

Summer read the letter again, this time taking in each word. When she was done, she did not cry or tear up the letter or crumple it. She put it back in the box.

She went to the closet and pulled out her battered old suitcase. Carefully she packed: tops, jeans, shorts, a couple of skirts, underwear.

She went to the bathroom and got her brush, hair dryer, shampoo, and conditioner. Toothbrush, floss, Tampax.

She zipped up the suitcase. Her hands were not trembling. Her lip was not quivering. She felt strangely, eerily calm, the unnatural quiet in the eye of a hurricane.

She got a phone number from her purse, then found Diana's cell phone and dialed.

"Juanita?" she said calmly. "It's Summer Smith. I've changed my mind about the live-in position."

When she hung up, she found a pen and a notepad. The first note was to Marquez.

*Marquez—*
*I am at 1304 Naples Avenue in Eden Shores.*
*Please come see me. Promise you'll go to coun-*
*seling tomorrow. Diver is really worried.*
*Don't worry about me. I'm fine.*

She got a fresh piece of paper. She thought for a while. At last she wrote:

*Seth and Diana—*
*I know everything. Do not try to get in touch with me.*
*Summer*

Succinct, to the point, no unnecessary emotion. It was a note to make Diver proud.

# 21

## Summer Returns

When the doorbell rang, he was already waiting, his left hand tightly clutching the arm of his wheelchair.

"Shall I, sir?" Stan, the butler, asked.

"Please."

The door swung wide, and there she was: the long tanned legs, the hair like yellow silk.

"Summer," he said.

Her face was drawn, pale. "Thank you for letting me come, Jared."

She stepped inside. Stan took her bag.

"The west wing, sir?"

"What color do you like?" he asked Summer. "Blue, yellow, cream? Your pick."

"I don't care," she said softly.

"Blue, then," he said, and Stan headed upstairs.

He held out his good hand. "I'm glad you'll be staying here with us," he said. "It'll be good to have you."

She took his hand and nodded. Her eyes were glassy. She looked as though she weren't quite sure where she was.

"I had a change of plans," she said.

"I understand."

Juanita came down the stairs. She glanced at Summer's hand in his disapprovingly, but he held on a little longer.

"Well, this certainly is a surprise," Juanita said. "But of course we're pleased to have you join the staff. Will you be having dinner with us this evening?"

"I . . . no. I'm not hungry, thank you."

"I wish you would," he said.

Summer looked at him. "We'll see," she said.

"You're all right?" Juanita asked. "You look a bit under the weather."

"I had a, um, a situation I had to deal with." Summer twisted the Kleenex she was carrying. "I'm okay, though."

"Perhaps after you're settled we can meet to discuss your duties," Juanita suggested. "I thought a regular schedule might be easier for Jared—reading in the morning, time in the garden in the afternoon, things like that. Perhaps we can put together an activities list."

"That would be fine."

"Juanita," he said, "let her rest. She just got here, and she's obviously had a hard day."

Juanita shrugged. "Fine. We'll meet in the morning, then. Nine sharp?"

"Nine," Summer said flatly.

"I'll be in the kitchen, Jared, if you need me."

"I'll be fine," he said. "Summer and I will be fine."

"All right, then. If you're sure." Juanita marched off.

Summer stood quietly in the foyer next to his chair. A shaft of light through the window made her seem to glow. Or maybe it was just his imagination seeing something that wasn't really there.

"Why don't we go out to the porch?" he suggested.

Summer blinked, momentarily confused, a stranger in a foreign land. "Oh," she said, "all right." She gestured toward the door. "After you."

He guided his chair to the porch. She followed behind him.

When they got there, she went to the screened window and stared out at the ocean.

"So something happened," he said, hoping he sounded gentle, not too prying.

She nodded.

"I'm sorry."

She turned. "Don't be. What happened . . . it's nothing like what happened to you. A small thing, really."

"Matters of the heart are never small."

He said it in that flat, asthmatic way he could not avoid. The way an old man would talk, waging a battle in his throat to form each word. Talking made him terribly tired, but he so wanted to talk to her.

She sat beside him. He could smell her, an alive, sweet scent that made him ache for all he had lost.

"How did you know it was a matter of the heart?" she asked. She smiled a little when she said the word *heart*.

"I had a few . . . matters of my own, before." Instantly he wished he hadn't made reference to the time before. It sounded self-pitying. The last thing he wanted was Summer's pity. "And I could tell. Your eyes look so sad."

She glanced down as if she was embarrassed. "My boyfriend and my cousin. I found out they had a . . . relationship I didn't know about."

He looked away, too, letting it all sink in, word by word. The quiet seemed unbearable. He knew he should say something, anything.

"You must feel very betrayed."

"I trusted them. I thought I was the one making all the mistakes, and then it turned out—" A catch in her voice made her stop—a sob, but not quite. "I'm sorry. To sit here, feeling sorry for myself, when you've gone through so much more . . . what a jerk I am."

He tried to shrug, which was hard, and wished again for the simple ways people communicated—a wave of the hand, a wink, a nudge. All lost to him, at least for the time being.

"Physical pain is different. You can fight it more easily because it's . . ." He didn't know where to go. He hadn't tried to talk about it before.

"I think I know what you mean," Summer said. "Because it's a thing outside yourself, in a way. Emotional pain is inside you. Is that it?"

He nodded. It was so good to talk to her. It was as though the electricity had gone off in a violent storm and now, in the space of a moment, the power was on again, the lights worked, the phone was connected. He was part of the world once more.

She was there in his house. There, after so long. After so much silence.

"For him to hurt you like this, he must have truly lost his way," he said. "He must have forgotten what matters. It can happen. Even when you don't mean to, it's easy to lose track of what's most important. . . ."

He could see the look of confusion in her eyes. He was saying too much too fast. He was scaring her— with his words, but no doubt with his physical self as well. He sometimes forgot how frightening he was. He'd had all the mirrors removed long ago.

"I think maybe I need to lie down," Summer said. "Would that be okay?"

"Of course. Your room is up the stairs, the first one on the right. If you need anything, ask one of the staff."

"Maybe later I could read something to you," Summer said shyly. "If you'd like."

"You rest tonight. There's plenty of time for that."

"It might be good. It might take my mind off everything." She stood. "No romances, though."

He laughed, or at least tried to. It had been so long, his face didn't remember how to laugh anymore.

"Well . . . I'll go unpack."

She paused at the door. She was looking at him with pity, he knew that, and yet it pleased him just to have such a beautiful woman looking at him at all.

"Have you read *Huckleberry Finn*?"

"Not in a long time."

"Maybe we'll start with that, Jared."

He watched her slowly climb the stairs. For a

moment he thought he could hear her voice lingering in the air, saying the other name, saying "Adam."

It had been so long since he'd heard her say it.

Maybe someday, when he had the courage, he would ask her to say it again.

# 22

## Diver Says Good-bye

Austin crossed the lawn wearily. His brain throbbed indignantly. After the abuse he'd heaped on it the night before, he couldn't really blame it.

He was almost to the porch when Diver emerged from the apartment. His sleeping bag and backpack were slung over his shoulder.

"Hey, where are you off to?" Austin asked.

Diver looked uncomfortable. "Thought maybe I'd do a little camping for a couple of days," he said. "You know, adjust my *wa* and all that."

"Does your *wa* realize you just started a new job?"

"Yeah, well . . . the people at work, they're cool with it."

"You're not moving out because I made a drunken ass of myself in front of your sister last night, are you?"

Diver smiled. "No. I didn't even know you'd made a drunken ass of yourself."

"I have no idea what happened. I mean, I'm a rational guy. I'm not some slobbering, incoherent fool who'd crash a party and completely humiliate himself. Or so I thought."

"I saw Summer a while ago. She didn't even mention it, Austin."

Austin couldn't help feeling a little disappointed. "Nothing?"

"Nothing. Hey, I gotta get going."

"Far be it from me to interfere, but you're okay, right, man?"

"Yeah. I just feel like taking a little break from the real world." Diver strode away. At the curb he stopped. "If you see Summer—"

"That's not too likely, I'm afraid."

"Well, if you do, tell her something for me, okay?"

"Sure. You name it."

"Tell her she was right about me all along."

He was lucky. There was a Greyhound leaving at seven for Miami.

He took a seat near the back. The bus was almost

empty: a couple of kids, a guy with tattoos weaving up his forearms, a grandmother type. The bus smelled of diesel fumes. The seat was sticky.

Diver felt right at home.

He'd done the dog a lot the last few years. Mostly he'd hitched, but every now and then he'd come into some cash and taken the high road. He liked the anonymous feel of the bus. People left you alone. They all had their problems—tearful departures, uncertain destinations, missed connections.

The bus growled to life, and the door squealed shut. They backed out onto the tiny main street that bisected Old Town. It was packed with tourists: families on rented bicycles, in-line skaters, couples strolling hand in hand and eating ice cream while they window-shopped.

It took Diver a minute to realize they were going to pass right by Marquez's apartment. As it came into view he considered ducking. But the windows were tinted, and no one would expect to see him there.

Then he saw her.

She was standing in front of Jitters, her waitress apron over her shoulder, a cup of coffee in her hand. She was watching the crowds pass by.

For a moment she looked at the bus, taking it in without knowing. The breeze moved her hair. She pushed it back with a gesture both impatient and graceful.

Diver reached into his backpack. He found the note he'd written. It was long by his standards, even rambling. And it was full of passion, full of pleas for forgiveness.

As if he deserved any.

He crumpled it up. He was glad he hadn't left it for her, and now he knew he wouldn't ever send it.

This time he understood that no note could ever undo the pain he was causing.

This time he knew he could not be forgiven.

You didn't walk out on the people you loved. You didn't run when things got complicated.

Summer didn't.

He did.

The bus turned, and he looked back one last time. The street was bathed in the orange light of sunset, erasing Marquez, blinding him.

The sky, he thought, looked as if it were on fire.

august

# 1

# How Not to Dot Your *I*'s

It was a simple enough note. No question what it meant.

And yet as she held it, the paper shivering slightly between clamped fingers, Diana found herself recalling an article on handwriting analysis she'd read somewhere. One of her mom's *Cosmo*s, maybe, something with a title like "Love Letters: How to Read Between His Lines."

Of course, this would technically come under the heading of a "hate letter." And it wasn't from a guy—it was from her cousin.

Diana studied the note again, as if the handful of words had been written in code:

> *Seth and Diana—I know everything. Do not*
> *try to get in touch with me.*
> *Summer*

The broad stroke across the *t*. The thick period, almost a dash, after the name. The sharp, hurried writing, nothing like Summer's usual silly, feminine loops. Summer, who'd been known to dot her I's with hearts. Yes, if the handwriting was any indication, Summer was most definitely furious.

That was, after all, what Diana had intended. It hadn't surprised her to come home to the apartment and see Summer's closet half emptied, her suitcase gone.

Everything was going according to plan.

Except for this note. Diana hadn't expected it. The words on paper made everything so permanent and official. She'd felt this way when they'd handed over her driver's license, the plastic coating still a little warm, the picture startled and not quite herself.

This was real. Diana had hurt her cousin in a way she could never take back. She'd wanted to hurt Summer, she'd had her reasons for hurting her, and yet now Diana couldn't take her eyes off the note in her trembling hands.

She heard a key fumbling in the lock. Seth, Summer's boyfriend, came in. He was carrying a package and a bouquet of roses.

"For me?" she asked sarcastically.

"Yeah, right." He tossed the roses aside. "Where's Summer?"

"You tell me." She held out the letter, vaguely noting the way it continued to flutter in her fingers like a trapped moth.

Seth grabbed the paper from her. She watched him take in the words, the permanent, official words, just as she had.

"You *told* her about us?"

"I have no idea how she found out," Diana said, snatching back the note.

*Unless, of course, it was the love letter I wrote you,* she added silently. *The one I left out so Summer would find it.*

Seth sank against the counter. His lips worked at forming words, but none came. She imagined those lips on her mouth, her neck, remembered the sure and gentle way he had of kissing.

"But how?" Seth said at last. "How could she have found out?"

"The point is, she was going to find out eventually, Seth."

"But not now, not when I finally thought we had things worked out. . . ."

Diana turned toward the sink, away from Seth's wounded eyes. "You've gotten through other stuff. Maybe she'll forgive you for this."

"She'll never forgive either of us."

"I know," Diana admitted. It was a price she'd been willing to pay to win Seth for good. Lose a cousin, gain a cousin's boyfriend. It had seemed like a reasonable exchange.

"Where do you think she went?" Seth asked.

"She left a note for Marquez. You could read it. Maybe it says something."

Seth marched to Marquez's bedroom. A moment later he returned. "Summer is at that new job of hers, taking care of that handicapped guy. I guess she's staying at his house." He gazed at the peach-colored roses on the counter. "You told her, didn't you?"

Diana didn't answer.

"I thought so."

"She loves Austin, Seth. Why can't you see that?"

"But she *chose* me."

The catch in his voice made her reach for him. She was surprised when he didn't push her away. She kissed him, hoping he might kiss her back, knowing he wouldn't.

"*I* chose you too, Seth," she whispered, pulling away.

"Then you chose wrong." He rubbed his eyes. They were both silent. Through the French doors came the sound of the ocean, sighing again and again over some great, unspeakable loss.

"I was going to head back to California tomorrow," Seth said. "But I can't leave now, not with things like this."

Diana stared at the note in her hand. Things with Summer, he meant. "What about things with . . ." With us, she wanted to say, but of course she didn't.

"With what?"

Diana turned away. Slowly she tore the letter into long, neat strips. She stuffed them into the garbage disposal. She ran the water. With a flick of the switch the disposal chewed up the paper, growling purposefully.

Diana turned off the disposal. She watched the water run. The note was gone, but she could still see the letters in her mind, the tight scrawl, the scribbled signature of the cousin she'd lost forever.

# 2

## "Betrayal" Is a Mighty Big Word

Summer woke from her nap in a room that was not her own. She blinked. For a brief, terrifying instant she had absolutely no idea where she was. She sat up, taking in the thick oriental rug, the deep blue wallpaper shimmering like satin, the Tiffany lamp sending jeweled patterns onto the ceiling.

Well, wherever she was, she'd clearly come into money.

Oh. She was at her job. Her brand-new, live-in companion job.

She was at her brand-new, live-in companion job because she couldn't ever go home again.

It was amazing, the way you could go to sleep and

leave your complicated life completely behind you. Of course, the waking up wasn't much fun.

She walked to the wide pair of doors that opened onto the balcony. It was nearly dark, and the air had a touch of coolness in it. The ocean view was stunning, endless black against a sky of velvety twilight blue, but her eyes were drawn back across the inlet to Coconut Key. The lights along the coast glowed yellow. The old lighthouse at the north end of the key swept its single eye over the dark water.

Running here to Jared's estate had made sense a few hours ago. It was the only place she knew of where she could avoid Seth and Diana indefinitely. And she was going to be working here every day, anyway. One whole wing was filled with assorted staff members.

But now, standing here on the balcony, it seemed crazy, almost pathetic. Summer had never felt quite so thoroughly alone. She was barely on speaking terms with her brother. Her best friend, Marquez, was caught up in her own problems. And Summer had just learned she'd been betrayed by her cousin and her fiancé.

*Betrayal.* It was a big, dramatic word, like something from her English class on Shakespeare. From the Cliff's Notes, anyway.

She smiled, just a little. It was too much like a soap opera to be her life. Of course, in soap operas the main characters didn't run off to hide and lick their wounds, not unless they were due to be killed off because the ratings were down.

She was surprised at how empty she felt. Shouldn't she be throwing things, vowing revenge, cursing the names of Seth and Diana? In a soap opera she would get even. She would steal Seth back from Diana, she would make Seth pay for his lies. Or at least get amnesia, adopt a new identity, and return to town as a redhead.

But all she felt was emptiness. It almost disappointed her. Was she such a wimp she couldn't even dredge up a decent anger high? Marquez would be outraged on Summer's behalf. Why couldn't Summer manage to feel anything?

She tried to imagine Diana in Seth's arms. Tried to imagine them laughing at how naive Summer was, how they'd faked her out. She felt like a computer in need of a bigger memory. A little more RAM—maybe then she'd see the whole picture. Maybe then she'd come up with the appropriate feelings.

She heard a soft motorized whir and looked down to see Jared, the guy she'd been hired to assist, moving slowly down the long cement path to the beach. He was swathed in bandages—his arms, his face, one leg. The other leg was in a cast.

He paused at the sand's edge, unable to go farther. He looked so alone, even more alone than Summer. She wondered why his family wasn't here for him. He had no friends, just the people hired to care for him. And now Summer was one of them, his paid companion.

When she'd come running here, suitcase in hand, she'd told Jared what had happened. *For him to hurt you like this,* he'd said, *he must have truly lost his way.*

Losing your way. It was a nice phrase. It was how she'd felt a lot this summer, since graduating. Lost. Faced with hard choices and no nice neat plan to guide her—just her hunches about what made sense. As if life were one humongous, unsolvable geometry problem. Which college to choose. Which job to take. Which guy to pick—Austin or Seth.

She'd picked Seth. Out of loyalty, and out of love. So much for hunches.

She went back into the huge bedroom. A large stone fireplace dominated one end of the room, but it was hard to imagine ever using it here in Florida. Around the fireplace dark wood shelves held thick, leather-bound books. She scanned the shelves, found a couple of promising titles, and pulled them out. She'd promised Jared she'd read to him tonight.

Summer headed down the long, winding staircase. The house was quiet, as immaculate as a hospital and just about as sterile. Even the perfectly manicured garden in the back seemed antiseptic—not a dying bloom or fallen leaf anywhere.

"Hi, Jared," she said quietly, hoping not to startle him.

He turned his bandaged head an inch or two. Again she was reminded of a mummy. Between the bandages covering his injuries from the car accident, the cast on his leg, and the expensive clothes, the only parts of his body visible were his dark, luminous eyes and his left hand.

"I thought you were napping," he said in the hoarse whisper caused by his injured vocal cords.

"I was. It was nice too. I sort of forgot everything." She sat on the white bench at the end of the path.

"I do that," Jared said. "Then when I wake up, I'm always sort of shocked by all these bandages."

Summer nodded. His problems were so enormous that she felt her own shrivel in comparison. "I brought *Huckleberry Finn*," she said. "And something about spies I've never heard of. I thought I could read to you, if you want."

Jared stared at her in that unselfconscious way he had, as if she were an expensive museum piece he'd just acquired. "We'll start tomorrow. You relax, sit here. You had a rough day."

"Not so rough."

"Your boyfriend and your cousin—" Jared began, letting the rest go unsaid. "That's pretty rough."

Summer's eyes stung, surprising her with tears. She

hadn't cried yet. But the sound of pity in a stranger's voice was like the starting shot she'd been waiting for. She looked away, down the thin white beach. The sky was the vivid, unreal blue of night starting. Gaslights in the garden glowed like huge fireflies.

"I just feel like such a fool," Summer said, still looking away. "How could I not have known there was something between them? I can even understand how Seth might have had feelings for someone else, because *I* do. Did, I mean. But to keep it from me, all these months . . ."

"Did you tell him?" Jared asked.

Summer turned to face him. He seemed to be straining toward her, leaning in his wheelchair with effort. She wondered if he was so intensely curious because he'd been starved for companionship for many months, or if he was just being polite.

"I told him eventually," she admitted. She managed a weak smile. "I know, I know. How can I be mad at him when I did the same . . . but it's not the same, not really. Diana's my cousin, Jared. For her and Seth to be together—I don't know. It feels different. Like a bigger betrayal."

Again that word. And again she wondered why she couldn't match her sad, small feelings to the big hurt it implied.

"I've done my share of betraying people," Jared

said. "It's much easier than you'd think. But cleaning up the mess afterward . . . that isn't so easy." The slight movement around his lips made her wonder if he was smiling.

The glass doors to the back porch eased open, and Summer turned to see Stan, Jared's butler. "A visitor to see Ms. Smith," he said in his clipped New England accent.

"Visitor?" Summer repeated. Marquez! Marquez had gotten her note and rushed over after work to commiserate. Summer felt a surge of relief.

"It's probably my roommate," Summer told Jared. "I hope you don't mind. I mean, we didn't really discuss whether it's okay for me to have guests—"

"Of course," Jared said. "It's your house too, for as long as you want."

She started down the long path that snaked through the garden. Stan was holding the door, waiting so stiffly that she felt a little like royalty. A figure appeared in the dim glow of the porch light. Summer gasped.

"Summer," Seth said. "We have to talk."

# 3

# First Love, First Good-bye

"I have nothing to say to you, Seth."

Seth rushed at her, grabbing her shoulders. His face was grim. "We have to talk. You have to let me explain."

Summer shook off his hands. "Please, Seth," she said.

She was terribly aware of Stan and Jared, perfect strangers watching her private drama unfold. She felt like an actor in a very poorly attended outdoor performance of *Laguna Beach*.

But Seth was adamant. "I'm not leaving."

"It's all right, Summer," Jared said, rolling toward her down the path. His voice was barely audible over the sound of the waves crashing on the beach. "I was just leaving."

When he reached them, Jared paused for a moment, the hum of his wheelchair suddenly quieted.

"Jared, this is Seth Warner," Summer said.

"Hi." Seth gave a terse nod.

"You okay?" Jared asked Summer.

"Fine. I'm sorry about this. Maybe we can read tomorrow."

"Tomorrow," Jared said. He tilted his head, eyeing Seth carefully, then headed toward the door where Stan was waiting.

Summer returned to the bench and sat stiffly. Seth joined her, careful to leave space between them. She realized suddenly that this could be the last time they saw each other. They would call it off. Seth would go back to California. Down the road they might run into each other—say, at a party for a mutual friend. She could picture the awkward, surprised glance, the cold, heavy feeling in her chest. She wondered if they would even acknowledge each other. Would they pretend all their time together had never happened?

"How did you find out?" Seth asked.

"A love letter. From Diana to you."

He gave a harsh laugh. "I never saw it."

"She never sent it."

"Diana wanted you to find out, you know."

Seth was staring at the ocean, not at her. "If we end things over this, it'll be just what she wanted to have happen."

Summer sighed. She had the strange desire to nestle close to him, not because she needed to, but out of habit. It seemed unreal, the two of them sitting there like strangers waiting for a bus.

"I can almost understand you wanting Diana," Summer said. She was surprised at how reasonable she sounded. "I mean, she's beautiful and smart and sexy and . . ."

"Not you," Seth finished. "She's not you, Summer."

"Maybe that was the whole point."

"There was no 'point,' it was just an . . . an accident. I didn't mean for it to happen—"

"Were you . . . together when she went out to California last week to visit?"

Seth squirmed a little. "We saw each other, yeah."

"Were you *together*?" Summer pressed.

He didn't answer. Well, duh, Summer. Connect the dots. She'd actually been naive enough to encourage Diana to visit Seth. They must have had a good laugh over that. Summer Smith, junior matchmaker.

"As I was saying," Summer continued in a prim lecturing voice that she'd never heard from herself before, "I could almost understand your going after Diana. The temptation and all. It's like Austin and me." She was glad when he winced a little. "But what I can't understand, Seth, is how you could have kept it from me all these months. How you could have let me feel so rotten and guilty about Austin when you knew what you'd done with Diana was every bit as bad. Worse, even."

"Why is it any worse?" Seth asked. "Why isn't it just the same?"

"I can't explain it—it just is. Because she's my cousin and my roommate, and you knew, you *both* knew, how much it would hurt me."

"You hurt me too, Summer. And I forgave you."

"Do you love Diana?"

"No," Seth said automatically. "Not exactly."

"Not exactly."

"I'm only *in* love with you. Doesn't that make it any better, Summer?"

"In a way it makes it worse, Seth. Because it means you were just using Diana. It makes me feel sorry for her."

"The using was mutual, trust me. You don't need to feel sorry for Diana. You think it was an accident I flew back here to see you? Diana's the one who told me you weren't wearing my ring anymore. She's the one who told me about Austin—" His voice cracked.

She watched the tears trail down his cheeks. It scared her how indifferent she felt. How numb. She'd only seen Seth cry a couple of times. But now, seeing him cry over her, it was like watching a movie where you'd already figured out the ending and you wondered if maybe you should go buy some more popcorn.

"Summer." Seth took her hand. "We can't let it end like this. This is crazy. We've been through too much together. We're engaged."

"We *were* engaged."

"What about everything you said last night?" Seth cried. He was growing increasingly frantic, but the more agitated he got, the more cool and centered she felt. "About how what mattered most was loyalty and faithfulness and all we'd gone through together? Are you telling me this is it? It's over?"

Summer thought for a while. The finality of it all began to penetrate, like a tiny flashlight in dense fog. "It just feels like we've gone through too much, Seth," she said softly. "It's like . . . like that car of yours that you finally sold to the junkyard for parts. That Dodge? Remember how you kept trying to patch it together and as soon as you did something else would go wrong—the back door fell off or the alternator died? And then that old man rear-ended you in the parking lot at Wendy's and you just said, okay, it's time to give up. This is like the final straw. This is our rear-ending at Wendy's."

She tried to smile, but the muscles wouldn't obey.

It occurred to her that only a few days ago, she'd told Austin it was over between them. In the space of a week she'd ended relationships with the two great loves of her life.

Last summer she'd come to the Keys just hoping to meet a cute guy, maybe even fall in love. She'd worried about her flirting technique and her dancing technique and her kissing technique.

And now here she was, polishing her breaking-up technique.

Suddenly she felt very old. Older than Seth. Older than her friends. Older even than those actors on reruns of *90210*.

Seth reached into his pocket. He held out something small and shiny in his palm, and she knew at once that it was another ring.

"I found it at Woolworth's today," Seth said. "A replacement ring for your replacement ring." He paused. "When Diana came to see me in California, she brought a ring with her. She said it was yours."

Summer gasped. "*She* found my ring and didn't tell me?"

"I was going to mail the real one to you when I got back to California. But now I guess you won't be needing it."

"No," Summer said softly.

Seth pressed the ring into her hand. "You might as

well take this. I've already got a real one. Besides, I'm not going back to California for a while."

"What? You have to go back and finish your internship. You said you were learning so much about boat building—"

"Screw all that. I'm going to go hang out with my grandfather on Crab Claw for a while. Finish up the summer there."

"Look, there's something you should know, Seth. I reapplied to Carlson College."

Seth looked at her blankly. "When?"

"Before this. Before I found out about you and Diana. I went for a visit, and I realized I was only going to UW to please you. Well, mostly I realized I was going there because I was afraid I wouldn't hack it at Carlson."

"I thought you wanted us to be together. So you were planning on breaking up with me all along?"

"No, no. I knew it was going to be hard, being at different colleges, but I thought you could try to reapply to Carlson next semester and—"

"What does it matter now?" Seth interrupted. "The point is, you were ready to give up on us."

"No." Summer closed her fingers around the little ring with its fake diamond. "I just wasn't ready to give up on myself. And you shouldn't be either. You should go back to California, finish out the internship."

Seth just shook his head.

"I'm glad for everything we had, Seth." Summer touched his damp cheek. "You'll always be my first love." She was glad she was being so generous. She didn't want to feel bad about this later. No scenes, no accusations.

"Maybe if we give it some time?" Seth said hoarsely.

She started to say, No, it's over, it's time for you to move on. But when she looked into his desperate, regretful eyes, she couldn't bring herself to say it.

"I don't know," she whispered. "Maybe."

The word was so small and sad, so pathetically hopeful. When Seth leaned over and softly kissed her, she felt something inside shift and crack.

She was almost relieved when she finally started to cry herself.

# 4

# Please Leave a Message After the Beep. . . .

Marquez marched down the sidewalk toward her boy-friend's apartment, her dark curls bouncing rhythmi-cally. She'd been calling Diver all evening without success. Now she was opting for the up-close-and-personal approach.

Her mind was reeling. After work she'd gone home to her apartment to change clothes, only to discover that Summer, her best friend, had moved out. Mar-quez didn't need a scorecard. She'd known all about the little game Diana and Seth had been playing, but she'd kept her mouth shut, hoping things would work out on their own.

Great. Marquez's boyfriend was AWOL, and her

best friend had run away from home. It was not a pretty picture.

She climbed the porch steps to the apartment Diver shared with Austin Reed. Her hand was trembling, but she couldn't tell if it was from nerves or because she hadn't eaten anything all day.

She knocked. "Enter at your own risk," Austin yelled.

Marquez pushed open the door. The room was dense with smoke. Discarded potato chip bags and bottles littered the floor. A tiny fan on a TV tray herded the thick air back and forth.

Austin was lying on the couch, ratty jeans, no shirt. He was reading a *TV Guide*. His half-grown beard was dark against his drawn face. His long brown hair hadn't seen a comb in many a moon. He always looked a little edgy—now he looked downright scuzzy. Still, Marquez could understand why Summer was so taken with him. Even when scuzzy, he was attractively scuzzy.

"Hey, Marquez, join the party. You're just in time. I've got *Grey's Anatomy* on DVD."

Marquez waved her arms to clear the air. "Since when do you smoke?"

"I don't. I'm just experimenting with self-destructive behaviors. Next I thought I'd try the all-doughnut diet. Or else take up skydiving. Of course, that would require moving off the couch, and I think

I may be permanently stuck here. I sat on a package of Oreos a few days back."

"Blythe told me you were late to work and McNair almost fired your butt."

"Yeah. I was very disappointed when he gave me a second chance to clean up my act."

Marquez cleared a spot off a chair and sat. "This is because Summer ended things, huh?"

"I know it's not very melodramatic, eating and drinking myself into a stupor and watching the Weather Channel. I ought to have the decency to fall on my sword or something."

"You may want to hold off on the sword. Summer and Seth just officially broke up. You heard it here first. Look, have you seen Diver anywhere? I've been calling all day—"

"I turned the sound on the machine off." Austin tossed his *TV Guide* to the floor. "Tell me more about this alleged breakup."

"First things first. Diver?"

Austin frowned. "Didn't he say anything to you?"

"About what?" Marquez asked impatiently. She couldn't seem to stop her knees from jiggling.

"He left around six or so. He had his backpack and his sleeping bag—which is to say everything he owns, pretty much. Said something about going camping for a couple of days, getting away from the real world."

Marquez leapt out of her chair like she'd been ejected. "Are you *sure*? He didn't say anything to me, Austin, and I know he would have. And he just started a new job, he's supposed to work tomorrow, this doesn't make any sense—"

"Whoa, calm down, Marquez." Austin sat up. "I'm sure there's a logical explanation. I did ask him about his job and he said they were cool with it."

"How could they be cool with it? *I'm* not even cool with it!" She grabbed his phone. "Can I use this?"

"Sure."

Marquez hesitated. "Damn. What's his boss's name? Linda something. Linda . . . Linda . . ." She pounded the receiver in her palm.

"Calm down, girl. You sneaking into the double espressos again at Jitters?"

"Linda Right? Linda—"

"Rice?" Austin ventured.

"That's it!" Marquez dialed information, got the number, and waited impatiently for the phone to ring.

"So anyway, about this Summer-Seth situation—" Austin tried, but she ignored him.

"Linda?" she said when a woman answered. "This is Marquez—uh, Maria Marquez, Diver Smith's girl-friend? I'm really sorry to bug you like this, but I was wondering if you could tell me if he's scheduled to work tomorrow."

Marquez listened, said thanks, hung up, and groaned. "He's scheduled for the next four days straight. She didn't know anything." She wrung her hands. Her pulse throbbed in her throat. She couldn't get enough air. It was like trying to breathe through a straw. "There's something wrong, Austin. He wouldn't just split like this unless something were really, really wrong."

Austin put out his cigarette and stood a little unsteadily. He put his arm around her. "Relax, kid. Nothing's wrong. Now, come here and sit down. Watch those Oreos. I'm getting you some water." He led her to the couch. "Take it easy, Marquez. You've had a hard week. I mean, you just got out of the hospital a little while ago."

She nodded, touching the Band-Aid covering her stitches. She'd felt a little like this that night—dizzy, lost. The diet pills, probably, or not eating. She'd fallen, hit her head.

"Austin, Diver tells me everything. He wouldn't just vanish unless something horrible had happened. You've got to think. Did he say anything else? Leave a note, anything?"

Austin handed her a plastic cup from Burger King filled with water. "I don't think so, Marquez."

"Did he seem okay?"

"Well, I don't know Diver that well. He's always

sort of . . . cryptic. But he did look a little down."
He sat down next to Marquez. "You know, he did
say something weird. A message he wanted me to pass
along—"

"To me?"

"To Summer, actually. He said something like,
'Tell Summer she was right about me all along.' Does
that mean anything to you?"

Marquez closed her eyes. "It means he wasn't
feeling good about himself, I can tell you that much.
Summer's not exactly her brother's biggest fan. She
blames him for her parents splitting up, for running out
on her family—"

*Running out.* As soon as she said the words,
Marquez realized the truth.

Diver, who had spent his life running from problems, could be running once again.

Without thinking, she reached for Austin's hand.
He held tight and pulled her close. "He would never
run out on you, Marquez. He loves you completely."

"How do you know that?"

"Because he told me so. In that Diver way he has.
Said you were the only woman who didn't disturb his
*wa.* Whatever the hell that is."

She leaned her head on Austin's warm shoulder.
The room was swimming in lazy circles around her.
She had to clear her head, get organized. First she'd

go see Summer, see if she knew anything. Then . . . well, she'd deal with then when she got there.

"Maybe he tried to call," Austin suggested. He reached for the answering machine on the floor, his arm still around Marquez.

The first four messages were all from Marquez. *Diver, where are you? Diver, call me. Diver, you said you were going to meet me after work. Damn it, Diver, where are you?*

The next was from their boss at Jitters, reminding Austin he'd better be on time for his shift tomorrow.

Then came the last one. *Diver, hon. I so enjoyed our little visit this afternoon. Can't wait to see what develops.*

That was it. No name, no number.

"That southern accent," Austin said. "That's got to be Caroline."

Marquez didn't have to be told. She'd watched Diver at the beach party last night, eyeing beautiful, blond, petite Caroline like a lovesick puppy. She'd seen the looks they'd exchanged, and she'd known what they'd meant.

And now Diver and Caroline had spent the afternoon together. "His leaving," Marquez whispered. "It's about Caroline, I know it is."

"Marquez, my darling, crazed Marquez," Austin said, planting a kiss on her cheek, "that frothy little southern magnolia can't hold a candle to you. Diver loves you."

Marquez looked at him. "Yeah, and Summer loved you," she said gently.

Austin gave a crooked smile. "You're making comforting you extremely challenging."

For a moment they sat together, considering their shared plight. At last Austin rose. "Come on. We'll go talk to Summer, see if she knows anything."

"I doubt Summer's in the mood for visitors right now, Austin."

"You can tell me all about it on the way. But first let me brush my teeth, assuming I remember how."

"A little Right Guard wouldn't hurt either."

He laughed. She watched him disappear into the bathroom. When he closed the door, she replayed Caroline's message on the machine. She listened for meaning, for clues in the sweet, musical lilt of Caroline's voice.

But there was nothing there to hear, no matter how hard she tried.

# 5

## It's a Dog of a Way to Get Around

It never hurt in the dream. The sizzling embers under his bare feet were as cool as wet stones. The fire licked at his skin, the fumes poisoned his lungs, but he couldn't feel a thing.

As the fire ate it away, Diver walked through the crumbling house until he found his father, his father who was not really his father, lying under a burning support beam. His clothes were on fire, his hair, even his skin. His mouth was contorted with pain.

He was screaming, but Diver couldn't hear him.

The dream shifted jerkily, like a badly spliced film. He was lying on the ground outside the house now, the fire behind him. The grass was damp and springy against his cheek. His head was bleeding.

He looked back. The fire was like a living thing. He heard sirens howling.

Somewhere nearby he saw a light come on. A shadow passed by a window.

He climbed to his feet and ran, the way he always did in the dream. He was moving wildly, propelled by fear and by the sound of his father's screams that now, at last, he could hear.

He turned the corner down the dark street. The sirens and the screams filled his head. And then, out of the corner of his eye, he saw the hand—a girl's hand, familiar and yet not, reaching out to him. The hand extended from the doorway of an old, rickety house. The house seemed to float over a blue, endless ocean.

The sirens grew louder, the screams tore at him, and then Diver reached for the hand.

Something shook him hard. A voice penetrated through the screams. "Wake up, man."

Diver's eyes flew open. He saw a beefy forearm layered with blue tattoos.

He was on the Greyhound. It was night. He was headed for Miami, or somewhere like that.

"You musta been havin' a nightmare, man." The owner of the tattoos returned to his seat on the other side of the dark aisle.

"Yeah." Diver ran his fingers through long, blond hair. "I guess."

"I get those real bad, man." The tattooed man shrugged. "Course, I'm usually awake."

When the Greyhound made a stop just south of Miami, Diver was grateful for the chance to stretch his legs. It was a seedy building, low-slung and dirty, with a small twenty-four-hour restaurant attached to one end.

With his fellow passengers, groggy and grumbling, Diver shuffled off the bus. The driver leaned against the bus, sucking alternately on a Coke and a cigarette, looking as bleary as the rest of them.

Inside, most of the passengers headed for the restaurant, which smelled of grease and bus fumes. But Diver found himself making his way toward the telephones, old-fashioned booths with accordion glass doors. He entered one, sat on the wooden stool, and held the receiver, still warm from its last use.

He wanted so much to call her. Just to hear Marquez's voice—hear her bitch at him and laugh at him and tell him how she didn't care what was wrong, just please get his butt home.

He could call, let her answer, hang up.

But she would know who it was. By now she was probably pretty worried. It would be wrong, cruel even, to call her like that.

As if running away from her without a word was somehow kind. He leaned against the glass. He felt something low in his chest, a tight place he associated vaguely with anger. He hadn't been angry much in his life. He hadn't felt much at all, actually.

His head hurt the way it had hurt in the dream. As if the dream had been real.

He laughed grimly. Of course, it had been.

He punched 411 into the keypad. "Directory assistance," a man answered.

"I need the number for Blythe, uh . . ." What *was* Caroline's roommate's last name? "Blythe Barrett, I think, in Coconut Key."

"Checking."

He waited, flashing back to his visit from Caroline this afternoon. *I didn't kill him,* he'd told her, but she'd known it wasn't true, and so had he.

The operator gave him the number. He listened to the dial tone hum. What could he say? *Yes, Caroline, you're right. I did kill him. I burned down the house with my father in it and then I ran like hell. Like I'm running now, so fast you'll never find me.*

He hung up the receiver. What was the etiquette when you were running from your blackmailer? Probably it would not be in your best interest to call and taunt her.

He was hungry. He wasn't thinking clearly.

He left the phone booth and went to the restaurant. His fellow travelers were camped out, each in separate booths, sullenly munching down day-old fries and burgers. Diver bought an apple and a granola bar and went outside.

The night wrapped itself around him, warm and damp. The bus was idling, filling the air with acrid smoke. Above the big windshield a sign glowed red. Miami.

He didn't have much cash. It wasn't the first time. After the fire he'd changed his name and lived on the streets. He could do it again, but the thought of dodging cops and sleazebags and dopers made him deeply tired. He could pick up odd jobs, get by. But he'd liked his last couple of jobs, taking care of injured wildlife at rehab centers. Lousy pay, great work.

A while back Summer had told him he had to get his act together, stop drifting, reacting. Grow up. He really had. He had a job, a place to stay with a roof and four walls, and, of course, his relationship with Marquez.

But a chance meeting with a girl named Caroline had ripped all that from his grasp.

He'd had lunch with Summer just today. It had been tense, like it always was between them these days. But there'd been a moment when she'd reached for his hand and he'd told his sister how much he loved her.

At least, he'd told her in his way. He hadn't exactly said the words.

He wolfed down the granola bar. It surprised him a little, the way he could still have an appetite while his life crumbled around him. How had Marquez starved herself all these months? Hoarding calories like gold, exercising to exhaustion, sneaking diet pills. He should have watched out for her better. He should have made her see how beautiful and perfect she was.

And now there was no one to tell her that.

One by one the other passengers returned to the bus. The driver tossed his cigarette. "Time to go, bud," he said.

Diver watched him climb the steps. The engine revved. If he got back on that bus, he'd fall asleep.

If he fell asleep, he'd dream again.

He waved the driver on. The doors squealed shut. The bus slowly pulled away.

The fire, the smoke, the screams would have to wait, for a few more hours at least.

# 6

# A Little Night Visiting

*Tap. Taptaptap. Tap.*

For the second time in one evening Summer awoke in a room that she didn't recognize. This time, though, it didn't take her as long to remember that she was at Jared's—or to remember why.

She checked the glowing digital clock. It was a little after midnight.

*Tap. Taptap. Taptap.*

Was it hailing? South Florida was famous for its sudden storms, but when she'd been outside with Seth and Jared, the sky had been clear. And why hadn't she heard any thunder or rain?

She climbed out of bed and went to the window.

As she pulled back the curtain the sharp clatter of stones against glass made her jump in surprise. She opened the window.

"Summer! It's me, Marquez!"

"Marquez?" Summer called. "Who's that with you?"

"But, soft!" came a male voice, "what light through yonder window breaks?"

"Austin? What are you doing here?"

"Auditioning for summer stock."

"Let us in, okay?" Marquez called.

"Wait there."

Summer threw on the robe she'd remembered to pack at the last minute. The hallway was dark. Silently she swept down the wide staircase.

Marquez. It would be so good to see Marquez.

She didn't let herself think about how it would be to see Austin.

It took her two tries to disarm the door alarm the way Juanita, Jared's nurse, had taught her before Summer went to bed.

Marquez and Austin were waiting on the wide porch. Summer pulled them in, enforcing silence with a finger to her lips. She led them upstairs to her room and shut the door.

"Be very quiet or they'll fire me for sure," she said in a whisper.

Marquez flew into her arms. "Summer, are you okay? I was so worried when you just left behind that note, and now with Diver—"

"What *about* Diver?"

Marquez burst into tears. Summer looked over at Austin, who was scanning the bookshelves. "Austin? What happened?"

He turned to her, his face grave. "He's gone, Summer."

"Gone?"

Marquez was sobbing—great gasping sounds that Summer had never heard her friend make before.

"This evening I ran into him as he was leaving my apartment," Austin said. "He said he was taking a couple of days off, and that they were cool with it at work."

"B-bu-but I called his job," Marquez sobbed. "And th-th-th—"

"They didn't know anything about it," Austin finished gently.

Summer led Marquez to the bed. They sat there together, Summer's arm draped over her friend's frail shoulders.

"I just saw him this afternoon," Summer said. "He was sort of down, but he didn't mention anything to me." She shook her head. "This would be just like Diver, to run out without a word. It wouldn't exactly be the first time. He didn't even leave a note, nothing?"

Marquez shook her head and sniffled. "But I know why he left. It's that Caroline girl. She left a message on Austin's machine. They got together today, and at the beach last night he couldn't take his eyes off her."

"Marquez," Austin interrupted, "Diver is not interested in Caroline. He's in love with you."

"Diver told me about her, Marquez," Summer said. "He and Caroline were neighbors when they were kids, that's all."

Marquez looked at her hopefully. "Really?"

"He told me at lunch."

"Still, he had to leave for some reason. . . ." Marquez's voice faded away.

"Damn it," Summer muttered, all her pent-up anger at Diver resurfacing. "How could he just walk out like this? I mean, before, when he left Minnesota, I could almost understand. It was a new place, and my family was new to him. It was a hard adjustment, sure. But *now*? Now, when everything's going so well? He has a cool job, and he has you—"

She paused, suddenly aware of her rising voice and of Marquez's soft sobs. There was no point in making things worse. "Marquez, you know Diver," Summer said, softening her tone. "He gets these whims. He's probably sleeping on the beach, doing his back-to-nature thing. Truth is"—she forced a laugh— "he probably couldn't hack living in a normal apartment with Austin."

"Wouldn't be the first roommate I've driven out," Austin agreed.

"And after all," Summer added, "before this, Diver was living in a tree house. He's not like other guys, Marquez. He's got this wild streak in him. He's sort of, well . . . uncivilized. Give him a couple of days without indoor plumbing or remote controls and he'll be back, good as new."

"You think?" Marquez asked.

"I know. He *is* my brother, after all."

"Still"—Marquez grabbed a Kleenex box off Summer's nightstand—"he should have told me. At least when you ran out, you left a note."

"Interesting," Austin noted as he thumbed through a thick book he'd pulled off the shelves. "You both pull a disappearing act on the same day. Perhaps this tendency to vanish runs in the family."

"I did not pull a disappearing act," Summer said sharply. "I was offered a live-in position and I chose to . . . to exercise that option. That's all."

"And what exactly prompted this . . . exercising?" Austin asked, smiling just enough to tell Summer he'd heard about her and Seth.

Summer sighed heavily. "Austin, if you already

know about Seth and me, why are you asking? And since we're getting personal, there's this newfangled invention on the market. It's called a razor. I've got one in my bathroom you could borrow, but I've already used it on my legs."

"Actually, that might be very exciting for me."

She turned her attention back to Marquez. "Are you going to be okay tonight?"

Marquez nodded. "I just feel so . . . you know, helpless."

"Tomorrow's your counseling session at the hospital, right?"

Marquez gave a terse nod.

"Well, I'll try to get off early here and when you're done at your session, we'll go on an all-out Diver search. We'll check all the beaches, talk to anyone who might have seen him. We'll track him down, Marquez, I promise. Who knows? He'll probably show up tomorrow, all happy and Zen again, before we can even start looking."

Marquez smiled with one corner of her mouth. "Yeah. That would be Diver, all right." She stood shakily, bracing herself on Summer's shoulder. "Well, we should get going. Nice place, by the way. I can see why you prefer it."

"How'd you find my room, anyway?"

"Process of elimination," Austin answered. "You had the lousiest view."

"It's not fair to leave me alone with Diana, you know," Marquez said. "I had to hide all the sharp knives."

"I know. But I just can't deal with her and Seth right now."

"We've been so busy talking about Diver. You sure you're holding up okay?"

Summer shrugged. Out of the corner of her eye she could see Austin watching her intently. "Just kind of numb."

Marquez looked down at her feet. "Summer. There's something I have to tell you. I, uh, I kind of knew."

Summer blinked. "Knew. You knew what?"

"Don't make this any harder than it already is. I knew about Diana and Seth. I saw this letter from her to him. Really nauseating stuff. I didn't tell you because I thought maybe it was over and I didn't want to mess things up between you and Seth. . . ." She rolled her eyes. "And now look. As usual, with my incredible insight into human nature, I've totally screwed things up. No wonder Diver ran off."

She started to sob again. Summer felt the choices rolling around inside her—yell, cry, be disappointed, be sad. But when she looked at Marquez, so frail and desperate, all she could do was hug her close. "It's okay," she said. "I probably would have done the same thing."

Austin put a gentle hand on Marquez's shoulder. "Come on, kid. How about you and me stop by I Scream? They're open till one, I think. I'll buy you a hot fudge sundae with Reese's Pieces."

"I'm not hungry," Marquez murmured.

"I know," Austin said. "But let's go, anyway. I wouldn't mind some company."

Marquez looked from Summer to Austin and back again. "I need some air," she said. "And I have the feeling you two need some too. I'll meet you downstairs, Austin."

When Marquez was gone, Austin looked a little uncomfortable. "About last night," he said, clearing his throat. "When I crashed your little beach party . . . I believe I may have been slightly inebriated."

"You lay on the beach and made sand angels. It took two of us to drag you home. I'd say 'slightly' is a slight understatement."

Austin winced. "In any case, thanks for lugging me home. And I apologize for my boorish behavior."

"Apology accepted."

"If you need help with Diver . . ."

"Thanks. I'll let you know."

Austin moved a little closer. He touched her hair and she shivered. "About you and Seth—" he began.

"Marquez is waiting," Summer said. "You should probably go."

Austin seemed to be debating whether to press on. "All right," he said at last. "We'll do this another time." He gave her a gentle kiss on the cheek. "You've got enough to deal with right now."

# 7

# Jared's Future, Jared's Past

"Glad you could join us."

Juanita was sitting in the breakfast room, a sunny, spacious area apparently reserved for the staff. She was just a few years older than Summer, a pretty olive-skinned woman with a halo of brown curls. As usual, she was dressed in a crisp white uniform. She sat at the table by a bank of windows overlooking the ocean, removing sections from a grapefruit with systematic care.

"I kind of overslept a little," Summer said apologetically.

"Deb, our cook, is out shopping, so you're on your own," Juanita said. "There's cereal over there in the cupboard by the sink, English muffins by the toaster. Make yourself at home."

Fumbling around in the huge, shiny kitchen, Summer managed to fix herself a bowl of Cheerios. She sat across from Juanita, feeling like an unwanted guest in a near-empty hotel.

"We were supposed to meet at nine to discuss Jared's therapy," Juanita said, opening a notebook.

"I'm really sorry—"

"But before we start, perhaps we should establish some ground rules," she continued. "Jared's family arranged for him to recover here so that he could have complete quiet. Jared's very generous with the staff. We're allowed to have guests and to use the grounds." She paused. "But that does not mean taking advantage of the situation. That does not mean, for example, having one's friends sneak into Jared's home in the middle of the night."

Summer gulped.

"By my count, you've already been visited by three friends, two of them"—she lowered her voice—"*male*. You're obviously a very pretty girl, Summer, and it's only natural that you would have . . . admirers. Including Jared, I suspect." She added the last part as if it were clearly a topic for *Unsolved Mysteries*. "But it is extremely detrimental to his recovery to be reminded of all he's lost. He's just a little older than you are, Summer. Imagine how hard it is for him to be around people his own age, living their normal lives." She paused to sip her tea. "I've spoken to Jared's mother on the phone. Apparently Jared was quite a handsome guy. She said he had no shortage of girlfriends. One in particular he was quite smitten with."

"I wonder where she is."

Juanita shrugged. "I've seen it before. People have an accident like this, it really separates the wheat from the chaff. So-called friends just vanish."

"Poor Jared," Summer said. "I'm truly sorry about my friends coming by. I promise to be more careful in the future."

Juanita smiled. "I'm glad we understand each other." She tore out a page from her notebook. "Now, I've put together a list of therapeutic activities. Jared's been going through a slump. He's very depressed, very uninterested in life. Most of the time he just stares blankly at the TV. Your goal is to help him reengage." She passed the list to Summer.

Summer scanned the section headed "8:00 A.M. to 12:00 P.M." "Wake at eight," she read. "Bathe, change dressings, eight to eight-thirty. Breakfast, eight-thirty to nine. Read newspapers, nine to nine-thirty. Read novels, nine-thirty to ten. Play chess or other board game, ten to eleven—" She frowned. "I know I'm not a nurse or any-thing, but isn't this kind of . . . you know, regimented?"

She heard a whirring noise behind her, the sound of

Jared's motorized wheelchair as he sped into the room. He was neatly dressed as always, in a crisp tailored blue shirt and khaki pants, hemmed at the knee on one side to accommodate his large cast. He had a heavy gold ring on his left hand, and on his good foot he wore an expensive-looking dark leather shoe—attempts, it seemed, to impose order onto the chaos of bandages and plaster.

"She's right," Jared said in his low, gravelly voice. "It does sound regimented." He rolled over to the table and cocked his head to read the list. "My entire future laid out before me." He narrowed his eyes. "What? You didn't bother to schedule in my breathing, Juanita?"

"I just thought a plan of activities would give you something to look forward to each day—"

"We'll wing it, right, Summer?"

"Sure," Summer said. "How about a walk around the neighborhood? A roll, I guess I should say?"

"Fine idea," Jared said.

"I'm not so sure that's advisable, Summer," Juanita said. "Jared's wheelchair is cumbersome, and the temperature is so high—"

"Relax," Jared said. "What's the worst that can happen?"

"The worst that can happen is your throttle will stick and you'll roll straight into the ocean," Juanita said with a reluctant smile.

"I'll take my chances," Jared said.

"Ready?" Summer asked, spooning down the last of her cereal.

"Wear your Nikes. I'm hard to keep up with," Jared advised.

Summer took her bowl to the sink. "There's one thing," she said. "I was sort of wondering if I could have a couple of hours off this afternoon."

"Of course," Jared said, but Juanita was scowling.

"It's this family emergency. My brother's sort of disappeared—"

"Diver's gone?" Jared asked.

"Yeah, he . . . how'd you know his name?"

"You mentioned him yesterday."

"I did? Oh, well, I guess I did. Yesterday's sort of a blur. Anyway, it's probably nothing, he's sort of flaky sometimes, but I was going to help his girlfriend try to track him down."

"No problem," Jared said.

"You seem to lead a very turbulent life," Juanita commented.

"Sometimes I do feel a little seasick," Summer said with a grim smile.

Jared wheeled to his bedroom and closed the door. He pulled his sunglasses out of his nightstand drawer and tucked them in his pocket. Summer was waiting in the foyer to start their walk.

Summer was waiting for him.

*Summer.*

With great difficulty he removed the burled walnut box he kept at the back of the drawer. He set it on the bed, then wheeled over to the closet. With his good hand he removed the key he'd tucked inside his tennis racket cover.

It was an elaborate precaution, but one he felt was necessary. Juanita respected his privacy, such as it was. But it was too easy to imagine her coming across the box and inspecting its contents.

He locked his bedroom door and returned to the bed. It took three tries, but he was finally able to twist the key. The catch released. Slowly Jared opened the lid.

The picture was on top, where he'd left it. A beautiful girl on a sailboat, blond hair shimmering in the Florida sun, smiling radiantly at the camera. A handsome young man, dark eyed and too cocky, his arm draped around her shoulders.

He touched his bandaged face. He hadn't been such a bad-looking guy, all things considered.

Of course, that was a year ago. A lifetime ago. Back when he'd actually thought he might someday hear Summer say, *I love you, Adam.* Back when he'd been the rich son of a powerful senator. Back when everything he wanted came with such sweet ease he'd never imagined life could be any other way.

He was still rich. But his father had retired from the Senate in disgrace. His brother, Ross, was dead.

And he wasn't the cocky guy on the sailboat anymore, the guy who was sure Summer would fall in love with him, like every other girl he'd ever wanted.

Summer had been different. Summer, *he'd* loved.

That had only happened to him once before.

He pulled another picture out of the box. A girl on the beach, hiding behind dark sunglasses. She was Summer's opposite, dark, complicated, her smile full of secrets, and yet they shared one important quality— they both believed in love in a way he never had and never could. He'd believed in loyalty. Family above all else. And he'd lost both girls because of it.

He put back the pictures, locked the box, hid the key. A knock at the door startled him.

"Jared?" Juanita asked. "You need any help?"

"I'm fine. Tell Summer I'll be right there."

He returned the box to its hiding place. He should tell Summer who he was, of course. This couldn't go on forever. But he didn't want to.

For today, at least, for right now, Summer was waiting for him.

*Summer.*

# 8

# Nice People and Not-So-Nice

The sign on the door was small, handwritten: *Eating Disorders Clinic.*

For the third time Marquez walked past the door, casually, indifferently. The hospital, even this part, the outpatient wing, stank of disinfectant. It was making her woozy and lightheaded. Or maybe it was the fact that she hadn't eaten in ages.

She headed for the lobby and sank into a chair. She should go home, work her shift at Jitters, then try to look for Diver. She and Summer could start with the beaches north of town. He liked those. She could imagine him baking in the sun, his shades hiding innocent baby blues, grinning when she finally tracked him down. He'd show her some shell he'd found, or some injured pelican, or whatever had distracted him from acting like a normal human being and telling her where he was.

That was the good version.

In the bad version, the R-rated one that had kept her up all night, he was having a secret rendezvous with Caroline. Marquez wasn't exactly sure where or how, but she knew why. He was with Caroline because she was everything Marquez wasn't: beautiful, petite, thin.

A nurse walked by, rustling in her uniform. She paused, glancing down the hall at the ED door and then back at Marquez.

"Can I help you with directions?" she asked.

"I'm just . . . you know. Waiting for someone."

"At the ED clinic?" She had a nice smile, Nice, but nosy.

Marquez reached for an aging *People* magazine to prove she really was waiting. "Yeah, She's in there, Jane. She's, um, one of those throwing-up people."

"Bulimic?"

"I guess. Me, I could never do that. I despise throwing up."

The nurse stared. Marquez looked down at her magazine. David Hasselhoff was on the cover. He looked very tan and very old.

"Well, they're nice people at the clinic," the nurse said gently. "I'm sure she'll like it there. They really know how to listen."

"She's not very talkative," Marquez said.

"They'll understand. Tell her to give it a chance."

"Yeah. I'll try. But she doesn't really listen to me."

"There's a counselor on staff here all the time," the nurse said. "You might pass that along."

Marquez flipped through the worn pages of her magazine.

"If you get thirsty, there's a machine down the hall," the nurse said, smiling that sympathetic smile again. "While you wait."

Marquez watched her leave. She was average weight, maybe a little big in the hips, probably some cellulite on the thighs. But still. Nothing like Marquez. Marquez, who made Shamu look like a runway model.

She stared down the hall, imagining the other girls behind the ED door. If she tried hard enough, she could almost believe the lie she'd told the nurse. She was just waiting for Jane. Jane, who was a pretty messed-up girl, who threw up breakfast so she could have another one.

She lingered over an article on some supermodels in L.A. who'd started a new restaurant. In a big color photo they were grouped around a table overflowing with food, enough calories to keep them all happy for a year. One of them, a model Marquez had seen on the covers of *Seventeen* and *Teen Vogue,* had a french fry poised delicately between perfectly manicured nails. Of course, she probably barfed it up after the photo shoot. They all did it.

Marquez had seen girls at school do it too. In the bathroom by the lunchroom, the one someone had dubbed the "vomitorium." Once Marquez had been in there, plugging her nose at the putrid smell, when Dana Berglund had emerged from a stall, primly dabbing her mouth with a piece of toilet paper, her eyes wet. She'd smoothed her cheerleader skirt and checked her blush in the mirror. Noting Marquez's rolled eyes, she'd defiantly declared, "Everybody does it," before slipping out the door.

And there'd been that anorexic girl Marquez's junior year. Marquez hadn't known her. She was a senior, very popular, a 4.0, pretty. Real thin, but she always wore big sweaters, flowing skirts. One day she'd just stopped coming to school. Rumors floated around: she had AIDS, she'd taken a job as a roadie with a band from Miami, she'd run off to have a baby. Marquez heard later that she'd died. Starved to death. She hadn't known that was even possible.

She put the magazine down and went back to the ED door. With her ear to the glass, she could make out the faint noise of a girl sobbing. She'd promised Diver she'd try this once. Summer too.

Marquez turned away. Diver had vanished and Summer had moved out.

She didn't owe them anything.


"Eighty-six the pecan pie," Blythe whispered to Austin. They were standing behind the coffee bar at Jitters. The café was quiet, but the lunch rush wasn't due to start for another half hour. "That guy on table five just noticed one of the pecans moving. Turns out it wasn't a pecan."

"The Roach War begins anew. This building's crawling with 'em." Austin sipped at his cup of coffee, his third this morning. He'd been up late with Marquez, then too buzzed with manic energy to go to sleep after seeing Summer. He was still buzzed, but it was solely the caffeine keeping his eyelids up.

"In my apartment I've learned to accommodate them," he said. "I split my food fifty-fifty, let them use the TV remote when I'm at work. I'm teaching some of the brighter roaches to play poker. The other day I lost forty bucks and half a bag of Doritos."

"In my apartment," Blythe said, "I drown them in Raid. That works too." She paused to artistically arrange sugar packets in a bowl. "Caroline just pulverizes them with her foot. I'm really glad she's decided to stay a while longer."

Austin smiled. He liked Blythe, a pretty African-American girl with an easy smile and an open manner. She was fun to work with, and she never shirked on the side work, like some of his fellow waitrons.

He glanced over at the corner booth, where Caroline was reading a book and sipping tea. "You and Caroline go way back, huh?" he said, wiping down the counter. "Camp counselors. Very wholesome."

"Yep. During high school, at this summer camp in Virginia. That's how we met." She paused, sighing. "She's changed a little."

"How?" Austin asked casually.

"Oh, you know." Blythe shrugged. "Just . . . we used to laugh so hard, we were constantly snorting milk out of our noses. Now she's going to this really snooty college. She joined this sorority, and she's not nearly so down-to-earth anymore. Like, I mean, she actually *cares* about the difference between a Mercedes and a Lexus, Austin. Her dad's a small-town lawyer and her mom manages this clothing store, but they're not rich or anything, and all of a sudden Caroline's so money obsessed." She sighed again. "It's kind of depressing when people change like that."

Austin reached for a pot of hot water. "Speaking of, it's time for a refill. Maybe I can get her to snort tea through her nose. You know, for old times' sake."

Caroline smiled broadly as Austin approached her table. "You read my mind."

"I live to serve." Austin poured hot water into her teapot.

"Hey, you ever been to Crab Claw Key?"

"Sure. It's just down the road a ways."

"I thought I might go on a little shopping expedition. Coconut's not cutting it for me. It's nothing but glitter T-shirts and Speedo swimsuits. I'm looking for something a little more checkbook challenging. Saks, Nordstrom's, something like that. Heck, I'd settle for a Gap."

Austin laughed. "You want that, you need to head for Miami. Don't get me wrong. Crab Claw has some money. I mean, Senator Merrick used to live over there and Mallory Olan—you know, Diana's mom, the romance novelist—has a place. The main drag has a few nice stores, but nothing that fancy. We're just simple ol' folk here in the Keys."

"You're teasing me," Caroline said, turning up the volume on the accent. She pushed her book aside. "Besides, you're a guy. What do you know about shopping? I tried Blythe, but she's shopping impaired. I ought to ask Summer or Marquez." She paused. "Is Marquez working today?"

"She's coming in later." Austin poured Caroline some fresh tea. "I think she's a little distracted, what with Diver gone and all."

Caroline studied her cup. "Gone?" she repeated.

"Yeah. Just kind of vanished. But then, you know Diver. I hear you two are old friends."

"Where'd you hear that?"

"Summer. Diver told her you two got together yesterday to reminisce."

Caroline shrugged. She poured sugar into her cup and slowly stirred. The spoon shivered in her hand ever so slightly, but her face was a mask of calm. "We weren't exactly bosom buddies or anything. But yeah, we knew each other." She lowered her voice. "To be perfectly honest, he always was a little, well, odd. It doesn't surprise me one whit that he's run off like this. Does anyone have a clue where he went?"

"Nope. He didn't leave a note or anything. Very weird. We thought about calling the police—"

"Oh, I wouldn't do that," Caroline said quickly. "I mean, for one thing, they wouldn't do anything, anyway. I doubt he'd qualify as a missing person for a while. He's over eighteen, he has a habit of acting strangely. And besides, they're busy catching *real* criminals—rapists and burglars and murderers. . . ."

"No one said anything about Diver being a criminal. Real or otherwise."

"No, of course not," Caroline said. "I just meant it would be a waste of time to bother the police. I'm sure Diver will turn up." She offered up another broad smile. "So. When do you get off?"

"Me? My work is never done."

"Your shift has to end eventually." She brushed her hair behind her ear, an innocent gesture that none-theless seemed scripted. "I thought maybe you might want to give me a tour."

"A most tempting offer. But I do most of my shop-ping at 7-Eleven. That includes my wardrobe and most of my home furnishings."

"Well, the offer stands," Caroline said, eyes sweep-ing Austin from head to toe.

Austin gave his best aw-shucks grin and headed over to a nearby table to clear away some plates. Caroline returned to her reading.

She was undeniably a very attractive girl. Too bad he had the sneaking suspicion she was also very bad news.

# 9

# Seek and Hide

Caroline browsed a rack of bathing suits without much enthusiasm. The shops on Main Street in Crab Claw Key were having a sidewalk sale. Nothing special. Certainly nothing worth suffering over in this ninety-degree temperature. The cement shimmered with heat like nothing she'd ever felt before. Even in her tank top and shorts, she was wilting fast. She had a new pair of sunglasses on, the kind all the girls at Tri-Delt were wearing, but even with the deep green lenses, she had to squint.

She moved on to a shoe shop, sorting through a pile of leather sandals. No luck. Which was probably just as well, since she was going to be short on cash soon. Unless she could con her dad into sending her another care package with a nice fat check in it, she might actually have to consider getting a job one of these days.

But it wasn't this summer that worried her as much as next fall. Nobody knew better than she did that she'd squeezed into her sorority because her mom and her grandmother had also been members. She had the birthright. She just didn't have the car, the understated gold jewelry, the ski vacations at Vail. At the sorority house, a grand, crumbling structure on the outskirts of campus, she was merely tolerated, like a stray cat no one had the heart to kick out.

Visiting Blythe down here in the Keys had seemed like a welcome respite from the stresses of college. She was so mellow and uncomplicated compared to Caroline's friends at school. Being around Blythe had made Caroline start to think maybe she'd just quit the sorority and move into a dorm. It would be a humiliating social defeat, but a survivable one.

And then she'd run into Diver.

"Need any help?"

Caroline looked up, startled. A guy with a nose ring was leaning against the doorjamb. He had the spun gold hair of someone who lived from dawn to dusk in the Florida sun. Like Diver's hair.

"No, I'm just browsing," Caroline said.

"That's cool, Give a yell if you need anything. The Aerosole shoes are fifteen percent off."

"Is there anywhere around here I could get a soda?"

"The Sandcastle, down the street. It's like right on top of the beach."

Caroline headed down the street toward the wide ribbon of white sand filled with sunbathers. She took a seat under a striped red awning that shaded an outdoor café and ordered a large lemonade.

She watched two guys in swim trunks pass by, surfboards under their arms. One paused, pushed down his shades to check her out, grinned, and moved on. He too looked a little like Diver. How would she ever track Diver down now? He was like all these guys, a beach bum, a nomad. He could be anywhere.

She sipped at her lemonade, then rubbed the damp glass over her forehead. She'd moved too fast, pushed too hard. She'd been so excited about her little blackmail scheme that she'd forgotten not to overplay her hand.

Without Diver she had nothing. With him she could have a nice little bundle of cash. She could buy the car, the clothes, the jewelry she needed to redeem herself.

Yesterday she'd been sure she'd had him hooked too. Something about the way he'd reacted to the talk of his father's death had made her wonder if Diver didn't really think he *had* committed murder. When she'd offered to tell the cops a nice little made-up story about how she'd watched from her bedroom window—as her neighbor—Diver—had bravely tried to save his daddy, she could tell Diver had no memory of what had happened that night. The guilt in his eyes, the resigned, desperate sound of his voice, told her he wanted to believe her story, but he didn't.

Funny, when you thought about it. Because the little made-up story just happened to be true.

Of course, the police had other ideas. They assumed Diver had torched his house to kill his abusive father and then run. But she could clear him of all that. And there'd be plenty of insurance money waiting for the picking.

She opened her wallet to leave money for the lemonade. All her friends had a Gold Card and fat checking accounts. She could have them too, if she could just track down Diver and get him to go along with her plan.

She'd offered him an eighty-twenty split on the insurance money. Maybe she should have been a little more generous. Of course, she was new to blackmailing. And it wasn't like there were how-to books available.

The surfboard guys returned, ogling her again. They weren't her type—no future, no cash.

Once upon a time she'd had a wild crush on Diver. Maybe she should go fifty-fifty with him. Then he'd have money to go with his looks.

First, of course, she had to find him.

Diver skirted the shore of Crab Claw Bay, keeping an eye out for anybody who might ask the wrong questions. Fortunately most of the expensive homes along the water seemed deserted. They probably were. These were vacation homes for the rich, and most people found south Florida in the summer way too hot for vacationing.

Diana's mom, Mallory Olan, was an exception. She lived here year-round, although she was often away, visiting friends in Europe or, like now, on extended book tours. Her huge house, a strange jumble of arched windows and fantastic turrets, stood across the bay from the Merrick estate. But Diana's house wasn't Diver's destination. Not exactly.

Pausing under a palm tree, Diver surveyed the area up ahead. It was quiet and still, as if the world had been stunned into silence by the thick, unending heat. He saw no one, no gardeners, nothing except his goal—the ancient stilt house on the edge of the Olans' property.

It was a homely, squat little bungalow, its white paint chipped and faded. From the center of the house a shaded stairway descended straight down to a small platform on the water. A rickety-looking wooden walkway ran a hundred feet from the grassy, shaded shore to the stilt house. The walkway wrapped around the house, forming a narrow deck lined with a railing.

Diver shaded his eyes, hoping to catch sight of his old friend Frank, a brown pelican. But Frank's usual spot on the corner of the railing was empty.

It was now or never. If Diver had timed it better, he might have done this under cover of darkness. But he'd had a hard time hitching back from Miami.

He could take the walkway out to the house, but that was more visibility than he wanted to risk. Hefting his backpack and sleeping bag onto his shoulder, he waded out into the warm water. When it reached his waist, he began to swim, doing his best to keep his stuff from getting soaked.

When he reached the platform under the stilt house, he hefted himself up. It was shady, if not cool. The tar-covered pilings surrounded him. The ripe, sweet smell of dead fish and saltwater filled him with a strange, melancholy joy.

He climbed up the damp wooden stairs. The trap-door in the floorboards was open. When it came to the stilt house, the Olans had never been much for security. Diana had told him that her mother would have torn it down long ago except that as a home to bootleggers in the twenties, it was considered a historic landmark, and she got tax breaks for keeping it more or less preserved.

Diver kept low, just in case he could be seen moving past the windows. The mattress was covered with plastic. The sharp smell of mothballs hung in the air. A thin layer of white sand turned the wood floor to sandpaper on his bare feet. It was hot and musty and mildewy and dirty.

It was home.

After the fire he'd been on his own for a long time, moving from beach to beach aimlessly. But when he'd happened on the abandoned stilt house, he'd known it was the place for him. He'd slept on the roof and used the kitchen and bathroom when he needed it. And the Olans had been none the wiser. That was, until Summer had moved into the stilt house. She'd discovered him, and slowly, irrevocably, everything about his life had begun to change.

He opened the front door and sat down on the old wooden walkway, his back against the wall of the house. Out here, facing the ocean, he was safely blocked from anyone's view.

He wasn't sure why he'd come here. He should have moved on, headed north. He was probably much more vulnerable here, although it was remotely possible that hiding out in Crab Claw would actually give him the upper hand. Who would come looking for him here? They'd all assume he was halfway across the country by now, not secreted away in his old hangout.

Besides, he realized with a start, he'd dreamed of coming here. This was the house floating over the water. The house with the girl's hand beckoning.

Of course, there was no girl. Just Diver, all alone.

He closed his eyes. The sun scorched his lids. The water licked at the pilings. He had never been so lonely. Even after the fire. It hurt so much more now because he'd lost so much more.

The air stirred. He opened his eyes. A pelican sat perched on the railing, his huge beak tucked under his wing. He blinked at Diver doubtfully.

"Frank," Diver whispered.

Frank tilted his head, ever dignified, then dropped a load of white poop onto the deck.

Diver laughed. The laughter kept coming, deeper and edgier, until it turned to sobs.

# 10

# Life and Other Games of Strategy

"Checkmate." Summer winced, her hand poised over a black knight. "That's, like, really bad, huh?"

Jared gave a slight, stiff nod. "That's, like, really dead. But you were fantastic, for your first lesson."

"You could have at least shown me a little mercy."

"Did you show me any mercy when we played five hands of gin?"

Summer grinned. "You're just lucky we weren't playing for cash or I'd have bankrupted you."

Jared leaned forward a bit in his wheelchair. "I prefer playing with you," he confided in a barely audible whisper. "Juanita always lets me win. She thinks I need the morale boost."

A rustle in the doorway made Summer turn around. Juanita was there, arms crossed, mouth pursed like she was sucking on a sour ball.

"Just tell me this. Is there anyone in the Keys you're *not* dating?" she inquired.

Jared smiled at Summer. "I'm pretty sure she's not talking to me."

"There's someone here to see you, Summer," Juanita said. "Again."

"Jeez, Juanita, I'm really sorry. Hardly anyone even knows I'm here—"

"It's okay, Summer," Jared interrupted. "Truth is, I'm beat."

"No wonder," Juanita said. "It's two-thirty, and you were due for your nap at one." She cast Summer a sidelong glance. "I'll take over here, Summer. Maybe we should consider setting a quota on your gentleman callers."

When Summer opened the front door, she found Austin sitting on the lawn, leaning against a palm tree and chewing on a blade of grass.

"Nice digs," he commented. "Even better in daylight." He patted the grass. "Take a load off."

Summer closed the door. "Why are you here?"

"I'm not here to seduce you." He paused. "Unless you're putting in a request."

"I'm working. And I've been informed I'm not supposed to have 'gentleman callers.'"

"*A,* I'm no gentleman. And *B,* it's about Diver."

Summer rushed over. "Did you hear from him?"

"No, nothing like that. Actually, this has to do with Caroline."

Summer gestured toward the palm-lined street. "Come on. I don't want to upset Jared. It's hard for him to see normal kids his own age. Not, incidentally, that you qualify."

They fell into step down the quiet street of manicured lawns, each one boasting tropical blooms in vivid pinks, oranges, and yellows. "So," Summer said, "what about Caroline?"

"Caroline was at Jitters this morning, and when I told her about Diver running off, something about the way she reacted didn't sit right with me."

"What do you mean?"

"She was just a little too interested in his disappearance. And her teaspoon was shaking."

Summer couldn't help smiling a little. "Her *spoon* was shaking?"

"You had to be there." Austin shrugged. "I know it's not much to go on, but since we know she saw Diver yesterday, she's our only lead. I thought about saying something to Marquez, but she's all worked up about Caroline as the other woman, and I didn't want to set her off."

"So what exactly do I do with this information?"

Summer asked as they turned the corner. A stretch of palms provided spiky shade, but no relief from the sizzling heat. Beyond a stately white home the ocean sparkled endlessly.

"I'm not sure. I know it's not much. But I tried."

"You could have just called, you know."

Austin stopped walking. A self-conscious smile tugged at the corners of his mouth. "There may actually have been another reason that I stopped by. I may have wanted to ask you something."

His words had taken on a different tone. Summer knew it very well, that whispery and insistent way his voice got, like the sound of a river moving.

"I think we've kind of said all the things we can say, Austin."

He moved a little closer. She refused to look at his face, with all its complicating charms.

"I'm sorry about Seth and Diana, Summer," Austin said. "You deserve better."

"Thanks."

"I know the rules here. I'm supposed to allow you to heal, maybe have a couple rebound boyfriends, then come back into play. But I've never been much of a Miss Manners kind of guy. And besides, there are extenuating circumstances."

"Meaning?"

"Meaning you just dumped me. And as a recent

dumpee, I don't think I'm up to waiting around. So I guess what I'm asking is, where does this leave us?"

She watched the bands of frothy white appear far out in the water, then vanish. "I don't know, Austin," Summer whispered. "I don't know anything anymore. I thought I'd made the right decision about Seth."

"Well, as you may recall, I offered a dissenting opinion on that one."

"If I could have been so wrong about him, how can I know anything?"

Austin took her hands in his. "Do you remember what I told you when you were trying to decide about whether to reapply to Carlson?"

Summer watched his fingers tangle in her own, trying to stay neutral, trying not to feel the feelings tangle up inside her in response to his touch. "Something along the lines of, 'Don't crap out on it just because you're afraid of failing.'"

"I'm sure it was much more eloquently phrased. Anyway, you see my point?"

Summer shook her head. "I need to go, Austin," she said, trying to pull away.

"My point is, I'm just another Carlson. You did the noble thing. You stuck with old Seth, who turned out not to be Old Faithful. But that was just a diversionary tactic to keep you from dealing with your feelings for me. So I'm giving you one last chance to claim your prize. It's the choice of a lifetime, Summer. Don't blow it again."

Summer smiled. "The choice of a lifetime, huh?"

"And don't smile all-knowingly like that. You know it's true. Besides, I find it incredibly sexy."

Without warning, Austin bent down and kissed her. The scorching sun and the heat of his body, pressed close to hers, made it seem like much more than a kiss, made it seem almost dangerous.

When he pulled away, a troubled expression had replaced Austin's confidence. "This is harder for me than you know, Summer," he whispered. "I'm not sure it's fair for me to try again like this. There are things about me . . . I don't know. I'm just saying I'm maybe not the best choice for you. I'm saying maybe I'm being selfish here. Hell, I know I'm being selfish—" His voice caught.

"I don't understand. What do you mean?"

"Nothing." He gave a helpless shrug. "Except, of course, what you already know. That I love you."

She watched him walk away without another word. Even when he'd vanished from her sight, she could still feel his fingers wrapped in hers, and she could still taste his kiss.

Austin walked home the long way, taking his time to skirt one of the less crowded beaches. He took off his shoes and let the waves cool his feet. The sun melted into his shoulders, and turned the waves to dazzling prisms. "The always wind-obeying deep," Austin mumbled. That's what Shakespeare had called it.

Austin smiled in spite of himself. Here he was strolling down a Florida beach—a lost, lovesick, poorly-groomed poet muttering Shakespeare at the waves. What would his brother say?

He hadn't talked to his brother in a while. The messages kept accumulating on Austin's machine. *I know what you're going through. It gets easier with time. Don't give up hope, man.* Variations on the theme of coping.

Not that Dave was coping all that well. But then, the knowledge that you were going to die early, in exactly the same slow, awful way your father was dying, was bound to wear you down. Dave's fiancée had dumped him, he'd contemplated suicide, he was drinking heavily.

Not that Austin was doing much better.

He was hardly one to preach to Summer about how to make hard choices. What the hell did he know about choices? All he knew was that the idea of being without Summer so filled him with fear that he couldn't let her go. He'd humiliated himself again and again, returning to her life, making his case like an overeager lawyer filing endless appeals.

Even though he knew the kindest thing, the right

thing, was to let her go. She didn't deserve to watch him get sick and die. She didn't deserve any of it.

Of course, that assumed a long and happy relationship together first. But he did assume that, like he assumed the sun would rise tomorrow and the ocean would still be blue and *Baywatch* would still be on the air. He loved her that completely.

It could be years, decades, before he had any symptoms. There was research going on, things were always changing. Austin had told his brother that after Dave had gotten the news. Dave had told Austin the same thing when Austin had forced himself to find out the truth about his own future.

Austin paused to toss a shell far out into the ocean. He watched it get sucked deep into the sea without a sound. The wind-obeying deep.

He liked that. Wind obeying. If the sea couldn't fight the wind, how could he? Whatever Summer decided, that would be it. He'd said it before, but this time he *felt* it. No more pleading, no more humiliating pitches like a desperate ad man. He would blow with the wind, let things fall where they might.

There was no point in fighting fate. It was up to karma. The great cosmic game plan. It was up to secrets coded deep in his cells. It was up to the wind.

It was up to Summer.

# Not Good Enough

Diana slapped the Cheerios box to the floor with a satisfying *whap*. "Gotcha," she muttered.

The door to the apartment opened. "Anybody call?" Marquez asked hopefully as she tossed her waitress apron onto the couch.

"Nope. Sorry. No word on Diver?"

"Nothing." Marquez dropped into a chair. "And not that you and I are speaking anymore, but why are you crawling around on the floor with a box of cereal?"

"Not that you and I are speaking anymore, but I've spent all afternoon in search of the elusive Moby-Roach. This building is such a dump. He kept me awake all night, scrabbling around on the floor."

"Sure it wasn't your conscience keeping you awake?"

Diana ignored the question. "He's trapped inside this box. Now I just need to get rid of him."

"Finally. A guy who's your type. You should have shopped other species a long time ago. If it doesn't work out with Moby, you might try a cobra. Or a rat. Maybe a weasel."

Diana stared wearily at the Cheerios box. She knew Marquez was spoiling for a fight, but she just wasn't up for it.

Seth had stopped by this morning to pick up a duffel bag he'd left behind. He'd spent last night at his grandfather's, he'd informed her. No, he was not going back to California anytime soon. No, he did not want to talk to Diana about Summer, or about anything else, for that matter.

Marquez tried again. "It took you a while, Diana, but I knew you'd realize Seth was out of your league."

"This isn't going to work, is it?" Diana asked softly. "Just the two of us here in this apartment, I mean. Without Summer here, it's like there's no buffer zone to keep us from killing each other."

"I'm up for it. Swords or pistols?"

"Maybe I should move. I could go back to my mom's."

Marquez fell silent. The sound of laughter coming

from the pool area in the backyard drifted through the window. "I gotta go look for Diver with Summer," she said, jumping to her feet.

Diana felt her will to stay cool in front of Marquez slipping. She bit down on her lower lip until it stung. "Look, could we at least just stop the fighting? I'm not up for it right now."

"You should have thought of that before you ruined Summer's life."

Marquez disappeared into her bedroom. She emerged a few minutes later, wearing what Diana had come to think of as Marquez's uniform—baggy T-shirt, baggy jeans.

In the old days Diana had gotten great pleasure needling Marquez about her tacky, too bright, *I'm extremely available* clothes. No more.

Marquez grabbed her car keys and her purse. "If Diver calls, tell him . . . I don't know, just tell him to come home."

She was almost out the door when Diana asked, "How was the counseling?"

Marquez paused, hand on the doorknob. "Fine, great. I'm a new woman."

"You didn't go, did you?"

"Actually, I did."

"I saw a counselor for a while, did I ever tell you

that? After all the stuff with Ross, with him trying to rape me. . . ."

Diana could feel Marquez's eyes on her. But she just plunged ahead, stringing one word after another, touching each one like beads on a rosary.

"I went to this counselor, Lori, this one who worked at the Dolphin Institute. She was already kind of a friend—I mean, I knew her, so it should have been easy. But I went to her office three times and sat in my car and cranked up the CD player. I just sat there. I couldn't go in."

"Diana, I need to go."

"It was like I was afraid if I started talking about the feelings, I'd just dissolve in them. Like, you know"—she smiled—"like the Wicked Witch of the West. Which you probably would agree is not a bad analogy."

"Diana." Marquez was less angry than mystified now. "Why *are* you telling me this?"

"You have to try to get help, Marquez. Because if you don't, it just kills you. You die a little bit at a time."

"I'm outta here." Marquez yanked open the door.

"I got to this point, this really low point, where I was sure I was going to kill myself. But then I thought about all the things Lori had taught me. You know,

how strong I really was, how things would get better."
She smiled a little. "And it turned out she was right. I
got through it. And so can you."

"Damn it, Diana!" Marquez cried. She slammed
the door shut. "Damn it, Diana," she said more softly.
"I don't need this right now."

Diana sighed. "I know where it's coming from, the
dieting and stuff."

"How could you know? You've never had an
excess ounce on your bod."

"It's not just about that," Diana said. "It's something else—it's like you have to clamp down and take
control of your life. It's like there's just too much . . .
stuff in your head, and you have to find a way to shut
it out."

Marquez said nothing. But she was nodding slightly,
looking away. "How could *you* know?" she said at last.

"There's this feeling. This feeling that you get that
you're not . . ." She met Marquez's eyes. "Not good
enough."

Marquez cocked her head. "What is with you?
You're not, you know, cracking up, are you? I mean,
this is not the most likely time to suddenly be baring
your soul to me."

Diana shrugged. "You're right. Go ahead, go.
I'm sorry. I'm sort of bummed out, and you were the
nearest thing to a human being I had around."

Seconds passed. Neither girl spoke. "I gotta find Diver," Marquez said at last.

"I know."

"You're okay, right? I mean, not that I care, but I don't want to come home and have to call the paramedics."

"Like Summer did with you?"

"I wasn't trying to kill myself, Diana. I was trying to improve the shape of my thighs. There's a slight but significant difference." Marquez opened the door. "Want me to dump the roach?"

"I'll do it. I don't have much else planned."

"Bye, then," Marquez said, but she still wasn't moving. She stared at Diana with a clouded, annoyed expression.

"You know the thing I always thought was really great about you, Marquez?" Diana said.

"My voluptuous figure."

"The way you actually believed you were the coolest person on earth."

"Yeah, well, it was an act, okay? Is that what you want to hear?"

"But we're all acting, one way or another. And if you practice the act long enough, you start believing it."

"Maybe."

"You need to start believing in yourself again, Marquez. Trust yourself that it's all going to be okay."

"The person I love most in the world just ran out on me. Forgive me if I'm not feeling all that much like the coolest person on the planet."

"This isn't about Diver." Diana sighed. "This is about sitting in your car, afraid to go inside. Try the counseling. Please try it."

"You know, I'm not the one who just destroyed her cousin's life. Maybe you should take your own advice."

The door slammed shut. After a while Diana took the Cheerios box down to the backyard. She watched the ugly, fat bug vanish into the grass. It was not particularly satisfying.

Still, she realized with resignation, it was the closest she'd come in recent memory to helping anyone.

# 12

# In Search of Diver and Other Babes

"I feel like we've searched every beach in the Keys." Summer sighed as she and Marquez trudged back to Marquez's old car. The air was rich with the smell of coconut oil and the salty tang of the ocean. It was afternoon, and so hot that most of the beaches were nearly deserted, which had made the search for Diver quicker than it might otherwise have been.

Summer eased onto the torn front seat, gingerly lowering her bare legs onto the superheated vinyl. "You sure you don't want me to drive?"

"Nah," Marquez said. "The only way I can take out my frustrations is with the gas pedal. By the way, have I mentioned this is really nice of you, dragging around with me like this? You sure it's okay with your job?"

"Jared was great about it. Although he did mention that my life reminded him of a soap opera."

"Guess it's better than telling you it reminds him of CNN."

"Or *ER*," Summer said. "So. We've done Turtle Beach, Smuggler's Beach, Las Palmas Cove, and most of Coral Island. What next?"

"Much farther and we'll end up in Key West." Marquez tapped out a nervous beat on the steering wheel. "Maybe it's time to call it quits. For today, anyway. Who knows, maybe he called."

"He might even be home by now," Summer suggested, trying her best to sound like she believed it.

Marquez looked at her hopefully. Her big dark eyes had shiny circles under them. She'd lost so much weight that her cheekbones and chin had taken on a strange sharpness. She didn't look like Marquez anymore, but more like one of those caricature sketches they did on the boardwalk in Crab Claw.

"Want to get something to eat?" Summer suggested.

"I'm not hungry." Marquez jammed the key in the ignition. "I ate before."

"Tell me some more about the counseling."

"I told you. It was okay, no biggie. Not like in TV movies. Pretty mellow."

"And you liked the counselor?"

"Yeah. She was okay, I guess. For a shrink."

"So you're going back for sure, right?"

Marquez gave her a *back off* look. Summer held up her hands. "Okay, okay. I'm being nosy. It's just that you're my best friend, Marquez. I want you to be okay."

"I'll be okay when I find Diver."

"I know. But in the meantime you have to take care of yourself."

Marquez closed her eyes. "God, Summer, why is he doing this? I thought . . . I thought he loved me."

"Diver loves you completely, Marquez. You know that."

"Uh-huh. You didn't see the way he was looking at Caroline at the beach party."

Summer recalled what Austin had told her about his encounter with Caroline that morning. "Whatever this is about," she said firmly, "it has nothing to do with how much he loves you."

"But why, then?"

"I don't know." Summer tried to keep her fury at her irresponsible, selfish brother out of her voice. There was no point in getting Marquez more worked up. "I guess we have to remember Diver's had a really messed-up life. He's so laid-back and calm, sometimes we forget all those problems have probably taken a toll on him."

"Yeah, well, now he's taking a toll on me."

"I know. I'm sorry."

Marquez clutched the wheel so tightly, her knuckles were white. "I thought I knew him. I thought I understood him. You know what I mean?"

"I do know. Too well."

"You're thinking about Seth."

Summer smiled grimly. "Trying not to, actually." She nudged Marquez. "Come on. Let's hit the road, crank this baby up to fifty."

"It starts shaking uncontrollably at forty-five."

Marquez pulled onto the two-lane road that skirted the beach. Summer watched two Jet Skis fly across the calm water. "Remember when we took the Olans' Jet Skis out for a spin and they ran out of gas and we thought we were going to drown?"

"It was your idea," Marquez said.

"Whoa. Reality check. That was so totally your idea!"

They fell silent, the hot wind whipping their hair into tornadoes. "Sometimes," Summer said at last, "I feel a lot older than I was last year. Not just a year. More like, I don't know, five years or ten."

"Five years," Marquez considered. "That would make you a college graduate. An official adult."

"Well, just older in some ways. It's like everything got complicated. It went from black and white to shades of gray. Last summer I was worried about not ever having a boyfriend. Now I've had two loves and lost both of them. Last summer I had a brother who'd disappeared before I was even born. Now I have a brother who—"

"Who's disappeared all over again," Marquez finished for her.

Summer squinted at a sign up the road. "Hey, would you mind taking a little detour? Could we run by Carlson for a second?"

Marquez put on the blinker. "When do you think you'll hear from them?"

Summer shrugged. "I have no idea. I reapplied so late. They'll probably reject me for being so indecisive."

"It'd be so cool if you went. I'll be right down the road at FCU. You could move back into the apartment, maybe, and then—"

"Not with Diana," Summer said darkly.

Marquez glanced at her. "I understand why you had to move out, but do you have any idea what it's like for me living with her without you? It's like having a pet scorpion in the apartment. I can't ever let my guard down."

"Maybe this fall, when the lease is up, we could get something. . . ." Summer let her voice trail off. "There's no point in planning on it. Carlson's a long shot."

"They thought you were good enough to accept the first time."

"It was probably a clerical error."

Marquez pulled into the manicured grounds of Carlson, down a winding avenue lined by huge palms. "Where to?"

Summer grinned. "Nowhere. I just wanted to fantasize for a minute."

"So you're walking across the campus and, let's see, some babe like Brad Pitt is carrying your Intro to Something Irrelevant textbook—"

"No, this fantasy is babe-free. I'm carrying my own book."

Marquez stopped the car in front of a string of low-slung brick buildings with a view of the ocean. The campus was nearly deserted. "Mind if I get out for a second?" Summer asked.

Marquez smiled. "Take your time. But I'd advise adding a guy to that fantasy."

Summer walked over to the nearest building and peered through one of the windows. Desks, blackboard, table. Nothing fancy. But Carlson was considered a fine college, one for motivated and tough-minded students. It was difficult. It was competitive. Staring at the empty desks, Summer felt a slight shiver of fear skate up her spine. Was she motivated enough? Tough enough? Smart enough?

All year she'd planned on going to the University of Wisconsin with her high-school friends—and, of course, with Seth. She'd applied to other schools, including Carlson, but when Summer was accepted to Carlson and Seth wasn't, that had sealed her decision to go to UW.

Until, that is, she'd visited the campus with Austin recently and decided to reapply.

It would mean going to a new school solo, no friends, no Seth. On her own, no backup. Of course, they probably wouldn't reaccept her, not at this late date. So there was no point in worrying about how absolutely terrified the idea of being all alone made her feel.

She walked back to the car. Marquez was leaning against the headrest. Dashboard Confessional was blaring on the radio.

They drove back through the beautiful, quiet grounds. Summer watched the brick buildings blur together.

"How was the fantasy?" Marquez asked.

"Kind of scary."

"Maybe it needed a babe."

"I don't know," Summer said softly. "Maybe so."

# 13

# Word on the Street

When they got back to town, the main street that bisected Coconut Key was bathed in the rich, unreal colors of the late afternoon sun. "I guess you don't want to come home and say hi to Vampira?" Marquez asked.

Summer shook her head. "You guess right."

"You know, all your stuff's there. . . ."

"I'll come get it sometime when Diana's gone."

Marquez smiled sadly. "I'd offer to do it, but it would be like admitting you're not coming back. Why couldn't Diana just move out instead?" She snapped her fingers. "I could slip a little arsenic into her coffee. Think they'd bust me?"

"They'd probably bust me. I definitely have motive and opportunity."

At a red light Marquez gasped. "Summer. Duck. I mean now. Jerk alert at two o'clock."

"What?"

"Crap. He saw you. Seth is over at the bus station, waving like a maniac. What do I do? Ignore him?"

"I thought he was at his grandfather's in Crab Claw," Summer muttered.

Marquez groaned. "Two red lights in this one-horse town and we get trapped by one! He's coming. Don't freak."

Seth wove through the maze of cars. A moment later he was peering through Marquez's open window.

"The light's about to change, Seth," Marquez said. "Make it quick."

Summer stared straight ahead, her heart ricocheting around in her chest like a pinball.

"It's about Diver," Seth said, just as the light changed.

"What? Tell me, what?" Marquez cried.

"I—" Seth began, but his voice was drowned in a chorus of annoyed honks.

"Oh, just get in already, Seth," Summer said.

Seth leapt into the backseat and Marquez hit the accelerator. He glanced at Summer, then quickly looked away. "Just take me around the block. My car's parked at the station."

"How'd you know about Diver?" Summer asked.

"I left my backpack at your apartment," Seth said. "I went over to pick it up this morning and Diana told me."

"Would you *tell* us already?" Marquez cried. "What about Diver?"

"It's not so good, Marquez. I've been kind of looking out for him all day. Checking out his old haunts, that sort of thing. I went over to his job, but nobody knew anything. Anyway, as a last-ditch try, I checked the bus station. One of the ticket guys remembered Diver. He bought a one-way to Miami yesterday."

"Miami?" Marquez echoed in disbelief. "Miami?"

"I'm sorry, Marquez," Seth said. "I wish I had better news."

"Maybe he just took a ride to clear his head," Summer suggested, knowing how lame she sounded.

Marquez pulled into the Greyhound parking lot. She dropped her head onto the steering wheel.

"Well." Seth looked at Summer again, his expression half resigned, half hopeful. "Anyway. I'll let you know if I hear any more."

Marquez pulled herself upright. "Thanks, Seth. For trying. You're a good friend."

"Well, then." Seth put his hand on the door handle, but he didn't budge.

Summer studied her nails.

"Well, okay," Seth said. Slowly he got out of the car. He closed the door, then put his head through the back window. "Summer, have you thought any more about . . . you know, what we talked about last night?"

Summer shook her head.

"Okay, then. Well. Okay."

"Seth," Marquez said with a sigh, "you're babbling."

"Oh. Yeah, okay. Well."

"Thanks again." Marquez pulled away. "What did you talk about last night, anyway?"

"Take a guess."

"At least the men in your life are within walking distance," Marquez said. "Miami, Summer! Who knows where Diver is by now? He could be in Alaska. Well, okay, not Alaska. But somewhere equally not here."

"Maybe. But . . . I know this sounds crazy, Marquez, but I just have this feeling he's not so far away."

Marquez paused at a crosswalk to let two bare-chested guys in-line skate across. "You're just saying that."

"No, I'm not. It's this feeling." Summer noticed a

petite blond girl on the far side of the street. She was gazing intently into a store window.

Caroline.

"Hey, drop me off here, why don't you?" Summer said casually. "I kind of feel like walking."

"But why? I'll take you to Jared's."

"I need to clear my head after seeing Seth, you know?"

"I understand." Marquez nodded. "You going to be okay?"

"Yeah. How about you?"

"Me? I'm invincible," Marquez said softly. "Permanently single, but invincible."

"Not permanently." Summer opened the car door. "I'll call you. Eat something nice and fattening, okay?"

Summer dashed across the street. The blond girl had vanished into one of the shops. Now Summer wondered if it even was Caroline.

And what was she going to say if it *was* Caroline?

She peeked into three shops, open late like all the Main Street stores. Nothing.

Summer was almost ready to give up when she spotted Caroline in a bikini shop called Swim Jim's. Summer sauntered in and pretended to browse a rack of markdowns.

"Summer? Is that you?" Caroline rushed over. "I

heard about Diver," she said, oozing sympathy. "You must be worried sick."

Summer nodded. "It's so strange, Caroline. I mean, I just had lunch with Diver. He told me about how he'd gotten together with you."

Caroline put her sunglasses back on. "Yes, we had a nice little get-together. Talked about old times and all."

"When you were kids in . . . where was it? Virginia?"

"Uh-huh." Caroline turned to the rack of sale swimsuits. "So what do you figure happened?"

"Well, we're still trying to piece everything together. Did he say anything to you, by chance?"

"Me?" Caroline put her hand to her chest. "Lord, no. It's not like we were ever *close,* Summer." She grinned. "Guess I didn't see his potential back then."

Summer hesitated. She was getting nowhere. Probably because there was nowhere to go. "So you two were never, you know, an item? Childhood sweethearts or something?" she asked, trying to sound casual. "Between you and me, I thought maybe you were trying to rekindle an old flame."

"We were just *kids,* Summer. And back then Diver never paid me a bit of attention."

"How about now?"

"Now? Well, he's got Marquez, Summer. I wouldn't have a prayer." Caroline pulled out a red one-piece and held it up. "Too blah, right?" She returned it to the rack with a sigh. "No, it's not like that with Diver and me. I have a beau back in Virginia. Kyle. He's a junior at my college." She cleared her throat. "So, anyway. You're saying there are no clues about Diver?"

"Not really. He might have gone to Miami."

"Miami?" Caroline demanded. She moved to another rack. "I mean," she added more calmly, "why Miami?"

"I don't know. Someone thinks he caught a bus heading that way."

"Lord, I hope not. For your sake, I mean. And Marquez's."

Summer hesitated. "Well, I have to get going." She started for the door. "If you happen to hear anything about Diver, let me know, would you?"

"Of course." Caroline smiled sweetly. "I can't imagine why I would, but I'll keep my ears open. And my fingers crossed." She held up another suit. "How about this one? Thirty percent off. I'm positively broke, but it's my size."

"Nice," Summer said. "Well. I'm sure I'll see you around, Caroline. Say hi to Blythe."

Summer stepped into the still-hot street. She'd heard nothing to suggest that Caroline had anything to do with Diver's disappearance. And yet she couldn't quite shake the feeling that Austin might just have been onto something with his shaky-teaspoon theory.

# 14

# Hiding Out

*So,* Diana thought as she sipped at her coffee, *this is dawn.* It was rather pretty, if you were into that sort of thing.

She sat in the breakfast room of her mother's huge, fanciful house. It reminded her of Sleeping Beauty's castle at Disneyland, lots of color and curlicues and excess. Not unlike her mother, Mallory, actually.

Diana watched the sun slowly grow, reds spreading like a bruise. On the edge of the property the old stilt house took on a pink glow. A pelican, probably the one Summer and Diver insisted on calling Frank, sat on the railing, looking positively prehistoric.

She wondered if she should try to get some sleep.

She'd come here in the middle of the night after lying awake and restless in the apartment, haunted by images of Seth and Summer. At last, in frustration, she'd jumped in her car and driven aimlessly along the highway skirting the ocean.

Why she'd ended up here, she didn't know. Mallory was away on a book tour. And it wasn't as if Diana had a lot of cozy Hallmark memories of this place.

But she'd needed to clear her head. She hadn't realized how confused and unhappy she was until she'd tried to talk to Marquez yesterday. Attempting to give her advice had made Diana realize how utterly unqualified she was for the task. She had her own problems, plenty of them.

She was obsessed with the idea of calling Seth and begging for another chance, and repulsed by herself for wanting someone who so obviously didn't want her. And disturbing her every waking moment was the image of Summer—or the lack of her, anyway. Her clothes still in the closet, her half-made bed, her shampoo on the edge of the tub.

Diana dumped out the rest of her coffee. Maybe she'd try for a nap and then decide what to do. She didn't want to move back to Mallory's, but she obviously couldn't keep living with Marquez for much longer.

As she turned to leave the kitchen a flash of movement out the window made Diana pause. Someone was climbing up the stairs under the stilt house. She saw dark, tan skin, a glimmer of golden blond hair, then nothing.

Diver. It had to be.

For a brief moment Diana considered letting him be. She understood wanting to be alone, and whatever was wrong in his life, she doubted she could help him, if her experience with Marquez was any indication.

An image came to her suddenly of Marquez, her thin body racked with sobs. Marquez, so not like the old Marquez anymore.

With a sigh Diana opened the sliding glass doors and crossed the wet grass in bare feet, tightening the belt on her mother's robe. She knew if Diver saw her he wouldn't try to run. There was nowhere to go. And she had a feeling some part of him might just want to be found.

Diver was on the deck, leaning against the railing. He nodded as if he'd been expecting her.

"Not the best hiding place, huh?" Diana said, joining him.

Diver smiled sadly, his eyes on the brightening sky.

"That is," Diana added, "if you're really hiding."

He turned to her. His dark blue eyes were sheened with tears. He was so beautiful, a not-quite-of-this-world beauty. It was hard to look at him without thinking of his sister, of her innocent gaze and shimmering prettiness.

"To tell you the truth, Diana," he said wearily, "I'm not sure what I'm doing. I thought I was running. But then I came full circle and ended up here. It's like gravity is pulling me back."

"I know the feeling. I had no intention of coming here either."

She draped her arm around him and he laid his head on her shoulder. His skin was cool and smelled of the ocean. He'd been out swimming, of course. Diver loved the water.

There was a time not so long ago—last summer, in fact—when Diver had held her just this way. She'd been worn down and desperate after all the problems with Ross and Adam. Diver hadn't said much. He'd just been there for her, quiet and kind, on a dark, warm, sad night.

"Is she okay?" Diver whispered.

Diana considered. "I'm not sure," she admitted. "I'm just not sure, Diver. Marquez wants to know why you left. She thinks it's her fault."

"Oh, man." Diver pulled away. "Oh, man, I was afraid of that. . . ."

"What did you expect, Diver?" Diana said gently. "You disappear without a trace, not even a note—"

"I wrote a note. I tore it up. It was crap. It was full

of excuses, and there aren't any." He wiped a tear away with the back of his hand. "There aren't any."

Diana touched his arm. "I could say something to her. If you're not ready to deal with everything, I could at least pass her a message."

"You don't understand," Diver cried, startling her with his sudden rage. Frank flapped off in a huff. "I'm screwed. I can't go back. I've lost Marquez, lost Summer. I've lost everything."

A slow smile tugged at Diana's mouth. "What?" Diver demanded. "What? You think this is funny?"

"Diver, no, no. It's not that. It's just that I could be saying those exact same words."

"I don't get it."

"Seth and I, we were . . ." Suddenly she felt embarrassed. Diver was so sincere, so innocent in some ways. "We were together for a little while, and Summer found out. They broke up and Summer moved out of the apartment and now I'm public enemy number one." She shrugged. "With good reason, I suppose. I just can't get anything right. I hurt everyone I care about."

Diana waited for Diver's shocked response. But all he said was, "You've never hurt me, Diana. I know you're a good person."

She let the words sink in, holding on to them as long as she could. "You're a good person too, Diver.

Whatever this is about, you have people who love you. We can find an answer."

"There is no answer. I screwed up, and now it's caught up with me."

"You sure you don't want to talk about it?"

He shook his head, jaw clamped shut.

"No matter how much you're afraid you've hurt Marquez and Summer, all they want is to have you back. If you explained—"

"Did you try explaining about Seth to Summer?"

She looked away. "That's different."

"Diana, you have to promise me something. Promise me you won't tell Marquez about this. It would just get her hopes up. And there isn't any hope."

Diana stared out at the horizon. Deep reds were bleeding into the ocean as the cloudless sky lost color. The day was going to be a scorcher.

Diver took her arm. "Promise me, Diana."

"I promise. If you promise me something."

He smiled, just a little. "Maybe."

"Promise me you won't ever say there isn't any hope again."

Diver didn't answer. He just gazed out at the placid, blue water, lost in his private sadness.

"Nice sunrise," he said at last.

## To Err Is Human, to Forgive Is Extremely Difficult.

"Could I speak to Summer Smith?"

"May I ask who's calling?" a man asked briskly.

Diana hesitated. If she told the truth, Summer might not come to the phone. "Just tell her it's Marquez."

"May I also ask if you have a timepiece at your disposal?"

"I'm sorry. I know it's really early."

"Indeed. One moment, please."

Diana twirled the phone cord around her finger. From her bedroom window she had a clear view of the stilt house.

She wondered how long Diver would stay before

moving on. She wondered if she was making a terrible mistake, calling Summer.

"Marquez?" Summer's voice was filled with hope. "It's so early! Did you hear something about Diver?"

"Summer, it's not Marquez. It's me, Diana."

Silence.

"Don't hang up, Summer. Just hear me out."

"I have nothing to say to—"

"Summer, I know where Diver is."

"If this is some kind of cruel joke—"

Diana sighed. "I'm telling you the truth. He's hiding out at the stilt house."

"You *talked* to him?"

"Just now. Look, I don't know how much longer he'll be here, so you need to hurry."

Summer fell silent again. "I don't have any way to get over to Crab Claw," she said at last. "I'll call Marquez. Maybe she—"

"No," Diana interrupted. "You can't tell Marquez."

"Can't tell her?" Summer's voice rose in indignation. "What gives you the right—"

"I promised Diver, Summer. I told him I wouldn't tell Marquez, and he trusts me."

"That was his first mistake," Summer said bitterly.

"Listen, I had real doubts about calling you, but my gut tells me maybe you can get through to Diver."

Diana drew in a deep breath. "I'll pick you up. I'll be there in ten minutes."

Summer hesitated. "Okay, then." She gave Diana directions. "I'll be ready. Diana?"

"Yeah?"

"Is he okay?"

"He's your brother, Summer. You'll have to decide that for yourself."

When Diana pulled into the wide drive, Summer was already waiting. A woman dressed in white was with her and a guy in a wheelchair. At least, Diana assumed it was a guy. It was hard to tell, with all the bandages.

Diana parked next to a large van. The side door was open, revealing a wheelchair lift.

Summer met her eyes warily. She had on a T-shirt and a pair of cutoffs, no makeup. Her hair was damp and a little tangled. Still, she looked beautiful. She was clearly Diver's sister.

And Seth's love.

"All set?" Diana asked. Her voice was off, shaking just slightly.

"Diana, this is Jared and his nurse, Juanita."

Diana nodded. "Nice to meet you. Summer, we need to hurry."

To Diana's surprise, Jared moved his wheelchair close to her window. He fixed his dark, intense gaze at her. "Hi, Diana," he said in a hoarse whisper.

"Hi," she said, feeling strangely uneasy.

"We should get going too," the nurse said. "We've got a long drive ahead of us. Jared has a doctor's appointment at nine."

"I'll probably be back before you, Jared," Summer said as she climbed into Diana's car.

"See you," Jared said softly. Even as she pulled out of the driveway, Diana couldn't shake the feeling that he was watching her.

"Poor guy," she said. "How was he hurt?"

"Car accident." Summer sat beside her rigidly, one hand gripping the door handle as if she might bolt at any moment. "He was in Germany when it happened. He went over an embankment, like a two-hundred-foot drop. He nearly died."

"Where's his family?"

"In New England. They never visit. They just, you know, pay the bills."

The conversation ground to a halt. Diana drove faster than was strictly necessary. The warm wind ripped through the windows. She wondered whose job it was to break the awful silence.

They were almost to Mallory's before Diana finally spoke again. "I'm not sure I'm doing the right thing."

"It must be hard to know, what with not having a conscience."

Diana let it go. "The thing is, I think Diver needs to tell someone what's going on, and you're probably the only one he'll talk to. He feels so bad about himself. About hurting Marquez and you. But something's really tearing him up."

"He didn't say why he ran off?"

"No. He didn't say much of anything." Diana turned down her mother's street. "Except that he didn't have any excuse for what he'd done. And that he'd lost you and Marquez for good."

Diana paused. She felt the words working their way to the surface. She could almost taste them, bitter and unwelcome as tears.

"That's . . ." She pulled into the driveway. "That's sort of how I feel."

Summer opened the door. Her face was blank. There was nothing there—no forgiveness, not even any anger.

"Thank you for calling me about Diver," she said. She closed the door.

Diana watched her run across the green, still-dewy lawn. She put the car in reverse, then hesitated. After a moment she turned off the car and went inside the house to wait, although she wasn't quite sure for what.

# 16

# Did He or Didn't He? Only His Sister Knows for Sure. . . .

The front door of the stilt house was ajar. The smell of mildew and ocean and mothballs made Summer instantly nostalgic. This had been her first home away from home. While living here, she'd met Marquez and Seth and Adam.

And Diver.

Diver, who by some amazing convergence of fate and circumstance and the alignment of the planets and the Quick Pick lottery numbers, had turned out to be her brother.

He was in the bathroom, splashing water on his face. When he saw her reflection in the mirror, he seemed more resigned than surprised.

"Diana works fast," he said. "I knew I shouldn't have come back here. I don't know why I did."

"I do," Summer said. "It's home."

"You shouldn't have bothered coming. I was just about to leave."

Summer followed Diver onto the porch. Frank flapped over to join them as they sat on the sun-warmed planks.

"Where are you going?" Summer asked.

"North somewhere."

"That would be ironic, since you ran screaming from Minnesota like a bat out of hell."

"Not *that* far north."

Summer leaned back against the wall and closed her eyes to the sun's heat. "So what is it you're running from this time, Diver? Or should I say who? Last time it was Mom and Dad and me. So who is it this time? Marquez?"

"I love Marquez," he whispered.

"Well, you sure have an interesting way of showing it. How could you do this to her when she's so fragile?" She opened her eyes. Her brother sat beside her, head bent low, his long golden hair half obscuring his face. "How *could* you?" she demanded in a voice choked by rage.

Diver's shoulders jerked convulsively. His soft sobs were almost drowned by the steady rush and retreat of the waves.

Summer stared at him without pity. He was an illusion, not a real flesh-and-blood human being. Like a movie star, she realized. A blank, beautiful slate, an image without substance. He came into people's lives and let them believe and then, when they needed him most, he vanished. He'd done it to Summer, to her parents, to Marquez.

"She believed in you, Diver," Summer said.

Long minutes passed before Diver raised his head. His eyes were bloodshot. His face was damp with tears.

"I'm going to tell you something," he said. "Because I want you to explain it to Marquez. So she understands. So she knows I love her. I did something, something really bad, a long time ago. Back when I was with my other dad, the one who kidnapped me. I was just a kid. I mean, it was a long time ago, okay?"

Summer nodded. "Okay."

"And this . . . this bad thing finally caught up with me. So I had to leave."

"And that's it? That's supposed to make Marquez feel better?"

"I know," Diver said hopelessly. He went to the railing and gazed down at the water. "Forget it. There's nothing I can do."

"I have a brilliant idea. How about fighting back?

How about confronting whatever this thing is? How about trusting that Marquez and I would stick by you?"

Diver looked at her doubtfully. "Would you? I wonder."

"Maybe if you told me what it was, maybe then—"

"I killed someone, Summer."

The waves kept coming, the sun kept shining, the breeze kept teasing the palms. But Summer was pretty sure that the world as she'd known it was suddenly forever changed.

"Maybe you didn't hear me," Diver said sharply. "I killed—"

"I heard you."

"Do you still want to tell Marquez? Are you still planning on holding my hand, sticking by me? You'd look nice in court, the loyal sister."

Summer stood. She held on to the wooden railing. It was warm from the sun, smooth and shiny from years of exposure to the wild storms that spun out of the ocean. That's how it was, here in the Keys. One hour it would be calm, a little too calm, and then suddenly the sky would open up and you'd wonder how the world could survive such a beating.

She turned to face him. "I don't believe it."

"Believe it. It's true. I even have a witness."

Summer crossed her arms over her chest. "Tell me."

"I can't. I've already told you too much."

"You're leaving, anyway. What do you care? It's not like I'm going to turn you in, Diver."

"No."

"If you don't tell me the details, I won't have any way to make it okay with Marquez. If you do . . . well, I don't have to tell her everything, but I'll be able to sell your story. You know, to make her feel like it's not her fault you left."

Diver pursed his lips. His brow was creased, his blue eyes so dark, they could have been black. "Let's go inside."

"Who's going to hear us? Frank?"

Diver managed a grim smile. "He's never been able to keep a secret. Besides, he's always thought highly of me. I'd hate to disillusion him."

"Why not Frank? You've done it to everyone else."

They went back inside. Diver shut the door, and they sat at the wobbly Formica table.

"So?" Summer prompted.

Diver sucked in a deep breath. "I'll tell you the whole story. But you can't tell the details to Marquez. I don't want her thinking about me this way. Just . . . just tell her I got into some trouble. Deal?"

"All right."

"There was a fire," Diver said softly, almost as if he

were reciting a story he knew by heart. "My mom had died of cancer, and it was just my dad and me then. He wasn't such a great dad."

"Well, duh, Diver. He kidnapped you, for starters," Summer said, almost exasperated. "Sometimes you act as if your growing up was normal."

"It was, to me. I didn't know anything else, Summer. And it wasn't all bad." He shrugged. "So, anyway, he beat me up sometimes. Well, a lot, actually. And one night I just got so sick of it that I burned down the house and he died and then I ran away." He said it casually, as if he were reciting what he'd had for dinner last night. "I was on the streets for a long time. Living here and there, and then I found this place"— he waved his arm—"which was like a palace to me. And then you came. Which was like . . . like waking up from a nightmare, in a way."

Summer fingered a plastic place mat on the table. "Are you sure he died?"

"I'm sure."

"How can you be sure?"

"I saw the papers. They were after me for arson and murder."

"But assuming you did it—"

"I *did* do it."

"Assuming you did it," Summer persisted, "you were just a kid, Diver. It was self-defense."

"It was premeditated," Diver said calmly. "I wanted him dead."

Summer got a glass out of the cupboard. The water in the faucet was warm and tinny tasting. She drank slowly, considering. "So how did you burn down the house, exactly?"

"I don't remember. It was a long time ago. Mostly I just remember it in dreams. I think I blacked out at some point. I remember coming to on the lawn. It was dark, the grass was wet. The fire engines were coming. I could hear my dad . . . screaming."

"But you don't know how you started the fire."

Diver was staring at his hands, as if they held the answer. "No. But Caroline said they found—" He stopped cold.

"I had a feeling she was involved in this somehow."

"She was my next-door neighbor. She recognized me right away, that night Marquez was in the hospital and I ran into her. I denied it, but there was no point. She knew. She knew all the details. She said they found flammable liquid at the site. She knew the cops were after me. She knew everything."

"And?"

Diver sighed. "There was some insurance money, I guess. She said if I went back and claimed it, she'd make up this story about how she saw me try to save my dad. How she'd been just a kid, too freaked out by the whole thing to tell the police at the time."

"Let me guess. In return Caroline gets a piece of the insurance money?"

"Something like that." Diver gave a harsh laugh. "She really believes people would buy her story about how I was a big hero, not a murderer. How I'd tried to save my dad, even though he beat the crap out of me almost every day of my life."

Summer put her glass in the sink. She didn't need this to be happening. Her life was plenty complicated already. She didn't need Diver's problems.

Truth was, she wasn't even sure she needed Diver. He'd disappointed her so many times. She didn't owe him.

She turned. Diver was looking out the window at Frank, smiling wistfully at the ugly pelican. Sometimes when he smiled that way, she could imagine Diver as a child, desperate and alone and yet still, against all logic, hopeful. Hoping that his life really was normal. That his parents really did love him.

She joined him at the window.

"I want you to promise me something, Diver. And I want you to mean it. This can't be like all your other promises. This can't just be something you say to make me go away."

Diver looked at her, waiting. Hoping.

"I want you to promise me that you'll stay put for

two more days. Right here. No questions. I'll be sure you have some food. You just need to lie low and give me a chance to figure things out."

"There's nothing to figure out, Summer. It's like I told Diana—it's hopeless."

"Do you promise or not?" she demanded. "Yes or no?"

Diver gave a small nod. "I promise. Just don't . . . get yourself in any trouble because of me, okay? You don't owe me anything."

"You read my mind."

He stared back out the window. "It's funny. I have those dreams again and again, but I never let myself see the worst part. I see myself leaving my dad. I see him burning alive, for God's sake. But I never let myself see the"—he cleared his throat—"the . . . you know. The lighting of the match. I can't bear to know that's inside me, I guess. I wonder why that is?"

Summer went to the door. When she opened it, the clean, white light was blinding. "I'll tell you why," she said softly. "It's because you didn't do it, Diver."

# 17

# The Plot Thickens . . .

"That was quick," Diana said as she opened the door. "I take it that it didn't go well with Diver?"

Summer almost smiled. Not unless having your brother confess to murder was good news.

"I need to talk to you," she said, stepping into the wide marble foyer.

Diana led her into the white-on-white living room, with its leather furniture and thick fake polar bear rugs. A spray of lilies graced the grand piano in the corner. Even when she was away, Summer's aunt insisted on having fresh flowers in the house.

Summer sat on the edge of a white leather podlike thing that only vaguely resembled a chair. Diana leaned

against the piano, her hands on her hips. Her dark
beauty was even more pronounced in the wintry living
room. It was impossible to look at her without imagining Seth in her arms. Summer could almost understand
it. Diana was exotic and difficult and elusive. She must
have seemed like the ultimate challenge.

"Diver's in serious trouble, isn't he?" Diana asked.

Summer cleared her throat. She didn't trust Diana
for a moment. Still, it wasn't like she had any choice in
the matter. Diver was hiding out here, and Diana knew
about it. And for what it was worth, Diana was the one
who had called her about Diver.

"Diver needs to stay in the stilt house for a couple
of days, maybe longer," Summer said carefully.

"He can stay as long as he wants."

"I'll need to bring him some food and blankets—"

"Done, This . . . trouble he's in. What are you
going to do about it?"

"I don't have a clue. Try to find a way to set things
right." Summer forced herself to meet Diana's eyes.
"Diana, no one can know about this. Not even Marquez. No one."

"Diver's been a good friend. You can trust me."
Diana gave a short laugh. "I know what you're
thinking. Let me revise that. On this, at least, you can
trust me."

"I don't have any choice, I guess."

"This is different. With Seth . . ." Diana shrugged. "I guess when I'm in love, I'm capable of doing just about anything to get what I want."

"Including lying about Austin and me? Setting me up and using my own engagement ring to do it? Flying all the way to California just to be with Seth and destroy what was left of our relationship?"

"Fine. Yes. I'm a witch, okay? But I was right about you and Austin. At least I'm a perceptive witch."

"Maybe they can put that on your tombstone. Loving daughter, caring friend, perceptive witch." Summer stood. "Look, I don't want to talk about Seth."

"What you don't want," Diana said, "is to believe that Seth might have felt something for me and I might have felt something for Seth. What you don't want, Summer, is to have to believe that you and I are alike."

"Alike! Please." Summer started for the door, but Diana moved to block her path.

"You wanted Austin enough to risk everything, even Seth," Diana said. "And I wanted Seth enough to risk everything. Even"—her voice cracked—"even my own cousin."

"I have to go, Diana."

"I guess it's too much to ever expect you'll forgive me," Diana pressed on. "But you expected Seth to forgive you for all your little indiscretions with Austin."

"I ended it with Austin—" Summer began, but Diana's dubious look gave her pause. She took a deep breath. "I have to go, Diana. There's no point in discussing this. If you want to talk about your—your *relationship*—with Seth, why don't you give him a call?"

"Are you saying you're not going to try to reel him back in?"

Beneath the sarcastic tone, Summer could hear a touch of hope. She considered all the hurtful, cutting things she could say. But she was way too tired. "I know this may be hard for you to believe, but not everybody goes through their life with such absolute certainty about what they want. I'm not you, Diana. Thank God."

Their eyes locked. Finally Diana stepped away and let Summer through.

Summer was almost to the door when she paused. "There's something else I need to ask you," she said, barely forcing out the words. "Another favor."

Diana crossed her arms over her chest. "On the heels of just thanking the Almighty that you weren't cursed with being me?"

"Okay, so it's really bad timing."

"What do you want? You've got Seth. You've got the stilt house. You've got my vow of silence. How about my car? My firstborn? I've got an extra kidney I don't use much. . . ."

"Remember how you proved Ross attacked you?" Summer said suddenly.

Diana blinked in surprise. "Why do you ask?"

"Adam kept telling you no one would believe his brother did it, right?"

"He was telling the truth too. Ross was a senator's son. And the Merricks had money to burn." Diana smiled, not at Summer, but at some private satisfaction. "Of course, I got the last laugh, such as it was."

"You got Ross and Senator Merrick to confess, and you videotaped the whole thing."

Diana clucked her tongue. "A shame, the way the tabloids got hold of that tape."

"I want to borrow your new videocamera."

"I'd lend it to you, really I would. But Mallory gave it to a friend of hers. She's having twins and taping it for posterity. Which is one film opening I'm personally not dying to see." She eyed Summer doubtfully. "Summer, you're not getting in over your head, are you?"

"I don't have a clue."

Diana went to the hallway closet and dug through a storage box. After a few seconds she held up a palm-size tape recorder. "You might want to check the batteries. Mallory dictates into it, and she always leaves the thing running. . . ."

"A tape recorder?"

Diana pressed it into Summer's hand. "I have no idea what you're up against, but it might come in handy."

"Thanks." Summer slipped the tape recorder into her purse. "Really. Thanks. This might just help."

"Sometimes it helps to be a perceptive witch."

Summer reached for the doorknob. "Where to?" Diana asked.

"I'll walk."

"Summer, you don't have a lot of time. Diver's probably not going to stay put much longer. And it's a long walk back to Coconut."

They walked to the car in silence. "So. Where to?" Diana asked again.

Summer thought. An idea was taking root in her mind, but she wasn't quite sure what to do with it.

"Back to Jared's?" Diana prompted.

"No." Summer hesitated. "To Austin's, if you don't mind."

Diana's look said she was not particularly surprised. "No," she said. "I don't mind at all."


"You shaved," Summer commented when Austin answered the door.

He grinned down at Summer's legs from behind the screen door. "The question is, can I safely say the same of you?"

Austin swung open the door. He was wearing a pair of pathetically dilapidated jeans. No shirt.

"I know it's early. Sorry," Summer apologized, avoiding eye contact with anything visible between his neck and the edge of his jeans.

"I apologize for the chaos. Showering's as far as I've gotten with my rehab."

"You're feeling better?"

Austin slipped his arms around her waist. He smelled like soap. "You gave me hope yesterday."

"I . . ."

"Don't worry. It was nothing you said. It was what you didn't say. You didn't say 'get lost.'" He kissed her softly, a sweet breeze of a kiss, then pulled away, smiling. "Can I assume you're here to tell me you've made your choice? You can't live without me, you need me every waking—"

"Actually, Austin, I kind of need your apartment."

"Well, living together is a big step, but—"

"Just for an hour or two."

He planted his hands on his hips. "You're living at the Ritz and you want to borrow a room at the Motel 6?"

"I can't use Jared's. And I can't use my old apartment because Marquez can't know about this."

"This?" Austin's smile faded. He cleared a spot on the couch. "Sit. What's this about, anyway? There must be something going on if Diana, the Other Woman, is serving as your chauffeur."

"It's a long story."

"I can be late to work. They'd lose all respect for me if I actually showed up on time." He sat beside her. "Tell me. Maybe I can help."

"The thing is, I can't tell you much, Austin. This is my problem, and I have to figure it out myself. Even if I get it wrong." She shook her head. "And I've been getting plenty of things wrong lately."

Austin studied her carefully. He reached into his pocket. "Here's the key. I've got an extra. You say the word, I'll be sure not to be here. Just one thing. You're not having some sleazy tryst here with a brooding stranger, are you?"

Summer took the key. "Let's just put it this way," she said with a smile. "Fresh sheets would be nice."

Austin laughed. "I'm a guy, Summer. Refresh my memory. What exactly are sheets?"

Summer tucked the key into her purse. "I'll let you know when I need the apartment. And thanks."

Austin reached for her hand. "Whatever it is, Summer, trust your instincts. It'll be okay."

"I hope you're right," Summer said. "But the way things have been going lately, I have my doubts."

Diana drove back to Crab Claw Key, feeling both exhausted and too hyper to sleep. After dropping Summer off at Austin's, she hadn't been quite sure where to go next. Back to Mallory's? Back to the apartment and the inevitable cold shoulder from Marquez? In the end she decided it didn't really matter. Diana was scheduled to volunteer later today, so even if she tried to get some sleep, she wouldn't get much.

It occurred to her that it would be nice if she could talk Marquez into going along with her to the Institute. Maybe if she saw other people going to therapy—kids in much worse shape than Marquez—it might do some good.

Nice idea. Too bad she and Marquez were barely on speaking terms.

Diana cruised down Crab Claw's center, past white clapboard buildings decorated with sun-faded awnings. The corner bakery was doing a brisk early morning business. Even from the car Diana could smell the yeasty aroma of just-baked bread.

She paused at a four-way stop and hesitated. Coquina Street. Seth's grandfather lived just down the block.

Mariah Carey was wailing on the radio. Diana turned her off. She needed to concentrate. Mallory's house was straight ahead. Seth's grandfather's house—and potentially, Seth—was to the right.

To turn or not to turn? That was the question.

Behind her an ancient woman in a Cadillac honked.

Diana scowled at the rearview mirror. The woman honked again, more convincingly.

Diana turned.

She'd only gone a few yards when she saw Seth. His back was to her. He was mowing the tiny lawn with an old-fashioned push mower. No shirt, his broad tan back sheened with sweat.

This was insane. She didn't want him to catch her spying on him like some lovesick kid. She braked, thinking she could pull a U. But the street was narrow, and she knew she'd just draw more attention to herself, trying to turn around. Better to cruise on by and act like she hadn't even noticed him.

But just as she passed the neat white house Seth turned the mower toward the curb. He looked at her. She looked at him. She told her foot to keep pressing the accelerator. But because of some unexplainable freak accident of brain wiring, her foot braked instead, and she pulled over to the curb.

Seth wiped his forehead with the back of his arm. He was just a foot or two away, close enough, almost, to touch. She knew he was going to say something ugly. She knew he was going to make her feel even worse than she already did.

"You're up early," he said neutrally.

She tried to swallow, but her mouth was dry as sand. "I don't know why I'm here," she blurted.

Seth shrugged. "I don't know why I'm here, either," he said. "My grandfather says I should go back to California, finish up the internship. He's really ragging on me to leave."

"He's probably right."

"Yeah. I know. I guess I'm just . . . I don't know. Hoping everything will still work out. Waiting to see how the story ends."

"Me too." She forced her mouth into a smile that almost hurt. "Unfortunately I think we're hoping for different endings."

Seth leaned close. She smelled the sharp, sweet smell of freshly cut grass. "Are you okay?" he asked softly.

"Like you care?"

He stepped back. "Forget it. Just . . . forget it."

Diana stared out the windshield, unable to look him in the eye. "Just tell me this, Seth. All those times we were together and you were holding me and telling me how much I meant to you and . . . was that all just a big act? *All* of it?"

"I think—" Seth paused. "I think it was the same thing for me that it was for you."

She forced herself to look at him. "For me it was real, Seth. Is that how it was for you?"

She didn't wait to hear his answer. She knew he would just say something awful.

This time her foot had no problem locating the accelerator.

# 18

# Fairy Tales and Other Lies

When Summer returned to Jared's, he and Juanita were still at the doctor's. Stan, the butler, had left a Post-it note on Summer's bedroom door informing her that her mother had called. Summer was to call home immediately.

As she dialed her mom from her bedroom phone, Summer's first thought was that someone had died. Her second thought was that somehow her mom had found out about Diver. Her third thought was that her mom had discovered that Summer had moved out of the apartment and into the home of a rich invalid.

Of course, there was always *D:* None of the above.

On standardized tests teachers always said to go with your first hunch.

"Why on earth did you move out and why on earth didn't you tell me?" her mom demanded as soon as Summer said hello.

So. It was *C*. No wonder she hadn't done better on her SATs. At least no one had croaked.

"It's sort of complicated, Mom." Summer went to the front window. The van was just pulling up. "I got this job as a companion to a guy who was hurt in an accident. It's a live-in position—"

"But you and Marquez and Diana were so excited about the apartment, hon."

"I know. But this is a lot more convenient." She attempted a laugh. "No commuting."

"Are you sure everything's okay?"

"Well, there is one thing. Seth and I . . . we kind of broke up."

"Oh, no. Oh, Summer, I'm really sorry. Are you sure it's, you know, over?"

"I don't know, Mom. I kind of think so."

Her mother sighed. "It's hard to admit, I know. I got the final divorce papers yesterday, but I still can't quite bring myself to say *divorced* without choking on the word."

Summer watched Juanita open the van door and slowly lower Jared's wheelchair to the driveway. She tried to let the word sink in. *Divorced.* Her parents were divorced. That meant two houses at Christmas. Two new phone numbers to memorize. Two separate people, strangers living different lives. Strangers who just happened to be her parents.

"I'm really sorry, Mom," Summer said. "I just wish you'd given it more time. You were both so upset about Diver leaving and all that."

"This isn't about Diver, Summer. It's about your dad and me and the way we look at the world. We're just too, I don't know, too different."

"But you weren't different, not until Diver came back and all the fighting started."

"That was just the excuse we needed, Summer. And I hope your brother doesn't feel he's to blame. Have you seen him lately?"

"You know Diver." Summer hesitated. "Even if you see him, you can't really talk to him."

Her mother sighed again. "Well, anyway, I'm so sorry about Seth. You always seemed like such a fairy-tale couple. Of course, that's what people used to say about your dad and me."

They chatted for a few more minutes. When Summer hung up, she realized her hand hurt from clenching the phone so tightly.

Her mother really didn't seem to blame Diver for the divorce. Of course, she was a mother. Mothers weren't supposed to blame their kids for big things. Just little things, like driving them to an early grave.

Talking to Diver today, Summer had been struck by the way he'd talked about his past as if it made sense. As if it weren't some awful, crazy, unspeakable melodrama. There were so many people in his life he'd had to forgive. Why was it so easy for Diver?

Why was it so hard for her?

Still clutching the phone, Summer opened her bedroom door and went to the top of the stairs. Juanita and Jared were downstairs in the foyer, Juanita fussing, Jared joking.

How many people had Jared had to forgive? Where were his family and his friends now, when he most needed them?

"Summer?" Jared said in his soft voice. "You up for a walk in the garden?"

"Be right there, Jared," Summer said. "I just need to make a quick call."

Summer returned to her room. She dialed Blythe's number.

Caroline answered. "Summer!" she exclaimed. "Any word on Diver?"

"Well, that's why I'm calling, Caroline. I was hoping we could get together. Maybe early this afternoon sometime?"

Caroline paused for a beat. "Get together?"

"I have a proposition for you," Summer said. "Something I think will benefit both of us."

"I don't—"

"Benefit us *financially*. I think you should hear me out."

"Oh. Oh, I see."

"Why don't you meet me over at Austin's place around two?" Summer suggested. "You know where it is."

"Two," Caroline repeated. "I'll be there. I'm glad you called, Summer. I have the feeling we can work something out."

Summer hung up. Two would be good. Jared would be having physical therapy all afternoon. She'd call Austin and make sure he'd be out of the apartment. She'd meet Caroline there, and then . . . well, she'd figure out that part when she came to it.

She was sitting across from him in the gazebo, reading out loud, looking as radiant as she did in that photo he kept hidden away. If he closed his eyes, it could almost be last year and Summer could be his girlfriend again, not his paid companion. He could be whole again, not trapped in a wheelchair because on one dark, unhappy, drunken night, he'd driven himself over an embankment, hoping, just a little, that he might die.

If he closed his eyes, he could be Adam, Senator

Merrick's son with the bright future ahead of him. Adam, Ross's loyal little brother. Adam, Summer's boyfriend and maybe even her love.

"Jared?"

"Hmm?"

"Are you bored? I could read something else."

"No, no. It's great. But maybe we could just talk for a while."

"Sure." Summer set her book aside.

"Any word on your brother?"

"No, nothing." She shrugged. "But I'm sure he'll turn up."

"I thought maybe your cousin coming over this morning had something to do with Diver."

Summer looked a little uncomfortable. "No. Diana just wanted to talk."

"To make peace?" He knew he was prying, but he couldn't seem to stop himself.

"I suppose. It's hard to tell with Diana. She's very, you know, complicated."

Complicated. He couldn't help smiling a little. Oh, yes, Diana was complicated, all right. That had been very clear from the moment they'd started dating. How long had it been now? Two? Two and a half years?

"Do you think she's still in love with Seth?"

Summer hesitated.

"I'm sorry. It's none of my business. I mean, I

hardly know you. It's just . . . I guess I've sort of been out of touch with that for a while. Dating and all."

"That's okay, Jared." Summer smiled. "It's no biggie. I was just wondering what the answer was. Yes, I'm pretty sure she's still in love with Seth. But you never know with Diana. Like I said, she's complicated."

Beautiful, complicated Diana. Maybe she hadn't always been so complicated. Maybe that night with Ross had changed her.

After all, it had changed everything else. It was the first time Adam had wished he wasn't a Merrick. And it was the only time he'd ever wanted to hurt his brother.

Diana had wanted to press charges, but of course, the Merrick clan had circled the wagons, threatening and cajoling and intimidating her. Family loyalty and all that.

It had destroyed Adam's relationship with Diana. It had nearly destroyed her. And a year later, when Summer had found out the truth about Ross, it had destroyed Adam's relationship with her, too.

But in the end, Diana had found a way to get even. The revelation that a Merrick son had attempted rape had been bad enough. But the revelation that the senior Merrick had tried to cover it up had done the senator in. He'd resigned in disgrace.

Still, it hadn't taken him long to think about a

comeback bid, running for governor in New Hampshire. And his son's drunken accident in Germany wouldn't have helped his chances any.

He'd visited Adam in the hospital, full of good cheer. Would Adam mind recovering quietly in Florida, he'd wondered, away from the prying eyes of the press? Would he mind doing it under an assumed name, just for a while, mind you?

Naturally, Adam had said yes. Family loyalty and all that.

"Jared? You okay?"

"Sorry."

"You were like a million miles away."

"I was just reminiscing about some old friends."

"Anybody you want to talk about?"

"No. They're long gone."

She reached over and gently touched his good hand. "Maybe not forever."

"Maybe not," he said, but of course he knew better.

# 19

## Dirty Laundry

"I have to admit I was surprised when you called me, Summer." Caroline settled demurely on Austin's couch. "You said you had a proposition?"

"It's about Diver." Summer sat on the chair she'd carefully situated right next to the couch. She glanced—subtly, she hoped—at the laundry basket by her feet. Tucked inside one of Austin's shirts was the tape recorder Diana had lent her.

Before Caroline's arrival, Summer had tested it out several times, talking at a normal tone of voice from various locations in the room. It had only picked up her voice when she was within a few feet, and even then the words had been muffled and hard to follow.

"So, have you found Diver?" Caroline asked hopefully.

Summer smiled. "Well, that sort of depends."

"Depends?"

"Diver told me all about you, Caroline. How you know about his . . . history. And how you want a piece of the insurance money in exchange for clearing his name."

Caroline stood up. "I don't think you have any idea what you're talking about," she said sharply, crossing her arms over her chest.

"No, no, wait," Summer said, hearing her voice rising. She cleared her throat. "Just listen for a second." She went to the window and made a point of shutting it, then returned to her seat. "I do know where Diver is, Caroline. And I'm willing to tell you, for a price."

Caroline narrowed her eyes. "What kind of price?"

"I want a piece of that money too."

Caroline stared at her in disbelief for what seemed like several hours. "Well, you certainly don't mince words, do you?" she finally said, allowing a faint smile. "And here I had you pegged as such a sweet little thing, Summer. I had no idea." Caroline clucked her tongue. "Your own brother. My, my."

Summer swallowed hard. She shrugged, trying her best to look casual. "There's no love lost between

Diver and me. Besides, there's plenty of money to go around. The insurance money from his mom's death, plus there's got to be a big bundle coming from the fire. Split two ways or three, there's still plenty."

Caroline watched her suspiciously for another moment. Then she leaned forward. "So where is he?"

Summer cast another nervous glance at the laundry basket. "What?"

"Where *is* he?" Caroline said, louder this time.

"Not so fast," Summer said. "We need to talk percentages here. It seems to me, since I'm the one who's making this work, I should take half. You and Diver can split up the rest however you want—"

"Please! No way are you getting half the money!"

Caroline walked toward the kitchen, away from the laundry basket. She got a drink of water, then paused in the doorway.

Summer felt her heart banging around in her chest. It was too far. She hadn't tested the kitchen area, but she was certain the tape recorder wouldn't pick up anything from that distance.

"If we're going to discuss this, Caroline, let's do it in the living room," Summer said in a slightly choked voice. "Someone might hear. The kitchen window's open—"

"No, it isn't," Caroline said dismissively. She arched an eyebrow and locked onto Summer's gaze.

"Look, Summer, if you think you can muscle your way in at this late date, you've got another thing coming. This only works if I can convince the authorities that Diver's innocent."

Summer grabbed the laundry basket and slid down to the far end of the couch, closer to Caroline. She pulled out a wrinkled T-shirt and carefully began to fold it.

"How domestic," Caroline observed with a sneer. "I guess you and Austin are still an item after all, huh?"

"What? Oh, this. I told Austin I'd do his laundry in return for borrowing his place."

"Does he know about Diver?"

"Nobody knows. Not even Marquez."

"Good. You need to keep it that way." Caroline sipped at her water, considering. "Look, here's my best offer. I'll take sixty percent. You and Diver split the rest."

Summer pulled out another T-shirt, folding it on her lap. She didn't want to overplay her hand, and she knew she wasn't exactly Meryl Streep. When her senior class had performed *Hello, Dolly!* Summer had been cast as Crowd Member Number Seven.

"Diver owes me, Caroline," she said. "I just talked to my mom today. She and my dad got their final divorce papers. If it hadn't been for Diver, well . . .

they might still be together. You understand what I'm saying? I'm *owed*."

Caroline pursed her lips. "Okay. We'll do it this way. Fifty to me. Forty to you. Ten to Diver. It's not like he has a lot of leverage, right?"

"Excellent point." Summer's voice sounded a little too eager. She cleared her throat again. "Okay, then. I can live with that."

Caroline joined Summer on the couch. The laundry basket sat between them. The little red light on the tape recorder glowed from under a shirt sleeve. Quickly Summer rearranged the clothes.

It suddenly occurred to her that it wasn't like she'd heard anything worth taping yet, anyway. Was this a total waste of time?

She wondered, in a searing flash of doubt, if she'd been wrong about Diver all along.

She reached for another piece of clothing. "You know, I do feel kind of funny about this," she said. "I mean, profiting off a man's horrible death."

Caroline tapped her fingers impatiently. "Somebody's got to take the money," she said. "It's just sitting there in some bank, getting dusty."

Summer sighed. "But I mean, Diver *killed* someone, Caroline. Don't you think he should pay for what he did?"

Caroline blinked in disbelief. "You don't actually

think . . . oh, man, you *are* brutal! Summer, you poor demented fool, Diver didn't kill his daddy."

"He . . . didn't?"

"Please! Diver? Sweet little Diver, with those beautiful baby blues of his? That boy couldn't kill a mosquito." She grinned. "It's funny, though. When I told him I'd go to the cops and tell them how I saw him trying to save his daddy, I sort of got the feeling Diver thought it was a made-up story. He was listening to me like a kid who wanted to believe in Santa Claus, you know?"

"I don't think he remembers very much about the fire."

"Well, I guess not!" Caroline said. "Truth is, I saw that boy run back into the fire three, four times easy, trying to save his no-good daddy, lord knows why."

"But why didn't you say anything at the time?"

"I was just a kid, Summer. Like anyone would have listened to me?" Caroline shrugged. "I suppose the truth of it is, I'd always had this mad crush on Diver, and he'd pretty much always treated me like the dorky little girl next door. I didn't exactly feel like I owed him any favors, you know?"

"But they accused him of murder."

Caroline shifted uncomfortably. "Well, it wasn't like he stuck around. It didn't matter what I saw, one way or the other."

"How do you think the fire started, then?"

"They said something about finding flammable liquid at the scene, and Diver's daddy—I guess I really shouldn't call him that since, let's face it, he wasn't—he was always refinishing stuff out on the porch. Painting, that sort of thing." Caroline hesitated. "Our yard was right next to Diver's, and we'd had a big barbeque that night. After the fire happened, I heard my daddy talking to someone about how he hadn't put the coals out properly. It was windy that night. I suppose one thing led to another and . . . well, I guess it doesn't really matter now, does it? The point is, everybody just assumed Diver did it. He had plenty of motive, after all. His daddy beat the hell out of him practically every day. And after the fire Diver vanished. It made sense for everyone to blame him."

"I suppose it did, at that."

"So." Caroline glanced at Summer out of the corner of her eye. "Where are you going to spend all that nice green stuff?" She reached for a T-shirt from the laundry basket. "I guess the least I could do is help you fold—"

"Don't!" Summer cried, yanking the shirt away. "I mean, you know. There's underwear in there. Austin would kill me."

"You know, I *have* seen male unmentionables before." Caroline shook her head, "If I didn't know better, I'd say you were actually blushing, Summer! So, what are you going to do with your piece of the money? I'm thinking about buying a car."

Summer reached down and clicked off the tape recorder. "I'm sure I'll think of something."

# 20

## A Visit to Flipper

"I really appreciate this," Diana said for what had to be the gazillionth time.

Marquez jerked her car into the left lane. "I believe you've already mentioned that."

"I don't know what's wrong with my Jetta. It was fine this morning. But the transmission was making this weird noise. Sort of like when the vacuum cleaner sucked up your sock the other day. Anyway, it's really nice of you—"

"Shut up already, Diana."

"I mean, I've never missed a day at the Institute. The kids get so they expect you to be there—"

"Look," Marquez interrupted. "I am not doing this

to bond with you. I am only driving you there so I can have the apartment to myself. I can spend a few minutes with you in the car or be stuck with you all day. Guess which one I chose?"

Diana rolled her eyes. "Okay, okay. At least let me pay you for the gas."

"Just tell me this. What part of 'shut up' don't you understand?"

Finally Diana seemed to get the message. They drove in silence for a while. After a few miles Marquez flipped on her blinker and turned down a long unpaved road bordered by sea grass and scrub pines.

Weird. The silence was almost worse than Diana's babbling.

"To tell you the truth," Marquez said, "I thought maybe you'd moved out when I got up this morning and saw you were gone."

"I just went driving around. I couldn't sleep." Diana held her wind-whipped hair back with one hand. "Maybe I should, though. Move out. If that's what you want."

"If you move out, I can't afford the apartment by myself. So no, I don't want you to leave. Purely for economic reasons."

"I'm touched."

Marquez braked for a huge blue heron, slowly crossing the sandy road like a dignified old man.

"So, what are your plans today?" Diana asked.

"Why do you care?"

"No reason. I just figured you'd probably given up on the Diver search. I mean, at this point you just kind of have to wait and see if he calls or turns up, right?"

"Yeah. So?"

"And you don't have to work till tonight, right?"

Marquez parked the car in front of the long, cedar-shingled Institute building. "What exactly is your point?" she demanded.

Diana reached for her purse. "Well, it occurred to me that I'm only going to be here an hour or two, and by the time you drive all the way home and then turn around and come back . . . maybe it would just be easier to stick around. There's a lobby with some magazines, or you could hang out here in the car. Or you could, you know, watch the dolphins and the kids. It's pretty interesting, actually."

Marquez checked her watch and did the math. Diana was right, of course. "*How* did I get roped into this?" she muttered. "You're rich—you could have just run out and bought a new Jetta."

"So"—Diana swung open the car door—"want to come?"

"I'll wait in the car."

"But it's so hot. At least come inside. It's air-conditioned, more or less. And out by the dolphin tank there's a covered area with bleachers where the parents sit. That's pretty shady."

"I'll wait in the car," Marquez repeated, shooting Diana her laser-guided *get lost* look.

"Okay, okay. But if you change your mind—"

"I won't."

Diana looked as if Marquez had somehow disappointed her. "Well, okay. I'll try not to take too long."

Diana headed into the Institute. Marquez sighed. If Diana wanted somebody to watch her play the saint, she'd have to find another audience. Marquez wasn't buying.

She moved the car to the far end of the parking lot, where she could at least get a view of the beach. The big tank behind the Institute was partially visible, very large and crystal blue. A few adults in bathing suits roamed around. Diana was there, talking to another woman in a red tank suit. A handful of kids hovered near one end, towels draped around their shoulders.

Marquez cranked on the radio, flashed past some nice reggae-sounding tune, and locked it in. She lay back against the headrest and closed her eyes, but that was dangerous these days. Whenever she closed her eyes, she saw Diver. Not some blurry, half-formed picture, but *Diver,* complete and in spectacular Technicolor 3-D, fully animated. Maybe it was because she was an artist. He was almost as real to her in her imagination as he would have been if he'd been sitting here, right beside her.

The familiar, awful ache came back, a sharp heaviness deep in her chest. Why the hell had she said yes to Diana? She wanted to be home in the cool darkness of her bedroom, hiding under the sheets.

Waiting for the phone to ring.

Marquez turned off the car and wandered around the beach outside the Institute. She could hear the musical laughter of the kids, the soft, reassuring voices of the adults. Every now and then a huge splash interrupted the steady ebb and flow of the voices. The dolphins showing off, Marquez figured.

She wasn't sure what it was Diana did in there, exactly. She knew the kids came from troubled backgrounds or had emotional or physical problems. They played with the dolphins and that was supposed to help them, although Marquez couldn't quite see what a big slimy overgrown fish, even if it did look like Flipper, could accomplish.

She sat on the front steps of the Institute building for fifteen minutes or so until she realized she had to find a water fountain or she'd die of thirst.

The lobby of the building was small and unpretentious. A wide window allowed a view of the dolphin tank. Marquez located a drinking fountain, then wandered over to the window. Diana was in the pool at one end, holding a little girl in her arms while a dolphin swam circles around them.

Marquez took a seat by the window. At least there were some well-worn magazines to look at. Of course, they were all granola magazines, things like *Wildlife Conservation* and *National Geographic*. On the plus side, the only models in these magazines had four legs and way too much body hair.

The front door opened and a pretty girl about Marquez's age entered. She smiled at Marquez, took off her sunglasses, and went straight to the window. "She's having so much fun," she murmured. She glanced back at Marquez. "My sister. Stacy."

Marquez gave a vague nod to show she was not particularly interested.

"You waiting for someone?" the girl asked.

"Yeah. Not one of the kids. One of the . . . counselors." Somehow using that word to describe Diana was like calling a vicious Doberman "Benji."

"They're great," the girl said as she sat across from Marquez. She had large green eyes set in a heart-shaped face.

She was a little chubby, Marquez noted, but pretty nonetheless.

"That's Stacy with that dark-haired counselor. Diana, I think her name is."

Marquez watched as Diana lifted the girl she'd been swimming with out of the pool. The tiny girl was stooped over, emaciated. Her bathing suit hung slackly off a body that might have been made of twigs.

"What's wrong with her?" Marquez blurted. She cringed at her own bluntness. "I'm sorry. It's none of my business. She just looks so, you know, frail."

"She's anorexic," the girl said matter-of-factly. "You think this is bad, you should have seen her a couple of months ago. She's put on seventeen pounds since then. Coming here's helped a lot, I think. And she's seeing a therapist. She was in the hospital for nine weeks. We thought she was going to . . ." Her voice trailed off.

"But she's so young."

"Fifteen."

Marquez went to the window. That delicate, breakable, line drawing of a human being was only three years younger than she was?

"I hate to drag her away, but she's got a doctor's appointment," the girl said. "She loves coming here so much. It's funny"—she started for the door that led to the pool area—"we had to practically drag her here the first few times. She was so afraid."

Marquez watched through the window as the girl walked out to the pool, greeted Stacy, and helped her towel off. Diana helped Stacy put on a sweatsuit. It seemed ridiculous in the ninety-degree heat, but of course, Stacy was probably cold.

Marquez was cold a lot too.

It wasn't the same thing. She wasn't like that. She wasn't ever going to be like that.

Stacy, her sister, and Diana entered the lobby. Diana didn't seem entirely surprised to see Marquez. "Stace, this is my, um, my friend Marquez," Diana said.

Stacy smiled shyly. Her lips had a bluish cast. Her blond hair hung in wet ropes.

"Hi," Marquez said. "Looked like you were having a good time out there."

"I rode one of the dolphins."

"Yeah," Marquez said awkwardly, "I can see how that would be pretty cool."

"We're late already," Stacy's sister said, checking her watch. "See you next week, Diana."

Diana gave Stacy a hug. "Take care of yourself, promise?"

"Yep." Stacy glanced at Marquez. "See you," she said.

"Yeah," Marquez replied. "See you."

Diana wrung out her hair. "I'll just be a few more minutes."

Marquez nodded, watching as the door closed behind Stacy and her sister.

"Is she going to be okay?"

"I don't know. Maybe. She's tougher than she looks."

Diana returned to the pool area, and Marquez went back outside. The heat felt good on her face. She watched an old Honda circle the parking lot. It passed her on the way out.

Stacy was sitting on the passenger side. She was looking at Marquez. She waved, and Marquez waved back.

Stacy smiled as if they were old friends.

As if they shared a secret.

# 21

# Reaching Out

For the third time Diver rewound the tape.

Summer stood next to him on the deck of the stilt house, waiting, hoping. Her face was flushed.

Diver fast-forwarded, then pushed the play button. Caroline's muffled laughter filled the air.

*Truth is, I saw that boy run back into the fire three, four times easy, trying to save his no-good daddy, lord knows why.*

Diver closed his eyes and he was there again, in that place the dream always made him go.

He could see himself running through the inferno. He could see his father lying under a burning support beam, his clothes on fire, his hair, his skin.

He could hear the screams.

Diver reached for his father's hand. He pulled, trying like he'd never tried for anything in his life.

There was nothing he could do. Nothing.

The sirens were coming. The fire was roaring like a thing alive.

There was nothing more Diver could do, except, just maybe, save himself.

He opened his eyes. The sun made diamonds of the waves.

In his dream there was always a hand, familiar and yet not, reaching out to him. There was always an old, rickety house, floating over a blue, endless ocean.

There was always hope.

Summer held out her hand. "It's going to be okay, Diver."

He took her hand, wiped away a tear, smiled a little. "You did all this for me. Why?"

"I don't know. I guess because it hurt to see you hurting." She shrugged. "And because you're my brother, Diver."

"I don't know what to do now."

"We'll go back to Virginia. We have the tape. We'll clear the whole mess up. Maybe Dad and Mom can meet us. It'll be fine. You'll see."

"I can't ask them to do that. Not after everything I've already put them through."

"What about all you've been through?"

Diver shrugged. "Not so much, really."

"I don't know . . ." Summer paused, frowning with concentration, as if she were searching for the very last word in a crossword puzzle. "I don't know if I'd be as kind as you are, Diver. If I'd gone through all you have, I mean. That's something I've had to realize this summer. I'm not very good at forgiving people. I sure haven't been very good at forgiving you."

He smiled. "Maybe I don't deserve it."

"Or maybe I needed someone to be mad at. Maybe I needed a reason for the divorce to have happened. That way, it kind of made sense. I didn't want to think that a relationship could just end for no reason."

Diver watched as Frank swooped past, searching for an afternoon snack. His life was so simple. Eat, sleep in the sun, survive. Sometimes Diver wished his life could be like that.

He looked at Summer, at his sister who'd loved him enough to help him. Enough to forgive him.

Sometimes he was glad his life was so complicated.

"I don't think relationships just end for no reason," Diver said. "Sometimes it's too complicated for us to understand. All these interconnected things have to be just right before you can have love. That's why it's so amazing when it happens. Maybe it shouldn't be so surprising when it doesn't last. Maybe we should just be astounded that it happens at all."

Summer nodded. "I'm sorry I blamed you for the divorce," she said. "I was wrong."

"I'm sorry I let you down."

"You didn't. I let myself down."

Summer laid her head on Diver's shoulder. They stared out at the water, bluer than the sky and just as endless. Frank scooped a fish into his massive beak and returned to the deck, preening and strutting just a bit to show he hadn't lost his touch.

Diver took a deep breath. "I'm afraid," he whispered. "I don't think I have the courage to go see her."

"Marquez loves you, Diver. All she wants is to have you back."

"But I ran out, I hurt her—"

"That doesn't matter. She'll understand." Summer grinned. "She's quicker at forgiving than I am."

Diver gave her a dubious look.

"Well, okay, she gets madder up front, but she gets over it faster." Summer pulled on his hand. "Come on. You can't hide here forever."

"No, I guess not."

They walked to Coconut Key together, savoring the sun, saying little. Diver tried to plan what he would say to Marquez, but he wasn't much for speeches, and besides, what could he really say except "I'm sorry"?

As if that would be enough.

When they climbed the stairs to the girls' apartment, his heart quickened. He grabbed Summer's arm. "I'm not ready. I can't, not yet."

"Diver, you have to. She needs you."

Before he could protest, Summer unlocked the door. Diana was lying on the couch. The TV was on. She sat up in surprise and clicked the remote control.

"Is Marquez here?" Summer asked.

"What happened?" Diana asked. "Diver, I thought you were at the stilt house—"

"It's okay," Diver said. "Summer worked things out. With a little help from your tape recorder."

"That's great news." Diana smiled. "Really great. Look, Marquez isn't here. I think she's scheduled to work tonight, though."

"Do you know where she is?" Summer asked.

"I don't think I'm supposed to know." Diana seemed uncomfortable. "I overheard her making a call when we got back from the Institute this afternoon. She was talking to the Eating Disorders Clinic at the hospital. I think maybe she went over there. I didn't want to push it by asking."

Summer looked at Diver. "You want company? I'll walk you over to the hospital."

"I think I can take it from here," Diver said. He kissed Summer on the cheek. "Thank you. For everything. You too, Diana. I owe you both." He paused in the doorway. "It's too bad you two hate each other. You make a pretty great team."

He got off on the wrong floor at the hospital and took two wrong turns before he found the Eating Disorders Clinic. The waiting area was empty. Diver took a seat, thumbed through a worn *People,* paced awhile.

He was so proud of Marquez for coming here, especially in the middle of the mess he'd created. How was he ever going to tell her that?

The clinic door opened. He saw a girl, too thin, too beautiful.

Marquez. Her back was to him.

How was he ever going to make her believe she could trust him not to leave again?

She was nodding, talking to a woman who was smiling. "Okay, then. I'll see you next week," Marquez said.

How was he ever going to make her believe how much he needed her? What kind of words were there for that?

She turned. The door closed. She looked past him, then back. Her mouth formed the word: *Diver.* She ran to him.

He took her in his arms and held her till she felt

like a part of him. She was sobbing softly, and so was he.

He kissed her, again and again and again.

"I love you," he whispered, and suddenly he realized he'd known what to say after all.

# 22

# Diana Meets Up with Her Past, Summer Says Good-bye to Hers.

The next afternoon Diana made her way down the winding garden path at the rear of Jared's home. Just as his nurse had said, Summer and Jared were sitting at the edge of the beach. Summer was on a bench, reading. Jared was in his wheelchair, staring out at the ocean.

Diana fingered the envelope from Carlson. Suddenly she regretted coming here. Yesterday, after all the stuff with Diver, it had almost seemed like she and Summer had reached a kind of uneasy truce. But if this was a rejection letter, Diana was going to look as if she'd come over to gloat.

Jared noticed her approaching even before

Summer did. "Diana?" he said in that whispery, odd voice of his.

"I'm sorry to interrupt," Diana said.

Summer turned and took off her sunglasses "What are you doing here? Is everything okay with Marquez and Diver?"

Diana laughed. "Are you kidding? I've barely seen them since Diver caught up with her at the hospital yesterday. This morning she was floating around the apartment like she was filled with helium." She held out the envelope. "This just came in the mail. I thought you might want to see it."

Summer took the envelope and read the return address. "It's too thin," she said flatly. "It's a rejection."

"They accepted you once, Summer," Diana pointed out. "If they reject you now, it's just because you reapplied too late and they were already full."

Summer stared warily at the envelope as if it contained plutonium.

"Well—" Diana took a step back. "I guess I should get going. Oh, we got the phone bill too. Your share's twenty-one bucks and some change." She smiled. "Good luck."

"Thanks for bringing this by," Summer said, not sounding altogether sure she meant it.

"Neither rain nor sleet nor heat nor gloom of night," Diana said. "See you, Jared."

"See you." He was gazing at her out of those penetrating dark eyes again. It was very unnerving.

"And Diana?" Summer said. "Thanks for helping with Diver."

"He means a lot to me too, Summer."

"Wait," Summer said. "You might as well stick around. You'll hear soon enough, one way or the other." She tore open the envelope. "Here goes nothing."

She pulled out the letter and scanned to the bottom. "Idiots," she muttered darkly. Suddenly she broke into a huge grin. "They're actually letting me in!"

"Congratulations, Summer," Diana said.

"Way to go." Jared held out his hand and Summer clasped it in both of hers.

"I can't believe it," Summer said, glowing. "I really can't believe it." She passed the letter to Jared. "Read it, okay? To be sure I'm not hallucinating."

Diana started to leave, then hesitated. She should have been thinking about other things, about how this meant Summer was staying in the Keys, or how upset Seth was going to be when he heard the news.

But something else was troubling her. Jared was holding Summer's acceptance letter in his uninjured hand. A heavy gold ring glittered on his finger, a lion's head carved onto either side of a deep blue stone.

There was something familiar about that ring. It was very striking. Expensive, unique.

She'd seen a ring like that once before. On the finger of Adam's brother, Ross.

Summer looked over at her. "You okay, Diana? You look like you just saw a ghost."

"Something like that," Diana said softly as she started down the path.

The Carlson campus was quiet, softened by late afternoon shadows. Summer walked the grounds, taking in trees and statues and buildings as if she owned each and every one. The initial high of being reaccepted had worn off, replaced by a tingling, edgy nervousness that was part anticipation, part dread.

It was like diving into a lake without knowing how deep it was. Sure, the admissions people had decided she could handle this school. Her high school teachers had told her she could handle it. But part of her was still convinced she was being set up for an elaborate practical joke. She'd show up for class the first day, laden with heavy textbooks, only to have the entire college leap up in unison and yell, *"April Fools!"*

The University of Wisconsin, with all her friends—and with Seth—seemed like such a comforting choice now that she'd sealed her fate and decided against it. She would have felt secure there, safe. Here she was going to feel utterly and completely alone.

She went back to the car, which Marquez had lent

her, and waited for Seth. She'd asked him to meet her here. She wasn't sure why. It seemed like the right place to say what she had to say.

A few minutes later he parked alongside her, smiling shyly. She led him to a bench beside a shimmering fountain.

"So," he said, "everything's going to be okay with Diver?"

"I think so. I talked to my dad last night and he's making some calls. And Diver called me right before I drove over here. He confronted Caroline today with that tape I made. I don't exactly know what he said to her. But I do know I haven't heard him laugh so much in a long time."

Seth dipped his hand in the fountain pool. "That's cool. I'm really glad. Diver's a good guy. Man, he's been through a lot."

Summer nodded. The fountain whispered, filling the air with the musical sound of first rain.

"I was wondering why you wanted to meet here," Seth said. "But then it clicked. You got reaccepted, didn't you?"

"Yeah. I just got the letter."

"And you're definitely going to go here? UW's out of the picture?"

"I'm going to try it for a semester, anyway. I have to try, Seth, or I'll always regret it."

Seth nodded, his expression stony.

"It's like your internship, Seth. You really should go back to California, finish it up."

"I know. I guess I was just . . . waiting. In case."

"I've been thinking a lot about us. About all the mess this summer, Austin and Diana and you and me. I realized when I was trying to help Diver that I'm not very good at forgiving people. What happened between you and Diana, it really hurt me, and I couldn't see past that to the fact that I'd hurt you too. I couldn't forgive you any better than I could forgive Diver."

"There's plenty of guilt to go around," Seth said with a grim smile.

"I think I'm ready to forgive you, Seth. I think I can even start to forgive myself for messing things up so badly."

Seth reached for her hand. "Then you want to get back—"

"No," she said gently. "When I got past the anger and the forgiving, I realized something else. I've changed this summer, Seth. I've started to see how complicated life is. My parents divorcing. Diver's problems. You, Austin, Diana. All the stuff with Marquez. I mean, I thought all I'd do this summer was get some minimum wage job and perfect my tan. But it's ended up being a little more work than that."

"So what are you saying?" Seth tightened his grip on her fingers.

"I'm saying that if life's going to keep being so damn complicated, I want some time to get my head on straight. I want to concentrate on school. And on knowing I can count on myself to get through the tough stuff." She looked away, fighting tears. "I don't want to have to devote all my energy to trying to fix us, Seth. The truth is, I think we're past the point of fixing."

He released his grip. "Okay. Okay, then. I hear you."

"Diver said something to me, about how it's amazing love ever happens at all. Think about it. Two people have to get their brains and their hearts and . . . other elements of their anatomy . . . all in sync. And then the circumstances of their lives have to be in sync too." Summer sighed. "It seems to me we got the first part right, but the timing on that second part, the other stuff in our lives, isn't quite on track."

"This is because of Austin, isn't it?"

"I do love Austin, Seth. Just like I think some part of you, whether you'll admit or not, is in love with Diana. But that's not what this is about. It's not about Austin. It's about me. I know that seems selfish. But if I'm not sure of who I am and how strong I am, how can I ever really be someone you can trust and love?"

Seth kissed her, an achingly soft kiss that made her wish, for just a moment, that she could take back everything she'd said. "I'll always love you, Summer. And I'll always trust you. But I think I understand why you have to do this. Just be sure *you* understand one thing."

"What's that?"

"I will always be there for you. I don't care if I'm in Wisconsin and you're in the Keys. I don't care if I'm on Mars and you're on Venus. It doesn't matter. I'll always be there."

He touched Summer's cheek. He gave a small, sad smile. And then Seth walked out of her life forever.

# 23

## The Pretenders

When Diana found him the next morning, he was in the bus station, duffel bag at his feet, dozing lightly.

"Seth," she said. She took the seat beside him.

He opened his eyes. "How'd you—"

"Summer told Marquez what went on between you two yesterday. I wormed it out of Marquez, then I called your grandfather this morning."

Seth rubbed his eyes. Outside, a Greyhound belched black smoke. A line of passengers was forming.

"I'm glad you're going back," Diana said. "It would have been a shame to blow off the internship."

He shrugged. "I didn't want the whole summer to

be a loss. Although it sure hasn't turned out like I'd planned."

"Me either." Diana smiled. "Not even close."

"I thought about calling you to say good-bye. But I figured you'd take it the wrong way."

"The 'wrong way' being—?"

"You know. Summer dumps me, so I grab the nearest phone and call Bachelorette Number Two."

"Yeah, I have to admit that's pretty much how it would have looked."

"But that wasn't why I was going to call. I was going to say, you know, I was sorry. I think I pretty much treated you like crap, Diana."

"Well, I wasn't exactly a saint," she admitted. She cocked her head, smiling at him a little. "So what brought on this revelation?"

Seth shrugged. "I don't know. I guess I wasn't even really surprised yesterday. About Summer, I mean. I was holding out hope, but I kind of knew. And as I was sitting there, listening to her tell me it was over, I sort of flashed on how you must have felt this summer, hoping maybe you and I would . . . you know. Work things out."

"You've always been pretty straight with me, Seth. I knew the deal. I knew you were in love with Summer." Diana sighed. "I just didn't want to believe it. I wanted to pretend things were different. Sometimes it's more fun pretending than it is just letting go."

"Yeah." Seth nodded. "But it hurts worse when you finally do let go. It hurts like major hell."

Diana rose to her feet. "Well, I just wanted to say good-bye."

Seth slung his duffel bag over his shoulder. "I'll run into you one of these days, I'm sure. Maybe at Christmas, who knows?" He stood. "Maybe sooner."

Diana stared at the floor. She wanted to touch him one last time, but she knew it would just be one more awkward moment in a long string of them.

On the other hand, what did she have to lose? She'd already lost Seth.

Diana reached for him and hung on longer than she knew she should have. She put her lips to his ear.

The words were out before she had time to stop them.

"Did you even love me a little?" she whispered.

Instantly she was sorry. It was an awful, humiliating, desperate thing to say. She knew so much better.

She let go and turned away quickly so Seth wouldn't see her face. But he caught her arm and pulled her back to him.

"You know I did," he said, almost angrily. "Did *you*?"

Diana's breath caught.

Tell the truth.

If she could just tell Seth the truth this once . . .

"Put it this way," she said at last. "I'm not quite ready to stop pretending."

When she left the bus station, Diana drove straight to Adam's. He was waiting for her on the front porch when she pulled up.

"How about a walk?" he said as she got out of the car.

"Where's Summer?"

"After you called, I told her she could have the day off. I think she went over to town."

Diana took the handles of his wheelchair. "How do you push this thing?"

"It's motorized," Adam said, zipping past her down the ramp and into the driveway. He stopped and turned to face her, his smile almost hidden in the layers of bandages. "I know how you love to control things, Diana. Sorry."

Diana fell into step beside him. The day was crystalline, almost too bright.

"So," Adam said softly, "what gave it away?"

"The ring. I was there at Ross's birthday party when your dad gave it to him. Remember?"

Adam groaned. *"Now* I do. Damn, I should have known. I figured Summer wouldn't recognize it, since she barely knew Ross and he hardly ever wore the ring." He held out his hand. "It *is* kind of ostentatious.

But I've worn it ever since Ross died, and I didn't feel right about taking it off. Don't ask me why."

"How long did you think you could keep up this charade, Adam? Summer was bound to find out eventually."

"I know, I know. It just . . . it just happened. I was already using a fake name, and then when she walked through the door that day to apply for the job, it was too good to be true. I had a little part of my old life back, you know?"

They turned toward the beach, going as far as Adam dared with the wheelchair. Diana sat beside him in the hot, sugar-fine sand.

"I knew your dad pretty well," she said. "And I hated him for the way he treated me after the stuff with Ross. But I have a hard time believing even the almighty Senator Merrick could dump you here under an assumed name when you were in this"—she gestured toward him with her hand—"this condition. I mean, sure, he didn't mind trying to destroy *me* if it meant saving his rear. But you're his son, Adam. I thought loyalty was everything to the Merrick clan." She couldn't leave a trace of bitterness out of her voice. "After all, when I needed you, Adam, you chose Ross over me."

Awkwardly Adam twisted his body toward her. The bandages forced her to look directly into his eyes—it was as if there were nowhere else to look. And his eyes were so sad, it was almost more than Diana could stand.

"Yes, we've always been big on loyalty," Adam said. "But I guess even the almighty Senator Merrick couldn't put a good press spin on Ross and me. One son drunk and drowned. The other one nearly dead and also, for the record, quite drunk most of the time. Talk about your family values." Adam made a soft sound, like a laugh dissolving into a sob. "I guess you think I got what I deserved, huh, Diana? Poetic justice to the max."

"No. I don't hate you anymore, Adam. The truth is, what your family did to me made me stronger. I wouldn't wish it on anyone, but I'm still here. I survived, and I'm tougher for it."

She hesitated, watching the waves come and go. Gently, slowly, she reached for his left hand and held it, covering Ross's ring. "You'll be stronger, too, when this is over."

"Maybe."

"You have to tell Summer, you know."

"I know. I've known all along. I just hate to see her quit, it was so nice having her around. Like going back in time." He paused. "She will leave, won't she?"

"It's hard to say. Summer's okay. She might just stick around."

Adam closed his fingers around hers. "How about

you? You think you might, you know . . . stop back and say hi now and then?"

"I don't know, Adam," Diana said honestly. "I'm strong, but I'm not sure I'm strong enough to forget everything that happened."

"That's okay. I don't blame you."

"Maybe, though," Diana added softly.

They started back toward the house. When she reached her car, Diana paused. "So you'll tell her soon?"

"Soon, I promise. I just want to hang on to the illusion a little longer, okay?"

Diana nodded. "I understand. As it happens, I'm pretty good at make-believe myself."

# 24

# You Can Go Home Again

After Jared gave her the day off, Summer spent a couple of hours just walking the beach, trying her best not to think too much. There was only one place she wanted to go, but it wasn't really home, not anymore.

After a while she headed for town. When she peeked through the window of Jitters, the café was nearly empty. Austin was wiping down a table.

She pushed open the door. "Table for one," she said, "if you can squeeze me in. I don't have a reservation."

"Right this way, mademoiselle."

He seated Summer by the window, then straddled a chair across from her. "You're looking radiant," he said.

"I'm feeling pretty radiant, actually."

"Marquez told me how things went down with Diver. I'm glad."

"I couldn't have done it without your apartment."

"Hey, I got my laundry folded. Too bad it was dirty."

"Eww."

"Just kidding. I think."

She reached into her pocket. "Before I forget. Your key."

"Maybe you should keep it. Just in case we decide to cohabit."

"Maybe I shouldn't."

"Hey, it was worth a shot." Austin lowered his voice. "By the way, Blythe told me Caroline's developed this sudden, inexplicable desire to head back to college early."

"Good. She'll be close by in case the cops need to question her. Diver's flying up to Virginia at the end of the week to work things out. My dad's paying for the ticket and meeting him there." She smiled. "Strange. It may do more to help cement their relationship than all those awkward father-son football tosses in our backyard."

"So." Austin crossed his arms. "Any other reason for the radiance?"

Summer reached into her purse and passed Austin

her acceptance letter. He smiled broadly as he read it.

"Congratulations. I'm not surprised, of course. This is the right thing for you, Summer."

"I hope so." She put the letter away. "I'm scared to death. I'm going solo. No spotters. No net."

"You'll have friends nearby." Austin gazed at her, suddenly serious. "You'll have me."

"I've been thinking a lot about that, Austin," Summer said. "I—I told Seth good-bye. I told him I loved you."

"A wise choice indeed. I knew you'd come to your—"

"I also told him," Summer pressed on, "that I need to be by myself for a while. I need to figure out who I am and know I can get by on my own. To not be part of a couple. Not Summer and Austin. Just Summer."

Austin gazed at her, his face solemn, slowly, almost imperceptibly nodding.

"It's funny," Summer said, trying to fill the quiet with words, "when I first came here to the Keys, all I wanted in the world was to be part of a couple. I thought that was the only thing that mattered in the whole world. I still think it matters. Being in love is the most wonderful"—she smiled—"and the most wonderfully frustrating thing in the world. But I think it only works if you know what you want out of life. So you don't get lost in the other person."

She paused. Austin was still staring at her. "Well?" she said.

"Well, I want to tell you that you've just made a really lousy decision," Austin replied. "But I'm not going to. Because although it really hurts to admit this, Summer, I think you're probably right." He smiled, a slow smile that started at the corners of his mouth. "I think it's cool that you're brave enough to go solo for a while. And to do it at a place like Carlson, a place that scares you. It's the kind of thing that just makes me love you that much more." He laced his fingers behind his head, surveying her with affectionate annoyance. "Which is a drag, you see. I love you because you're stubborn and willful and independent, but of course it's exactly those qualities that are getting in the way of me sweeping you off your feet with my incredible charm."

"Oh, you swept me pretty good, Austin."

"This is just for a while, right? This isn't like some freaky hermit thing where you've sworn off human companionship till the end of time?"

"I'm sure we'll still run into each other. Even freaky hermits go to the movies now and then."

Austin sighed. "I told myself I would leave this in the hands of fate. And it appears fate has spoken. That bastard really gets on my nerves sometimes." He leaned across the table and kissed her sweetly. "But I can wait.

I have a whole lot of *Baywatch*es on DVD. And I figure you'll come to your senses eventually."

"It could happen." She stood. "Hey, before I go, could you load me up with three sticky buns and three orange juices to go?"

"Sure. Where are you off to?"

Summer smiled. "In search of some human companionship."

The apartment was quiet. Diana's door was closed, and so was Marquez's. Summer put the food from Jitters on the kitchen counter. She made as much noise as possible, searching for plates and forks.

Both doors opened at the same time.

"Summer?" Marquez cried.

"Summer?" Diana said. "What are you doing here?"

Summer placed the plates on the coffee table. "Hey, I paid a third of the rent—I have rights."

"Are you moving back in?" Marquez asked hopefully.

Summer shrugged. "I just wanted a little company, is all. Girl talk." She smiled. "Human companionship."

"And *Diana* came to mind?" Marquez sneered.

Summer sat cross-legged on the floor and grabbed a fork. She patted the couch. "Come on, you guys. They're still warm. Sit."

Diana and Marquez looked at each other warily.

"I promise to intervene if there's a significant loss of blood," Summer said. "Come on. Let's just hang out and talk. Like the old days."

"I don't know," Diana said, leaning against the counter. "It's been a long, hard summer. What can we all possibly agree on to talk about that won't lead to armed combat?"

"Guys?" Marquez suggested.

"No way," Diana and Summer said at the same moment.

"Food?" Summer suggested, holding up her plate.

"Pass," Marquez said.

"I have an idea," Diana said. "Let's talk about this fall. I caught another roach this morning the size of Nevada. I love this apartment, but if Summer's going to be at Carlson, and Marquez and I are going to be right down the road at FCU, I was thinking maybe we could look for something a little less roach infested when our lease is up. . . ." Her voice trailed off. "Sorry. We're not exactly ready for that, are we?"

Summer looked at Marquez. She looked at Diana. She smiled.

"Go get the want ads," she said.

## About the Author

After Katherine Applegate graduated from college, she spent time waiting tables, typing (badly), watering plants, wandering randomly from one place to the next with her boyfriend, and just generally wasting her time. When she grew sufficiently tired of performing brain-dead minimum-wage work, she decided it was time to become a famous writer. Anyway, a writer. Writing proved to be an ideal career choice, as it involved neither physical exertion nor uncomfortable clothing, and required no social skills.

Ms. Applegate has written more than one hundred books under her own name and a variety of pseudonyms. She has no children, is active in no organizations, and has never been invited to address a joint session of Congress. She does, however, have an evil, foot-biting cat named Dick, and she still enjoys wandering randomly from one place to the next with her boyfriend.